LEWIS
WARNER
Finds the
DOOM
PROPHET

LEWIS WARNER
Finds the
DOOM PROPHET

UNDER THE BRIDGE TO THE SEEDS OF LIGHT
Part II

REV. PHILIP RIGDON

TATE PUBLISHING
AND ENTERPRISES, LLC

Published by Tate Publishing & Enterprises, LLC
127 E. Trade Center Terrace | Mustang, Oklahoma 73064 USA
1.888.361.9473 | www.tatepublishing.com

Tate Publishing is committed to excellence in the publishing industry. The company reflects the philosophy established by the founders, based on Psalm 68:11,
"The Lord gave the word and great was the company of those who published it."

Book design copyright © 2015 by Tate Publishing, LLC. All rights reserved.
Cover design by Maria Louella Mancao
Interior design by Gram Telen

Published in the United States of America

ISBN: 978-1-68142-569-6
1. Fiction / Fantasy / Contemporary
2. Fiction / Fantasy / Paranormal
15.05.25

Contents

1

What Is There That Lemon Pudding Can't Fix?

Silence.

He wondered if he was in a tomb. What else could it be? There was no sound, no movement of the air, no room to move his body. Sure, he could wiggle his right foot slightly. He was able to pivot his head a bit. His jaw was unrestrained enough, allowing it to open and close. Nevertheless, as it mattered, he was frozen in place, trapped beneath large heavy rocks. He could tell the rocks were not natural, not those just having rolled down a hill or hewn from some primeval mountain. No. He was pinned under an unimaginable weight of man-made stones, persistent, relentless, and unmercifully committed to keeping him in place. Each time he tried to come up to his knees or stand, the callous stones punished him for it. Their rough edges scratched his skin or bruised his muscle. The stones wouldn't negotiate at all. He was stuck.

Aside from this, he could barely breathe. The pressure of the rocks covering his chest allowed only for the slightest breath, very shallow. What's more, there was fear in breathing because each time he exhaled, the stones above pressed down farther, crushing his chest and shrinking his lung capacity. Soon he wouldn't have enough air to sustain his consciousness. His lungs would be too small, his ribs too far bent. What good was the air, anyway? The man-made stones that formed his prison filled the air with a fine, foggy mist of rock powder. It tasted rough and bitter. The powder gathered increasingly on his dry lips with each new breath. It coated his tongue, so too his lungs.

He guessed that the stones were white or gray. That's all he could do. The thick impenetrable darkness kept that fact from his awareness. Eyes open or closed, he saw the exact same thing—murky gloom. So he lay there, helpless. He closed his eyes, ceased any further efforts to move, surrendering to the proven mastery of the rocks. This next breath was smaller than the last, less satisfying. He ran his fingers into the cool fine earth on which he was lying, a blind reaction to the misery of his predicament.

His lungs were a bit smaller now. He gathered saliva in his mouth to spit out the stony powder and did so after gathering it together with his tongue. This next breath was the shortest yet. Stars formed behind his eyelids; it wouldn't be long now. *Please, just a bit more air*, he thought. His crushed ribs and burdened lungs granted him but a little air. His chest barely moved. He forgot where he was. More stars now. His brain told his lungs to breathe. But nothing, no movement at all, and…

Silence.

* * *

"Did you enjoy the park today, sweetie?" a young mother asked her son. She had to curl her head around her husband to see the boy. She was walking arm in arm with her husband who was holding their son's hand gently, but firmly.

"Yes, Mama," he responded respectfully. There was no "yeah" or "uh-huh." It was "Yes, Ma'am," "No, Ma'am," or nothing at all. Indeed he did enjoy the day at the park. The weather was a perfect specimen of summer—warm, sunny, with just enough clouds to create elusive passing shadows on the paved sidewalk. When the boy saw the shadow pass on the ground before him, he would look up into the sky to see if the cloud's shape matched the shadow on the ground. They did with near-perfect consistency. Almost immediately, the child returned his gaze to the ground before him. The sun above was fierce and unrelenting. The large yellow ball overhead would not tolerate stares from little boys of the earth.

The child's left (and in this heat of the day, slightly sweaty) hand securely clinched a vibrant bouquet of helium balloons. The blue, red, green, and yellow globes were tethered to their owner by six lengths of white woven chord, which, under the unpredictable influence of the summer breeze, were left twisted and tangled. The multicolored team of floating gems seemed to exercise a life of their own, creating round shadows on the ground, making a hollow— *buddah-du-bub, bubbah-du-bub*—as they bounced off one another, and tugging slightly on the little boy's hand in their helium-induced effort to fly up into the blue summer sky.

His right hand was consumed in the spacious skin, bone, and flesh of his father's left hand. His father's palm and fingers were warm, comforting, and strong. He could tell they were strong. History assured him they were strong. These mighty hands had frequently lifted his son onto his broad elevated shoulders. These mighty fingers had tickled him to the point of hysterics more than once. These hearty hands covered the boy's tender ears against the sonic booms of July 4 fireworks. They were Daddy's hands. Certainly the little boy loved his mother tenderly, sweetly. However, he drew strength from his father. It was that kind of love. As long as his father was in sight, the little boy believed he was untouchable, vacuum-packed and hermetically sealed against all harm. It was that kind of love.

The little boy pulled his father's hand over to him and leaned his head toward the hand so that they met. His father's hand was snug against his cheek. His young skin felt the hairs on the back of the hand, the full-grown knuckles, and the metallic slightly cool smoothness of his wedding ring. Keeping his face cozied up to his father's consoling hand, the little boy closed his eyes and continued walking. He trusted the rhythmic gait his parents followed down the sidewalk and let them lead. The sun laid its heat in perfect portion on his supple young face. His ears took in all the activity before and behind him, on the grassy areas to their right, and the hum of traffic in the street to their left. He was peaceful and happy.

The little boy strolled down the concrete sidewalk with his parents in this fashion for nearly two minutes until he felt his father's arm tense up to prevent his proceeding further. He opened his eyes and looked up at his father.

"Hang on, little man," his father spoke through a warm smile. "We have to cross the street."

The young boy panned down from his father's face and took in the surroundings. He and his parents had reached the corner. He could see cars of all shapes, sizes, and varieties driving in four directions. Traffic lights hung in helpless suspension overhead, keeping time in reds, greens, and yellows. To his immediate left, the child saw a perfectly wooden, cylindrical pole rising up high and suspending electrical wires. It was covered with paper fliers of a seemingly endless variety of colors and purposes. There was a pale yellow advertisement for a rock concert that took place three years ago. This lay under three copies of the same flier, asking for help in locating a lost Lhasa apso. The page contained a black-and-white image of the dog, a number to call, and enlarged bold letters that spelled L-O-S-T D-O-G. His tender child's heart sank slightly as he wondered if that dog was ever found.

The boy's peaceful reflection was broken crisply by a terrific crash that occurred in fact over two blocks away but seemed by its volume and shock to happen nearby. A reckless speeding driver smashed into a nearby car, creating the most terrifying cacophony of bending metal and pulverized window glass. Following the terrifying crunch, which was audible for blocks, the wildly erratic car slowed only slightly and then continued speeding toward the intersection at which the little boy and his parents stood transfixed. Everyone within earshot of the car stared in fear and gave close attention to the sound of the engine, revving to its apex and then falling as it moved from gear to gear.

The little boy gave a start and turned sharply toward the noise of the oncoming automobile. So helplessly hypnotized was the child that he released his hands, both right and left. He pulled his right down from his father's hand and then yanked it in close to himself for protection. Then he dove unabashedly into the sanctuary space under his father's legs. He did the same with the left but only after allowing the white chords attached to the balloons to slip through his fingers. The colorful bunch of rubber-inflated jewels floated in a slow, relaxed pace toward the sky, not in a direct ascent, but rather diagonally, up and to the side.

Immediately after rushing with all intent to the security of his father's legs, the boy noticed that his precious balloons were floating away slowly, quietly into the summer sky. His fear of the oncoming car was overcome by the terror of losing his only recently acquired balloons. With a child's impulsivity, he released his desperate grip on his father's leg and ran into the street, away from his parents, off the sidewalk, with no other goal than that of retrieving his beloved balloons.

"Sweetie, no!" his mother screamed.

The boy ignored her. He blocked out everything else but his fixation on the balloons, even the oncoming car, now travelling at top speed and less than one hundred feet away.

"Son!" the father cried in abject terror, seeing that the speeding car showed no signs of stopping or even slowing down. And his one beloved child stood almost immediately before it. The boy's father dropped his wife's hand and moved speedily toward the street after his child, almost jumping toward him with energy and desperation. He took two leaping steps toward the curb. And in understandable haste, he lost his footing and fell down to his right knee, breaking his fall with his two hands. His palms and knee were raw and abraded, but he was not mindful of the pain. He rose to his feet and tore out once again toward his child.

By this point, the boy had walked fully from the curb and was standing in the middle of the street, both hands stretched into the air in the vain hope of reaching the white strings that dangled helplessly from the newly liberated and slowly ascending balloons. Having come to the heartbreaking realization that the balloons were gone, he stopped walking, lowered his arms to his sides, gave an about-face toward his mother and speedily approaching father, and crunched his facial expression as salted, bitter tears welled up in his eyes. He squinted, pulled his nose down toward his mouth, and bent his pursed lips into a frown.

Still the car kept coming, and it was nearly upon him. The boy was oblivious. Tears that expressed a mixture of anger and cruel disappointment filled and overflowed the corners at his eyes and then rolled gently down his young supple cheeks, curving around his nose to the ends of his mouth. His chin pulled open his mouth to let forth the most tragic wail.

"Naaaaahhhhh!" the boy cried.

His mother was crying too but for a completely different reason. "The car, the car!" the boy's mother yelled in fevered desperation. "Sweetie, come back!"

The child could taste the salted liquid invade his lips and pass into his mouth. The savory tang slid past each territory of taste buds on his palate: sour, sweet, salty. Still consumed with his lost balloons newly abducted by with wind and sky, he turned ignorantly toward the oncoming car, looming in malicious aggression and now less than fifty feet away. The little boy stopped crying instantaneously and froze in place, his mouth now relaxed and eyes widening.

The car's fully-taxed engine bellowed out a thunderous roar. Its front had sustained multiple dents and scrapes centered on the driver's side, which was also missing its headlight. Additionally, the front bumper was dangling down and dragging on the street, barely attached to the car on the passenger's side. Together with the car's engine, this hanging length of metal produced a hellacious harmony of metallic growls and shrieks, like a grizzly bear newly shot and making a desperate effort to escape while dragging a steel trap from its leg.

So shocking and terrifying was the little boy's situation that, mentally and emotionally, he stood outside of time and experience, disconnected from the approaching doom. It happened with such rapidity as to detach him from his own capability. He was helpless in fear.

"Get him! Get him!" his mother yelled.

He understood that this command was meant for his father as opposed to himself. Torn away from the car's increasingly large face for a moment, he saw his mother's horror-stricken expression in the corner of his left eye.

His father dominated the remainder of his view, leaping toward him, reaching out with both hands, his face displaying without reservation every ounce of fear, endangered hope, and love that one human heart could muster. The boy, tender and small—the beloved object of all his mother's devotion and self-sacrificial commitment, the focus of all his father's dreams and hopes even before birth—turned to face two tons of speeding metal, and...

* * *

"Brrrzeet, brrrzeet, brrrzeet, brrrzeet, brrrzeet," sounded the alarm.

Lewis Warner shot up from his deep slumber with a sharp and powerful start. His ten-year old heart was pumping with a rapid and frantic pace. A small amount of perspiration glued his pajama shirt to his chest. The material bore a sports pattern with a light blue background covered in intermittent clusters of footballs, baseballs, and basketballs. It felt cool and sticky, quite uncomfortable. Small pools of liquid dotted the shirt so that it appeared that Lewis had spilled something all over himself at dinner. His bed was a twin-sized mattress lying over a rectangular box of springs that creaked with mournful age at the slightest lean to one side or the other. A key-lime colored fitted sheet wrapped the mattress snugly and matched the loose sheet that draped over it. Over this lay a collection of blankets, each with its own pattern, colors, and history. Most were older than Lewis.

Once Lewis had calmed slightly and realized fully that he was no longer dreaming, that this safe place was his reality, he took in his surroundings—nothing that he had not seen before for a number of years now. A dark blue, but not quite navy blue, paint covered his bedroom walls from ceiling to floor, which was lined with a wooden trim. The walls bore the scars of unplanned movements of furniture and accidental digs and scrapes resulting from toys tossed across the room. Lewis observed a particularly obvious scrape and wondered if his grandmother had seen that one yet. On the wall opposite his bed was a poster featuring capital cities from around the world: Sao Paulo, Cairo, Berlin, Rome, Moscow, Beijing, Tokyo, Washington D.C. Lewis received this map as part of an issue of *National Geographic*, which highlighted cities of the world that month. He loved that poster and was often lost in anticipation and reverie at the idea of visiting one or more of those places.

Underneath the poster sat a wooden desk and chair. The desk dutifully bore the weight of a lamp, a few copies of *National Geographic*, and an open mathematics textbook covered in paper and pencils, Lewis's unfinished homework. Were one to open the desk drawer, he would discover a pile of pencils, markers, and pens, and multiple marks all over the inside of the drawer left unintentionally from uncapped pens and markers. To the right of the bed was a window, complete with blinds and curtains, that opened into the front side of the house and yard.

Still affected by the dream, Lewis hung his head slightly down, pulled the disheveled covers off his legs, swung them off his bed, and down onto the chilly wood floor. The nerves in his feet sent a message to his brain, making it perfectly clear that the floor was cold, that it was still January, and that slippers would indeed be a great idea. Lewis understood all of this, but he didn't care. The power of the dream left him numb to the cold of the floor, the winter chill in his bedroom, and the light of the sun that still had not entered through the window. Like an aimless zombie, Lewis Warner stood on his feet, walked to the door that adjoined his bedroom to the hallway, turned its handle with a practiced motion, and passed into the living room.

Imelda Warner kept everything. At least that's what her home suggested. Every available space was occupied with items. There were stacks of magazines and papers piled overwhelmingly in every table and on each piece of furniture. Her upright piano had plants strewn across its back divided by pictures, both black-and-white and color, of family, friends, and bygone days. Two solid but timeworn hutches seemed to brace up the wall and held countless glasses, plates, pictures, porcelain figurines, and other such items. A couch that was past its prime, but still wonderfully comfortable, laid against the other remaining wall. Underneath all the blankets and comforters, it was a wooden frame, upholstered and covered in a lattice-patterned beige cloth. Both Imelda and Lewis had enjoyed many perfect naps on that couch. Like Imelda herself, it was evidence that age does not always diminish value.

While Imelda's home was overfilled, let the reader be clear that this elderly woman's abode was never dirty or unkempt—far from it, in fact. She took pride in her home, cleaning it more regularly than most and taking great pains to assure that it was always supplied with those things that rendered a house a home: safety, good food, and love. If there was anything strange in Imelda's practice of keeping nearly all that she obtained, it was not a pathology with which she entered the world. Rather, Imelda grew up in a time when few people had much money. Imelda's family and all those she knew struggled to buy food, clothes, and to keep the heat on. In such circumstances there was no waste, no throwing things away.

"Good mornin', sweetie," offered Imelda warmly to her grandson.

That was what Lewis needed, a good morning, a warm morning. It was January. Not only was it cold outside, snowy and frozen; it was also dark. It was dark when Lewis came home from school, dark when he went to bed, and still dark when he rose from his slumber. *Ugh*, he thought, and believed that certainly the expression came forth from his mouth.

"Mornin, Grandma," returned Lewis, making an effort to be cordial despite his tight muscles, lingering fatigue, and heavy heart over his dream.

Imelda was seated on the couch like she always was when present in the living room, centered on the couch and comfortable. Imelda was Lewis's paternal grandmother. She had taken charge of Lewis six years earlier when his mother died of cancer. His father passed away before that. So now it was just Lewis and Imelda Warner against the world. Imelda stepped up to the task decidedly and strongly. She took care of Lewis just as she did her own son, Lewis's father. She made sure Lewis had a safe warm place to live. Imelda provided stability, making sure that Lewis knew right from wrong, went to school, and put forth his best effort in all he did. All this was easy for her.

Her hardest task was finding the right spot for Lewis between his pain and what he needed. Lewis was quite young when he lost both his parents. Imelda too had lost a son and daughter-in-law. Her heart ached as well. So she had to meet Lewis's need to hurt and recover. At the same time, Imelda knew that life had to continue. It would be no blessing to allow her grandchild to get lost in his pain, or to become bitter over the life he had and what was taken away. Her heart, her shoulder was eternally soft, her ears forever open. Nevertheless, she worked hard to give Lewis structure. She expected him to work and grow. Oh, how taxing this second task was for her.

Lewis was hungry. His stomach made muffled petitions for food, but it was too soft for Imelda to hear, and Lewis already knew he was hungry anyway. He desired to keep walking to the kitchen and fix his breakfast t, but at this moment he pined more for something else. It was only a few chilly steps over to the couch and the anticipated support of his grandmother. He sat down next to her and felt the couch take on the burden of his growing eleven-year-old body. Imelda was reading one of her books on gardening. She had read the book many times before but wanted to review, to look over the colored photos, and make plans for what she might plant when the murderous frost allowed the ground to soften and accept seeds.

"How are you this fine mornin'?" she asked, having a pretty clear sense already that something was wrong with Lewis.

"I'm fine," Lewis lied.

This simply meant that he either wasn't ready to talk or wanted his grandmother to try harder. He looked over at the book that she was reading and noticed that the pages were shaking. He followed the quivering pages up to his grandmother's fingers and saw that, in fact, her fingers were shaking. Lewis had seen this before. He knew something was wrong but didn't understand, nor did he wish to ask. Lewis eventually leaned his head over to the right and left it on his grandmother's soft old shoulder. He relaxed and watched her turn page after page. She read about which rose seeds to choose, when to plant, how far apart to set the rows, how far down on the stem to cut, etc. When Lewis's hunger overcame his desire to extend his sleep into rest on the couch, he silently stood up, walked to the kitchen, and prepared his food. Imelda looked up from the pages of her rose book and watched Lewis step away, knowing his young heart was in pain.

Lewis followed his routine. Opening the refrigerator door allowed added light to illuminate the semidark kitchen. He removed the milk and orange juice. He opened the pantry in the hope that his favorite flavor of instant oatmeal, maple with brown sugar, would be there. He loved it! To relief and delight, the box of assorted instant oatmeal flavors still contained two of his preferred taste. Lewis gave an unnoticeable smile, grabbed the packet, and moved over to the kitchen cabinet and stove. He found a suitable-sized bowl and filled it with the contents of his oatmeal packet, watching the oatmeal and powder produce a small dust cloud as they were poured out. He put the kettle of water on the stove, applied it with heat, and filled a dark green-colored drinking glass with orange juice. When all was prepared, he grabbed a spoon and took it all into the dining room.

Like always, Lewis chose the chair that faced away from the kitchen, leaving his back to his grandmother. Once there and seated, Lewis looked at the mount of still dry oatmeal and flavored powder that stood in the center of a pool of near-boiling water. He bowed his head a bit and gave thanks. Lewis poked his spoon into the pile and mercilessly stirred it into the already softening oatmeal and anticipated this delightful mixture that so often made up his breakfast. The warm air that rose from the oatmeal and hot water caressed his face and gave him a slight blush that begged Lewis to release the tears. He was still thinking about the dream. He lowered his head again and started to sob quietly. Beyond his notice, his grandmother had walked up behind Lewis. She curved around slightly to his left side and wrapped her right arm about him. Lewis was surprised but not displeased. He looked up at his one source of stability and love. Imelda knew what was wrong. Lewis had had the dream a number of times before.

In her left hand, Lewis's grandmother held a small bowl of lemon pudding tart, sweet and smooth. Like his maple brown sugar instant oatmeal, Lewis loved his lemon pudding. She laid the little bowl on the table next to Lewis's orange juice. As she did, Lewis pivoted to the left in his chair, extended his arms around his grandmother's waist, and buried his face safely in her side. He wept.

2

Ming Lee's Language Barrier

Lewis felt better. He finished up his breakfast (he saved the lemon pudding until last), returned the dishes to the sink, and walked back into his bedroom to get changed and ready for school. His spirits were lifted a bit. Crying does that. A small amount of sunlight was peaking over the horizon as well, mixing with the January morning darkness and creating a murky blue at the top of the sky and then descending into complete blackness. His grandmother loved him. His belly was full. The sun was coming. That was good enough.

After he worked through his morning regimen of toothbrushing, face washing, and other tasks, he changed his clothes, collected all his books and papers into his backpack, and came back into the living room. Imelda Warner shifted back and forth within the kitchen, now preparing her own breakfast, pressing two pieces of white bread down into the red-orange heat of the toaster, stuffing a strong amount of breakfast tea leaves into her metallic tea basket, filling a mug with boiling water, and withdrawing the strawberry jam from the refrigerator. Lewis could smell the toaster. Its potent heat rendered a pacifying, hunger-producing aroma—a mixture of the new fresh bread recently slid inside, and the remnant crumbs burning from a long history of bread toasted in the past. Had he the time, Lewis could have found room in his belly for that toast and jam.

While addressing each element of her breakfast, she swayed back and forth to the slow soft rhythm of her own voice. She was singing softly like she didn't have a care in the world. In the early morning cold of winter, she was singing. Lewis wondered if she knew he was standing there. Regardless, he was sure that had she known, she would have sung anyway. She was untouchable. At that moment, although he could not imagine ever being as old as his grandmother, Lewis envied her. He deeply envied her detached joy. He questioned in his mind if that comes with age, as if nothing could truly, deeply trouble a person anymore after they've lived so many years. He marveled at Imelda. While her bread toasted and her tea water boiled, she pivoted gracefully in place and raised her singing voice slightly,

> Many moons and red sunsets ago,
> You breathed those words of promise "You'll be mine,
> you'll be mine, forever."
> Ocean waves and breezes blow,

Bearing forever your pledge so sweetly "You'll be mine, you'll be mine forever."
Life comes a callin', you're suddenly fallin' out of love.
No hope deceivin', I'm done believin' "You'll be mine, you'll be mine forever."

Within the safety of his own head, Lewis pondered the idea that perhaps his grandmother heard that song when she was a young lady. Maybe she sung it then too. Maybe the words remind her of some bygone time when she was surrounded by friends, living each moment as if she had a million years to live. Perhaps she sang that song dwelling on some boy who broke her heart. Either way, she seemed blissful and pacifically lost in that melody, suddenly transferred to another time and place when she first sang it. Lewis's envy slowly turned to love and gratitude. He was grateful to have Imelda as his grandmother. He smiled.

Lewis returned to his preparation for school. From head to toe, he transformed himself from a eleven-year-old boy into an arctic traveler, ready for whatever the frigid air and bottomless snow could bring against him. He slid his feet smoothly but firmly into his coal black rubber boots, and fastened the three clamps that ran in-line up the front of each. Then he covered his body with a thick puffy green winter coat, so bulky that it looked more like a sleeping bag with a hood attached. He completed this thermal suit of arctic armor with a red stocking cap, decorated with white snow men and a pair of heavy gloves that matched the coat. He was ready.

The fully vested Lewis zipped up his coat from the bottom edge to his neck, and the sound woke Imelda from her tranquil trance. She turned to see Lewis preparing to venture into the winter world. She walked over to her grandson with a warm smile growing on her face. Even though Lewis had each part of his winter suit situated just as he liked it, Imelda felt it necessary to make some adjustments. He tolerated it although he seemed to like her changes less and less. She pulled the stocking cap further down over his ears, drew the sides of his hood closer together, and did the same to the chest area of his coat as if somehow crunching the materials would provide added warmth. She gave him a kiss on the cheek right before he reached down for his bag.

"Have a great day, sweetheart. I love you," Imelda offered.

Lewis opened the cold door to reveal what they both expected. The bright pale-yellow sun was fighting to shine over the lingering midwinter darkness and through the frost that covered most of the screen door. Imelda Warner's grandson turned toward the frozen day and reached out to clasp the metal screen door handle that certainly would have been painfully cold had Lewis not been wearing gloves.

"Aren't you forgetting something?" questioned Imelda, wearing an impish grin and clasping her hands together in front of her.

Lewis didn't know what she was referring to. He had already kissed her good-bye (or at least allowed his grandmother to kiss him good-bye). "What?" he returned in genuine ignorance and growing curiosity. His grandmother stood there perfectly still with the exception of her eyes that she used to gesture diagonally down and to the left toward the piano bench. Lewis realized almost immediately what it was. The piano bench, in addition to supporting Imelda when she played, also served as a processing station for all mail coming into the Warner house. There on the bench beneath a couple of bills—two sheets of coupon fliers and department store advertisements—and three pieces of piano music by three of the jazz greats from the early twentieth century was Lewis's new copy of *National Geographic*, recently arrived and still wrapped in sheer transparent plastic.

With unrestrained excitement, Lewis tore off the bulky glove protecting his right hand and reached down a bit to the bench. He dexterously slid aside the electric bill and "Ain't Misbehavin'" by Fats Waller and pulled the magazine off the bench without causing the bench's other burdens to fall off. Standing up straight once more, he offered his grandmother a satisfied smile, stowed the magazine in his backpack, and walked out the door. Lewis loved that publication, marveled at its pictures, and became lost in its detailed maps. He had received a subscription to it each year for his birthday since he was nine. Somehow, with his cherished new magazine, the weather seemed a few degrees warmer.

Since Lewis had taken a rather slow start to his morning, it wasn't long before his school bus arrived in all its snowy yellow-orange grandeur. It pulled to a stop, giving its snow-caked wheels a rest. Lewis was amazed the wheels moved at all, given the vast amount of snow packed between the tires and the curved fenders that surrounded them. It gave a frosty *screeeeech*, flapped out its stop sign, and allowed Lewis to board. Once aboard, Lewis made his way down the narrow aisle that ran between two rows of green seats. It was a filthy wet mess with thin rivulets of dirt-polluted slush-water, running in every direction under the seats. Ignoring the other kids, even those he knew well enough to sit with, Lewis plopped himself in the nearest available seat and ripped off the flimsy plastic from his magazine like some ravenous grizzly bear shredding a state park picnic basket in barbaric fury. One girl two rows back reviewed her spelling words for that day's test. Two boys sitting across from her were having a pinching contest. Another boy immediately behind Lewis licked his name on the frozen moisture that covered his window. It read "Dalio" but was intended to be *David*. Not bad though, given that his face was two inches off the glass, and he was using his tongue. To all of this, Lewis was oblivious. For the duration of his trip to school, his eyes didn't once leave the magazine's pages.

When Lewis's bus pulled to a noisy stop in front of James Madison Elementary School, he groaned slightly, wishing the driver had driven more slowly or taken some lazy circuitous route, anything to allow him more time to digest the beautiful photos and engaging articles in his new magazine. Alas, there was no avoiding school. He exited the bus using the treacherously wet steps down and took his well-traveled path up to his fifth-grade classroom.

Underneath Lewis's mournful attitude over leaving his reading lay a firm pride about being in an upstairs classroom for the first time. All the kids from kindergarten to fourth grade studied in the first floor classrooms and were considered "children" by everyone upstairs. Lewis had graduated to the "big kids" upstairs (Lewis often mused that this was ridiculous and confusing since a few of the fourth graders were taller than a few of the "big kids" upstairs). In fifth grade, he was at the bottom rung of the ladder, but at least it was the second ladder.

In his heavy coat, winter hat, and gloves, and with his backpack slung loosely over his left shoulder, Lewis reached the second floor, slightly winded and with a few drops of sweat gathering under his arms. This was also due to the unpredictable heat produced by the building's furnace. In some areas of the school, you'd feel like an earthworm crawling on a blacktop in summer. In other areas you could freeze meat! Although the custodian of the building swore by his every relative, dead or living, that the furnace was indeed operating, the air in certain places was chilly and damp. The boiler was decrepit and inconsistent; facts are facts.

Lewis entered his classroom as he had each day this school year since late August. It was a comfortable place, full of color and warmth. The floor was a standard checkerboard tile design of marbled black and maroon. The walls were covered with screw-attached bulletin boards, rectangular and caramel orange in color. The wall opposite the entrances was dominated by windows, six in all, that opened inward and seemed to allow every single honeybee in during the warmer months of the year. Naturally, the room also contained a desk for each of the class's twenty-four students, a teacher's desk, and an area for coats in the back.

The classroom was buzzing with activity and decoration. Christmas had passed, and the heavy snow of January covered the ground outside. Within the classroom, there was also snow, but the paper variety, cut artistically with scissors, spread out and hung from the ceiling, walls, and bulletin boards. Additionally, every student had recently offered their impression of winter life rendered on French vanilla-colored paper in chalk. Joseph Acker, Lewis's teacher, labored busily at his large heavy wooden desk, checking over his lesson plans for the day, organizing his photocopies, and drawing the occasional sip of increasingly cool coffee.

Each student present in the classroom prepared for the day in their own unique manner. Julianne Benotti hurriedly replaced the caps on each of her markers. She was obsessive. Each marker had its own cap. There could be no mismatches. There would be no dried-out markers. Donny Vanderhill sat contently at his desk, covering his left palm in a thin coat of white glue. Then he blew gentle cool air over his palm in order to speed the drying process. Without reservation, he pulled the sheer opaque shreds of dry glue from his hand, marveling at how effectively they reproduced the skin underneath. After smoothly panning his head back and forth to check for onlookers, Donny slowly placed a shred of glue-skin on his tongue, closed his mouth, and let it melt, flavored with all the dirt and sweat that the glue had drawn from his palm. With an understated, satisfied grin, Donny relaxed, believing he had consumed glue shreds without anyone noticing. When in fact, everyone present had seen him do it a hundred times and was trying to ignore him. Eduardo Padilla and Marcus Upshaw sat on their desks (forbidden in Mr. Acker's classroom) bartering over collectable cards.

It was 8:17 a.m. School started at 8:30 a.m. Lewis had to go to the restroom. If he hurried, Lewis could complete the task before the buzzer started the day. Lewis rapidly shaved off his coat, boots, and other cold-weather items, pitched his backpack over to his desk, and darted across the hall into the boys' restroom still carrying his new *National*

Geographic. Lewis leaned into the heavy wooden door to the boys' restroom with his shoulder, pushing it open with the combined force of his back, shoulder, and legs. The old door gave a whiney *creekeeheh*, which echoed off the vacant walls and the uncarpeted floor. He tucked the pristine smooth-covered publication under his right arm and headed for the last stall (although each had its own door, Lewis felt more secure in the stall nearest the wall).

As he spun the circular metallic door lock on the stall with his left hand, Lewis was slightly startled to hear the restroom door open again behind him. It gave the same high-pitched whine but was accompanied by three obnoxiously loud voices, giggling wildly with incoherent speech. Each of the three spoke over the other two, interrupting and increasing in volume to gain dominance. Lewis froze, knowing who had just entered the restroom with him. They were not welcome. Dylan Pierce, Wyatt McKinney, and Jeremiah Strickland were the uncontested scourge of James Madison Elementary as unanimously described by student and teacher alike. Each had repeated at least one year in school. Collectively, it was six. They held the top three spots for most time spent in detention. Each was a successful experiment in getting through school with the least effort possible.

Individually, Dylan Pierce struggled primarily with authority. The vast majority of his entanglements with teachers and other adults pertained to his overwhelming desire to be in charge. To his parents, teachers, and other authority figures, Dylan consistently mouthed off; once, he even pushed the gym teacher. With other *kids*, there were two choices: submit to Dylan or get hurt (one choice, really). That was it. Dylan exploited his large eighth-grade physique, his prematurely deep voice and (like all bullies) fear to dominate others.

Wyatt McKinney seemed in many aspects an exact replica of Dylan. Wyatt was disrespectful and confrontational to all authority figures and ruled over all those smaller or weaker with an iron fist. Yet, his motivation differed greatly from that of his friend Dylan. Where Dylan was aggressive with others for the sheer sake of being the master, Wyatt mimicked Dylan's behavior out of envy; he wanted to *be* Dylan, to command the same respect, to produce the same terror. Wyatt was utterly unsatisfied with himself. He wanted Dylan's life.

Jeremiah Strickland stole everything: money from his father's wallet, pencils from his classmates, and toys from the local mall, just to give a few examples. Sometimes he stole things he didn't even need or enjoy. Once, he shoplifted a small bottle of nail polish remover from a convenience store and then threw it in the dumpster around the back. For Jeremiah, the main thing was the exciting fear that came from the possibility of getting caught, and then the satisfaction of getting away with it.

"Fancy meeting you here," said Dylan in a cruelly sweet voice.

"Yeah," began Wyatt, "you better hurry, Lewis. You're going to be late for school!"

Wyatt followed the taunt with string of high-pitched laughs, looking to Dylan for approval.

"Hey, Lewis, are you finishing up or just getting started?" questioned Jeremiah. "Don't let us interrupt."

Lewis realized that the doorway to exit the bathroom was blocked. He wouldn't be able to simply walk past them. At this point, he still had a bit of courage and annoyance to bolster himself. He released a deep breath and dropped his head in submission as he spoke, "Guys, just let me go. I don't want any trouble." Lewis didn't really expect they would let him pass untroubled. He anticipated having to endure some beating, pushing, or other twisted ritual designed to humiliate him and provide the three with enough of an ego boost to make it through the day. He was right.

"Well, Mr. Lewis Warner, trouble wants you!" returned Dylan, leaning his head in toward Lewis and speaking in a falsely caring tone, like some twisted devil fussing over a baby in stroller.

Each of the three closed in on Lewis in perfect unison, stepping at the same speed, not too fast, desiring to increase Lewis's fearful suspense and to prolong their pleasure in this moment of control. Lewis tensed up fully, pulling his arms to his chest, squinting, and stepping backward. After a few steps, Lewis's back met the panel of the first stall. His fear overshadowed the surprise and slight pain produced by the collision. Pulling his arms over his chest brought his magazine into unavoidable view of the three villains.

"What have we here?" queried Jeremiah, knowing full well the magazine's title. "Mine hasn't come yet this month. How 'bout you guys?" he continued, turning slightly to face Dylan and Wyatt.

"Oh, the dog ate mine, hah, hah!" added Wyatt. He patted Dylan lightly on the back, hoping for a good laugh.

With a vicious lack of consideration, Jeremiah reached out to Lewis and yanked the magazine from under his arm. He stepped back slightly and began flipping the pages with mocking pretense as if he were actually interested. Jeremiah stopped about halfway through. "I already read this article," he said, and tore the article from the magazine from top to bottom. The other two wailed with laughter that encouraged Jeremiah like a singer's standing ovation. He flipped to another. "Looks like I read this one too. Uh-oh!" Just like the first, Jeremiah stripped the pages from the binding and tossed them over his left shoulder.

Dylan was amused, but Jeremiah had been the center of attention long enough. His ridiculous smile was replaced by a severe, flat expression as he stared at Jeremiah. Dylan stood up straight to remind Jeremiah that he was larger and then extended his hand. He could have yanked the magazine like Jeremiah had from Lewis, but making Jeremiah hand it to him would once again assert his superiority, even over his friend. Jeremiah obediently dropped his silly grin in an instant, shrunk slightly, and gently passed the magazine to Dylan.

Dylan wasn't trying to be original. Once he had the magazine, he flicked through the pages as did his fiendish friend a moment earlier. "Oh look, they found some pretty flowers in Norway," began Dylan. "I'm on the next plane tonight!" Then he peeled the glossy photo-covered pages out and pitched them away. The other two cackled and howled. They both found it amusing but also laughed from a terrified obedience to Dylan. "What do you think of that, Warner?" asked Dylan, taking another step toward Lewis. Wyatt and Jeremiah followed suit. By this time, Lewis could barely be seen from outside the nightmarish human noose that Dylan and his friends created. Lewis was shrinking down more and more. He just wanted to crawl into a ball and wait until it was all over. Dylan reveled in Lewis's distress and dread, in part because he had caused it, in part because it soothed his own self-hatred to see another weaker person suffer.

By now there wasn't much left inside the magazine, but Dylan wanted one more poke. "Hey, Lewis, they found your grandma's bones in Shanghai!" Wyatt and Jeremiah roared with laughter louder than before. They bent over slightly to emphasize the humor of the remark, all the while looking at Lewis in order to savor his anguish.

"上海," (Shanghai) sounded a voice coming from behind. "你說它錯了." (You spoke incorrectly)

The unexpected sound stole the collective attention of Lewis and his torturers. The three bullies wrinkled their faces in reaction to what they heard but clearly did not comprehend. Each turned around in unison to investigate the new voice's source. Lewis, relieved that, at least for the moment, their attention wasn't on him, relaxed just slightly and gazed through the opening, which his captors created as they turned.

"What?" questioned Wyatt, staring at the newcomer.

Dylan gave Wyatt a viciously patronizing stare, sending the message that he would pose such questions first.

"什麼嗎," (What?) said the young man, mimicking Wyatt's grossly exaggerated expression. There in the doorway, having just entered the bathroom, stood Ming Lee (or Lee, Ming, we'll get to that later). Ming was just over five feet in height, slightly overweight, and somewhat unkempt in his appearance. His left blue-and-white gym shoe was untied, dragging its lace behind. He covered his T-shirt with a button-down dress shirt, which he wore untucked, dangling over his belt. This belt sustained a nice pair of blue jeans that hung off his legs like curtains, loose and airy, due to the fact that Ming's waist demanded a slightly larger size pants than his legs. At Ming's home, a brush sat on his bedroom dresser, unused.

As the three locked their gaze on Ming, an added level of tension left Lewis. He leaned forward off the stall wall and lowered his arms all but completely from his chest. When Dylan and his cohorts in evil had fully committed their attention to Ming, it was as if the wind carried Lewis's fear over their heads and wrapped it around him. Ming's hands began to shake unnoticeably, and he stepped back just a few inches.

"Well, look who's here, Mr. Fried Rice himself, Ming," taunted Dylan.

"好, 看看是誰在這裡, 炒飯先生, 明," (Well, look who's here, Mr. Fried Rice himself, Ming) responded Ming, mimicking Dylan's expressions almost perfectly.

"What did he say?" asked Jeremiah.

"他說了什麼?" (What did he say?) returned Ming.

"I think somebody just got off the boat," said Wyatt.

"我認為有人剛下船," (I think somebody just got off the boat) Ming returned responding.

Dylan was out of patience. He was by no means afraid of Ming. But to hear him speak in a language he didn't understand put Dylan out of control. He wouldn't have it. Using every ounce of his intimidating, prematurely muscular physique, Dylan shot up into Ming's face with lightning speed. He snatched him by the T-shirt, crushing the garment's material into his large sweaty hand. Dylan's arm yanked Ming effortlessly up to just inches from Dylan's mouth. Ming received an immediate, comprehensive education on the condition of Dylan's teeth, gums, and general oral hygiene, including the spare remaining pieces of the bully's breakfast still stuck in the crevices. As Dylan spoke, Ming suffered a full volley of his warm, moist breath, thick with the smell of Dylan's half-digested morning meal.

"You start speakin' English now, or I am gonna break your face!" demanded Dylan. Making every effort not to vomit, Ming closed his eyes, tried to pinch his nostrils together with the muscles in his face and bravely responded.

"啟動現在說英語, 或我會打破你的臉," (You start speaking English now, or I am going to break your face!) said Ming. Ming didn't open his eyes. He knew what was coming. There were no illusions. Bullies are all the same.

"That's it!" asserted Dylan as he pulled his right arm back and into a curl. He tightened his fingers into a solid mass of bone, skin, and muscle. Wyatt and Jeremiah stepped back and out of the way. Wyatt smiled gleefully. Dylan threw back his shoulder slightly and leaned back on his right foot. Ming tightened his jaw and face and crowded his shoulders up around his neck in a vain effort to protect himself.

With marvelous rapidity, the bathroom door flew open! The door swung with such force that, had Mr. Acker not been holding it, it certainly would have bashed into the wall and left an awful gash. At this point, Mr. Acker wasn't aware of what had taken place in the boy's restroom. "Boys, it's 8:30 a.m. What are you doing in here?" he asked. With speed that rivaled Mr. Acker's breeching of the restroom entrance, Dylan released his murderous grip on Ming's shirt and stepped away. Mr. Acker walked into the main chamber of the restroom and surveyed the scene.

Joseph Acker was no fool. He was in the middle of his twenty-first year of teaching. Besides, even if the floor wasn't covered with ragged-edged magazine pages and Ming's shirt wasn't crushed into a wrinkled wad, Lewis's tense expression made it clear that something suspicious had just taken place.

"What happened to Lewis's magazine?" asked Acker, staring back and forth at Dylan and his friends. This was no snap judgment. Lewis was Mr. Acker's student and had seen Lewis tote and read his *National Geographics* on numerous occasions.

"Who knows," answered Dylan, enjoying the taste of the lie as it passed his lips, "they don't make magazines like they used to."

Jeremiah and Wyatt offered a repressed giggle, which was soon snuffed out by Mr. Acker's severe stare. "Lewis," began Acker. "What happened to your magazine?"

Lewis contemplated his options for what seemed like an eternity. To rat out Dylan and his stooges would provide the much desired justice for his magazine; but he would certainly suffer all the more later, on the playground, in the locker room, wherever. Lewis rolled both eyes to the right, away from Mr. Acker and shrugged his shoulders. Dylan, Jeremiah, and Wyatt were all staring right at Lewis and exhaled just below everyone's notice. Dylan looked at Lewis with a devilish smile as if he had just struck a deal for his very soul.

Mr. Acker knew quite well what had happened and was disappointed that Lewis gave into fear. Without any admission of guilt or claim from Lewis, his options for discipline were limited. Like Dylan and the other two, Joseph Acker gave a sigh, more to release frustration than to signal relief. Despite his limited options, he wasn't willing to let these three just walk out the door. He wouldn't have it! "Dylan, Jeremiah, Wyatt, pick up the pages and throw them in the trash," ordered Acker.

"But we didn't—" started Dylan.

"Pick up the pages and throw them in the trash!" repeated Acker, interrupting Dylan and adding volume and gravity with the repetition.

It was the least they could do. After a brief hesitation, the three miscreants knelt down, retrieved the pages from the floor and pitched them defiantly into the garbage just feet from Mr. Acker. He glared at the three with a gaze both concentrated and blazing. First Jeremiah and then Wyatt walked slowly passed Mr. Acker and finally out the door. Before taking his leave, Wyatt turned back to check in with Dylan as if (he were) taking his queues from him rather than Mr. Acker. Dylan gave a nod, and Wyatt looked back at Acker, and then walked out the door. Dylan leaned over the garbage, spit, and then strolled in front of Acker with a falsely calm manner.

"Boys, are you all right?" probed Mr. Acker changing his tone from stern to soft.

"Yeah," they both answered in near unison.

But Acker knew better.

3

Tones For Lunch and Tones Before Supper

Lewis returned to the classroom and was received by the staring eyes of his classmates. They just looked at him, not knowing if he was the culprit or the victim. They knew, however, that he was at the center of it. Lewis returned their glaring gaze for an instant and then retreated to the relative safety of his desk. Mr. Acker entered the classroom almost immediately after Lewis and his presence set the students back into a mode of learning. Each of them, including Lewis, took out their mathematics texts, laying them out and opened on top of their desks. Mr. Acker checked a few things at his own desk, jotted down a few notes related to the incident in the restroom, and then walked over in front of the students to begin his lesson.

Lewis did his best to put the encounter behind him, but it was so troubling. His hands trembled helplessly as he turned to page 196 in his book. His arms and legs were cool and stiff. Lewis tried his best not to dwell on the fear and humiliation. He tried to focus on the mathematics lesson but couldn't. Those three monsters manhandled him and destroyed his new magazine. All the while, he was powerless to fight back and hopelessly outnumbered. It was terrifying to be at the mercy of others. More than once he had to fight back tears that welled up in his eyes, half from distress and half from anger. Each time they came, he took a deep breath and wiped his eyes before the drops grew too large, acting as if his eyes simply itched.

By the time morning studies were completed and lunch period began, Lewis was feeling better, more stable. Down in the cafeteria, he had a group of friends with which he normally lunched, but today he sought out Ming. In the course of Lewis's traversing the cafeteria, Ming noticed that he was coming and enthusiastically waved him over. There were a couple of unoccupied seats near Ming, and Lewis sat down across from him, laying his royal blue lunch tray on the table. "Hey, thanks for coming in this morning," began Lewis. "Those three apes could've taken us both, but what you said kept them busy long enough for Mr. Acker to arrive."

Ming beamed back at Lewis with a warm smile. "No sweat!"

"What were you saying to them?" asked Lewis. "Was that your family's language?" Lewis finished the last syllables of his question as he raised his corn dog from the lagoon of ketchup he poured onto his tray. After widening his mouth enough to avoid a mess, he chomped off the end, taking in more corn than dog.

"Yeah," answered Ming. "My family is Chinese. We speak Mandarin at home all the time. My father insists." As Ming mentioned his father's insistence, he shook his head slightly and rolled his eyes up and over, like a cow jumping over a moon.

"We'll, what did you say?" pressed Lewis.

"Nothing special," returned Ming rapidly, sensing his new acquaintance's impatience. "I just repeated what they said." Ming finished his response with a proud, sly grin pasted across his face, like a mouse that had successfully taken the cheese from under the cat's nose and returned home safely.

"That is so cool!" marveled Lewis. "Teach me some, please!" he begged. "How do you say 'hello'?"

Ming placed his fork back in its place and ignored his corn. "Nee-how," he said, leaning his head forward intently like the master teacher.

"Nee-how," repeated Lewis.

"That's great, Lewis," said Ming. "But you said it too flat. You have to use the tones."

"What does that mean?" shot back Lewis, contorting his expression to register confusion. "What's a tone?"

"Tones are what make the language sound right," answered Ming. "See, you go up with your voice when you say 'nee' and then you go down and then up when you say 'how'. Listen!" Ming said effortlessly in perfect intonation, overemphasizing somewhat for Lewis's sake.

"Nee-how, nee-how, nee-how, nee-how," parroted Lewis.

"That's pretty good," encouraged Ming. "Think of it like a rabbit that jumps up over the fence, lands, digs a hole under the ground, and then comes back up. That's what my Mom taught me."

Lewis didn't notice, but Ming's expression when referring to his mother was the polar opposite of that of his father. Ming's entire air was warm and appreciative when talking about his mom. Had Lewis been a bit older at the time, he may have guessed what he'll discover further along in the story—Ming does not have the best relationship with his father.

"Hey," shot out Ming, "what do you think of Alexandra Reiniger? Is she not the prettiest girl in the whole school? I mean, *vroom, vroom*! She really gets my engine running!"

"Yeah, I guess she is pretty," agreed Lewis. He looked down slightly and pressed up his bottom lip to elevate his upper lip, indicating that agreement was merely partial.

"You *guess* she's pretty?" mimicked Ming. "Alexandra Reiniger is the jelly to my peanut butter! She is the butter to my bread! You know what I mean?" Ming's face bore an expression of such animated delight, as if he just won a shopping spree to his favorite toy store. His eyes were lidless, opened as far as his skull would allow. An excited smile pulled his cheeks into fleshy wads immediately below his eyes.

Lewis and Ming continued talking, eating, and growing more acquainted with each other as the lunch period progressed. They chatted regarding their teachers, sports, and favorite video games. Ming took a brief break from the conversation to watch Alexandra Reiniger walk from the kitchen with her food tray over to the other eighth graders where she sat down. He was mesmerized. In his mind's eye, Alexandra was not merely at school in the lunch room, she was rather passing through the iron gate that surrounded her castle and waving to the adoring common folk as she made her way to the royal jewel-encrusted chariot that awaited her. In Ming Lee's heart, she was a queen.

Eventually, lunch ended and the teachers signaled to their students to gather their trays, pass through the service line, and return to their classrooms. Lewis and Ming continued to gab as they walked, pitching used napkins and empty milk cartons into the black wide-mouthed trash cans that guarded the cafeteria's exit. They marveled at the ability of the other kids to ignore the rules, dumping spoons in the garbage, carelessly blasting ketchup and other slimy remains everywhere except in the trash, or lazily delivering their tray, paper, food, and all up to the overworked, underpaid kitchen staffer receiving the trays armed with a dish sprayer in her hands and a ferociously hateful expression on her face.

"Lewis, I'll see you at play rehearsal later today," said Ming.

"What do you mean," asked Lewis. "You're not in the play."

"Yeah, I am. Well, not really in it. I help out in the back with the lights and sounds and stuff," returned Ming as he knocked his blue plastic tray carelessly against the inside of the trash can, hoping to dislodge the stubbornly clinging items.

"Oh okay," responded Lewis. "Did you know that Alexandra is in the play?"

"Why do you think I'm helping?" rejoined Ming with a sly grin.

* * *

Sandy LaGrange was a perfectionist and immeasurably passionate about theater. She believed that the answer to all the world's problems could be found on stage, in the music of a robust chorus, a heartbreaking soliloquy or a colorful piece of background scenery. She was single, childless, and nearing retirement. In addition to teaching first grade—having done so for over thirty-five years—she was the faculty supervisor for all things theatrical, including the winter musical. This year's event was entitled *I Like Ike and Elvis: A Musical Tribute to the 50s*. This dramatic spectacle involved nearly the entire student body of James Madison Elementary and featured the voice and instrumental talents of the school's best and brightest, including Lewis Warner.

As the teachers led their respective classes into the gymnasium (which doubled as the auditorium), Ms.

LaGrange scanned the row of incoming students, pulling out her singers and musicians. The remaining students filed past her and took their seats in the wooden bleachers that lined the northern side of the auditorium. When she had all her kids extracted from the others, she directed them to their places. She stood tall and proud on the gym floor in her black dress boots, like some sort of pirate captain. She also wore black dress slacks, a red sweater with black polka dots over a black-and-white striped-dress shirt. Both the sweater and shirt were rolled up nearly to the elbow, intended to indicate that she was dynamic and powerful. Her neck, ears, and wrists were decorated with her usual collection of large jewelry, which was usually purchased in some foreign country. On this particular day, her jewelry ensemble bore a black-and-white tiger pattern to match her outfit.

"All right everyone, quiet down. We need to begin," mandated Ms. LaGrange in her calm, smooth voice. She didn't talk like most people do to one another. She usually spoke like she was hosting a dinner party, using a deep melodic tone as if she were paid much, much more than James Madison Elementary could afford. Group by group, student by student, the children took their seats in the bleachers and settled into place.

"Whenever you are ready, Lewis." She turned to the student orchestra and gave a heavy nod to signal that it was time to start the music.

Lewis had the quite important role of Dwight D. Eisenhower. He walked slowly across the stage trying his best to appear powerful and presidential. The idea of this scene in the play was to present the history of Eisenhower's life. Lewis was dressed in the uniform of a US Army general, very much as Eisenhower dressed as he visited the troops, following the American invasion in France during World War II.

Lewis walked in front of a group of third graders dressed as the baseball players on Eisenhower's Abilene, Kansas high school team. Next, he paraded before some seventh-grade boys, doing their best to portray military combat in Germany in 1944. On the far end of the stage, Lewis finished his walk by passing in front of a group of children from various grades, holding signs that read "Ike," and "We Like Ike." The children waved them back and forth and up and down in an effort to give the appearance that Eisenhower had just been elected president.

"Wonderful, wonderful, Lewis!" began Ms. LaGrange, attempting to express approval and encouragement to Lewis while still maintaining her air of calm professionalism. "But I need more movement from you, and emotion! Remember, you are now the leader of the free world!" She directed her attention to the third-graders playing Eisenhower's baseball team. "Boys, you can't just sit there. You're baseball players! Wave the bats like you are hitting a ball. David, try winding up for a pitch just after Lewis passes by. Craig, stop flicking his ear. Stop it, or I can find someone else for your part. Very good! Very good! Now it's your turn, Agnes."

Agnes Reiniger was Alexandra Reiniger's younger fourth-grade sister and was considered rather strange by her classmates. This was not as a result of her appearance. She stood the normal height for a girl her age, had straight light-brown hair that she wore just below her shoulders and ended in a slight upward curl. It always contained a shiny ribbon with cleft ends. She dressed normally. Today she was vested in tan suede ankle-high boots, pink jeans, and a long sleeve aqua flannel blouse, patterned in vertical and horizontal lines of various shades of blue. She unnerved everyone, including her teacher, because she never ever spoke.

A year earlier, Agnes had undergone some sort of traumatic experience from which she had since recovered in every respect, except for speech. She played, read, studied, watched television just like all the other girls her age—but never spoke. Nevertheless, she retained her dulcet, melodious singing voice. And did she use it!

Ms. LaGrange had recruited Agnes to play Peggy Lee, a favorite singer from the 1950s. Today, Agnes was dressed normally. On the evening of the play, however, she planned to mimic Peggy Lee's appearance as much as possible. Agnes's mother had prepared a brilliantly white gown, a platinum-blonde wig, and a fake fur scarf to wrap around Agnes's neck, all to assist her in playing the role.

Agnes strolled confidently from behind the curtain and across the front of the stage toward its center. As she did, Ms. LaGrange cued the musicians to begin the accompaniment. Agnes gently reached her prearranged spot on stage and let loose the most vibrant and sweet tones imaginable. She threw out her arms like a set of a butterfly's wings in a manner that seemed to give her voice greater power and height. The diminutive fourth grader sang these lines from W. C. Handy's "Beale Street."

> I've strolled the Prado, I've gambled on the Bourse
> The seven wonders of the world I've seen
> And many are the places I have been.
> Take my advice, folks and see Beale Street first.

Lewis watched his fellow cast member from offstage behind the curtain. As always, he was quite impressed with how effortlessly Agnes sang and danced. She seemed to float across the floor and to bring a sudden and irresistible halt to all activity when she sang. The song lyrics also fascinated Lewis, and he wondered if this song's author knew any of his grandma's favorite songwriters. Agnes moved from point to point on the floor with practiced elegance, all the while hitting each note flawlessly. So she continued until such a change came over her appearance and behavior as to leave Lewis petrified with surprise and fear.

Agnes stopped her fluid movements and angelic song. She halted altogether and became rigid from head to toe, drawing her feet together and pinning her arms to her sides like a soldier. Her mouth went closed and silent, and she stared straightforward. Lewis pulled his head back in shock and waited for Ms. LaGrange to ask Agnes why she had stopped singing. He heard nothing from Ms. LaGrange and, panning over to see her, saw no change in her at all. Sandy LaGrange was smiling in utter delight, nodding at Agnes with enthusiastic approval as she directed the student orchestra. Lewis returned his attention to Agnes, who remained stiff, like a freshly hewn statue of marble. She was motionless. Thousands of lightning-fast sensations shot down Lewis's back like electrified worms as he tried to comprehend what was transpiring before him. He stepped forward just slightly and pulled the dark green curtain back to see if the students and teachers in the bleachers saw what Agnes was doing (or wasn't doing). They had not reacted at all. The entire student body present and every teacher in the auditorium were behaving as if Agnes was performing in her normal manner. Lewis didn't understand! This wasn't part of the play. *Why doesn't Ms. LaGrange stop the practice and talk to Agnes*, questioned Lewis to himself.

"Lewis!"

Lewis turned immediately to Ms. LaGrange, expecting to be met with a coarse and intense stare. She was probably wondering why he was pulling the curtain back and disrupting the rehearsal. To his mystification, Ms. LaGrange wasn't looking at him at all. She was grinning at her golden girl on stage and waving her arms in orchestration toward the student musicians.

"Lewis!"

This time it was unmistakable. The voice was stark and clear and seemed to pull Lewis's head and eyes. The sound came from Agnes, and yet, her head had not turned. Lewis didn't notice as he gripped the velvety curtain with sharp and terrific strength like a drowning man on a tethered life preserver. His heartbeat doubled its pace, and the electric tingles poured over his skin a second time. He gave Agnes his complete attention like a defendant awaiting the jury's verdict.

"Lewis, Lewis, Lewis!" spoke Agnes in a dangerous and smoky voice. Then she slowly swiveled her head to the left at a perfect, uniformed speed.

Lewis noticed that her eyes were closed. As the muscles in her neck rotated her head, her body followed suit in a crisp, almost robotic fashion from top to bottom, first her shoulders, then her waist, her knees, and finally, her feet. When she had completed the turn and faced Lewis fully, Lewis instinctively withdrew and fell backward over his own feet. Pulling his head and shoulders up off the ground high enough to see Agnes, Lewis saw her eyes crack open at the bottom to reveal a pure luminous fire, burning with crackling flames on the right and the left. The glowing reds, oranges, and yellows illuminated the lines and curves of Agnes's tender smooth face; and yet the fire did not burn her.

Lewis's mouth dropped open, and his lower jaw hung limply. He remained in place, slavishly attentive to Agnes. As her eyes continued to produce the lovely and yet harrowing flame, Agnes opened her mouth with the same mechanical manner she displayed when she turned. Her head remained firmly in place. Only her jaw moved to open her mouth. The same rich glimmering flares that erupted from her sweet child's eyes now crackled out the rim of her lips. The flames began small deep in her throat like a spark at the bottom of an oil well. From there, they grew ravenously as a heated red tornado, consuming the oxygen in her mouth and launching forth with a vengeance.

Daring to take his eyes off Agnes for a split second, Lewis panned to the left, thinking that certainly now Ms. LaGrange must notice Agnes's behavior. By now, the children and teachers in the audience must be shrieking in terror and running for safety. No. Ms. LaGrange continued to shine an affectionate smile toward Agnes like a sunbeam at the dawn of a perfect spring day. Her arms fluttered back and forth in view of the orchestra, keeping them gently in time. Lewis suddenly felt completely alone, as if the whole world has turned black, and he was the solitary white spot. His mind began a slow and steady crawl toward madness. It was beyond fear now.

In desperation, Lewis shot to his feet with the sharp fleet movements of a fifth-grade boy. Without hesitation, he shot over to the front center of the stage, looked directly at Ms. LaGrange and yelled, "Ms. LaGrange, don't you see Agnes? Look at her! There's fire coming out of her eyes!"

Ms. LaGrange gave a sudden jump, throwing her flowing arms into the air in shock. Her conductor's baton slipped from her nimble fingers and dropped slowly to the gym floor. Most of the sound from the orchestra ceased immediately. From a few students—those who were in the middle of producing a musical note—came a flurry of final instrumental groans and squeaks.

Lewis now had the attention of the entire gym. In his peripheral vision, he could see that every eye among the students and teachers was on him. The waves of attention felt heavy and hot, like opening the door to a car, with its windows rolled up on the muggiest day of summer. Lewis's eyes were glued to Ms. LaGrange, and she would not allow them to escape.

She drew in and released a deep breath, her thin arms posted at her sides like sentries there to contain the anger brewing in her gut. She leaned her head just slightly forward and spoke slowly, trying to remember that she was a professional and was standing in front of the entire school. "That's an interesting line, Lewis. But I don't think it's in the script!" she said in a controlled voice.

Lewis's emotions were a turbulent mixture of fear, anger, and frustration. He knew he was in trouble now. He was thoroughly embarrassed in front of the whole school. Yet, he knew what he had just seen. It happened!

"But didn't you see?" he asked with a beggar's expression on his face.

"Lewis, get off my stage and go to the principal's office, now!" Ms. LaGrange demanded.

Lewis's heart sank. He was done. Imelda Warner's grandson turned to the right to walk off the stage with his head hung so low he could barely see in front of himself. As he passed by, he slowed just slightly to look at Agnes. There were no glowing flames bursting from her eyes. There were no glimmering sparks crackling from the rim of her lips. Agnes Reiniger stood in the right place, the spot prearranged by Ms. LaGrange, the spot where she had sung her song at every rehearsal prior. There was every indication that while Lewis saw her with flames and flares, Agnes was, in fact, singing her song normally.

Lewis walked off stage, passing by the velvety green curtain and the stage hands and other actors tucked behind it, and he descended the stairs that led to the hallway, like a prisoner newly condemned to death. Once on the main level, he again turned right and began the slow march to the principal's office. He didn't know what to expect. He had even less idea of how to explain what he had done wrong.

Lewis played the encounter out in his head. "Mr. Cohen, Ms. LaGrange sent me to see you. I am very sorry. While Agnes Reiniger was singing her song for the school play, I ran out on stage and yelled at Ms. LaGrange, claiming that Agnes's face was on fire. It was very naughty, and I promise to never do it again."

"Oh, that's fine, Lewis. Don't give it a second thought. It happens all the time," said Mr. Cohen in a warm consoling tone.

"But, Mr. Cohen, I'm not in trouble?" asked Lewis in disbelief.

"No, no. In fact, why don't you take the rest of the day off? There are two nice men here who will help you into a nice white suit. They'll take you to a soft white room where you can be all by yourself, peaceful and quiet," explained Mr. Cohen.

Lewis's mind returned to reality as he approached a drinking fountain stationed in the hallway next to the boys' and girls' restrooms. He wasn't particularly thirsty but was willing to do anything to postpone his encounter with Mr. Cohen. *I better drink deeply*, he thought. *This may be my last one.* Lewis drew close to the white basin with its arching metallic water emitter and leaned forward in a curved motion to take in the gurgling liquid. At the same time, his left hand smothered the faucet handle that released water to the emitter, giving it a turn. The barely clear cool water hit his lips.

"Lewis!"

Lewis stopped drawing in water immediately, choking slightly on the liquid that passed through his throat. He pulled his head up and backward with phenomenal speed, like a chef retracting a newly burned finger on the stove. As he turned around, he assumed it was Ms. LaGrange, having pulled up right behind him with a mouthful of wrath to pour out on a lowly fifth-grader, who disrupted her rehearsal.

It wasn't. Ms. LaGrange was in gymnasium, pulling herself together and making every effort to salvage the remainder of the rehearsal. It was, in fact, Agnes Reiniger standing before Lewis. *What was she doing here?* Lewis pondered. *Is she angry at me for interrupting her song?*

"Agnes," Lewis started. "I'm sorry for—"

Before Lewis was able to complete his apology, Agnes took three long assertive steps toward him and snapped her left arm out to the side in a crisp rapid motion, like a dutiful soldier coming to attention before her commander. She stared at Lewis but remained silent. Although she was shorter and lighter than Lewis, Agnes genuinely created fear in Lewis's heart. He knew what he saw and heard in the gymnasium—fire in her eyes and mouth, her loud commanding voice as she demanded his attention. Lewis wondered if she were here to use that same flame to melt Imelda Warner's grandchild into smoking jelly on the hallway floor.

"Agnes," Lewis started once again. "What do you—?"

Again, Agnes shocked Lewis. However, this time, there were no flames, crackles, or fast-moving arms. Agnes didn't even shout out Lewis's name. Instead, she sang. The melodic pitches passed her tender vocal chords, resonated within her mouth, and were shaped by her slightly pink lips before escaping beautifully into the open air. Using the arm that already pointed toward the wall, Agnes extended her hand, aiming her finger in the same direction. Agnes Reiniger's tuneful voice flowed out like honey and carried these words.

> The heavy snows will soon arrive, and then will gently lay,
> Their frosty burden on the trees, to keep the spring at bay.
> The winged birds in flying herds are feathered to keep warm.
> On treetop crests they build their nests and safe remain from harm.
> I, too, could wait for spring that way, but why would I bother?
> I am my father's father.

Even if Lewis had given Agnes's lyrics his full attention, it is unlikely he would have comprehended their meaning (at least at this point). Lewis was, rather, awestruck by what appeared on the wall where Agnes pointed. As she sang, her words were inscripted in sparking crackled flames. Each new letter exploded in luminescent flame, cutting permanently into the white-painted cinder block. When the flame completed one word, it proceeded to the next with purpose and passion. Agnes continued her mournful tune.

Long before my father's arms my tender frame were keeping,
An older man chose evil's way and left his maiden weeping.
His actions broke a mother's heart, two if truth be noted,
And left two children fatherless, on whom their love was doted.
Like Dad, I, too, could choose the good, but why would I bother?
I am my father's father.

Lewis watched the wall faithfully as this second set of verses was burned into the stony blocks. When the last letter's flame sputtered into popping sparks, he curved to his left and examined Agnes, hoping to gain some sort of understanding. Agnes's face, to this point covered with a neutral expression, now turned severe and demanding. She pulled her brow together and downward, nearly uniting the two light-brown strips of hair that lay above her eyes. As her expression altered, she tensed-up her extended arm and reasserted the finger aimed at the wall. Lewis understood.

Timeless, I signal this fevered plea, from days still yet to pass.
To learn my story clean and clear, like tempered sheets of glass.
Can you withstand the coming chill, the blightful, winter wrath,
And harken to this supple child, who, silent, speaks the path?
I could, this instant, end the threat, but why would I bother?
I am my father's father.

Agnes's final sweet pitch faded into silence like a tired soul into sleep. She slowly and peacefully lowered her arm into a normal relaxed position at her side. The severe dominating expression left her face, and she looked at

Lewis with full serenity. To her left, the final orange-red sparks gave their ending pops and mutated into billows of gray smoke, crawling carelessly upward into the air. Before Lewis could muster even the first question, the gym door leading into the hallway waved open.

"Aggie, what are you doing? C'mon, Ms. LaGrange wants to run through your song again," said Agnes's sister, Alexandra. She stood tall in the doorway, still dressed as the Statue of Liberty.

Agnes dutifully turned to her sister's familiar voice and speedily returned to the gymnasium. As Agnes walked through the door under her sister's arm that held it open, Alexandra turned her attention to Lewis, giving him a look both puzzled and hostile. She was curious about Lewis's strange outburst, but even more, she was angry that it involved her little sister. She certainly had questions for Lewis and, if nothing else, wanted to give him a rather large piece of her mind. Finally, however, she was mindful of her obligations inside the gymnasium and released Lewis from her oppressive gaze.

Lewis stood motionless. He had just finished filling his belly with water but was thirsty again, nonetheless. Nervousness left his throat parched. He was shaking like a Chihuahua in a kennel full of Rottweilers. What was he to do? His mind was racing with questions, most of which pertained to Agnes and her recent display. He still seriously considered the idea that he was losing his mind. How could he ever know he wasn't? No one else saw what he had seen. Agnes didn't talk. If he were to ask, "Hey, Agnes, just out of curiosity, has anyone else seen your face catch fire before? Do you burn words into the walls at home?" people would think he really was crazy.

It was quiet enough now in the hallway that Lewis could hear and feel his heart pounding like a piston in a race car. Lewis took a deep, long breath. He felt a cool wet drop of sweat creep down the side of his head, ease past his ear, and curl underneath his face. Another made its way down his back in the same fashion. He stepped cautiously over to the fountain, gorged his belly on water, and leaned up straight as he wiped the excess drops of liquid from his mouth. Then he did the only thing he could, Lewis turned toward Mr. Cohen's office, dried his moist hands on his pants and walked.

4

Are You Thankful For Me?

Earlier that same year…

A rounded Honda two-door compact car pulled up to the house. The vehicle was painted purple and kept in near-perfect condition, which was quite a feat, given its ten years on the road. Its small but peppy engine came to an anticlimactic halt after the tires ground down the gravely driveway. While the car was still in motion, Ming Lee released the latch on the inside of the passenger side door and pushed it open, causing his mother to apply the brakes earlier and with more fervor than she had planned. Ming wanted out of the car.

"Ming, slow down! The car is still moving," demanded Ming's mother, trying to keep her son in the car while simultaneously putting the transmission in park and yanking the key from the ignition.

"No, Mom. I have to show Dad!" returned Ming with fulsome, nearly desperate joy. He stepped carelessly out of the car, pushing the door open to its full expanse. Hitting its apex, the door bounced back vengefully, slowing slightly his advance toward the house. Ming gripped a white eight-by-eleven-inch sheet of paper tightly in the left hand and dashed toward the front door at top speed, nearly leaping with each stride. He had fantastic news for his father, and nothing would get in the way.

The Ming family lived comfortably at 928 Broadleaf Drive. Unusual but attractive faded green paint covered the exterior walls of the house. The front was adorned with steps leading up to a white wood-planked porch that lay underneath a swing of the same color. A small but steady maple tree kept silent vigil in the front lawn, suspending its sad, empty limbs. A strong autumn's wind blew intermittently against the tree, bending the tree's sixty-year-old trunk. It appeared as if the tree was looking down at its fallen leaves in a pitiful lament forward, then backward, then to the sides, gazing on its prodigal children promised to return in the spring.

Ming jumped broadly from the gravel up to the first wooden step, leaving a bare divot in the chalky stoned driveway. He landed firmly on the wood, both feet landing simultaneously. His weight produced a predictable *creeeeeeeek*, which ceased as he ascended to the next step. As he dashed to the front door, he ignored totally the pile of dead leaves ushered into the corner by the relentless November wind. He missed utterly the wooded-porch swing, swaying forward and backward in a broken rhythm, as if two kindly invisible spirits were sitting in it, passing the afternoon sharing memories of their life in this house. Ming was oblivious to the very air around his head, chilly and filled with the first tiny snowflakes of winter.

His gloveless fingers wound rapidly around the storm door's aluminum handle. The metal sent a cruel bite through his skin, which he barely noticed. Ming wrenched the storm door open just far enough to position his body between it and the main door. He turned the old iron knob on the main door and pushed it open with zeal, like an archeologist having finally reached the chamber containing some lost ancient treasure.

Upon entering, Ming felt the man-made indoor heat mix with the cool outside air. He allowed the storm door to slam behind him under its own weight and failed to close the main door, darting down the hallway as if being chased. His young energized legs took him promptly past the house's front bedroom, through the hallway connected to the stairs, in and out of the kitchen and small dining area, and ultimately into the living room.

"Dad, Dad! Look what I did! Look what I got!" cried out Ming with a bright, warm excitement that could have filled the room.

Ming's father sat comfortably in his favorite chair, a large leather-upholstered reclining armchair. Today, however, he was sitting straight up, his attention fully focused on the task at hand. He wore a pair of neatly creased gray dress slacks and a long sleeve, blue button-down business shirt, complete with a necktie. The tie's colors matched the slacks and shirt perfectly, with its diagonal pattern. While outdoors, Mr. Lee wore black leather dress shoes, perfectly clean and polished to a mirror shine. However, as was oriental custom, his shoes sat peacefully at the front door, replaced by comfortable wool-lined slippers. Mr. Lee was reading a single piece of white paper, much like Ming's. He ignored Ming completely.

"Dad, look!" demanded Ming, widening his eyes and thrusting his own white paper forward.

Mr. Lee, who habitually sat with one leg over the other, pulled his right leg from under the other and laid it gently on top of the left. He pulled his gaze up from the paper in a slow methodical manner, a movement that Ming perceived as a sign that Mr. Lee would finally bestow his son with his full consideration. Mr. Lee was now staring in Ming's direction but not precisely at him.

"It's the coolest thing in the world, Dad," Ming began, renewed with youthful vigor and ready to forget his father's distance. "Ms. LaGrange wrote this letter about me. She thinks that I have real…"

Still not quite looking at Ming, Mr. Lee cracked a warm proud smile. He rested the arm that supported the paper on his lap and extended the other outward, as if to greet a welcome visitor, yet still gave no mind to Ming.

"Dad, who are you—" started Ming.

"Hey, idiot," groaned a disturbing but familiar voice. Its very sound caused Ming's skin to crawl and seized every muscle in his back. It felt as if each bone in Ming's young spine suddenly grew by two hundred percent and began to bulge through the skin. He was tense and silenced. Ming drew upon every dignified bit of strength within, breathed out a portion of his anxiety, and gave a full turn to the rear.

"Putting on a few pounds lately, huh?" he asked. There stood Ming's older brother, Hui- Cheng. What he asked wasn't a question at all. It was a statement intended to offend, merely disguised as a question. Hui-Cheng was a junior at Lakeland Preparatory High School and appeared as a walking billboard for their athletic program. His feet sported perhaps the most expensive pair of tennis shoes ever purchased and went well with his stone-washed blue jeans, faded intentionally to give the appearance that they faded unintentionally. A warm wool sweater covered his upper body, gray with dark blue at the shoulders, fashioned in some Americanized version of a Norwegian design.

Over his torso, he wore a Lakeland High letter jacket with all the trimmings. Four shadowy orange chevrons adorned his right sleeve, pointed downward like a row of dutiful soldiers. They signified one of Hui's many accomplishments, about which Ming understood little and cared even less. On the jacket left side was a large "L" of same sunset color, decorated with tiny golden pins, each representing an activity in which Hui excelled. The pins included a basketball, a foot with two attached wings at the ankle, a bat and baseball, and a treble clef, among others. Ming wondered if there was anything at which Hui didn't excel. If so, he thought, it would be humility and common sense, represented by a tiny golden brain. Yes, that fits.

Hui-Cheng was standing in the entryway that adjoined the hallway to the living room. As Ming had dashed down the hallway past the kitchen, he missed Hui lurking there, heating up a cup of green tea in the microwave for his father. Hui's face wore an expression of false benevolence as he stood there in a purposeful pose, as if he were at some shoot for a fashion magazine, leaning slightly to the left with his head cocked in the same direction.

In a nauseatingly cute manner, his arm brought his hand up to his head to scratch an ear that didn't itch. His other hand was occupied with ferrying a steaming mug of green tea from the kitchen to his waiting father, enthroned in his leather armchair. The tea's near-boiling liquid produced a steady steam as it evaporated into the air. Hui maintained a contemptuous eye on Ming as he walked around and past him; the tea gave a short-lived trail of vapor as he strolled by.

Ming turned to follow Hui as he passed, stopping when he reached their father. Hui dutifully leaned over to hand his father the heated ceramic cup with a gross smile as if he were waiting for a tip. The cup itself was covered in a gentle off-white glaze and trimmed with mistletoe, red berries, and Chinese characters that expressed wishes for good luck and prosperity. Hui returned to a fully upright stance and pulled around behind their father as if the two were posing for a family photograph. In drawing so near behind their father, Hui intended to give Ming the impression that his older brother and father were paired off against him.

"Ming," his father started, "I didn't see you there. Come see what your brother received in the mail today."

"No, Dad. I want you to see what I've got," Ming said as he snapped his own letter up to waist level, pushing it forward for his father to receive.

"Ming!" shot out his father with mild frustration. His proud, peaceful expression transformed almost instantaneously into fierce dissatisfaction.

"No, Dad. I was here first!" asserted Ming.

Technically, this wasn't true. But it was the quickest way his mind could express what was in his heart.

"Ming!" shouted his father.

Mr. Lee's bark was so loud and severe that Ming's mother heard it upstairs. Ming himself was greatly shaken and felt his heart speed up to a double pace. He knew what it meant to anger his father, how wrathful he could become, and what would happen after.

Ming dropped his eyes to the floor, closed his mouth, and pulled in a deep full breath. Instinctively, he released the air to calm himself ever so slightly. He felt as if he could explode at any moment, as if a savage burst of emotion waited just under his throat, ready to spew out in infernal vivid color. Inside his young form was a volcano of anger, hurt, and fear.

Over and over again, time after time, his father poured love and attention onto Hui like a chef basting a choice piece of meat on rotisserie, smiling as the salted juice soaked into the animal flesh. Everything Hui did was perfect. Every mistake was minimized or completely overlooked. Hui was intelligent, athletic, good-looking, and popular; and his father made sure the whole world knew it. How many letters had Hui received in the mail, acknowledging him for some great achievement, or cordially welcoming him into a select group of honored students? Ming rarely received mail, and even more rarely, special honors for outstanding achievements. *Why did Hui have to get another letter today*, Ming thought bitterly.

Unable to look either his father or brother squarely in the eyes, Ming stepped forward just enough to place himself with his father's arm's reach. Almost touching his father's crossed legs, Ming extended his empty hand to receive the letter from his father regarding Hui. Grasping hold of the white crisp sheet, Ming felt as though he was receiving orders for a suicide mission. After years of disapproval and neglect, what possible interest could he have in his brother's success?

After years of being compared in every respect to Hui's perfection, how could he be expected to find delight in Hui's triumphs? Every desire in Ming's heart yearned to unfold the letter to its full length, pinch it with two fingers at its top center, and tear it slowly in two. What a feat of satisfaction that would be! Finished, of course, with a dessert of shoving one-half of the letter down his father's throat, and the other half down Hui's.

Ming savored the vivid dream. Then he tucked his own note under his left arm and used both hands to unfold Hui's letter. Ming could tell from the paper's texture and color that it was more fine and expensive than average. He glanced carelessly over the letter's introduction, the whole "Dear Mr. and Mrs. Lee" portion. All of Hui's letters read that way.

Ming gave the letter's message just enough attention to grasp its basic message. He ached to return the letter to his father as quickly as possible. It was a letter of acceptance to Columbia University Business School. *What's the big hairy deal*, Ming thought. Hui had a number of other similar letters on his desk upstairs. Besides, Hui didn't really want to go to Columbia anyway.

Ming looked up numbly and handed the letter back to his father in a slow emotionless manner.

"Aren't you proud of your brother, Ming?" asked their father with a sickeningly sweet patronizing smile.

"Oh yes," began Ming with a tone, dripping with scornful sarcasm. "Can I quit school and start a Hui-Cheng Fan Club? Can I hang the letter on my bedroom wall? Please?" Ming spoke the words in an overly emotional, mocking tone. The effect produced a surprised and dejected expression on Hui's face, much to Ming's delight.

Their father, on the other hand, leaned on his elbows in order to push his torso up straight and tall in the chair like a king cobra expanding its body to intimidate an enemy. Mr. Lee peeled his lips off his teeth, drew in a deep, dramatic breath and pressed Ming with two eyes that conveyed imminent doom, like thunderous storm clouds just off in the distance.

"Perhaps if you spent more energy on school and less on wisecracks, you might be a success like your brother!" shot out Mr. Lee, trying to restrain his anger.

Ming looked down again and swallowed. His father's response to his sarcastic remarks put him down, but just barely. Ming was furious with hurt, but he knew he had pushed his father far enough. His muscles were taut and shaky. Warm blood flushed his smooth light-brown skin. In his peripheral vision, he could see Hui's hurt expression change to vengeful contentment, like a husband hearing the judge sentence his wife's murderer.

All three were silent and motionless for an instant, waiting to see who would act first. Suddenly, Ming spun around and headed back the way he came. He just wanted to go to his room and sulk. As he walked toward the kitchen, he imagined the two of them quietly joking at his expense. When Ming had traversed the kitchen and reached the staircase, Mr. Lee broke the silence.

"Ming?" spoke his father in a more calm but no less distant tone.

Ming stopped in place but didn't turn around.

"Was there something you wanted to show me?" asked Mr. Lee pretending as if all were peaceful. Ming let his fury control the hurt. He could feel his angry sweat soaking into the letter under his arm. He turned around just enough so that his father could see his lips speak.

"No, nothing," replied Ming calmly. Then he turned his head back in-line with his body and walked up the stairs.

* * *

Thanksgiving dinner was always quite an event at the Lee residence. It was a beautiful, well-prepared mixture of American and Chinese culture and food. This year was no exception. Within the few days that had passed after Ming's unpleasant encounter with his father and brother, extended family had arrived from out of town: Ming's paternal grandmother, his maternal grandfather, and his aunt and uncle with their two girls.

Throughout the late morning and afternoon Mrs. Lee's cooking sent tempting smells to every corner of the house, teasing everyone's imagination and causing their stomachs to cry out with increasingly loud groans. When she finally called the family to dinner, all came immediately, dropping with enthusiasm whatever activity currently held their attention. Ming's father bent over his newspaper and discarded it to the floor, Ming and Hui shot up from the carpet and left their football game, Ming's cousins temporarily stopped breaking his toys, and his grandparents took a much-needed respite from their broken, meaningless conversation intended to give the impression that they were comfortable with one another.

Every member of the family pranced through the kitchen with ravenous anticipation and entered the dining room. The decorated table was as sumptuous as the food. Perfectly positioned in the middle of the dining room was a long wooden table, complete with matching chairs, carved in the same style. A soft white eggshell cloth covered the table, with its ends dangling helplessly off the sides down toward the floor.

The Thanksgiving feast included a generously full bowl of steaming, slightly moist, Chinese dumplings placed near a small container of savory brown sauce used for dipping; a wider but more shallow bowl of cooked Chinese cabbage, full of vibrant greens and flavorful; a large broiled fish laid out on a plate, complete with its head and tail, and a pot of Chinese beef noodle soup, full of seasoning imported from China and still yet too hot for serving.

The table also supported a full array of traditional American foods: a bowl of snow-white mashed potatoes crushed to a perfect smoothness, with a liberal hunk of butter melting into a warm golden pool at its top; a small dish of home-style cranberry sauce, complete with unprocessed berry chunks (Ming liked the canned variety); a plate of flawlessly baked sweet potatoes, murky orange and individually wrapped in aluminum foil; puffy round bread rolls, baked with a crispy light-brown shell, which contained a reservoir of steaming flavor; and rich savory stuffing.

Magnificent as they were, each of these dishes played a secondary role to the brilliantly prepared bird, which sat in the middle of the table like a regal queen. Mrs. Lee's Thanksgiving turkey was indeed a sight to see. From head to toe, the bird bore an even golden brown hue. From top to bottom, it dripped glistening hot juices, the same liquids with which she had spent hours basting. In its beauty and grandeur, the turkey towered over the other foods, seeming to demand their tribute of respect.

Instinctively, each member of the Ming family took their seats at the table without giving any attention to choosing their places, retracting their chairs to sit. Each was enraptured by the turkey's transcendent beauty. The family surrounded the table thusly—at the table's head sat Mr. Lee, broad and glorious (much like the turkey itself). To his right were Hui, then Ming and the grandparents. Mrs. Lee sat at the other end, wearing a proud, warm smile, gleaming with joy to have her family together. To her left followed Ming's annoying and destructive cousins. His aunt and uncle completed the circle.

Everyone cast their eyes over the parade of luscious culinary delights displayed across the table. Hui pawed at his silverware and pondered which food he would try first like a race car driver revving the engine and waiting for the checkered flag. Initiating the conversation in Mandarin Chinese, Ming's uncle spoke up. "Before we enjoy this wonderful food, I think we should go around the table and each share what we are most thankful for. I'll start!"

Everyone around the table reacted with a positive, appreciative smile at the idea (or at least indicated a neutral attitude). That is, except for Hui, who gave off a cynical, pained expression as if he were a resident in some third world prison camp, tortured and starved for days at a time.

"I'm thankful for my new job and getting rid of the stress and fear of being unemployed, and I'm thankful for my beautiful wife and wonderful children," offered Ming's uncle.

When Ming's uncle expressed thankfulness for his children, Ming looked over at his cousins in stupefaction. He thought that if he's thankful for those kids, he must also be thankful for headaches, vomiting, world hunger, and armed robbery.

Everyone's smile grew slightly as Ming's uncle completed his sharing and Ming's aunt reached over to take her husband's hand. The older of Ming's cousins took the next turn. "I'm thankful for pbthpbthpbth!" he said, pressing his tongue between his lips and blowing. His younger brother began to howl with laughter. Mr. Lee looked at his wife's family with contempt. Ming's aunt leaned over and spoke softly but intently into her son's ear, conveying the warning to either shape up or be spanked.

When the disruptive effect of Ming's cousin's juvenile display had all but passed, Ming's aunt shared regarding those things for which she was thankful. And things continued in this way until everyone had taken a turn sharing.

Mr. Lee was last. He waited not out of courtesy for others at the table, but in order that he would be the one to complete the activity, that his words would linger on everyone's minds the longest. He extended his arms long and wide, laying his hands on the table where he could find space amidst all the food. Panning his gaze across each face at the table, he drew a deep breath and began to speak.

"I am very lucky man. I have so much to be thankful for. But there are three things in this world that I treasure more than anything else, more than this house, my job, our cars, vacations, whatever. These three things I love more than any of that. All those things could just fade away, and I would still be the richest man on earth!"

At first, Ming was confused but then he began to smile just a bit and sent a guarded expression of love toward his father.

"First, I am thankful for my wife. She has been my faithful partner in life all these years. She does so much, and I often thank her so little. She's a fantastic cook and homemaker, and she's been patient and tolerant with our frequent moves for my job. I love her," said Mr. Lee tenderly.

Then his smile widened slightly as he gazed proudly at Hui. "My son, we gave you the name Hui Cheng because it means splendor and success, and you have certainly lived up to that name. Each year of your life, and in every way, you have made your mother and me so proud! You've been a success in school your whole life, excelled in sports, and had many friends. You've grown up strong and handsome. No father could ask more from a son. I love you, Hui!"

Ming began to beam with joy and excitement. He stared unreservedly at his father; the anger and resentment from the other day melted away layer by layer. His heart softened as he gripped the sides of his chair with anticipation. *He said he was thankful for three things.* Ming thought joyfully. *I have to be number three! And he saved me for last!*

His father began. "Finally," he said, looking over at those seated to his right. "My heart is aglow this evening," he continued, turning to those on the left. "I am very, very proud," he said and then paused. "Hui got into Columbia business school!" In one fluid motion, Mr. Lee reached under the table and produced the letter he received regarding Hui from Columbia University. Mr. Lee raised his arms excitedly as if he had just won a million dollars. He shot his gaze intently around to everyone at the table, almost as if he were demanding they express similar exhilaration at the letter.

"Now, let's enjoy this wonderful food!" exclaimed Ming's father. He heaped a generous portion of Chinese dumplings on his plate and passed the remainder to Hui. Hui received the bowl and spooned twice his father's portion onto his own plate. Almost simultaneously, everyone at the table grabbed the nearest dish and passed it on after helping themselves to more than they could ever eat. The dishes and bowls spun around the table swiftly as almost everyone shared in the delightful food and company.

Ming sat in his chair motionless and silent.

Up in Ming's bedroom, on his desk lay a letter—white paper and black ink. It was addressed to Ming's parents. It read:

Dear Mr. and Mrs. Lee,

I would like to take this opportunity to express my appreciation for and unique pride in your son, Ming, and his special artistic talent.

As you know, three of Ming's works were included in our annual art fair, one of which won first prize! Let me be the first to share with you that this same painting has been selected to represent James Madison Elementary in the state competition later this year!

Ming has an exceptional gift for artistic expression and a strong willingness to develop his skills. He is polite and well-behaved in class. As his art teacher, it has been my pleasure to teach and see him grow. He shows extraordinary promise, and with you I look forward to seeing what accomplishments await him.

Sincerely,
Ms. Sandy LaGrange
Art Instructor and First-grade Teacher
James Madison Elementary

5

A Quick Trip to the Car

Lewis bore a great deal of resentment toward Sandy LaGrange. It wasn't because she sent him to the office; rather, that she insisted on a Friday afternoon practice. Good enough was just never good enough for Sandy LaGrange. He wondered how many times he would have to dress like Dwight Eisenhower and walk across the stage, waving his hands and smiling. He was tired of hearing the musical pieces over and over again and listening to Ms. LaGrange pick out all the minute mistakes in the singing, acting, or choreography. She was like a monkey, pulling bugs out of another monkey's hair, errors the audience wouldn't notice anyway. Nevertheless, here he was in the gymnasium, and it was Friday afternoon.

"Ughhh, can we please go home?" moaned Lewis. "I so don't want to be here. I mean, look at the snow outside! It's really coming down, perfect weather for building snow forts and snowball fights!"

"Speak for yourself, Lewis," added Ming. "Any chance to spend time with Alexandra Reiniger is time well spent, umm-umm!"

"Has she ever actually spoken to you, Ming?" questioned Lewis in a tone that suggested he already knew the answer.

"Yes! We had a conversation. Three months ago at lunch, her napkin fell off her plate as she was walking up to the garbage can. I picked it up off the floor and threw it away for her," related Ming, speaking as if he had retrieved Alexandra's golden ring from a secret treasure cache, after slaying an evil dragon and saving the kingdom from everlasting darkness.

"Yeah, but did she speak to you?" queried Lewis.

"Sure she did," returned Ming. "She said thank you."

Lewis didn't speak. He simply stared at Ming with pinched eyes and an expression of incredulity. The dreamy appearance left Ming's face as he returned to reality, and the two friends turned in unison to look out the window at the snow. It was indeed snowing heavily. Large bulky snowflakes had begun to fall around lunchtime and had not ceased. Instead, the rate and density of the precipitation had grown as the hours passed. Snow covered everything. The leafless tree branches appeared as pretzels encased in white chocolate. All of the parked cars supported a shell of five-inch-deep snowfall. All of this together made traveling increasingly dangerous. The heavy snow with its bleached blinding whiteness made it seem as if everything in view was one giant object; and the thick speedy snowfall filled the air like a frozen fog.

"All right, everyone," began Ms. LaGrange. "Let's gather around for just a minute before we begin." She stood in place and made eye contact with each of the children present. She extended her arms and made inward waving gestures with her hands directing everyone to draw in closer, like an all-star quarterback at the two-minute warning. "First of all, thanks for staying after today. I know it's Friday, but we really do need the practice."

As if we had a choice, Lewis thought to himself.

Now the children were gathered in close. The circle included Lewis, Ming, Alexandra Reiniger, and her sister, Agnes. "We're only going to stay for an hour and a half. So we need to be efficient and give our best!"

Lewis reflected on how nicely Ms. LaGrange always dressed. Today was no exception. She wore tan slacks with a precise crease, a blue, pink, and white-patterned blouse covered by a heavy pink woolen sweater, and comfortable but stylish casual walking shoes. As usual, the ensemble was ornamented with relatively expensive jewelry, befitting a childless, single career woman nearing retirement. She began giving directions.

"Ming, we obviously don't have the chorus or orchestra with us today. So I need you to man the sound system and play the recorded music at the right time. Do you think you can handle that?" Ms. LaGrange expressed the directive to

Ming as if she were verifying that a kindergartener could replace all eight crayons in the correct box.

"Sure," responded Ming, listening to Ms. LaGrange but simultaneously giving Alexandra a quick glance.

"Alexandra, Agnes, can the two of you just have a seat for a bit while I work with Lewis?" asked Ms. LaGrange. In the course of her question, she looked at both Alexandra and Agnes but only expecting a response from Alexandra.

"Yeah, we'll just sit over here?" asked Alexandra. Agnes nodded.

"That would be perfect. Thank you so much," returned Ms. LaGrange, drawing in her arms and interlocking her hands in one smooth, überdramatic motion, tilting her head to the left simultaneously. She was all smiles to Agnes, but Sandy LaGrange secretly was deeply relieved that Alexandra was here as an intermediary. She valued Agnes as a student and treasured her golden, honey-soaked singing voice. Nevertheless, Agnes's silence gave her the creeps.

Just as the sisters turned toward the bleachers, a fierce low-pitched wind wound up and battered the windows of the gymnasium. The slightly rusted old frames creaked sorrowfully under the pressure of the gale; but the glass panes remained intact. The wind's power quickly reached an impactful apex and then abated. Everyone in the room gave their immediate attention to the occurrence, wondering what might happen next. Sandy LaGrange returned from the trance first.

"Now then, Lewis!" started Ms. LaGrange, pivoting in place. "Don't worry about wearing the costume today. We don't have time for that. I'd just like to walk through your part a few times. I think the timing needs a little work."

Lewis had no idea to what she was referring. He just nodded obediently and figured he would practice his part until Ms. LaGrange was satisfied or it became 5:00 p.m., whichever came first. "Ms. LaGrange," Lewis started, "what are they doing over there?" He raised his right arm and pointed over the bleachers. Dylan Pierce, Wyatt McKinney, and Jeremiah Strickland were over by the bleachers. Dylan meandered around, in and out of the bleachers, carrying a black garbage bag in his left hand and occasionally picking up pieces of paper and other refuse from the ground. Of course, this only happened intermittently between making jokes to the other two or lazily loafing around.

Wyatt and Jeremiah were a partnership in uselessness. Wyatt walked up and down the floor underneath the bleachers with a wooden broom in his hands, while Jeremiah followed bearing a charcoal gray plastic dustpan. Naturally, their intended goal was to gather piles of dirt with the broom and brush them into the dustpan. Nonetheless, the pair succeeded at nothing more than moving the dirt into new arrangements under the bleachers, spilling what dirt they did accumulate, and poking each other with broom and pan amidst endless giggles.

"No need worrying about them," answered Ms. LaGrange warmly. "They made some unfortunate choices yesterday, and the bleachers needed cleaning before the musical."

By "unfortunate choices," Ms. LaGrange meant that the boys misbehaved. Lewis knew that, and he wondered why teachers didn't just say "they got in trouble" or "they misbehaved." With regards to Dylan, Wyatt, and Jeremiah, he couldn't have been more pleased. It was high time that they received just punishment for something. He pretended in his mind that their current castigation had been imposed for the treatment he and Ming had received in the bathroom. It was a sweet contemplation.

"Hey, Dylan," began Wyatt, leaning up straight from his ineffectual sweeping. "Why don't you come here and sweep for a while. I'm getting sick of swinging this broom." It was a relatively common occurrence for the three of them to endure punishment together. Wyatt didn't like that Dylan also seemed to assume the easiest or least uncomfortable part of whatever the chastisement happened to be. Privately, he believed himself superior to Dylan, certainly to the dull Jeremiah. Even more so, he wanted Dylan's position of dominant leadership, his authority among the three of them.

"Hey, Wyatt," returned Dylan. "Why don't you come over here and let me shove that broom down your throat. I'm getting tired of hearing your mouth!" Dylan wasn't at all worried over the reaction his response might provoke.

He was confident in his power and authority. He gave a wicked, self-satisfied smile and then returned to what he was doing. Wyatt, on the other hand, envisioned Dylan as a broom—his neck, wooden, slender, and easy to grip. He squeezed the broom in his hands, still staring at Dylan.

"Stop talking and get back to work, or you will spend the weekend here!" Ms. LaGrange reprimanded. Of course, she could never actually impose such a threat. However, she spoke it in a stern, ironclad voice practiced over decades of teaching; and it left the boys unsure if she could or not.

Within the course of Ms. LaGrange's sharp reproach, another dreadful wind buffeted the windows, this one stronger than the first. As before, the wind pressed fiercely against the windows and made the iron rectangles groan. So robust was the gale that it pushed open the window closest to Ming. It had been left closed but unlocked. Ming rose instinctively, passed over to the window, closed and locked it.

"Lewis, make your way up on stage, please," directed Ms. LaGrange, changing from a grim tone of voice to one more congenial. Lewis quietly left the gymnasium, staring at the windows as he walked, and passed into the hallway where the side entrance to the stage was located. He pulled opened the hollow outdated wooden door and ascended the shadowed stairs to take his place at stage right just behind the curtain.

"All right, Ming," began Ms. LaGrange politely, keeping her eyes on the stage but gesturing to Ming in unison with the command. "Start the music, please."

Ming dutifully pressed play on the screen of the computer that accompanied the sound system and pushed up the volume to an appropriate level. Militant, patriotic music sang from the speakers to the right and left of the stage. In reality, it was the same music that the students in the orchestra played. Alexandra reflected on how the recorded version was more precise and confident but also less entertaining than listening to the students play.

Hearing the point in the piece that was his cue to begin, Lewis left the dark safety of the curtained darkness and began his dramatic march across the stage, trying to get himself into a Dwight Eisenhower frame of mind.

"Not too fast, Lewis!" shot out Ms. LaGrange.

Lewis slowed a bit and pictured in his mind the other actors in this scene pretending to be Eisenhower's baseball teammates and political supporters. During the portion that featured Eisenhower's military victories in World War II, the music included booms and crashes played by drums and cymbals, intended to simulate bombs and explosions during combat.

With the music playing at a high volume, no one could hear the wind battering again against the windows. No one noticed its gusts slamming against the glass panes like a siege ram working at a castle wall. No one perceived the wind's angry howl, furious in its frustrated inability to break through. *Boom*, went the music.

Ms. LaGrange produced an energized smile on her face. She was in her element, like an eagle soaring through the cool upper air, far above the stony mountains. *Boom*, crashed the music once again. Sandy LaGrange began to wave her arms like a conductor. She gave direction to an orchestra that wasn't there. She was in a trance of pure bliss, like a dolphin gliding through the blue brine, popping up from the surface with grace and ease.

Boom!

Ms. LaGrange returned from her deep musing with a start. She could tell immediately that this boom was not in sync with the recorded music. The explosion came from the window in the back corner of the gymnasium. Glass flew inward with terrific speed in every direction following a thunderous blast. Blustering snow and frigid air poured in through the now-empty rectangular iron frames. Monstrous gusts of winter wind charged in with a chilly vengeance, working to assert their victory over the resilient glass.

All eyes turned in one breath toward the snowy hole.

"Whoa," offered Ming with a growing smile of delight. He turned around to see Lewis's reaction.

"That was so cool!" said Lewis, now completely out of character.

Alexandra and Agnes were more surprised than delighted and looked over at Ms. LaGrange obediently.

Dylan, Wyatt, and Jeremiah were transfixed by the pile of broken glass sprayed all over the floor. Their miscreant minds pondered the fantastic mischief they could do with shards of sharp glass, smashing the larger pieces against the wall, and what they could cut. Sandy LaGrange released a deep breath of relief to see that no one was hurt. With the snow, the heavy winds, and now-shattered windows, she wondered if scheduling this practice was such a great idea.

"All right, all right. Is everyone all right?" asked Ms. LaGrange.

Everyone nodded or spoke up in the affirmative. Lewis wondered how many times Ms. LaGrange used the word *all right* in one day, considering that the Guinness Records committee might be interested. Like a crowd at the scene of an auto accident, everyone in the gymnasium began walking toward the window.

"Now, everyone just stay where you are. Stay out of the glass!" mandated Ms. LaGrange, gesturing away from her body to reinforce the words of her directive. She walked steadily but slowly over to the empty frames that previously held glass panes and now merely conducted freezing air. The winter air pouring into the gymnasium made the space rapidly and noticeably colder. She guessed that certainly the temperature had dropped.

As Ms. LaGrange drew close enough to the window to see outside, the others closed in behind her. Her ears heard them step on the glass, a clear indication that they were closer than she wanted. But Sandy LaGrange was mesmerized by what she saw. Snow was falling now at least twice as fast as before, a change that occurred only within the few minutes since Lewis and Ming conversed while gazing out the window.

Now the wind blew the snow more violently and erratically. Visibility was such that driving would be impossible, even walking would be treacherous. Without exception, white heavy snow covered everything in sight. Blanched wintry powder was piling heavily even on the ground so that the tires of cars in the school parking lot were buried nearly to their midpoint. The storm was blinding.

Eventually, Ms. LaGrange leaned back slightly, stood up straight to her full height, and turned around. "The snow has gotten much worse. We need to get all of you home right now," asserted Ms. LaGrange, trying to convey calm to her students. "I thought I told all of you to stay out of the glass!" she said, remembering her earlier order. Everyone backed out of the glass slightly but not completely. "Let's get to the office so that we can call your parents," she added.

"But Ms. LaGrange," begged Lewis. "What about those kids outside?"

"What do you mean, Lewis?" returned Ms. LaGrange. "There are no kids outside."

"Uh-huh. They're over there by that bunch of cars," said Lewis respectfully.

Ms. LaGrange turned her gaze back out the window, leaned forward a bit and squinted, working to squeeze every ounce of clarity from her close-to-retirement eyes. Her brain succeeded at separating the snow in her vision, and eventually she did indeed spot distinctly at least three children playing out in the wintry tumult. Through the tempest, however, it was impossible to even guess their ages.

"What are they doing out there?" asked Alexandra.

"It looks like they're just playing," responded Ming cautiously, not wanting to give offense to the object of his affections.

"Out in that snow?" returned Alexandra. "Who could have fun in that? They need to go home."

"It's gotta be more fun than bein' in here!" offered Dylan.

"Dylan, you are in here because of the choices *you made* in my class yesterday. If you don't like it, shape up!" asserted Ms. LaGrange. "And I told you to get back. Dylan, Wyatt, and Jeremiah, get back over by the bleachers right now."

"I am afraid I can't do that, Sandy," responded Dylan.

Ms. LaGrange turned to Dylan with an angry, offended expression. "Dylan," she began, trying hard to remain professional. "You will call me Ms. LaGrange."

Dylan dropped his garbage bag and looked right into Ms. LaGrange's face contemptuously. "No, I will call you what I like, Sandy," responded Dylan.

Ms. LaGrange's face turned to the red of a serious burn. Her willingness to remain composed ebbed away. "Dylan

Pierce, you pick up that bag right now! Or, so help me, you will spend the summer cleaning this building," she answered, nearly shouting.

At this, Dylan finally relented. He tried hard not to withdraw too fast, not wanting to appear weak. He cleared his throat to get rid of some of the anxiety, picked up the garbage bag, and walked slowly over the bleachers.

"C'mon, guys," ordered Dylan, attempting to give the impression that Wyatt and Jeremiah were ultimately under his authority and not Ms. LaGrange's.

Just then, all those present in the gymnasium heard another crash of broken glass. This time it was faint and far-off. Everyone had a sense that it came from outside in the storm somewhere. The sound pulled everyone's attention over the window again.

"What was that?" asked Jeremiah, half-curious and half-fascinated by destruction in any form.

"Bleachers!" asserted Ms. LaGrange.

And the boys obeyed.

All eyes at the window remained peeled and inquisitive until Alexandra spoke up, "It looks like they just broke the window on that car."

"Ms. LaGrange," began Lewis. "Isn't that your car?"

"Oh my! Yes it certainly is!" responded Ms. LaGrange.

Ms. LaGrange stood up straight and tall, taking and releasing a deep, somewhat pacifying, breath. "I am going out to my car and deal with this. You four stay here in the gymnasium and stay out of the glass!"

Ms. LaGrange walked away from the window, corralling the four children like sheep away from a patch of thorny bushes. She walked quickly, but without panic, over to the stage where her coat and purse lay. In a hurried instant, she pulled her coat over her back and arms and curled her designer scarf around her neck.

"I'll be right back," assured Ms. LaGrange, talking to the four but giving the bleacher boys only a stern look. Pulling her brown supple leather gloves over her thin dainty hands, she bolted out the side door into the cold and snow. As a matter of course, the four turned and darted back over to the window just as soon as the heavy metal door closed behind Ms. LaGrange. The four closed in on the enormous gap in the wall that was once a window, crunching shards of broken transparent glass noisily under their feet.

Unconsciously, the four drew close together against the bitter chill as they looked out the steel-framed aperture. Each pulled their arms in and began to rub their upper arms and hands, attempting to create friction, and thereby, heat. Almost immediately, they spied Ms. LaGrange trekking into the wintry blast, her tree brown winter's coat creating a stark contrast against the overwhelmingly pure white. She left the entryway to the school building and walked rapidly but safely out into the parking lot.

The four could no longer see her head and face since she had pulled up the coat's hood. As she made her way to her car and the children by it, the thick, heavy snow made it tough for Lewis and the others to see clearly what was happening. The frigid howling wind had the same effect on their ability to hear. Their youthful eyes were able to see that she had stopped about twenty feet from the children to address them, but were unable to discern clearly or even hear the conversation. As she spoke to them, she extended her arm, obviously referring to the smashed passenger's side window. Then she drew her arms up to her head and pulled the sides of her brown hood closer in an effort to allow less wind to her face.

As she began to speak, two of the children turned away from the car and focused their attention fully on Ms. LaGrange. The third gleefully smashed his arm through the windshield, and gave a terrific cackled laugh. He had no rock or iron pipe, just his empty hand. Although it sounded like just a whisper to Lewis and others, Ms. LaGrange shouted "Stop!" This third child ignored her, pulled his arm from the windshield, and proceeded to rip the windshield wipers from the window.

In the course of these events, the snow took on a sharp increase, falling even more briskly and densely. Now it was hard to see anything at all, but the four in the gymnasium were able to see that two of the children with Ms. LaGrange stepped away from her car and toward her. She gave a start and stepped backward. In the ever-deepening snow, Sandy LaGrange lost her footing and fell onto her back, the white fluff cushioning her collapse. With leopard-like rapidity, the two children leapt onto Ms. LaGrange, offering hideous wails of delight, terrifyingly loud to her but inaudible to the four in the gymnasium.

"Oh no!" cried out Lewis.

"We have to go out and help her!" asserted Ming bravely.

Agnes, characteristically, said nothing but gave her sister's arm a mighty squeeze and pinched the skin of her face in a teary-eyed, despondent expression. By now, the snow fell with such freakish density that the four saw nothing but a couple of dark shapes. They couldn't be sure if it was the children, Ms. LaGrange, or both. Steadily, the thick snowfall changed the dark indiscernible figures into dark indiscernible shapes. After that, they faded in and out of visibility within the snow that fell like white bed sheets hung out to dry and waving in the strong, spring breeze.

And then, nothing.

6

First Time to the Principal's Office?

Cold, icy wind howled, whistled, and cried as it blew over the deepening snow in the parking lot. Lewis and the others could see nothing clearly. It was now impossible to discern the boundaries of the sidewalk, street, and parking lot. Everything blended together in one blanched image. Snow was falling at an uncanny rate. With the wind, drifts of white frosty snow leaned up against the school building like siege ladders inclined against a castle wall. Blowing snow from just such a drift began to bite at Lewis and Ming's fingers that rested on the window's opening.

"We gotta go out there right now!" asserted Ming once again.

"Yeah," added Lewis. "She's out there freezing to death, and those kids got her!"

Agnes squeezed her sister's hand to express agreement with Lewis and Ming. Alexandra was the oldest, and with Ms. LaGrange at least temporarily out of the picture, she assumed a natural responsibility. Alexandra Reiniger continued staring out the window into the white waste.

But in reality, her gently rounded brown eyes focused on nothing. She slipped into a moment of reflection, shutting out the opinions of the others in order to make her own decision.

"We need to call our parents," declared Alexandra.

By now, the four had turned away from the window and in toward each other for comfort and warmth.

Lewis dropped his arms to his side in defiance. "No! What about Ms. LaGrange?" he started. "We can't just leave her out there."

"I want to help her too, Lewis," replied Alexandra. "But she's an adult. She can take care of herself. Besides, what can we really do for her?" Her question was rhetorical.

"I don't know. Can't we just put on our coats and check on her?" suggested Lewis.

"No, Lewis," returned Alexandra. "Look at the snow outside. Who knows if we could even reach her. And if those kids attacked her, they might do the same to us."

Lewis turned sharply to look out the window, taking in the severity of the storm, and noticing that snow was now blowing off the drift and over into the gymnasium. Then he turned back toward the others and bowed his head down, registering that he agreed but didn't like it one bit. Ming had his opinions and largely agreed with Lewis. He was ready to brave the cold and venture out after Ms. LaGrange. However, he was lost and paralyzed in his crush on Alexandra Reiniger. Ming loathed the idea of disagreeing with her publicly because he believed that doing so would put distance between the two of them. On the other hand, allowing her to make the decisions, and at least passively supporting her, would increase the chance that she would like him and perhaps—in his middle schooler's mind— have feelings of affection for him someday.

Ming marveled at Alexandra, fixing his unchanging gaze on her like a preindustrial villager watching an astronaut descend from the clouds for the first time. She stood high and slender, taller than most of the other girls in her class. She shared her sister Agnes's coloration crowned with coffee brown, straight hair that hung with a slight wave against her shoulders and upper back. The locks were divided perfectly at the center top of her head, seemingly without one strand on the wrong side.

Ming Lee decided that Alexandra's salmon-pink striped three-quarter-sleeved sweater was without doubt the most exquisite article of clothing every created; her white shirt, the finest collection of thread on earth. In some faraway land, a cadre of sleepy clothing artisans sat mildly in quiet joy, knowing that Alexandra was wearing their masterpiece outfit. He dreamed that one day the moonlit night sky might be as richly blue as her jeans, and how gratefully the ground supported her every footstep, wrapped in beige leather casual shoes. In reality, Mrs. Reiniger shopped for all of her daughters' clothes at one of the local malls like most every other family.

"Okay, Aggie?" asked her silent sister. Alexandra didn't expect that Agnes would respond verbally. She just held her hand, looked for an agreeing nod. Agnes reluctantly gave it. Agnes kept a special warm spot in her heart for Ms. LaGrange. Like most people, Ms. LaGrange was vexed by Agnes's unrelenting silence. However, Sandy LaGrange saw far enough through her own discomfort to reach Agnes's beautiful singing voice. Although Agnes never expressed it, she deeply loved Ms. LaGrange.

"Let's head to the school office," directed Alexandra, "there's a phone in there." Alexandra gave Lewis and Ming a look intended to convey that it was time to move. Keeping Agnes's closely gripped warm hand, she turned toward the hallway door. The others followed.

"Hey, wait a minute," shot out Ming. "Where are Dylan and the other two?"

The other three panned over to the left, and with Ming realized that Dylan, Wyatt, and Jeremiah were gone. All that remained by the bleachers was a black, plastic bag, a broom, dustpan, and four sloppily amassed piles of dirt and snack wrappers.

Suddenly, Alexandra felt a sharp heavy pull on her arm. Agnes was looking at her and demanding her attention. As soon as her sister had offered it, Agnes shot out her arm like a crossbow bolt and pointed over to the floor near the stage. Ms. LaGrange's orange floral-patterned purse was off the stage and dumped on its side; the contents spread out erratically from its zippered opening. Hurriedly, the four walked over the purse to investigate. The innards of Sandy LaGrange's purse lay chaotically about: her telephone, painkillers, a small travel-size packet of tissues, sunglasses, pen, and a few other unremarkable items. Most importantly, her black leather wallet rested on the floor amidst the fray. Ming doubled over to retrieve it from the floor.

"Well, there's no money it," began Ming with an embittered tone. "And the credit card slots are all stretched out. So those are probably gone too." Ming passed the wallet to Lewis for further examination. Lewis agreed with his friend's assessment and took a brief moment to indulge his curiosity. There was Ms. LaGrange's driver's license, complete with picture, height, weight, donor status—just like Grandma.

Alexandra and Agnes took it all in.

"Gee, I wonder who did this!" said Ming with obnoxious sarcasm.

"Oh, I'm sure it was Jeremiah first and foremost," avowed Alexandra. "I know he's been in my locker and bag more than once."

"Wul where did they go?" questioned Lewis.

"I don't know, Lewis," responded Alexandra with a reservedly hostile air, remembering everything she had lost to Jeremiah Strickland's light fingers. "And honestly, I don't care. We need to get to the office."

Just then, a particularly loud and haunting howl of winter wind was heard.

"Did you hear that?" asked Lewis, addressing his query to no one in particular.

"Yeah, Lewis," offered Ming calmly. "It's just the wind."

Certainly, the wind was blowing. However, Lewis picked up on a sound that was more intentional, almost vocal.

"Poah nuh, poah nuh, poah nuh," it went.

"I don't think that's the wind, Ming," said Lewis confidently.

"Poah nuh, poah nuh ma, poah new mah," came the sound again, more loudly this time.

"I think you're right, Lewis," agreed Alexandra. "It seems to be coming from the broken window."

All four turned in unison back toward the window. Lewis and Ming were the group's vanguard, motivated by curiosity and unmindful of whether or not Alexandra and Agnes followed. Alexandra moved to follow the two but felt a sudden and strong jerk in the opposite direction. Agnes was pulling, nearly yanking, her sister's arm. All the while, Agnes shook her head back and forth vigorously. Her tender, cold-reddened face wore a fearful expression, almost as if her fear was beyond the general, but rather based on the specific as if she had some idea of what produced the unidentifiable sound.

"Aggie, what is it? Quit yanking on my arm!" said Alexandra with an increasing level of annoyance.

"Poah new mah, pah new mah, pa new mah," emanated the sound again.

As Ming and Lewis drew closer, the sound became more clearly enunciated. The wind continued to cough flurry-filled frozen air through the aperture, producing lonely howls.

Upon reaching the opening, Lewis and Ming saw nothing unusual. The snow had reached the window level fully and now gathered there in chilled crystallized piles. Outside it was still an empty white waste.

"Is there anything there?" questioned Alexandra, trying to ignore her sister's yanks and hoping to keep her arm in its socket.

"No. Nothing strange at all," responded Ming, assuming that his love must certainly have intended to address him.

"Raughh!"

In abject terror, Ming turned his head away from Alexandra and back out the window. Immediately before Ming, less than a foot from his face, stood an indescribable horror. Ming gave a startled, "yeaagh!" and fell backward onto the gymnasium floor. On top of the snow bank that leaned against the outside wall stood a revolting small creature, about the size of a child from what Ming could take in. A dark-colored hood cloaked a wrinkled ruddy face. Folds of rough dry skin imposed themselves around the creature's piercing eyes, and cheek muscles pulled up oddly red lips to reveal a set of unnaturally sharp rotten teeth. The creature's hot breath escaped its mouth in muggy puffs of steam.

"Pah new mah!" belched the creature.

Ming's eyes, now lidless, expressed the boundless dread that ruled his heart. He instinctively got up on his hands and shuffled backward, trying to distance himself from the creature without taking the time to stand. Lewis, still on his feet, stepped back just as quickly.

"What is that?" questioned Lewis senselessly.

"I don't know, but I don't like it!" responded Ming, jumping to his feet and stepping over toward his friend.

For a moment, the creature remained more or less still and quiet. It appeared rather crushed in its position and posture at the window. The head, shoulders, and upper arms were visible about the sill; but rather than invading the opening with its arms and hands, the creature pulled up its gnarled bare right foot and rested it confidently on the sill, dexterously avoiding the remaining shards of broken glass. In turn, it produced the other foot and did the same.

Half-transfixed with fascination and half-frozen in fear, Lewis and Ming remained in place, watching the creature intently. It looked at Lewis and uttered, "pa new mah," and then panned over to Ming, giving the same creepy utterance. It continued in this fashion back and forth, staring at each of them in turn and speaking *pa new mah*. With each expression, the creature widened its eyes, much like a starved wolf upon cornering its meal. After bouncing its gaze back and forth four or five times, the creature straightened up a bit, revealing more of its torso.

Underneath the decidedly dark cloak, the creature wore a pair of blue jeans, slightly faded and near-torn on the left knee. On its upper body, it wore a sweatshirt in colors that Lewis and Ming recognized immediately. It bore the words JAMES MADISON ELEMENTARY SCHOOL. This uncanny revelation drew Lewis and Ming's collective minds away from the distress of their situation just enough to ponder this new mystery. Whatever this creature was, why was it dressed like a student at James Madison?

Just as the distraction of this question brought their hearts to slightly slower pace, the creature belted out, "Pah new mah!"

Lewis and Ming tore off toward Alexandra and Agnes like grease lightning. In their peripheral vision, they observed the creature press off its monstrous hands and launch itself over the sill and onto the gymnasium floor. At top speed, the two shot passed the girls while frantically shouting, "C'mon, time to go!" Agnes, already pulling her sister's arm in the same direction, let go of the hand and released her momentum to run with Lewis and Ming. Alexandra followed, pausing just briefly to take in the vision of nightmarish creature that now stood solidly on the gymnasium floor.

Lewis crashed out the door first, pushing it so hard as he ran through that the door hit the outer wall making a loud, humming *wung*. Ming followed close behind but stopped briefly to hold the door for Alexandra. Whatever love points he endeavored to score were lost on Alexandra as she passed briskly through the doorway right after Agnes. Having already decided to call home from the school office, the four ran in that direction, blasting through the school corridor at a desperately vigorous pace, and finally reaching their destination.

Pushing past the main office door, the four gathered before a second, made of wood and glass, and labeled Mr. Abelard Cohen, School Principal. Lewis rotated the knob back and forth to its full extension in both directions. Nothing. He pushed and pulled on the knob with all of his youthful might. Still nothing. The door was locked. Down the carpeted corridor of the office area sat the desk of Caroline Lively, the school secretary. Ming darted down the corridor and around her desk to reach the telephone. The receiver was light tan and unwieldy, encumbered by the ergonomic shoulder rest that was convenient if one was typing but bulky in the hand of a junior high kid.

Before Ming could begin to discern how to get a line out, he realized that it was dead—absolute empty silence. Slowly, and with an expression of despair, Ming replaced the receiver. "It's dead. There's no sound."

"The snow must have broken the phone lines," speculated Alexandra.

"And if the phone at Mrs. Lively's desk is down, it's likely that the others are down too," Agnes's sister thought out loud.

"Well, we might as well try to get out…or find a place to hide," suggested Ming in a weakened and quivering voice. Not waiting for anyone else's approval, Ming speedily returned from Mrs. Lively's desk and launched past Mr. Cohen's door and the others. Upon reaching the main office area door, he yanked on the lockless handle, fully expecting it to swing easily open and grant them access to the main hallway. It didn't. The door didn't budge, not even a creak or bend. "What is going on?" demanded Ming. "This door doesn't even have a lock."

"Lewis?" sounded a gentle and diminutive voice, little more than a whisper.

Ming continued tugging at the door, trying to change fear into strength. "Why won't it open? It's supposed to open!" he shouted with increasing panic.

"Lewis? Lewis?" sounded the voice again, this time a bit more insistent. Neither Lewis nor Alexandra gave it any attention; their collective auditory sense consumed in Ming's anxious hollers.

"Lewis!" roared the voice. Now it was unmistakable. Lewis, Alexandra, and even Ming turned and gave Agnes their full attention. Agnes was staring exclusively at Lewis and met his gaze as he turned.

Alexandra was overcome by a mixture of surprise and relief to hear her sister speak again. "Aggie?" she began with a furrowing brow and moistening eyes. "How are you talking?" She couldn't believe it but was in for so much more.

As Agnes did in the hallway with Lewis, she became unyieldingly rigid. Her facial expression was stern and empty. Less dramatically than before, her eyes and hair took on a more understated, but no less frightening, flame. Yellow flickers grew into bright flares, initiating at her roots and extending to the tips of each strand of hair. Brilliant orange sparks began near her tear ducts and created luminous, fiery circles around her eyes.

Ming released his desperate grip on the main door handle and turned around toward them. He could feel the heat emanating from Agnes's face and hair. The fire lit up the other three's expression of unrepressed astonishment. As before, Agnes was not consumed.

Behind Alexandra, Mr. Cohen's door gave a barely audible click and opened with an inoffensive, unoiled *creeeeeeeek*. Alexandra completely ignored the previously-locked-now mysteriously-opened door. Agnes's unanticipated speech and fiery features left her sister transfixed. Agnes's brilliant oranges and luciferous yellows danced on Alexandra's soft cheeks and frolicked aimlessly in her chestnut tear-moistened eyes. Both Lewis and Ming noticed that the door was now open. However, that surprise was still less compelling than their diminutive companion's blazing countenance.

When Agnes was sure that she had captured Lewis's total attention, she raised her delicate left arm in a purposeful, crisp movement and pointed directly into Mr. Cohen's office. The other three followed her gesture almost immediately, looking in. At this point, the heat and flames that ornamented Agnes's head began to diminish slightly, yet her extended arm remained straight and firm. Lewis and the others remained in place.

"Lewis!" shouted Agnes insistently. As she did, the fire swelled to a heat and brightness greater than before. She snapped her arm out again, demanding Lewis to enter Mr. Cohen's office.

"Okay!" responded Lewis, taking a short vacation from shock and confusion to express frustration at Agnes's impatient, inexplicable mandates. "Maybe, just 'will you please go in the room?' How about less fire and yelling?" Agnes disregarded the request.

Lewis stepped cautiously into Mr. Abelard Cohen's functional, but otherwise unremarkable, office. Alexandra followed, then Ming. It contained a desk, centrally located and burdened with paper piles pertaining to unresolved administrative issues, a picture of his wife and children, and a personal computer. A bookshelf rested passively in the corner, full of textbooks and monthly magazines on teaching methods and office management techniques.

The majority of Mr. Cohen's decor expressed his passion for fishing and included pictures from various fishing expeditions, most of which featured him holding a huge fish, wet, helpless, and wishing it could return to the water. He also showcased a large preserved fish on a shiny wooden placard that hung noticeably on the wall behind his desk. On the wall opposite the bookshelf stood a tall charcoal-steel file cabinet.

Before any of the children could muster up a coherent expression of any sort, the steel cabinet's bottom file began to shake tightly but rapidly and grew quite hot. Unknown to the four children, this file drawer was the only one locked, and after shaking and burning, its front spat out the locking mechanism like a cork on a boiling kettle. In succession, the lock hit the side of Mr. Cohen's desk, and the drawer shot out to its full length and stopped, pulling the whole cabinet forward slightly. It gave a violent *raaaa chat*!

Then multicolored documents from various folders in the file slid out and flew straight up into the air. Initially, the papers soared about in seemingly indiscernible arcs and patterns—some moving alone, and others in trains. Then, every page, alone or in group, flowed obediently together into one extended serpentine chain. Apparently, under its own direction, the chain proceeded to fly to every corner and crevice of the room, sewing itself under Mr. Cohen's desk, behind his bookshelf, and everywhere else. As this continued, Agnes broke into song, just as she had when alone with Lewis in the hallway outside the gymnasium.

Hall to hall and room to room, obey the mop and hear the broom!
Growing dust and paper piles, push the garbage down the aisles.
See this work, my life's endeavor, nothing fancy, nothing clever!
Seen my face? Not yet, not ever…

Shine the mirror, scrub the sink, powder up that vomit stink!
Like the windows clean and streakless, like me in my quiet meekness?
Shake my hand, a small endeavor, Just a greeting, "Morning!," never!
Learned my name? Not yet, not ever…

Just a sip, perhaps a swallow. I'm alone; did someone follow?
Found the bottle carefully hid. Learned my secret. Yes, they did!
Sign the page, the form, whatever! Take my job, my lifeline sever.
Think I'm done? Not yet, not ever!

As soon as Agnes stopped her song, the long slender paper trail gave one final twisting spin around the office and then headed directly for the same file from which it came. Although unnoticed by the four, each sheet of paper did not merely return into just any file. They each slid smoothly into the exact same folder from which they came. All but one. While the paper parade slithered back into the file like a serpent returning to its hole, one lonely sheet glided out from the paper trail and spun in the air all by itself. It continued in this fashion until the others had fully reentered the cabinet. Finally, the file rolled slickly back into the cabinet and gave a confident *slam*!

The solitary sheet ceased curling in midair, and then, like a tired autumn leaf, floated carelessly to the floor right at Lewis's feet.

7

I've Never Received Mail Before

"Um…what?" asked Ming in total bewilderment.

"Yeah, that was totally weird," added Alexandra.

Agnes stood gently still. She took her sister's hand.

"Okay, I have, like, a thousand questions," began Ming. "Why was the door to the hallway locked? How did Mr. Cohen's door unlock itself? Why do papers fly all over the room? And what was that shrimpy freak that tried to eat my head?" He shot the queries out like machine-gun fire. Part of him earnestly sought answers; another part just wanted to vent.

"I don't know about the hooded guy. But I think that I have some explaining to do," offered Lewis.

The others were willing to put aside their shock and questions for the moment in order to give Lewis their attention.

"I think I can answer one of those questions," started Lewis. "'Member that day at play practice when I kinda went nuts and acted like Agnes had fire comin' out of her eyes and flaming hair and all that?"

The others nodded.

"Well, see, I did really see that. And Agnes sang to me in the hallway after that when Ms. LaGrange sent me to see Mr. Cohen. She sang and pointed her finger at the wall, and flames burned words into the wall and everything."

Alexandra and Ming returned Lewis's explanation with expressionless faces. Given what they just witnessed in the gym and here in Mr. Cohen's office, they were not entirely incredulous but were still quite confused.

"Agnes," started Lewis, turning to her. "You did that, right?" Lewis asked the question with hope, fully expecting that Agnes would support him and explain it all. Agnes smiled reservedly at Lewis and continued to hold her sister's hand tightly. "Agnes, c'mon. Tell 'em," he begged. Agnes gave no response. Lewis dropped his shoulders and exhaled laboriously in frustration. "Well, I don't understand what she did then or what happened in here, but I think it's connected somehow."

There was a brief moment of silence.

"That's all you've got?" asked Ming with an unmistakable air of aggravation. "That doesn't get us anywhere. That's no explanation!"

"Just wait," commanded Alexandra, asserting her age and height. She released her sister's hand, turned and knelt down to face her. "Aggie, sweetie, what's going on? Is it true what Lewis said? Did all that really happen? Are you the reason Mr. Cohen's door opened? Did you make the papers fly around?"

Agnes looked directly at her sister and gave the warmest, most tender smile one sister could offer another yet said nothing. Alexandra wrapped her hands around Agnes's shoulders in a firm but inoffensive manner. "Aggie, why won't you talk to me?" she began. "You just spoke to Lewis out in the hall?" Alexandra pulled her sister in close and added, "I'm so sorry. I'm so sorry for what happened. Why won't you talk to me?"

Lewis and Ming were a bit taken aback by Alexandra's sudden and candid display of emotion. The two wondered what Alexandra meant by her repeated apology to her sister. Agnes never spoke to anyone. Why would Alexandra be sorry about that?

"I don't think we're going to get any answers from Agnes," started Ming. "It appears she only talks when she wants, or when something weird is about to happen. I just really think that we need to get out of here and go home. Ms. LaGrange is outside and can't help us. The phones are dead. I think we should get our stuff and try walking home."

"Well, I guess we could try that," added Lewis. "I don't live too far away. I've walked a few times before. What about you, Ming? Do you live far away?"

"No, not too far," he returned.

Tuning into the conversation, Alexandra released her desperate and loving hold on Agnes and stood up to her full height. She began to shake her head in disagreement as she moved up. "No way! You two may live pretty close. Aggie and I live almost ten miles away. It's outside the city in the country a bit. We can't walk that in this snow! It would be tough even in the summer."

Ming was torn. In part, he still hesitated to displease Alexandra because of his crush and natural admiration for her height, age, and beauty. However, he was scared, frustrated, and getting hungry. "Look, can't we just try? Why don't we walk until we get to somebody's house, or maybe a gas station or somethin'? Maybe the phones are working there. We can call your parents or mine and get a ride home. We won't have to walk all the way."

Alexandra realized that she was responsible for her sister no matter what they decided. She considered staying. *Maybe we should just sit tight and wait for people to come here,* she thought. *Someone might come, but then again, maybe not for some time.* On the other hand, she considered the snow and cold outdoors. She and her sister were dressed warmly enough to walk from Dad's car to the school building, but not so to walk for miles through a deep and ever-worsening blizzard.

Ming looked at Alexandra and perceived her indecision. "We won't walk far. We'll just go until we come to a place where we can call," said Ming, trying to be as persuasive as possible.

Alexandra looked down at Agnes, not exactly looking for approval, certainly not an opinion. She knew Agnes wouldn't respond. Her glance was more to size up her sister. Would Agnes be all right to walk out in the snow? "All right," Alexandra agreed with reservation. "We stop at the first place we can call, and I decide which way we walk, got it?" She stared at Lewis and Ming, less to gain their approval than to impress upon them, these two younger boys, that her compliance to venture into the cold and snow meant that she called the shots and that this was nonnegotiable.

Lewis first, and then Ming, nodded their heads. Ming decided Alexandra was even prettier when angry.

So consumed with the recent amazing events and considering what to do next, no one gave any attention to lone sheet of paper resting passively at Lewis's feet. It was the one sheet that *didn't* return to the folders in the file cabinet at the end of the paper storm. Having determined their plan of action, Ming turned his attention to it. Agnes was staring at it devotedly and had been doing so during their entire conversation. "Lewis, what's that paper at your feet?" asked Ming.

Lewis had forgotten all about it. He reached down to retrieve the rather ordinary eight-by-eleven-inch sheet of white paper. It reads as follows,

Mr. Abelard Cohen, School Principal
James Madison Elementary School
8719 Red Knot Run
Steeple Grand, Indiana 46412

Franklin Bristol Jenski, Head Custodian
421 Baden Point
Steeple Grand, Indiana 46412

Dear Mr. Jenski:

This letter serves as your notice of termination as head custodian effective immediately.

James Madison Elementary strives to provide the best education possible in a safe and nurturing environment. Working toward excellence requires each employee to maintain the highest level of job performance and strict adherence to behavioral standards.

Your conduct over the last two years makes it impossible for James Madison Elementary to continue your employment. I have included a list of the most outstanding offenses and disciplinary measures below.

- Frequent tardiness over a three-month period: Verbal Reprimand.

- Willful verbal insubordination toward principal: Verbal and Written Reprimand.

- Possession of alcoholic beverages on school campus: Written Reprimand.

- Public intoxication on school campus: Termination.

The School Board and I believe that we have met the requirements spelled out in the employee handbook regarding discipline and have provided opportunities for improvement. While James Madison Elementary will not be able to provide you a positive reference for future employment, we wish you the best of luck in subsequent career endeavors. For our records, we will keep a copy of this letter on file.

Regards,
Abelard Cohen, School Principal

"Well, what does it say, Lewis," asked Ming impatiently.

"It's a letter from Mr. Cohen to some guy named Franklin Bristol Jenski," responded Lewis, bearing pinched face and confused expression.

"Who's Franklin Bristol Jenski?" inquired Ming.

"I dunno'," offered Lewis, dropping his letter-carrying hand to his side in resignation.

"He was the head custodian here until about five years ago," dropped in Alexandra. "Here, let me see the letter," she demanded.

Lewis passed it over obediently. Alexandra scanned the letter quickly using every ounce of her youthful wits and developed reading skills.

"It says he was terminated for willful verbal insubordination and public intoxication," explained Alexandra.

"What does that mean?" begged Ming.

"It means he smarted off to Mr. Cohen too many times and was drunk here at school," she returned.

"Why was that the only paper that didn't fly back into the drawer?" asked Lewis.

"Yeah, and what does that have to do with us?" probed Ming.

"I have no idea. What I do know is that it's getting dark out. And if we're going to try to reach a phone outside, we need to go now," asserted Alexandra.

Neither Lewis nor Ming voiced any objection.

"Okay, let's go down to the main doors, and we walk out to the street from there. I think there's a gas station not too far," directed Alexandra. As she spoke, Lewis's eyes landed unintentionally on Agnes. Up to this point, Agnes offered little more than a kind, unaffected expression. Now she was staring directly, unmistakably at Lewis with a haunting, piercing gaze. Once she had Lewis's attention, her fixation left him just long enough to glance over at the letter in Alexandra's hand. Then she returned her drilling stare to Lewis. Then again she panned over to the letter and back to Lewis.

"Lewis, c'mon!" ordered Ming. "Let's go, Mr. Daydream."

Ming's poke woke Lewis from his stupefaction. By this time, Alexandra was heading through Mr. Cohen's office doorway, pulling Agnes along. She laid the letter on Mr. Cohen's desk.

Upon reaching the main hallway, the four turned sharply left and walked through the central welcome area of the school. Distracted by the intentionality of the plan and the hope of getting home, no one, least of all Ming, noticed that the door connecting the office area to the main hallway, previously unlocked but impassable, now pulled open just as easily as always.

From the central welcome area, the four traversed a set of doors leading to four stairs down and then the main doors. As they opened the connective doors and got a full view of the main exterior doors opening to the school parking lot, each froze instantly in place, as if the cold outside wind itself found its way through the glass and iced each of them over.

"You have got to be kidding!" offered Lewis in heavy, deliberate speech.

"Look at that!" added Ming.

In the few minutes they had spent inside the school office, the snow had continued to fall at an ever-increasing rate and still did presently. It was more than any of them had ever seen, stacked up at least eight feet high, and drifted another two atop that. The four glass doors that led to the school parking lot were twelve feet in length from bottom to top. Only a few feet of uncovered glass at the top remained.

The four stepped slowly down the stairs to the door level in order to more closely investigate the beautiful yet harrowing marvel. Under normal circumstances, such an offering of snow would mean multiple days off from school. But they weren't at home, still in their pajamas, eating breakfast, and watching the television for news of school delays and cancellations. They were *at* school, and this much snow meant they weren't going home.

"Whoa!" spoke Lewis, stepping up close to the glass to investigate the snow. Stacked up so high against the door, the frosty wall appeared almost as an anthill made of snow rather than sand. Lewis imagined ants crawling up and down through vast networks of passages and holes. Alexandra looked at the top of the snow as it drifted against the window. For a moment, she put aside the reality of their situation and reflected on how the piling snow looked like an hourglass, with its moments of snowy sand accumulating in unplanned white frosted hills. She wondered poetically if this was the sand in their hourglass. Was their time running out?

Ming placed his bare palm against the glass. Not surprisingly, it chilled his soft skin. He pulled away. Ming put on his gloves and wrapped his hands around the door's metallic silver crash bar. He had no illusions about opening it to produce a passable aperture but was curious if it would move at all. As he expected, the door cracked ever so slightly, barely an inch. The goliath wall of snow on the other side of the door would give no more, and returned the offense with a blast of cold air and pinch of white powder, dropping in from the door's top to its bottom.

"What are you doing?" asked Alexandra in an annoyed tone. "Do you really think you're gonna get that door open?"

Unnoticed by the others, Ming's complexion took on a slightly reddened tone as a blush of embarrassment fleeted throughout his body. It troubled him greatly that Alexandra disapproved of his efforts. He wished he had the strength to push the door open with one swift movement, casting aside the frigid wall that barred them from freedom. He longed deep in his youthful heart for her approval. "Uh…no," he stuttered out in tense mortification. "I was just trying to… uh…see if the door was frozen shut," Ming returned in the calmest and most confident tone he could muster.

"Look, we're not going to get out this way. The snow is too high," asserted Alexandra. "We might as well head back up and look for another way out."

At that, Ming released his body weight from the chilled glassy door. Its metallic weight, added to that of the snowdrift behind it, caused the door to pinch the white melting powder between the door and its frame. He turned in place and headed obediently up the stairs. Alexandra took Agnes's hand and did the same. Lewis stood in place for an instant more, fixing his keen attention on the remaining sky still visible over the growing snowdrift.

"Did you guys notice the sky?" asked Lewis, raising his right arm and pointing up at the top of the glass, built in above the doors.

"What do you mean?" probed Alexandra, registering an unabashed impatience in her voice. "Let's just go!"

More inclined to take interest in his friend's discovery, Ming turned back and looked in the direction that Lewis's hand pointed. Alexandra wasn't interested and continued toward the door. "Alexandra, I think you should look at this," suggested Ming.

Expelling a full irritated sigh, Alexandra turned and offered Lewis a moment of indulgence. When she did, she saw it. The sky, which was barely thirty minutes earlier, bright and white in snowy overcast with the sun burning relentlessly behind it, was now pale purple. This was no dusky purple, like one finds on the horizon when the suns sets slowly, resisting the coming moon. This was full, even purple, and it was uniformed in tone and shade from the horizon all the way up to as high as the eye could reach. It was pale and yet still vibrant, like the colored paper the school secretary shoved insistently into the side of the office photocopier.

For a moment, all four were transfixed by the phenomena and stared incessantly at the sky through the glass. No one spoke, and a calm silence fell over the scene, silent enough to allow the arctic gales blowing outside to make themselves heard. Unconsciously, each of the four took a step closer to the doors as if one step closer to the sky might help to discern the mystery in which they currently found themselves.

"Blagh!" belched out the creature in a hideous yell. Whatever this beast that bashed through the gym window, it now vexed them here at the main doors to the school. All four children shook and screamed in shock and horror, backing away from the doors and moving awkwardly backward toward the stairs in an instinctive retreat. The creature seemed to know they were there and stared down from the top of the snowdrift with a malicious gaze.

"Pneuma!" cried out the creature. It squatted down slightly on its tiny feet and lifted up its enormous hands to bear in the glass. "Pneuma!" it yelled again and bashed its gigantic hands against the pane with furious strength. The glass absorbed the shock, giving off a low vibrating hum. "Pneuma!" barked out the grotesque beast and again slammed both hands in herculean unison against the glass. This time, the window hummed again but also surrendered to the creature's robust blow, cracking just slightly at the spot where the diminutive's monster's right fist had fallen the hardest.

This was more than enough for the four. Without hesitation, discussion, or mutual consent, each of the four tore up the stairs, yanked open the doors leading to the welcome area, and shot fleet-footedly down the hallway toward the office area.

8

Tell Me What You Really Think

"Okay. Well I guess we're not getting out that way," stated Ming in a sarcastic tone, fully aware that he was simply stating the obvious. He arched over for a few breaths, rested his hands on his knees in order to allow his lungs to work more efficiently. He wasn't used to sprinting, but that is exactly what the four did at the sight of the horrific creature.

"Even without that huge-handed weirdo, the snow was way too deep against the glass. There's no way we could open the door, let alone dig our way out," let out Lewis, projecting his speech through labored inhalations and exhalations.

As the other three continued to recover from their impromptu sprint from the main school entrance back to the main hallway, Agnes stood up straight and tall, drawing her feet in immediately next to one another as would a soldier in formation. She turned stiffly toward the door that led into the classroom closest to the main office and by which the four stood. So stark and rapid were her movements that the other three could not help but notice.

"Agnes, what do you need in your classroom?" interrogated Alexandra, finishing her own last huffs and puffs. "You have your coat. We don't need to go in there."

At this, Agnes lifted her right leg from the ground nearly to the height of her other knee. Upon reaching this apex, she slammed her foot down with all the might she could muster. Her petite muscles and soft-soled shoe didn't produce much sound, but the effort and force caused the rest of her body to shake. Alexandra interpreted this as nothing more than a child's immature tactic to get her way.

"No!" asserted Alexandra. "I don't know what you need, and since you aren't going to tell me, the answer is no. We have to get out of here!"

Lewis and Ming, fully recovered from the recent dash, stood by in quiet indifference, allowing the family drama to pass naturally. Agnes, unaffected by her sister's unyielding attitude, repeated her attempt at intimidation. This time she lifted the same leg to a height greater than before and smashed it down in the tile with even more furious fervor.

Alexandra leaned into her sister with a patronizing, almost motherly, posture. She extended her index finger to a level perfectly parallel to Agnes's soft round nose and took in a chestful of oxygen like a machine gunner loading his weapon. "Agnes! I am done!" blasted Alexandra, waving her finger in Agnes's face. Her finger waved up and down like a carpenter's hammer. "It is time to grow up. I need you to—"

One final time Agnes lifted her leg and pounded it down. This time she coupled the action with an intense snap of her arm toward the door. All the while that Alexandra scolded Agnes, stepping up to her with a punitive finger, Agnes never relented, never changed her posture.

Despite Alexandra's harsh words and raised voice, Agnes remained unmoved, unaffected. As Agnes's foot impacted the hallway floor in this final instance, the phenomenon that followed did so in such a seamless fashion as to suggest that her arm's snap triggered it. Soft pale purple light seeped through the space under the door at which Agnes pointed. The hypnotic glow started as a bright dot at the center of the bottom edge of the door and extended out in both directions, until it appeared as a purple beam seamlessly attached. Eventually, the light flowed onto the hallway floor, suggesting that the illumination had its source at some point inside the classroom.

"Whoa," offered Lewis. He simply stared at the unnatural glow like a camper transfixed by a fire's pops and upwardly licking flames. Ming followed suit. Still staring directly at Agnes like a seasoned police detective interrogating a suspect, Alexandra didn't notice the new light immediately. Upon hearing Lewis, however, Alexandra was sufficiently distracted from Agnes so as to catch a peripheral glimpse of the purple light reflecting off her left leg. She then paused briefly in bewildered disbelief and subsequently gave the door her full attention.

At this, Agnes broke into her increasingly familiar voice and sang these words.

> Hey, can you see it there behind wooden doors?
> Wood, glass and iron hinges, ceiling to floor?
> It's the fear you must now set aside.
> To see the visions I confide.
> Courage will follow through. Will you come, too?
> Hey, it's a history of evil laid bare,
> Haunting the corridor, the classroom and stairs.
> While the lesser heart will run and hide,
> Come see the visions I confide.
> Danger will follow through. Will you come, too?
> Hey, what you're thinking, is it true, is it real?
> Lost to the shadows, what they say will reveal.
> Flowing unrestrained, a thoughtful tide,
> The truth alone we here abide.
> Courage will follow through, will you come, too?

In the course of Agnes's song, the purple light that shone underneath the door grew such that it now was glowing from all four sides of the rectangular entrance, and through the glass portal window cut from its center.

"This is getting a little nuts," put in Ming. "Is anyone making any connections between Agnes's flaming hair and creepy songs, the creatures outside, and all this snow? It doesn't make any sense to me." Ming didn't mind sharing candidly his ignorance and lack of understanding. He was all but sure that neither Lewis nor Alexandra had any better grasp that he did. He didn't know what to make of Agnes. He looked at her and then back at the door as a severe cold fear shot up his spine. Whatever was going on, Agnes continued to creep him out. She had displayed powers he only encountered in comic books and cartoons. Agnes was no mere fourth grader; and he planned to keep his distance.

Lewis kept his thoughts to himself. His young mind supposed that there certainly must be some connection between Agnes and the other strange occurrences. No doubt, she knew more than she had shared. What he feared telling the others was that somewhere in the unclear, unreachable depths of his mind, parts of what the four were currently experiencing was familiar to him. Yet, he had no context, no frame of reference for it. He tried hard to grasp the place and time from where the memory came, but he couldn't.

"I think one way or the other, we need to go into that classroom," asserted Lewis. "It appears that Agnes won't leave until we do."

"I just want to see what that cool purple light is!" offered Ming without hesitation.

Alexandra drew in a deep calming breath and expelled it while still staring scornfully at Agnes. Her patience was gone. As the redness began to leave Alexandra's face, she pulled back from her sister and again stood up straight, regaining her full considerable height. "All right, Aggie, we'll go in," conceded Alexandra. "But then we're getting out of here, and I don't care if you stomp holes in the ground!"

Motivated in tandem by an anxious desire to investigate the glowing hue behind the door and a wish to be Alexandra's gentleman, Ming stepped enthusiastically up to the doorknob and wrapped his olive brown fingers around the cold black rounded metal.

"Don't even think about it!" shot out Alexandra, simultaneously giving Ming a dominating stare, and extending her left arm to keep him at bay. "I'm going in first."

"Okay," returned Ming in a mockingly submissive tone. He looked away from Alexandra's glare, still too infatuated with her to make eye contact for more than a second or two. He stepped gently back and waved his left arm toward the door while bowing slightly as a hotel doorman might when welcoming a king, or perhaps, the president.

As Alexandra opened the door, Lewis and Ming worked to peer over her high shoulders, working to get an immediate glimpse of whatever was producing soft lilac light. Surprisingly, and to Ming's great disappointment, the light died just as Alexandra had opened the door widely enough to allow entry. And at this, the classroom appeared as nothing more than it had ever been. Mrs. Naomi Fuller taught third grade in this room. The desks were aligned in neat equidistant clusters of four. Mrs. Fuller placed her desk at the front near the chalkboard. The chalkboard itself was a deep green, freshly cleaned and even in color from edge to edge.

"Move in!" demanded Ming, letting his curiosity overcome his desire to impress Alexandra. "I want to see!"

"There's nothing to see! So cool yer' jet's buster," returned Alexandra confidently.

The four made their way at various speeds into the room. Along with education, Naomi Fuller studied art in college and, as a consequence, spent more time than other teachers teaching it. The interior reflected her prioritization of the subject. The wall of the classroom on the side where they entered was covered with Christmas tree pictures, produced by weaving together strips of red and green construction paper with a black background. Lewis remarked to himself that a few were quite good. Alexandra considered them each one by one and imagined how she might improve on them.

Another wall featured the students' rendition of a Christmas star. Fundamentally, each piece was the student's attempt to paint a yellow star on navy blue paper. From there, each was to decorate their star with golden glitter. A number of the projects reflected a great deal of patience and care, just enough glue and glitter to accentuate the painted yellow star and add scintillating sparkles. Amid the pleasing pieces were interspersed an equal number of artistic train wrecks that featured sloppy glue squirts and poorly sprinkled glitter.

Far from bringing to mind for the spectator a calm, meditative Christmas night, these projects instead suggested that a crazed cow had chewed up a bar of gold, then broke into this classroom, and simultaneously sneezed and blown its nose all over the papers.

Finally, the ceiling sported the most interesting efforts of Mrs. Fuller's little beasts. Over each student's desk hung a two-dimensional snowman made of construction paper. Each snowman showcased the artist's personality and talents. One carried a football and wore a helmet. Another had long blonde hair and was vested in a pink skirt. Still another sported what appeared to be a black leather vest, a fierce tattoo and horns where its ears might be located. Mrs. Fuller imagined that a parent conference was soon to follow.

"See. I told you," started Alexandra in a vindicated tone. "There's nothing here."

"Oh, there's nothing here. Aren't you Miss smarty pants!" added a voice.

"Aggie, are you making fun of me?" interrogated Alexandra, spinning around in a rapid circle to face her sister directly. "Now you decide to talk, huh?"

For the most part, Agnes remained still. In response to her sister's assertive question, she only offered silence, a slight shake of the head and furrowed brow intended to express her innocence.

From this, Alexandra turned determinedly to Ming and Lewis each in turn. "Okay then. Who said it? I am not stupid or deaf!"

"I didn't say it!" offered Lewis, raising his outwardly turned hands up to his chest in a defensive posture.

"I didn't say it either. But boy, you sure are cute when you're angry," expressed another voice.

"Ming," shot out Alexandra as she turned toward Ming and pressed him with a fierce gaze. "I know you have crush on me, but it's time to grow up!"

Ming tensed up under the intimidating weight of Alexandra's stare. Instinctively, he pulled his arms into his sides and tucked his head down a bit. "I didn't say anything, Alexandra. Believe me!" Ming was embarrassed and little angry. He did indeed have a crush on Alexandra, but she didn't need to throw it out into the open. Ming turned away from the others in shame.

"Look, I didn't mean to make you feel bad, but I don't need that right now," began Alexandra in a repentant tone. "You did say it though. I heard you. It was your voice."

Ming reflected on Alexandra's words. He didn't say those words to Alexandra, but he did hear what she did, and it was in his voice. He was sure of that. Ming turned back to the others with a lost pensive expression.

"Well, I don't care what you think you heard. I don't like you being mean to my friend," offered a voice in an acidic tone.

"Now, you?" interrogated Alexandra, turning to Lewis. "Don't you start in too!"

In posture, Lewis reacted to Alexandra's accusation but not as strongly as before. He looked away, deep in thought.

"I heard Ming speak, but his mouth didn't move. I heard my voice, but I didn't speak either. What the heck?" said a voice.

"I am not talking!" asserted Lewis. "I did not talk just now!"

"Yeah, I know," granted Alexandra. "I saw your mouth and it was closed, but it was your voice."

"I would rather hear your sweet voice," spoke a voice in a soft loving tone.

"Ming, cut it out, or so help me you will eat my fist!" threatened Alexandra, offering Ming a thorough view of her tightly squeezed right fist.

Ming pulled his hand over his mouth. "Uh dumma suh nuttum!" he mumbled through his young fingers. He pulled his hand away and repeated the defense, "I didn't say nuth'in!"

"Now just wait," Alexandra demanded in slightly raised voice. "Everyone just stop for a minute."

"Yeah, that's it, Alexandra," started another voice. "Tell everyone what to do. Take charge! We know what happens when you are in charge, don't we?"

"Aggie, do we really need to bring that up right here and now?" asked Alexandra in tender wounded voice.

Agnes shoved her hands out in front of herself and waved in proclamation of her own inculpability. Her eyes widened, and she shook her head. Now Alexandra stood in the center of the other three.

"Can you two keep the drama at home?" asked a voice.

"I don't want to hear it, Lewis!" shot back Alexandra instantaneously. "We will bring the drama here whenever we feel like it!"

"There wouldn't be any drama if you cared about anyone but yourself, Alexandra," offered another voice.

At this, Alexandra swung away from Lewis and faced Agnes once more. Alexandra felt like a lamb surrounded by three wolves, keeping them each barely at bay.

"Yes, yes, poor little Agnes," began Alexandra in a bitter teasing voice. "Oh no, I've been traumatized. I've been traumatized. I don't talk now. Everybody, look at me! Everybody, pay attention to me!" Alexandra stopped speaking and placed her hands on her hips, leaning to one side in with unabashed sass. Yet another voice sounding just like hers continued.

"I wish you would have just stayed traumatized, or maybe not even come home," sounded the voice.

Finally, there was silence.

A hard, heavy hush came over the whole room. Whatever had passed between the two sisters, Alexandra knew that she had said too much, gone too far. She regretted it immediately. The air in her lungs rushed out like residents from a burning building. Her shoulders dropped down in burdensome disgrace, and she cupped her hand over her mouth as if by doing so, she could somehow recall what she had said.

Agnes did the same with her own hand, but for another reason. Salty water welled up in her left eye and then her right. She could feel the heat intensify in the skin and muscle around her eye sockets. Agnes was mortified. Her beloved older sister had all but wished her dead. She had said as much. What's more, she did so in front of other people. Grief pulled her cheeks down the sides of her mouth, and her throat knotted up like a dammed river. Although it seemed much longer, only a few seconds passed before Agnes began to cry. The tears overflowed the tiny crevices under her eyes and rolled over her cheekbones like spring-melted snow down a woodland stream.

"Oh, Aggie, sweetie, I am so sorry. I didn't mean it. Please forgive me," produced Alexandra in one long verbal stream. She launched herself toward Agnes in penitence.

Agnes retreated backward out of her sister's peace-seeking reach. As she did, the sadness over her sister's ill-considered remark was overtaken by humiliation, and then changed into fierce anger. Agnes pulled her hand away from her mouth as if she were about to speak. Still, she did not.

"Has it been so very hard for you, Alexandra?" asked a voice with a stern biting tone. "Do you carry such a heavy burden? Does your guilt trouble you? Do you know what

I have been through? Do you know what I have seen? Would you speak if you had seen it? I will speak when I have a voice!"

While a voice that sounded like Agnes's was heard, a transparent image began to pull up away from her body. The image appeared as an exact duplicate of Agnes in features, size, and even clothing. Pulling up and away as Agnes's voice was heard, her transparent duplicate even mouthed the last words. The duplicate continued up until it hung in the air, entirely detached from Agnes herself. This see-through floating Agnes had no tears of sadness at all. It expressed pure unrefined wrath toward Alexandra. Agnes stepped forward a bit and turned around and up to get a fuller glimpse of her ethereal double. She marveled and was terrified.

"Why don't you take it easy on your sister, Alexandra?" asked a voice that clearly sounded like Lewis's. The utterance was sharp and accusatory. "It's clear you have done something very wrong to her. Don't you feel horrible? Aren't you ashamed?"

Terrifically impressed by her wispy doppelgänger, Agnes moved very naturally into her sister's waiting arms and pacifying embrace. They both looked intently at Lewis. As had occurred with Agnes a moment earlier, a floating transparent double of Lewis peeled away from the original and lifted freely away into air above him. Lewis's double turned toward Ming and continued.

"And aren't you pathetic?" the airy being snarled. "Oh, I am so in love with Alexandra! Like she would be interested in a wimp like you. As if you stand a chance!"

More rapidly than the first two, Ming's double shot out from him like a pouncing lion. "You're calling me pathetic? Who was the wimp that almost got killed a few days ago in the bathroom? Remember that?"

Agnes tucked her diminutive form underneath her sister's body. Alexandra responded to the movement by pulling her in closer and wrapping her arms around her tiny sibling. The sisters closed their eyes. Ming and Lewis stood motionless in bewildered amazement as the loud, violent bantering continued. Back and forth, Ming's double to Lewis, Lewis's double to Agnes, Agnes's to Alexandra. So it persisted until Alexandra's own double burst from her body like a deranged jack-in-the box.

"I am disgusted with the lot of you!" it barked. "Get yourselves home. Deal with your own problems. Leave me alone!"

Boom!

No sooner than had Alexandra's crazed wisp let forth its frenzied exclamation, a thunderous crash came from the hallway outside the classroom. With it, came a destabilizing impact that shook everything in sight. Mrs. Fuller's favorite coffee cup popped up off her wooden desk and smashed into unredeemable shards and powder on the hard floor. Ceramic pieces that once composed the message, TEACHERS

Make A Difference Today And Tomorrow, in stylized font and florid colors scattered in every direction. Every piece of chalk and dry erase marker jumped from the tray and fell. A few of the loose hanging art pieces fell as well.

Boom!

A second impact smashed against the other side of the wall, this time further up the hallway. So grand was the force that it broke the cinder block wall and indented Mrs. Fuller's classroom. Lewis and Ming fell to the floor. Alexandra drew Agnes in even further and pulled in two lungs full of air. "Help!" she yelled.

Boom!

9

You're Getting Warmer

Beep, beep, beep, beep, beep.

The machine monitoring the young patient's heart rate sounded off in a steady, if abnormally, rapid pace. A medium-pitched beep emanated from the rectangular device in sync with a spectacle of blue, yellow, and red lights. Like the beep, the lights flashed on and off, on and off. Very near, and slightly above this machine, hung a transparent plastic bag filled with a clear liquid, suspended by a tall, slender frame. Through an equally transparent plastic tube fell drops of a liquid labeled Dextrose 0.5. The tube ran down the length of the metal frame and came eventually to lie on the bed, terminating underneath a well-fashioned wad of gauze and medical tape. The intravenous needle pieced the girl's tender skin, allowing the liquid to flow uninhibited into her veins.

"How is she doing? Have there been any changes?" asked Mrs. Reiniger.

"She's stable, and it's good that she's here now," began the nurse. "We're getting some fluid into her and trying to raise her body temperature as well." A professionally dressed doctor looked up and down from a chart, absorbing information from the papers attached to the firm board, and then returning his attention to his juvenile patient. "Do you know how long she was outside?"

"Not exactly," Mrs. Reiniger started. "I know it was at least overnight."

"Well, that explains quite a bit," returned the physician. "Your daughter is suffering from severe dehydration and hypothermia. Judging from the color of her fingers and toes, I'd say they were exposed for at least a number of hours."

"Is she going to be okay?" asked Mrs. Reiniger in a desperate, weakened tone.

"I think she will be, eventually. She's unconscious right now, which is normal given her condition. But I think that will pass too. We just need to give her time." The tall, slender doctor stood confidently in his well-pressed white coat.

Although unable to read them, Mrs. Reiniger noticed the doctor's name and the hospital embroidered in green at chest height into the snowy white coat. Additionally, the doctor's coat was ornamented by a rectangular plastic identification badge, which gave more information regarding his training and assignment in the hospital. His hair was an ashy mix of jet black and middle-age gray; his beard too. Nevertheless, his eyes bore a youthful sharp shimmer. His hair and eyes together created a comforting warm impression that patients and family liked.

Just as the doctor's statement ended, a retirement-aged nurse entered the room, carrying a thick heavy-looking blanket attached to an electrical cord. From head to toe, her nurse's clothing reflected years of experience through a long career. Her feet sported a near-new pair of lady's tennis shoes decorated in a rainbow array of hues and highlighted with her favorite color shoe laces. The shoes housed a pair of well-used support pads, which reduced the impact of twelve-hour-work shifts on her feet and controlled the natural foot odor.

Her legs were vested in a comfortable pair of pants, tinted in deep green and suspended at her waist with stretchy elastic, allowing space for the weight gained due to advancing years and too many "comfort" cheeseburgers in the hospital's basement cafeteria. From there to her neck, she wore a breathable loose shirt cut from a fun, light-hearted undersea cloth print, which featured tropical fish, sea horses, and octopi.

She walked purposefully from the door to the girl's bed and proceeded to spread the electric blanket over the patient in a gentle but thorough fashion. As she drew the blanket up near the girl's face, she smiled. A heart replete with warmth and care pulled her soft motherly cheeks up near her compassionate eyes. She wasn't sure if the little girl sensed her presence, but she smiled nonetheless. Pulling back to the foot of the bed, the nurse grabbed the temperature control device and began pushing buttons.

"Let's start with the temperature fairly low, okay?" asked the doctor in an unassuming voice. In reality it was a mandate, but he made effort to give his orders as kindly as possible.

"Sure," agreed the nurse, focusing her vision through the bottom half of her bifocal glasses. She set the temperature with a series of button presses and left the device lying on the bed near the girl's left leg.

The doctor turned his attention back to Mrs. Reiniger to make few final remarks. "She's lost a great deal of her fluids, Mrs. Reiniger. That's why her blood pressure is low. But her heart rate is high. Her heart has to work double hard because it's pumping less liquid. So we need to get that taken care of, and I think the dextrose will do the trick. With regards to the cold, all we can do is wait. When she does wake up, don't be surprised if she says some things that don't make sense. Disorientation is normal with fluid and heat loss. I am just glad you got her in when you did."

Mrs. Reiniger mentally jotted down everything the doctor said. Nothing focused her mind like her daughter's welfare. All of what he said was important, but it was the last remark that triggered the emotion: "I am just glad you got her in when you did," he had said. She sat on the edge of the upholstered chair and cradled her little girl's right hand, caressing it with smooth tender strokes. She stared at the rough red skin that covered the palm, back, and knuckles, leading up to the purple fingertips and at the ends, almost black. The left hand was in the same condition but tucked snugly under the blankets.

"Probably best to leave that hand under the covers," suggested the doctor.

Mrs. Reiniger complied immediately, lifting the heavy mound of soft blankets up just enough to move her daughter's listless right hand underneath. The girl's face had fared much better. Coarse patches of flaky skin covered her cheeks, nose, and lips but there was no purple. An even angry red covered most of her face and upper neck, more intensely so near the rough patches. She lay presently unconscious, with her pretty hair lying chaotically over the pillow. Her mother, needing to connect with her daughter, raised her left arm over the girl's head and began running her own fingers through her bangs and gathering them gently to the sides.

"That's where we are for now," stated the doctor, wanting to close the conversation and leave. Even after fifteen years, he was still slightly uncomfortable with the powerful emotions that accompanied his work, the vulnerability and desperation. "The nurses will check in to make sure things are moving in the right direction, and I'll be in personally tomorrow."

"Thank you so much, doctor," offered Mrs. Reiniger, feeling the burn of salt in her tear-burned eyes and struggling to give the doctor and nurse the most polite expression she could muster.

As the nurse and doctor left the room in unison, Mrs. Reiniger allowed her head to fall unsupported onto to her daughter's. The tears flowed more now like gushing rivers having just broken through a dam. She closed her eyes and produced heartbroken sobs and fearful groans for her beloved, and now endangered, child. Partially disregarding the doctor's orders, Mrs. Reiniger slid her right hand under the thick warm covers and held her daughter's hand. It was still quite cold but warmer than before.

For a few moments, she shut out the world, the beeping machines, her husband and other daughter in the hallway, the doctors and nurses, and simply held her daughter's hand. She took comfort in the room's quiet, the touch of the young girl's calloused but youthful fingers, and the soft toasty electric blanket, which wrapped her daughter's body and soaked up her own tears.

All the while, the girl lay still in passive unconsciousness. Air flowed in and out of her nostrils in a steady pace as she laid peacefully, her body working feverishly to raise its internal temperature and to heal the rough skin and flesh, damaged by the rigid cold.

Eventually, Mrs. Reiniger's eyes exhausted their store of tears. She drew in a few calming deep breaths and raised her head from the blankets. Underneath the linens, mother and child were still holding hands. Still maintaining her intimate grip on her daughter's tender fingers, Mrs. Reiniger rose up to her feet and noticed two quarter-sized wet spots where her tears had soaked the blanket. Briefly, a hint of embarrassment forced its way into her consciousness amid the fear, sorrow, and anger.

Yes, the anger. Somebody was responsible for her little girl's night alone in the dark cold. That person was close, too close. There is no stopping a mother's love for her child and no quelling the herculean wrath due anyone that puts the child in danger. Mrs. Reiniger affectionately loosed her angel's hand and turned purposefully toward the door. She gripped the privacy curtain that divided the entryway from the room proper and walked past the sink, sanitizing lotion dispenser, and soiled-robe receptacle, which were located near the door. As she did, the despairing, weakening sorrow for her child transformed itself into confident fuming rage. Mrs. Reiniger grabbed the door handle and pulled it open with resolute rapidity, nearly yanking it.

It opened to a busy hallway of hospital traffic. Doctors passed intently from room to room, nurses punched buttons at the station computer, a diminutive custodian moved unobtrusively down the hall, pushing his plastic-wheeled cart full of rags, paper towels, brushes, and cleaning solutions. He seemed pleasantly detached and set apart from all the activity and, under other circumstances, might have appeared as a vendor selling snacks at the county fair or a prison trustee, offering books and magazines to inmates.

Mrs. Reiniger noticed none of the ambient activity. She looked directly at her husband, who was standing nervously against the wall. To the mother's right, stood her other daughter Alexandra Reiniger. Her mother intentionally gave Alexandra no notice. Instead, she moved decisively into her husband's embrace. Alexandra turned to look at them both, opened her mouth to speak, but finally said nothing. Mrs. Reiniger threw her arms around her husband and fell onto his strength, squeezing out a few more tears. "She's going to be all right," she whispered.

Having dropped her head in shame, Alexandra looked up with renewed intent and moved within a few feet of her parents. "Mom, I am so sorry," she began, immediately looking away in search of her next words. "I didn't mean for her to get lost. I—"

With her face still turned away from Alexandra and lying warmly on her husband's strong chest, her mother pushed her hand out toward her daughter's face. Alexandra stopped talking immediately and retreated slightly, snapping her head backward. Her mother pulled gently but quickly from her husband's embrace and turned her scornful countenance at Alexandra like a weapon. "I don't want to hear it, Lexie. You better leave me alone cuz' I don't want to talk to you right now."

Whatever doubt her mother's words may have left, her aggressive expression dispelled. This was not the time for Alexandra to try to explain herself.

Keeping her hand up toward Alexandra in a wordless expression of disdain, her mother walked away and down the hallway in a faked calm. Mrs. Reiniger needed to cool off. She continued down the hallway, lost in a bewildering tornado of emotion, unsure of what to do next. As she curved slightly to the left with the hallway, she arrived at a small room labeled "Vending." Still carrying a few loose bills in her pocket from breakfast in the hospital's basement cafeteria, Mrs. Reiniger pivoted uncertainly toward the room and walked in.

The vending station was undecorated and practical, accommodating five machines: four offering food and one for making change. Normally, she used a credit card for even minor purchases, but her purse was back down the hallway with her husband and daughter. She wasn't going back there now. Her hand dove blindly into her right slacks' pocket and produced three bills, a five and two ones. Mrs. Reiniger returned two to her pocket and pushed the five dollar bill—slightly twisted and crushed as it was—into the machine, offering chips, gum, candy bars, and other sundry items.

She focused her emotion-heated eyes on the touch pad and pressed N and then 7 in succession. She wasn't really hungry; fear and anger had taken care of that, shaking and contorting her insides without mercy. Nevertheless, she needed something to do. The machine responded with detached robotic swiftness, pushing the next bag of potato chips forward. She stared at the colorfully designed bag and anticipated just a bit the salted, oil-soaked goodness that would soon gratify her palate.

The bag moved forward and then stopped, snagged helplessly on the end of the silvery ring, which suspended it. "What!" Mrs. Reiniger said out loud. She closed her eyes and leaned forward with her forehead against the machine's glassy façade in passive defeat, but only for an instant. In the darkness of her closed eyelids, the volcanic resentful terror and frustration lathered up like a neglected pot of boiling spaghetti.

"No!" she shouted. Then again, "No!" bellowing out as she pushed against the machine with her left arm on which she was resting. All of the items inside the mindless automated contraption jiggled slightly, but her chips remained unreleased. "No! No! I will have my chips!" she hollered, pushing again with increased force against the glass. As before, all the snacks vibrated and swung, but the machine was relentless. "Give it! Give it!" she cried, now banging against the glass more than pushing.

In the corner of her peripheral vision, within the typhoon of her frustration, Mrs. Reiniger noticed Alexandra, standing to her left at the room's entryway near the change machine. Alexandra did not speak, but her mere presence was sufficient to rescue her mother from further hysterics. Her mother became suddenly silent, lowering her arms away from the machine and turning deliberately toward Alexandra. The two spent the next moment speechlessly, briefly daring to make eye contact, and then turning away for safety.

"I'm sorry, Mom," said Alexandra.

"Sorry for what?" returned her mother. "Sorry for not watching after your sister? Sorry for being more concerned with your friends than your own family, huh?"

The anger came from the same place, except it was turned toward its intended target rather than the vending machine.

"I know I screwed up," began Alexandra. "I should have been more careful. I'm sorry, okay?"

"Just what are you sorry for, Lexie?" shot back her mother rapidly. "I want to know if you know. I want to hear it. Are you sorry that Aggie was out in the cold overnight in the middle of winter? Sorry that she could have died and nearly lost her fingers and toes?" Now her mother was pointing her finger and making no effort to control the volume of her voice.

Alexandra was silent. She realized her mother was not really interested in hearing an apology. She hung her head but not for the reason her mother would have guessed. Alexandra was regretful that Agnes was lost out in the cold, and especially that she was hurt. But that was not the complete inventory of her feelings.

"How about it, young lady?" taunted Mrs. Reiniger like a courtroom lawyer. "Why are you sorry? That you terrified your father and me? That—"

"Fine, I'm not sorry!" blasted Alexandra like a besieged enemy returning cannon fire. "Is that what you want to hear?"

Her mother reacted with silent shock.

"Aggie wasn't my responsibility! She's always pushing herself into whatever my friends and I are doing, like some lost little dog," continued Alexandra. She enjoyed the high of yelling back at her mother. In doing so, she felt strong and less like the villain.

"She's your sister," exclaimed her mother. "You're older than she is. You're supposed to look out for her."

"I didn't ask to be an older sister," stated Alexandra. "Nobody asked me. I wish I didn't have a younger sister."

At this, her mother was again silenced. She stared at her daughter with a mixture of fury and hurt. Alexandra knew she had gone too far, said too much. As such, she stopped talking as well. Her mother had enough maturity and composure to put an end to it and almost immediately, she walked toward Alexandra with unrelenting purpose. For an instant, Alexandra didn't realize her mother's true purpose in coming at her. Did her mother have in mind to take the argument to another level?

"Get out of the way, Alexandra," demanded her mother with a manufactured, restrained calm.

Alexandra stepped to the left, creating an aperture large enough to allow her mother to exit the room but just large enough. She didn't want her mother to think she was surrendering completely. Alexandra watched her mother leave the room and realized that her father was standing just outside the room—and probably had been for some time—hearing the entirety of the exchange and waiting to see how far it would escalate. Behind her father stood a couple of concerned nurses, curious (and brave) enough to investigate the familial dispute. Alexandra's father did his best to convince them that everything was fine.

It was quiet again. Mrs. Reiniger turned right and went down the hallway toward Agnes's room. Alexandra's father remained for a moment and looked at his daughter. She perceived a strange mixture from her father. In part, his expression conveyed a deep saddening disappointment at her selfishness and irresponsibility. At the same time, his face communicated an unchangeable steady love and an extreme relief that, more than likely, all would soon again be well. Satisfied that Alexandra was all right for the present, and that he had conveyed the emotions which he intended to, Mr. Reiniger turned to follow his wife and left Alexandra to calm herself.

Lost in her thoughts and consuming passions, Alexandra stood at the entryway for just an instant after her father had walked away. Then she stepped backward and leaned unconsciously against the change machine, ignoring its uninvitingly stiff metal frame. There she stood for a time, which she didn't measure, working through a long chain of deep relaxing breaths and replaying her words with her mother. With each mental replay, she tried harder to convince herself of her own innocence, and if she had any words to take back, they were only spoken in response to what her mother said first.

Eventually, Alexandra pushed herself off the change machine into a full upright stance. She pivoted in place and took the few requisite steps over the food machines, surveying their offerings. She spotted the dangling bag of potato chips and guessed this must certainly be the same bag over which her mother had made such a scene. She pulled a dollar bill and some coins from her own pocket, delivered them dispassionately into the tall rectangular machine. Her finger pushed N and then 7.

As she expected, the machine dropped not one, but two bags of chips: that which her mother purchased and her own. For a brief moment of maturity, Alexandra considered walking down the hall and offering one bag to her mother, or at least to save it to offer her later. Then she reconsidered. Alexandra tucked herself into the back corner of the room and ate her own bag of chips. Then, opening the second bag with impish delight, she proceeded to eat her mother's as well, savoring each chip with self-justified pleasure.

10

The Dream Seemed So Real

Boom!

Lewis and Ming, still slightly dazed and lying on the classroom floor, were the first to turn toward the powerful, relentless crashes pounding on the other side of the wall. Alexandra was still kneeling with her arms, her very body wrapped around her beloved younger sister like a cocoon of bone and flesh. Lewis and Ming gave a start as the yet-unidentified force again blasted against the concrete. They marveled at how easily the concrete gave way. The bulletin boards affixed to the wall surrendered to the herculean might of whatever was on the other side, bending inward along with the broken and displaced concrete cinder blocks.

Boom!

This time the thunderous crash was not so loud and impacted with less force. The blow did crack the wall but failed to create an observable opening. Nevertheless, small piles of debris continued to form on the floor beneath the wall. A mixture of paint chips and crushed concrete composed the piles and created a wintry white and gray frosting on the classroom floor. Alexandra leaned her head up and took in what Lewis and Ming already had seen. Agnes followed suit. The four guessed that whatever was causing the rumble likely hit the opposite side of the hallway.

Boom!

"What the heck is going on," demanded Alexandra. She released her protective body grasp from around Agnes and stood up to her full impressive height.

Neither Lewis nor Ming had any answer. They both rose cautiously to their feet and began walking closer to the wall. Agnes, for the moment, remained huddled down on the floor. It seemed that only Agnes was still mindful of whatever ghostly creatures menaced them just a brief moment ago.

Alexandra, Ming, and Lewis continue to hear and feel the pounding against the walls, but it was clear by now that its source had moved down the hallway. A few additional hits sounded off and then it stopped. The three looked at one another expectantly as if some helpful information might suddenly appear on their foreheads.

"C'mon," started Ming. "Let's check it out!"

At this, Lewis and Alexandra followed Ming over to the door closest to the source of the pounding. Alexandra's cautious caretaking instinct resisted, but like the other two, she was curious.

"Aggie. C'mon, sweetie. It's okay," said her sister, reaching out her hand.

After a brief hesitation, Agnes rose slowly to her feet and joined the others. The four gathered tightly at the door, and Ming wrapped his hand enthusiastically on the knob.

"Wait, wait, wait!" whispered Lewis intently. "Don't open the door. We don't know what's on the other side."

"How are we going to find out what's on the other side unless we open it?" returned Ming in a slightly startled and sarcastic tone.

"Stop talking and *listen* at the door," instructed Alexandra.

Agnes stood back from the other three, standing in between the south wall of the classroom and the coat area. She scanned the random items on the floor and shelves left behind by the children at the end of the day before they went home. Various mittens and gloves littered the floor and shelves. Most of them needed their twin. The metal hooks supported a few coats and hats. Crushed and folded papers also lay strewn about all over the area. They included a number of homework assignments that Mrs. Fuller's students claimed had been lost, left at home, or destroyed by a nonexistent animal or sibling.

Ming leaned in close to the door, nearly pressing his ear against the brown wood. Lewis leaned in over him, trying to work his ear as close as possible to the door while maintaining his balance and not falling forward. Lewis was close enough to hear Ming's whispered breathing and obtain a near view of his friend's coarse jet black hair. Too polite to mention it, Lewis also noticed slight evidence of body odor wafting gingerly from Ming. No doubt it was produced by sweat from running. Fortunately for Alexandra, she was tall enough to hang slightly over the two boys and still get close to the door.

They listened.

"Give me your shoes, I must have them," came a terse demanding voice from down the hall. It sounded familiar but none of the four could quite identify it.

"No! You've got your own! Shut up!" returned another voice.

"Give me your shoes! And give me your face. I must have your face now!" insisted the first voice again.

Ming looked over his shoulder at Lewis with a questioning expression. Lewis returned the same. "Is that Wyatt?" asked Lewis.

"Yeah. And I think he's talking to Dylan," answered Ming.

Alexandra leaned back a bit and nodded in affirmation. The three agreed but were puzzled. The voices sounded strange, chaotic, and feral.

"Ming, open the door a little. I want to see what's happening," whispered Lewis.

Ming looked up at Alexandra for approval. She looked back at Ming and gave a quiet labored expiration. Then she nodded. "Okay, but quietly."

Ming pulled his hand off the door knob and regripped it with his fingers. He nimbly rotated the knob to the right until it would no longer turn. Then, with great care, he slowly pushed the door open, creating an aperture of nearly two inches. Given the location of the classroom door and the design of the hallway, the three couldn't see much more than the other side of the corridor.

"Open it a bit more, Ming," suggested Lewis. "I can't see anything."

This time, without checking with Alexandra first, Ming pushed the door open. To his surprise, and Alexandra's immense relief, it offered no creak, not a sound. Encouraged by the door's silence, Ming dared to press the door further until it allowed the three to step into the hallway. They did but only as much as needed to see clearly. This is what they saw.

Dylan Pierce and Wyatt McKinney stood toe-to-toe at the end of the hallway. They bore each other an aggressive stance and hateful expression. For the most part, the two appeared exactly as they had before with a few notable exceptions. Both were slightly hunched over, and Wyatt's arms were longer and hung down. Lewis mused that his arms reminded him of the ropes that hung from the ceiling in gym class. Dylan, who previously stood taller than Wyatt, had shrunk. He was still taller than Lewis or Ming but was now shorter, smaller, and generally more diminutive in stature. He *felt* tinier to Lewis and the others.

Most remarkable were the changes to their faces. Dylan's head was more rounded than before. The edges of his jaw appeared smoothed over, and he no longer had a prominent chin. What's more, his facial features were no longer distinctive. His nose and ears were generally fatter and seemed to have melted into his face, like the edges of an ice cube in the midday summer sun. His lips were almost completely gone. All that remained were two narrow slightly pink lines around his mouth, one above and the other beneath. Finally, his hair was thinning. In fact, his scalp was balding in patches, one in front above the forehead, another in the back, and smaller spots on the sides. All of the patches revealed smooth white skin, lighter in tone than normal even if one shaved their head.

For Wyatt, all of his features and hair were present. However, he didn't quite look like himself anymore. He was still Wyatt but not completely. The children recognized him but something was different, like when you paint your white room into beige, or wear a rose-colored dress instead of a pink one. The difference was present but not pronounced. More importantly, Wyatt's behavior with Dylan had changed—it was more confident, aggressive. Certainly, Wyatt had challenged Dylan before, but it was always in check. Wyatt knew how far he could push Dylan. Now Wyatt stood up to Dylan without reservation. His words and posture toward Dylan were bold and belligerent, as if he wanted a confrontation.

"Give your face, your eyes, your nose!" demanded Wyatt, raising his monstrous hands up to Dylan's face with intimidation.

"Are you some kinda' freak?" asked Dylan, stepping back and turning away.

"I must be you! I am you!" asserted Wyatt. Then he threw his dangling arms back over his arched shoulders and smashed them against the hallway wall immediately to Dylan's left. Wyatt's left forearm produced a dent in the wall nearly two feet in diameter. His right elbow struck the wall directly and nearly caved in the cinder blocks. Lewis, Ming, and Alexandra were transfixed. They had never seen Dylan fall back in fear.

Under any other circumstances, Lewis and Ming would have watched in spellbound fascination. Dylan and Wyatt looked like two characters from a favorite movie or video. Here they were in battle. However, Lewis and Ming knew Dylan and Wyatt. And—while had no love for either one of them—they pitied them for the grotesque alterations they had undergone. Both Lewis and Ming held secret desires to one day see Dylan and Wyatt in the same type of abject terror that those two had dished out to so many. But this was too much. They didn't want this even for two such inveterate bullies.

None of the three could begin to account for the changes present in Dylan and Wyatt. Nevertheless, the source of the pounding in the hallway was clear. Whatever changes had taken place in Wyatt, they were more than met the eye. No one, not even the strongest eighth-grader, could smash dents and holes in concrete walls.

Utterly consumed in the violent display down the hallway, neither Lewis nor Ming, not even Alexandra, noticed a whispered unobtrusive voice singing sweetly behind them.

> How long have you labored in his shadow,
> Craved his strength and mighty stance?
> Pined to lead and forward stepping,
> To set the beat and choose the dance?
> Is the mirror disappointing,
> Your own endowments to decline?
> Is his mind so worth obtaining
> And His features rare and fine?
> Then, they shall be yours,
> Your driest thirst to slake.
> And fill your gut with emptiness,
> This dearest wishing which you make.
> But will you want your wish's end,
> Or some reversal seek,
> When your new eyes see amber flame,
> Your nose, the burning reek?

Back down the hall, Wyatt's exercise in terrorism continued. "Give me your face, your head, or I will crush it! It is mine, mine! *I am you!*" Wyatt had pulled his arms from the wall and its fresh dents. He returned to waving them before Dylan in a dance of coercion and browbeating. He towered over Dylan in mass and height. He hunched over his former leader in frightening girth. "You are not so big now, are you Dylan?" Wyatt added. "Who runs the show now? Who drives the emotion? Does your heart beat in fear over me? Let it beat, *beat*, *beat*!"

At this, Dylan fell to the floor before Wyatt in total submission. There was not further contest. Dylan pinched his lashless, browless eyes in a vain effort to shut out his coming demise. His thin pink lips retracted to reveal his teeth and to allow shallow, rapid fear-induced breaths to pass uninhibited in and out of his mouth. As Dylan's entire body began to shake, more chunks of his hair dropped in various sizes from his pale scalp. Now his head appeared as a corpulent dalmatian puppy or a soccer ball, dappled in white and black.

"I don't understand what you want, Wyatt!" exclaimed Dylan. He then proceeded to pull his arms over his head in self-preservation.

Suddenly, Wyatt ceased his petrifying rampage. He reached out with his hand in bloodcurdling tenderness and placed it slowly in Dylan's head. Then, transfixed by the hair that had fallen from Dylan's head, extended his other arm downward toward the floor in order to grasp a small pile of it. Holding Dylan's pale head effortlessly in firm position, Wyatt pulled the fallen lock of Dylan's hair up close to examine it. He gave a creepy smile of satisfaction and then attempted to add the hair to his own. When it fell, Wyatt's placid expression changed to disappointment. He reached down a second time, hoisting up another handful of hair and tried to affix it to his own. His faced was adorned with a briefly sweet smile, almost like a child's. Like the first, this patch of hair dropped helplessly like an autumn leaf.

Dylan made no effort to resist Wyatt's goliath grip on his head. He merely stared at his captor and quivered fearfully in a lukewarm covering of sweat from head to a terrified toe. After a third attempt to affix Dylan's hair to his own scalp, Wyatt dropped his head slightly in bitter disillusionment. Then an initially soft grumble sounded off from his mouth. As he raised his face and gave a piercing stare at Dylan, the gentle growl flourished into a volcanic yawp.

"*Raugh!*" shot out Wyatt. His herculean lungs produced enough wind as to blow Dylan's few remaining hairs to and fro like summer wheat on a gusty day. "Your hair is mine! I am you! Pick it from the floor! Stick it to your head! I must have it! I must be you! I am you!" Further growls seeped through Wyatt's monstrous clenched teeth. Still cradling Dylan's head with his left hand, Wyatt solidified the grip with the other as well. So large were Wyatt's colossal hands that neither Lewis, Ming, nor Alexandra were able to see much of Dylan's pasty whitened head.

Wyatt glared into Dylan's terrified face like a long-clawed eagle about to crush a field mouse. Dylan began to feel increasing irresistible pressure on the sides of his head. "Uh…uh…no…naugh…ploosh," begged Dylan, unable to create discernable speech with his jaws under such force. The pressure continued and grew.

Then, inexplicably, Wyatt stopped. He released the immense pressure on Dylan's skull until he was once again merely holding it, cradling it. Wyatt examined Dylan's head regretfully, like a child having nearly knocked a bird's egg from its nest. Satisfied that Dylan's head remained undamaged, Wyatt released him to the floor like a rag doll. In sheer despondency, having realized that he would have neither Dylan's hair nor the cathartic outpouring of his own wrath, Wyatt closed his eyes, cast back both his head and arms, and threw his arms crashing against the wall above Dylan's limp body like battering rams against an enemy's castle door.

So deep was Wyatt's anger and so powerful his arms that they did not merely crack or dent the wall, they broke through it. A thunderous boom rolled down the hallway and gave Lewis, Ming, and Alexandra a potent start. As Wyatt's tree-like arms pieced the cement wall, chucks of dislodged and broken cinder blocks fell to the floor in the classroom on the other side. Pulverized cement fell from the wall on both sides like the first pristine snowfall of a harsh and heavy winter. Dylan was now nearly flat on the hallway floor at Wyatt's feet, pulled together in the fetal position in total surrender, and convinced of his own imminent end.

With his arms hanging over the wall into the open air of the classroom on the other side, Wyatt undertook to retract them with the full intent of smashing again in an effort to expel his profound bitterness. His arms would not come.

They were stuck between the broken cinder blocks in the cavity his murderous rage had created. He gave another stronger yank. The wall was unwilling to surrender his arms even an inch. He drew a third time, still nothing.

Dylan, still cradling his own puny form on the cool tiled-floor, peered out briefly over the horizon of his left arm. Realizing that his assailant was stuck, Dylan rolled courageously onto his bottom and sat upright. Over Dylan's hairless head, now nearly without color and covered in a light dusting of flurried cement powder, Wyatt worked feverishly to remove his arms from the gaping aperture he had created in the wall. Wyatt produced a pathetic cacophony of growls and yells. As he yanked, twisted, contorted his limbs in a desperate struggle for liberty, he sounded off with ferocious bellows of anger, followed by supple whimpers like a bear cub snapped in a hunter's steel trap.

Seizing an unexpected opportunity from a situation he was sure to produce his demise, Dylan crawled frantically out from under Wyatt's suspended arms. Wyatt stopped pulling to give Dylan his full attention. "*No*! Don't go! I am you. You can't leave. You must not leave. I must not leave!" cried Wyatt. Falling into yet even deeper frustration, Wyatt raised his right foot up against the wall in order to offer more force. He pulled and pulled and pulled.

Without an instant's hesitation or looking back, Dylan rose weakly but swiftly to his feet and tore down the hallway toward the stairs leading up to the second floor. "Where are you going? Where am I going? *I am you!* I cannot leave. I cannot leave!" yelled Wyatt. Dylan reached the stairs and dashed up, taking them two by two. He was gone.

At this, Wyatt turned his face toward the shattered wall, leapt up slightly, and braced his left foot against the wall as well. With both legs offering their full might, Wyatt held his breath, tensed every muscle from head to toe, and pulled. After what seemed like an eternity to Wyatt, the wall relinquished their hold on his arms. Wyatt had built up such a great force with his body that, when his arms did finally pop loose, he flew backward in the air, landed on the solid floor with a painful thud, and slid to the other side of the hallway like a bowling ball reaching its pins.

Jarred slightly, but only slightly, Wyatt rose to his feet undeterred and darted down the hallway and up the stairs after Dylan. "You cannot run! I cannot run! I must have your legs, give me your legs!

11

Famous Last Words

The last few remaining leaves hung spitefully from the maple tree limbs, blown in every direction by the cool autumn winds. The trees themselves seemed cold, laid bare by the change of season, and promised nothing else until the springtime. They stood tall and thin, with broad bent-over limbs poking into the air. Nothing more heartening came from the early evening sky. Overhead, it was nothing but sad, gray clouds floating through a sea of sooty sky.

The ground was better. In every direction, the eye was flooded with the blazed reds and oranges of newly fallen maple leaves. Their color was brilliant and proud, and the broad leaves created a healthy crimson-flushed carpet as far as the eye could see. The beauty of the fallen leaves was fine recompense for the dismal sky and lifeless trees.

"If it's time for me to go back, it's time for you too," asserted Agnes.

"No, Agnes," Alexandra refused. "It's getting dark, and you have to go back home."

Agnes, Alexandra, and their three cousins, Audrey, Brooke and Madeline, stood facing one another in a broad circle. October brought not only autumn, but also the annual visit to Dad's brother. Uncle Aaron was a corn and soybean farmer and, in addition to acres of cropland, owned spacious tracks of wooded areas. The forest was perfect for prolonged games of hide-and-seek, tag, or just endless wandering.

"Mom said that we had to come home when it gets dark. So that means you too," added Agnes.

"You're wrong, Agnes," returned her sister. "Mom said that only after she forced us to take you along."

The three cousins were closer in age to Alexandra, and so created a natural foursome. Just as naturally, Agnes consistently wished to make it five. Trying to be polite, Audrey, Brooke, and Madeline stood quietly with their wind-chilled hands tucked snugly in their coat pockets. All five wore dresses or skirts made from heavy materials like corduroy or denim. For the most part, the thick fabrics served to ward off the chilly winds and left only their hose-covered ankles to face bold icy breezes unprotected.

"Well, then we have to go back," said Agnes. Even with her few tender years, Agnes Reiniger understood the reality of this situation. Her mother did in fact instruct the other girls to take her along under resistance. She did direct them to return home with the coming of the evening dark. More than likely, this was for Agnes's sake alone. Alexandra and her cousins had traversed the woods numerous times in the past and would be fine returning on their own. Agnes understood the bitter truth that her older sister wanted her to return to the house in order to be freed from the obligation to return home at dark and, finally, to be liberated from her annoying younger sister.

It hurt. Nevertheless, Agnes considered it a small price to pay and was willing to spend time with her older sister and cousins, all the while knowing that they had no real interest in her company. She admired them for their age, height, beauty, maturity, and a host of other qualities she observed but could not describe. They were older. As far as she was concerned, their presence was the place to be. Whatever they were doing was the thing to do.

"No, *you* have to go back, Agnes," said Alexandra, leaning forward a bit as she referred to Agnes. "We're going to stay out for a while."

"C'mon, Lexie," began Agnes with a slight but increasing whine. "Let's just stay out for a little while longer. I don't want to go back yet. It's boring there."

"Yes, Aggie," returned Alexandra with a whine of her own. "You have to go or we're going to get into trouble. If you go back, then Mom will be fine with us staying out longer."

"Just let me stay a little longer. Mom won't notice. And if she does, she'll know that I am with you."

"No way, Agnes," shot back Alexandra, growing slightly impatient. "We were nice enough to let you come with us for a while, but that's it. Now go back!"

Agnes did not enjoy the feeling of being rejected. Nor did she like the reminder that she was younger than Alexandra and, therefore, excluded from her socializing activities and adventures. She was tempted to cry a bit and even felt a warm salted tear pool at the bottom of her left eye. Agnes did not respond at first, and for nearly a full minute, she glanced up and down, to the left and right, stalling as long as possible, and trying to avoid eye contact with Alexandra who was staring at her with unrelenting expectation. Agnes spoke up with the first thing that popped inside her fledgling mind.

"I'm not going back. And I don't care what you say!" she asserted.

"Well, you are not coming with us," responded Alexandra immediately.

Agnes expected this. "Fine, I'll stay right here. You can go, but I'm not going to go back."

Now Alexandra was in quite a bind, and she knew it. She didn't want to take Agnes along, but she also knew that, ultimately, she was responsible for her younger sister. The cousins weren't responsible for Agnes, and she wasn't responsible for herself. Not in this situation. "Agnes, just go back, okay? We're not gonna be out that much longer."

"No," returned Agnes with new resolve. She could tell from Alexandra's tone of voice and body language that she was conflicted. Agnes stood her ground, hoping to turn her sister's heart.

"Look, Agnes. I know you want to spend time with us, but we want to be by ourselves. If you go back now, later we'll spend time together, the five of us, and we'll do whatever you want." Alexandra thought that certainly such a generous offer would placate her sister.

"No," responded Agnes, believing she still had a foot in the door.

Agnes's sharp, stubborn response triggered the latent percolating frustration in Alexandra's heart and mind.

"Agnes, go back!" Alexandra's sudden burst of viscera gave her cousins an acute start.

"No," said Agnes, with a slight and naughty grin. Agnes reveled in her newly found control. It was a game now.

Alexandra paused.

"Fine!" said Alexandra. "Stay here all night long. But we're leaving."

Brooke, cautious of her cousin's wrath, spoke up intently but softly, "Lexie, maybe we should—"

"No way," said Alexandra, shaking her head in stern refusal. "If little Aggie is old enough to spend time with us, then she is old enough to get back on her own."

Alexandra's solution and her cutting words gave Agnes a shock, so much that she looked up from the ground straight into her sister's face in sheer unmistakable disbelief. She wondered if Alexandra would actually leave her out in the middle of the woods. The hard, resolved expression left her face instantly and was replaced with tender vulnerability. Everyone was looking at Alexandra now. Her three cousins stared at her from their different locations in the circle.

"C'mon, girls, let's go!" directed Alexandra in a commanding voice, turning her head as she did to catch each of the three cousins in the face as she spoke. Part of Alexandra wondered if the three would follow her or might instead have compassion on Agnes and refuse. At the same time, her frustration with her little sister squelched such concerns and provided Alexandra with a sturdy steadfast resolve. Despite this firm doggedness, the compassion in her own heart demanded that she give Agnes a final look as if to offer one ultimate opportunity to relent and return home. Alexandra hoped Agnes would do so and offered a relatively soft expression as she looked directly at her little sister.

Agnes was conflicted as well. She hated being at odds with her sister. Agnes not only looked up to her sister; she also loved her. Agnes wanted her sister to think well of her. What's more, she wasn't sure that she could successfully navigate her way back to the house. At the same time, she greatly desired their respect and had a nagging urge to demonstrate her own strength and self-reliance if for no other reason than to convince the girls that she had the capacity to join their ranks. Ultimately, this second sentiment won the day. Agnes steeled herself and refused to move. She crossed her arms in one overly dramatic motion and even raised her right foot slightly, bringing it down again as if to express immovability.

"Okay," said Alexandra, attempting to soak her voice with manufactured indifference.

With that, Agnes stood in place, and Alexandra turned and began to walk away. One after the other, the cousins followed. Audrey first, she was the youngest of the three and most apt to follow. Madeline followed, walking backward and looking into Agnes's face, hoping that she would change her mind and walk home or at least follow the girls. They could walk her home and still have some evening left over to explore on their own. Realizing Agnes's dogged intransigence, she eventually turned and followed as well. Brooke was the last. She stood in place and watched Agnes even after the other three girls had turned and were committedly walking away.

"Agnes?" she said in a most affectionate, almost aching voice.

This touched Agnes deeply. Her cousin's tone and willingness to remain opened up a place of warmth in Agnes's young heart that put away the buffeting cool winds of the autumn evening and, even more than her sister's efforts, tempted her to yield. However, Agnes would not be coaxed. Perhaps her cousins' sweet effort led Agnes to forget the chilly winds and the coming dark. Perhaps it was Agnes's irrepressible wish to be respected by her sister. Who can discern the unfathomable motives of a young girl's mind?

"You can go," said Agnes. "I'm fine."

Brooke looked to the ground, breathed out the entirety of the air in her lungs, and unconsciously clinched her hands together as she decided what to do. After an instant, she gave Agnes one final look, shoved her chilled hands into her pockets, turned and followed after the other girls. At this, Agnes was affected by a sharp sensation of fear and loss. She stared undistractedly at the girls as they vanished from sight. It didn't take long. The combination of the thick formations of maple trees, the gloomy gray overcast sky, and the setting sun afforded little light by which to see.

At first, Agnes was exhilarated. She basked in the glow of her new freedom. Who needed the other girls? The woods were hers to explore, and she was more than capable of navigating their ligneous depths with complete independence. Her solitude and lack of outside interference made every sensation that much sweeter and more potent. She welcomed the chill of the autumn winds that curled around her soft cheeks and sought to break through her fall weather coat. Her eyes marveled at the glum choreography of the trees swaying to-and-fro in their leafless dance. Her cold-reddened ears soaked in the symphonic whirls and crackles produced by the wind and weakened tree branches. As the breeze whipped up the bright red maple leaves intermittently, Agnes imagined she was walking on the sun, watching the solar flares curl up in regal pomp and then casually dissipate. These sensory treats helped to assuage Agnes's hurting heart, her loneliness, and sense of inadequacy. It also helped her to forget that she was alone.

Agnes wandered in this manner for nearly half of an hour although it seemed much longer to her. She even ventured from the clear paths and still-wild trails cut through and prepared by Uncle Aaron and the farm's previous owners of generations ago. This brazen defiance of convention and safety served to enhance Agnes's sense of self-sufficiency. *What did she need of trails?* she thought. When the time came, or more accurately, when *she* was ready, the path to return would become clear. She would waltz back to Uncle Aaron's house in a careless fashion, disregard her family's unnecessary concern, and watch in amusement as they slowly realized how wrong they were to doubt her ability, her smarts, her *maturity*.

The time did come, and sooner than she expected. The evening dark seemed to creep up suddenly like a friend tapping you on the shoulder from behind, or the abrupt, insistent ring of the morning alarm clock. Her fascination with maple trees' gray and brown bark had distracted her from the setting sun. The few creatures she saw scamper about had so engrossed her imagination as to divert her attention from the increasingly late hour and thickening of the woods as she strayed farther and farther from the well-defined paths.

Agnes took an extended look into the sky and realized its darkening state; she saw the innumerable overarching tree branches so enmeshed and intertwined as to nearly block out the sky. The branches seemed to come together in an almost purposeful manner, concentrated intentionally only over her head. Agnes decided it was just her imagination.

She was ready now. It was time to go back. Still convinced of her own navigational skills, Agnes stopped in place, took a thorough look around, and decided upon a direction that would take her back to the safety of Uncle Aaron's house and family. She walked at brisk pace in relative confidence. At the same time, she felt a growing doubt creeping up her mind and crawling down her spine like an annoying summer bug or ice water, dripping from a slush ball recently smashed against her winter head.

Agnes walked in the same direction for approximately the same amount of time that she guessed had passed since she left the last trail. She was deeply disappointed to find nothing familiar. *Perhaps I haven't walked far enough,* she thought, trying to calm the nudging panic. She stopped a few times to look around to verify that she had not walked past the trail or some other recognizable marking. This served only to confirm that she wasn't traveling in the correct direction. Agnes examined the sky and identified the brightest portion where the sun was still setting, dying out like the end of some saccharin, romantic song or a southbound bird. She had no practical reason for choosing this direction. She didn't know in which direction lay Uncle Aaron's house. She didn't see her sister and cousins walk this way. The light was comforting; it seemed to convey hope. She needed it.

Agnes followed the setting sun until it was gone. All the while she saw no trails, nothing familiar, nothing to suggest that she had come any closer to her mom and dad, Alexandra or her cousins. She stopped cold and surrendered to the despair and panic that had been pounding on the door of her heart for some time. Partially from hopeless resignation, and partially from fear-weakened knees, Agnes dropped to the ground and began to sob, wishing desperately for her parents, Alexandra, someone, to come and take her home.

By now, it was almost completely dark. The last vestiges of the setting sun waved good-bye to the evening like a shiny coin sinking to the bottom of a murky lake. Amidst the relentless sound of her sobbing, Agnes missed the strange change that took place around her. One by one, the ambient sounds ceased, not simply came and went, but stopped altogether. The cicadas brought an end to their soothing unified buzz. Wind ceased to blow through the trees and halted the strained creaking of autumn tree branches. No longer did the squirrels and other animals dash through the leaf piles or dart up the tree trunks. There was silence.

After a bit, Agnes did notice the change. The silence was at once thick and hollow like the sound against your ears underwater. Agnes looked up attentively from her nearly fetal position.

"You," said a low unidentifiable voice. It was soft and wispy and seemed to come from nowhere in particular, filling the empty silence.

Agnes shot up to her feet. Her heart jumped to a sprinter's pace, like a bird having spied the ravenous feral cat. She looked around frantically and saw nothing. If there was something there, she couldn't see it anyway. The evening darkness had graduated into thick impenetrable night. Her eyes could discern little more than the trees and leaf-covered ground immediately before her. Agnes wrapped her arm around the tree on which she was leaning to regain some modicum of safety and waved her head back and forth to its maximum radius in order to avoid being caught off guard.

"You will," moaned the voice again.

"Who are you?" Agnes demanded in a terror-soaked shrill cry. "What do you want?"

The instant Agnes finished speaking, a large face— nearly the size of a bedroom window—shot out at her from the wooded darkness. It was gray, nearly transparent, with crooked facial features on prematurely wrinkled skin.

"You will break your leg at the age of forty two!" shouted the voice. The flying phantasmal face passed over Agnes's head with terrific speed.

Terrified and utterly confused, Agnes released the tree and ran straight in the direction she was facing. She had no plan or destination. She simply wished to be away from the horrific apparition that she encountered. *Pash, pash, pash,* went her nimble feet as they carried along her light frame. She sped through the wooded darkness, barely avoiding each tree just an instant after becoming aware of it, like a frantic driver avoiding cars on a rainy pitch-black highway.

Then another face, similar to the one she just encountered, emerged from her left side, beginning small and then growing. Like the first, it spoke as it passed Agnes by. "Your husband will die of cancer!" moaned the face, finishing the statement as it swished past Agnes.

Agnes continued running aimlessly through the woods. The stygian night seemed tangible, and its depths, endless.

"Leave me alone!" she demanded in helpless desperation.

This time from the right side, a third face broke from the obscurity. "You and your best friend will in time simply grow apart!" croaked the pale lifeless countenance, passing over Agnes like the other two. Like a horse driven again with the whip, Agnes increased her running speed in the hope of escaping the ghastly criers. She continued running in this manner for nearly a minute. Her lungs were burning with the hyperventilated cold autumn air. In contrast, her neck, scalp, and back were heated and wet with sweat from the intense, impromptu sprinting.

When a bit of time had passed with no further bellowing faces, Agnes wondered (or rather hoped) if perhaps they had stopped. She slowed to a panting stop, drawing in chilled air from the top to the bottom of her petite lungs. Between gasps of breath, she pinched her eyes together and cried, releasing the stress, fear, and anger that stood entrenched around her heart and mind like a besieging army. Instinctively, she leaned over and rested her hands on her knees, trying to rest and to slow her breathing.

She pictured Alexandra and the cousins sitting comfortably in Uncle Aaron's house, wrapped in the blissful warmth of blankets and hot cider and playing games at the dining room table. Agnes wished with all her heart that she has surrendered to her sister's wishes and returned to the house. Everything would be fine now. *Why do I have to be so stubborn?* she wondered. Right now, she would gladly admit her mistake to her sister if only she could be there with them.

Opening her eyes, she recognized what running through the uncharted woods in the dark had done to her clothes. Her shoes were caked with a soft light-brown mud from the puddles she failed to avoid. Only now did she begin to feel the cool soiled-puddle water that reached the mouth of her shoe and made its way inside. The leaves and sticks fallen from the trees left her socks pocked and full of holes, covered with a variety of seeds, nettles, and slivers of bark.

Just as Agnes began to catch her breath, she heard a whispery passing of air behind her. As she turned around to investigate the source of the sound, it became louder and more distinct. Without a doubt, it was a voice like those of the flying faces. This one sounded like a man breathing in air through dry pursed lips. In an instant, the source of the breathing was apparent. Agnes saw another face, this time far away and quite small. The face continued to inhale as it pursued her.

Agnes turned and ran. Her most heroic effort to run created a small distance between her and the haunting face. However, it was at her heels again quickly. When it reached her, Agnes cried out in acute terror. "Go away! Leave me alone!"

"Do you know how long you will live?" asked the face in a passionless empty tone.

Agnes ignored the question and poured on another level of speed, one which she had never previously reached. Her tensed pounding legs carried her a slight distance forward from the apparition.

"I will tell you how long you will live, girl!" declared the pale, ash-colored countenance.

Agnes tried to shut out the voice and focus exclusively on running. Her bent arms pulled forward and then back. She raised her knees up higher and higher, trying to move faster and escape. "No! Leave me alone!" she demanded. Her words flew from her taxed, expanded lungs and through her air-parched throat. She held her mouth wide open to its greatest expanse, allowing the fullness of each inhaled breath to fuel her lungs and heart. The crisp air wafted smoothly through her teeth, leaving them with an unwelcomed chill.

"You will die when…" spoke the swiftly moving face.

Agnes didn't hear the end of the declaration. Her running was interrupted by the lack of ground beneath her feet. She shoved her left leg down, searching for the ground and reached nothing. She did same with the right leg. Instinctively, Agnes extended her arms in front of her in an effort to reach something, or at least to prepare herself for whatever lay ahead. Her mind and heart experienced a stark and potent change in focus. Almost instantaneously, she forgot about her wispy pursuer in favor of an all-consuming lack of orientation. Her youthful, healthy eyes saw nothing in the dense, impenetrable dark. Her delicate blood-warmed hands and feet met nothing but cool emptiness.

For almost exactly a second time, Agnes paddled her arms and legs in the empty dark. She was aware that she was falling. Her body landed flatly, nearly face first in a pool of water filled with large rocks half-submerged in the frosty liquid. Her right knee came down hardest on one of the stones, sending a violent throbbing pain to the ends of her leg. She instinctively pulled her hands up to her chest and pressed down in order to lift her face from the water. When her mouth once again reached the open air, she breathed in deeply and released an agonized wail that expressed the shock of the cold water and the abrupt new pain in her leg.

"Mommy," she cried out into the void. "Lexie, where are you?" she asked desperately. "I'm sorry!" Her tearful howls met nothing but the black night.

Agnes was soaked from head to toe. Only the center of her back and the back of her head remained dry. Unbeknownst to her, she also had numerous scratches in her palms and knees as a result of the landing. Agnes used her arms to transfer her weight onto her legs and, despite the relentless throbbing in her right knee, managed to stand. Her head spun around, rapidly searching for some piece of landscape by which to orient. It was still impossible to see. She could hear the water moving. In certain places gurgled, tied up in miniature pools of rocks. In others, it flowed freely. Its depth rose to a height somewhere between Agnes's ankles and knees.

Agnes wanted out of the water. The inscrutable darkness offered no sense of direction. Agnes had to choose; unfortunately, she chose incorrectly. Merely guessing, Agnes turned to her left, walked a few painful steps and, upon bringing her right foot down on a large rock lubricated with moss, slipped and fell forward. This time she landed on her side and rolled.

She remained in contact with the ground as her body spun. In the course of her descending movement, the rocks became smaller and fewer, dwindling to the occasional stone. The rocky stream was replaced by a smoother track composed of stony earth. Agnes rolled and tumbled helplessly until the course of earth and stone deposited her in a small alcove cut out (whether naturally or otherwise, Agnes didn't know) of the earth.

Agnes had sustained no further injuries in the course of arriving at the rocky pocket, and she sensed that she was now below the stream into which she had fallen. The sounds of flowing water and her deep irregular breathing echoed off the hard moistened walls. Agnes lifted her head from the earth. Her entire body was covered with small chunks of dirt and murky brown-gray water. Her face was pocked with soil pellets in disorderly constellations. She groped around in the darkness until she felt the solid wet wall.

Agnes curled her diminutive body inward and moved gently into the stony curve created by wall and floor. She was wet, tired, dirty, hurting, thoroughly miserable. She listened to the echoes of her soft moaning and surmised that the chamber in which she now lay was bigger than her closet, but not as large as her bedroom. She thought about the times she had hidden in the closet from Alexandra while playing hide-and-go-seek. How she longed to be there now, waiting for Lexie to find her.

Agnes was sure that no one could ever find her here. She pulled her legs up close to her body and slowly leaned to her side until she was flat on the chamber's floor in the fetal position. With no options and nearly witless with fear and hopelessness, Agnes closed her eyes and began a series of deep, soulful cries. Her already wet eyes produced a full flow of salted pain-soaked tears. She continued in such a state until, wearied and affected by all that had happened, she surrendered to a deep, potent sleep.

Agnes woke to a warm pulsating white light. The glow throbbed in slow, unobtrusive beats. Opening her salt-stung eyes, she identified the source of the soft pulsating light. It came from under the surface of the ground, apparently a foot or so. The muffled glow under the earth appeared like a firefly held in a tinted glass jar. Unlike everything that had recently happened to her and her present rough surroundings, the light was soothing, almost welcoming. Agnes ignored the relentless pain coming from her knee and the unpleasant sensations produced by her dirty wet body and focused on the pallid glow.

She crawled over toward the buried light, trying to disregard the intermittent agony produced by the rhythmic pressure of crawling on her knees. The warm light wrapped a moony pale mixture of light and shadows on her wet cherub face as she hung over the section of earth. Overcome with ravenous curiosity, Agnes stabbed her water-wrinkled fingers into the soft dark-brown earth. As she removed the covering earth in a series of rapid scoops and throws, the light increased in brightness as she drew closer to it. She worked through nearly twelve inches of wet pebble-filled earth and reached the source of the warm glowing light.

There, in the bottom of Agnes's hand-burrowed hole, lay a small canvas sack. The sack itself was simple enough, roughly four inches long and pursed at the top with a piece of twine. Something *inside* the sack produced the hypnotic illumination. Agnes snatched the sack up from its earthen cradle. It was wet and rough. So intense was the radiance in her tiny extremity that it shone through the skin, flesh, and bones of her palm and fingers, like a camper's flashlight pressed tightly against the hand. Without a thought, Agnes poked her right-hand finger into the pinched top of the sack in an effort to work it open.

She inverted the open sack and poured its contents into her left palm. Her left hand received a small pile of glowing, but otherwise simple seeds. She marveled at the seeds' scintillating brilliance and, for a moment, forgot her bleak, helpless state. Keeping a firm protective hold on her newly discovered treasure, Agnes carefully moved herself back against the wall from where she had come. She opened her left palm and stared again in fascination at what she had found.

Initially under her notice, Agnes's skin began to dry, not uncomfortably so as when winter cruelly cracks your lips, but she merely lost the cold dirty water, which soaked her body as a result of recent events. The same happened to her clothes. In an unnaturally short period, her whole body, face, hair, and clothes were as dry as when she, Alexandra, and the cousins had set out early that afternoon. What's more, the numerous cuts, bruises, and scratches that riddled her young form closed and faded away. Most importantly, and most noticeably, Agnes's tender damaged knee ceased to throb. She extended the leg and found that it was as strong and pain-free as ever.

Agnes couldn't help but smile.

However, she was still very cold and alone. The light from the seeds quite effectively illuminated the chamber in which Agnes now sat; it was approximately the size that she had guessed. The opening to the chamber led out briefly and then almost straight up. Agnes surmised that she had fallen from the stream, and then down through this opening, until she landed here. She could hear the stream's water flowing above and could make out just a basic shape of the opening. However, it was still too dark, and the way too slippery to attempt to climb out. She was stuck. If help was to come, it would have to come to her. She could not meet it halfway.

Chilly, but at least dry, Agnes returned to the back wall of the hole and refocused her attention on the seeds. She counted them, rolled them around in her hand, examined their shape, all the while transfixed by their inexplicable, unnatural, and yet beautiful glow.

After some time had passed, she grew sleepy. Returning every seed to the sack, she pursed it closed and tied the twine. Pulling the small canvas sack to her chest like an old familiar teddy bear, Agnes leaned over on her right side, tucked her arm underneath her head, and closed her eyes. Despite her fear, the relentless cold, and a new and increasing thirst, Agnes surrendered quickly to sleep, lost in the stream's calming lullaby and the joy of her new treasure.

12

I Sure Hope That Memory Comes True!

"Okay," whispered Ming. "We really need to get out of here."

"Shush," responded Alexandra. "Be quiet. We don't want Wyatt to come back this way."

The four waited patiently for nearly half a minute until they were sure that Wyatt had cleared the corner and made his way up the stairs after Dylan. Slowly, and with a pronounced cautious silence, they stepped out from the safety of the classroom doorway and crept down the hallway to survey the damage Wyatt had created.

Arriving at the scene where Wyatt had accosted Dylan, the friends stood marveling at the two gaping holes in the cinder block wall and the piles of shattered and powdered cement on the ground. Ming stepped up to the damaged wall and peered through the hole. He stepped back, turned around, and spoke what everyone was thinking. "All right, how was Wyatt able to punch his fists through the solid cement wall? Even if someone could get their fists into the cement, it would break every bone in their hands!"

For a brief moment there was silence.

"I'll bet she knows something about it," asserted Ming in a voice slightly raised in pitch and volume. "I'll bet Agnes knows a whole lot about it!" Ming stared directly at Alexandra's silent diminutive sister with his pointed finger extended like a soldier's spear.

"Ming, calm down," asked Lewis in a low, even voice. "Take it easy, she doesn't know anything."

"I think she knows more than she's telling us," responded Ming. "She walks around not saying anything at all. Then she sings and makes papers fly all over the place. She knows plenty."

"Ming," started Alexandra. "Whatever she knows, she's not going to tell you. Aggie stopped talking a long time ago. If she doesn't talk to me, she won't talk to you."

Ming almost responded verbally, but then reconsidered. His affection for Alexandra was such that her words cut him to the quick. He rolled his frustration over in his head, reflecting on Alexandra's unexpected statement. He might have anticipated a more pure, visceral response like, "Ming, that's my sister! Back off!" or "Take that finger out of her face, or you'll count to nine for the rest of your short life!" Alexandra's response was measured. It seemed to convey Alexandra's own frustration with Agnes and a dull resignation at the futility of coaxing her to speak.

Lewis politely raised his hand as if he were in a classroom.

"What, Lewis?" asked Alexandra with exasperation. "Just speak up!"

"Well, I have a couple of ideas. I agree that Agnes knows more than she's saying," started Lewis, cracking a bashful smile as he pondered the obviousness of such a statement, given that she wasn't speaking at all. "You know how Dylan and Wyatt are friends but not really? I mean, they hang around together, but they're not really nice to each other."

Ming looked up at Lewis with squinted eyes, conveying his confusion.

"I mean…like… me and Ming are friends. We may joke with each other and make fun, but Dylan is downright *mean* to Wyatt. He doesn't respect him at all. And Wyatt, well, he looks up so much to Dylan. He wants to be just like Dylan. He's like his idol," explained Lewis.

Alexandra dropped in. "You're right about Dylan and Wyatt. But what does that have to do with Wyatt punching holes in the wall and growing so big?"

"Getting so big and having superstrength, I don't know," admitted Lewis. "I guess that has something to do with the crazy creatures outside, the flying papers in Mr. Cohen's office, and the flames that come out of Agnes's head. I think that's all related, somehow. But I'm talking more about Wyatt and Dylan and the things that Wyatt kept on saying."

"What do you mean?" asked Ming.

"You know," started Lewis, "All that, 'Give me your head! Give me your face! I am you!'" Lewis did his best to emulate Wyatt's voice and mannerisms. "It's like Wyatt wants so much to be like Dylan that he wants to take all his parts and *be* Dylan. Does that make sense? I know it sounds weird."

"Yeah," began Ming in a carelessly sharp voice. "It kinda' does. I mean, yeah, it sounds weird, and it does make sense a little. But that doesn't get us anywhere."

Lewis dropped his face slightly, believing that he had disappointed the others with his ideas. He felt ashamed. A warm tingling flush washed over his face. It was an emotional amalgam of shame and anger. He wondered why his friend would choose to embarrass him in front of the others. *I was only trying to help*, he thought.

"Boy, that was real nice, Ming," scolded Alexandra. "He's just sharing his ideas. Why do you have to talk to him like that?" Alexandra lifted her hands to her hips and slanted her stance slightly to add emphasis to her speech. It worked. Ming's olive brown skin took on a hot ruddy tone. He dropped his head even lower than Lewis's.

In the course of the interchange between the other three, no one noticed Agnes as she moved unobtrusively over to Lewis. By the time Alexandra had finished her reprimand and Ming was drooped in disgrace, Agnes was standing next to Lewis on his left side with gentle intimacy. When her arm was immediately connected to Lewis's, Agnes gracefully and purposefully leaned her head over onto his shoulder. In reality, given Agnes's shorter height as compared to Lewis, she was only able to touch the top of her head to the corner where Lewis's shoulder and upper arm met.

At any other time or set of circumstances, Agnes's sudden affectionate behavior would have appeared as act of honeyed, puppy-love endearment. However, Agnes's mien and facial expression ruled that out. Her countenance was markedly sober and her movements measured. Her close physical distance and inclination to Lewis indicated a kind of approval rather than romantic affection. It appeared as if Agnes wanted the others to know that she was in full support of Lewis's ideas. Alexandra endeavored to verify her suspicion.

"Agnes, do you agree with what Lewis was saying?" Alexandra began earnestly. "Is he right?"

Agnes made no response, either verbal or physical, to affirm her sister's words. She merely continued leaning into Lewis with her head hung uncomfortably onto the ultimate crest of his shoulder. For Lewis's part, he stood motionless with a polite stiffness. He didn't exactly mind having Agnes's head on his shoulder, but he was ready to have it off. He allowed it, and it reminded him of a time his second-grade class took a field trip to the zoo at year's end. Lewis "volunteered" his shoulder as a perch for the gargantuan parrot they encountered in the aviary. Lewis remembered painfully the bird's viselike claws pinching into his tender second-grade flesh. Images of multicolored wings beating carelessly against his head flooded his imagination.

Imelda raised her grandson to be as courteous and cooperative as possible. And so he was.

"See!" blasted Ming, drawing on his residual anger. "I told you she knew more than she was saying."

"Ming, how old are you?" asked Alexandra.

"Eleven," stated Ming in a cool and curious tone.

"Do you want to see twelve?" she asked.

Ming's eyes widened with horrific surprise. His last remark was the final time he accused Agnes. Lewis gave a silent and demure smile, nodding his head slightly in satisfaction at Alexandra's sense of justice. *Not exactly, Take that finger out of her face or you'll count to nine for the rest of your short life!* Lewis mused. *But it was close enough.*

The uncomfortable tension of the confrontation was broken by a disturbing, but increasingly familiar, sight. As had occurred just recently down the hallway, a bright, glowing purple light began to shine from under the door to the classroom opposite the one that suffered Wyatt's destructive fury. Just as before, it was warm and inviting, initiating at the center of the door's bottom at the floor, and then ascending up both sides of the wooden rectangle simultaneously in a perfectly synchronized movement of light. Alexandra, Ming, and Lewis each gave the light their respective attention in turn, mesmerized by its hypnotic glow. No one noticed, but Agnes remained casual and unaffected at the light's advent as if she knew it was coming.

All four watched the soothing lavender light surround the wooden door and encase its frame. They knew what to do.

Being nearest the door, Alexandra took the two requisite steps and reached out to grasp and pull the door's metallic handle. The music came first. Like a switch, the action of pulling the door's handle produced an onset of rather loud popular music, the variety one might hear on the radio during a school dance. So blaringly loud was the music that, upon pouring out into the school hallway, its waves bounced off the cinder block walls and created a startling echo. The four paused briefly, taking in the full effect of the echo's wavy, repetitive effect, and then entered the classroom.

As much as their ears were hijacked by the raucous music pounding in its relentless rhythm, the collective vision of the four friends was overtaken by a parade of flashing multicolored lights passing in an undulating procession of radiance. The flashes came in blues, then reds, yellows, and greens. In fact, the beats of music and the flashes of luminosity occurred in tandem. The light display was tied in to the music.

Alexandra walked in far enough to allow the other three to take in the view fully. In addition to the mind-numbing pulse of the music and lights, a low hum captured their senses. The source of the hum was difficult to discern initially as, apart from the cascading flashes of tinted glow, the room was decidedly dark.

When their young eyes had quickly adjusted, the mystery vanished into clarity. Wheels crafted on colored fiberglass rolled over a wooden floor. School-aged children roller skated clumsily in misshapen circles under a huge blinking lamp located at the center of the rink. The skaters circled the lamp aimlessly if dutifully, as if they hoped to appease some electric deity by offering their endless skated circles in humble obeisance. The four stood at the entrance to a roller skating rink. What's more, it was not just any rink, but the one that they normally attended for school skating parties.

"Apparently, gym class has gotten more interesting," remarked Ming in an unmistakably sarcastic tone.

Alexandra turned around just enough to give a disapproving look to her younger companion. "Don't be an idiot," she said in a tone intended to repress Ming, like a trainer gently yanking her dog's tensed leash.

Ming's ironic tone was appropriate. Aside from the fact that this space was normally a grade-school classroom, a skating rink could never fit into an area this size. The lack of windows allowing in the outside snowy winter's white light added to their conviction that this was some sort of unnatural occurrence.

The interior decoration of the rink was warm and functional but in desperate need of updating. The wooden rink floor was surrounded by a cement barrier about waist high to a normal-sized man and was intended to keep errant skaters from smashing into the folks standing in the walkways. Antiquated carpet from the 1970s covered the walking spaces on the outside of the rink itself. The flat worn-out carpet bore a random variegated design. It had a row of colored and black stripes flowing in one direction with the same type of stripes flowing in the other. Some stripes were curved and others rounded. Strips of old steel-gray duct tape mended the broken sheets of carpet and held it in place against the walls where it had begun to curl up.

Inside the facility, a vast group of children and adults were abuzz with activity; and the four recognized almost all of them. On the raised platform in the corner of the skating rink proper, a young undersized man bounced with unnecessary vigor to the beat of the music he produced for the skaters. He wore a slender spotty moustache and goatee to compensate for his diminutive stature and what he perceived to be an unnaturally high voice.

In addition to the unbroken circular stream of skaters on the wooden floor, the food and game areas of the rink were also busy. Nearly all of the video games stacked up against the wall of the building held a player entranced by a harmony of mesmerizing lights and sounds. At two of the machines stood eighth-grade boys, experts at the games, accompanied by their eighth-grade girlfriends.

As you might expect, the girls were bored out of their respective minds. However, they remained dutifully at their boyfriend's side, making empty repetitive comments like,

"Wow, you're really great at this game!" or "Great job! Yeah!" Ignorant of the reality regarding their girlfriends' state of mind, the young men continued to dump game tokens in the machine's bottomless gullet, living inside the electronic adventure, and believing that reaching the high score might actually endear them to their female counterparts.

Near the entrance to the facility, a young teenage girl stood behind a counter, receiving and distributing pairs of rented roller skates. She rolled them across the carpet-covered counter in muffled hums, calling out to the kids over the all-absorbing din of dance music. "Thank you!" she said in a repetitive and perfunctory tone. "What size do you need?" she asked. "Six? Why don't you try six?"

Busy as the evening was, the youthful female was inundated with returned pairs of skates, unable to single-handedly keep up with the load. She tried desperately to stem the tide of impatient middle and junior high students, passing out one pair and then working to return three or four. "Okay, seven. Seven and a half. Eight. Nine, nine, okay, nine," she spoke softly to herself.

Nearly thirty yards to the girl's right, a line of hungry wound-up kids stood querulously at the food bar. One boy held a sweaty wad of bills and coins in his right hand, banging the quarters against the metal bar that stood off the food counter and served to corral the customers into a servable line. Two kids behind him, spun uptight on sugar and caffeine, rolled their skates forward and back within the space provided between the serving counter and the metallic guide bar.

One in front stuffed her change into her pocket, pinched a box of overpriced sour candies between her left hand middle and ring fingers, wrapped her other hand around a jumbo-sized paper container of cola, and pushed off on her roller skates toward the tables in the eating area. The elderly overweight man behind the serving counter took money, scanned credit cards, popped corn, and took slow, often indiscernible, food orders from sugar-addicted, overindulged school kids. In misery, he pondered the definition of retirement and wondered if he could have withstood a few more years at the steel foundry.

The carpeted food area included a fleet of simple picnic-style tables fashioned from wooden planks and curved bars of coal-gray metal. Each table bore a distinct history of multilayered wads of dried sugar, the result of spilled soda, pop and soft candies pressed into the crevices of the wood's surface. Each table's underside was a filthy universe of age-old dirt illuminated with a constellation of chewed bubblegum. Once chiseled into clean squares and rectangles, firm and covered with delectable powdered sugar, each affixed piece of gum was now a blob of time-hardened goo, tasteless and pale, a monument to the owner's teeth, gums, and saliva.

Three fifth-grade girls sat in a intimate triangular huddle at one of the eating tables in the food area. One counted the remaining pieces of candy in her small yellow box, while other two spoke intermittently between slurps on their favorite soda. They mused regarding the cutest boys in junior high and shared ideas on what life might be like married to each of them, the type of house they would live in, cars they would drive, number of children, etc. The sweet mutual sharing of confidences regarding their romantic dreams covered an undercurrent of insecurity and resentment. One of the gals drinking soda scanned over the other's facial features, comparing them to her own and working to convince herself that any good-looking boy would certainly prefer her. The remaining girl spoke confidently of her own good looks and personality but secretly was sure that no boy would ever find her interesting.

All of this seemed quite normal to the four companions standing at the classroom door, which was now also the entrance to the local skating rink. They took in the reality, or rather, *unreality* of it all. This was until they spied three sadly familiar miscreants walking in some obnoxious gait into the men's restroom. They were none other than Dylan Pierce, Wyatt McKinney, and Jeremiah Strickland.

"What the heck are they doing here?" asked Lewis. His forehead wore a field of wrinkled skin, conveying his frustrated confusion and curiosity.

"What *could* they be doing here?" added Alexandra. "We just saw Wyatt in the hallway."

As if this wasn't enough to bewilder and befuddle the four, a familiar young boy walked calmly out of the restroom as Dylan, Wyatt, and Jeremiah walked in. It was Ming. He wore a different set of clothes, but it was unmistakably him. Naturally, the three bullies each took a turn to physically intimidate Ming. Dylan used his larger size to simply mash Ming up against the wall, producing a sharp pain in his arm as it pressed suddenly against the cold cement wall leading into the restroom. Wyatt bowed back his own right arm and gave Ming a healthy punch that landed between his elbow and shoulder. Looking to impress the other two with his originality, Jeremiah stuck out his left leg and endeavored to trip Ming. When Ming stopped moving forward, Jeremiah resorted to using the same leg to merely kick Ming in the shins.

"Hey, that's me!" exclaimed Ming. "This is weird."

"I wonder if I'm here," spoke Lewis. He didn't fully grasp the absurdity of his statement. He was consumed in scanning the interior of the facility, looking for himself.

"What are we looking at?" asked Alexandra. She was thinking the idea in her own mind as much as speaking it out loud.

Naturally, Agnes had nothing to say.

"I've been to these skating parties before," began Ming. "And I recognized the kids here. But I don't remember wearing those clothes."

Ming looked sharply at the clothes his roller skating mimic wore. Certainly, the clothes fit his body, and perhaps, were clothes he might choose. However, his young flawless memory could not recall ever wearing or even purchasing them.

Dylan, Wyatt, and Jeremiah, satisfied that they had effectively crushed Ming's spirit and reminded him of his lower place in the world, traversed the remaining distance into the restroom. Ironically, not one of them actually needed to be present in the restroom for it normal uses. Immediately upon entering, they initiated their nefarious designs.

Dylan entered the far stall and yanked the roll of toilet paper from its holder. As fast as his mind and hands could manage, he unrolled the soft blanched paper and threw it down in fist-sized wads into the toilet. He continued in this manner, unravelling the paper, wadding and stuffing, until his malevolent psyche sensed that the toilet was sufficiently stuffed in order to malfunction. Soaked in water, the paper looked like shaving cream poured into a white cereal bowl. Dylan flushed the toilet and waited with wicked anticipation. The victimized toilet started its normal flush. Then it gagged and gurgled, finally offering a petite bubble before surrendering to a block-up halt. Dylan howled with contented joy.

Sharing in Dylan's diabolic laughter, Wyatt approached the neighboring stall and kicked the door open. It swung with unnatural speed and gave a sharp *whump!* as it hit the inside wall of the stall. Wyatt, like Dylan, grabbed the toilet paper but for a different purpose. He pulled it gleefully in white curvy stream over to the sinks on the opposing wall. With the toilet paper and his pleasured expression, Wyatt looked like a four-year-old, running a rainbow stream of colored ribbons over a grass-covered springtime meadow.

Reaching the sinks, he opened the water faucet while still pinching the toilet paper's end in his fingers. He proceeded to pull the paper into a soft, fluffy ball in his arms until he had accumulated the perfect amount. The paper went under the faucet water until it was damp but not sopping. From there, Wyatt compressed the wad, tore in into moist, fibrous handfuls and threw them up to the ceiling. Each one stuck as expected, sending a web of water spurts in every direction all over the ceiling as it impacted. Uproarious laughter bounced off the solid cement walls and tile floor.

Breaking off from the toilet paper theme, Jeremiah laid his body down on the cool floor, his back coming into contact with its supreme filthiness. He scooted gracelessly across the tiles until he was under the stall from which Wyatt had drawn the toilet paper. Jeremiah regained his feet and cried, "Watch this, guys!" He pulled the door shut, locked it, and dropped to the floor again, bumping like a sleepy elephant into the toilet and stall walls. Jeremiah quickly rose to his feet on the other side of the stall and looked to the other two for an affirming laugh. Wyatt started a giggle that matured into a full obnoxious wail.

"That was stupid," said Dylan, staring at Jeremiah with stone-cold disapproval.

Of course, and in truth, Dylan found Jeremiah's prank endlessly funny. However, Dylan's relentless desire to deprecate others won the day. Wyatt stopped laughing immediately. Dylan, Wyatt, and Jeremiah, at least subconsciously, understood that friendships among the cruel are never genuine. Whatever shallow camaraderie they may provide, this always gives way to senseless mean cuts and jabs. The cruel despise all others and most especially themselves. Ultimately, Dylan cared nothing for the other two. Nor did he respect them. He abided with them for his own, selfish purposes. Believing them to be dull and undesirable, Dylan supposed that their presence would elevate his own standing in the school.

Lewis continued to scan the activity bustling around the rink, searching for himself. Still nothing.

Movement over in the food area answered Alexandra's curiosity. She saw herself stand up from one of the far tables and walk gracefully over to the section of wall that divided the rink from the video game area. There she stood, demure and patient. Facing the rink, the lights from the ceiling and walls flashed with rhythmic brilliance against the contours of her tender face. She displayed a nervous habit, drawing shapes and lines on the top of the cement wall, attempting to look calm but in reality making it clear that she wasn't. For the most part, she looked out and downward. Then she would raise her head and look around as if she were waiting for something or some*one*.

At this point, Lewis and Ming picked up on the skating rink version of Alexandra. "Alexandra, look!" exclaimed Lewis. "There you are, standing by the side of the rink. It's you!" Ming was enraptured as usual. From his perspective, the only thing better than one Alexandra Reiniger would be two. He pictured himself walking confidently up to Alexandra and taking her hand as if it were a matter of course. He would gently take her hand and lead her into the blinking storm of variegated electric lights, just as the slow music began, which introduced the current popular, romantic song.

As the singer toned out the song's lyrics, the couple would round the curves of the skating rink, staring deeply into each other's eyes, lost in blissfully true love. Naturally, all of the other skaters would leave the rink, allowing him and Alexandra to parade around the rink alone in regal grandeur.

The sweet dream ended when Ming saw someone else walk up to Alexandra. He half expected that his skating rink counterpart might be the suitor, just having exited the restroom, and rubbing his wounded shoulders after the encounter with Dylan, Wyatt, and Jeremiah. However, this young man was wearing a letter jacket. Initially, he wondered if it might be his own brother. *What is Hui doing here?* Ming thought. *Don't they have enough girls in high school? Maybe he just wants to tell all the grade-school kids that he got into business school!*

"Hey!" shouted Lewis. "Isn't that—?"

"Yes," interrupted Ming. "It's Brandon Meyer."

Ming was relieved, but not entirely. Certainly, Brandon Meyer was an improvement over his brother, but Brandon was tall for his age and good-looking, not the kind of kid he wanted near Alexandra. Brandon had a face of masculine but gently cut features, and a head crowned with the most radiant blonde hair, which always seemed to lay in a perfect formation of gilded locks. What's more, he had deep, soft blue rounded eyes, the kind that would melt the heart of any junior high girl newly consumed with the concept of boys and budding romance. To boot, Brandon was a nice guy. He was one of those successful, confident, intelligent athletes who actually *didn't* flaunt their talents and skills or lord their strength over others. Generally speaking, he was nice to everyone, even Ming and Lewis.

Brandon's manner of leading Alexandra to the rink was not nearly as smooth or theatrical as Ming imagined his would be. Nevertheless, it was just as, if not more, sweet and romantic. Brandon approached Alexandra, and his arrival produced a reserved but effectual smile from her. He did indeed take her hand, but rather than leading her smoothly to the rink, the change in position caused Alexandra to lose her balance. She slipped on her skates and leaned forward at an alarming rate. Ever vigilant, Brandon tensed his arm and pulled up slightly, giving Alexandra the foundation that she need to regain her balance. She did.

"I didn't know you and Brandon were a thing," started Lewis. "Oooooewwww," he mocked. It was unlike Lewis to make fun, but he couldn't resist.

"We're not!" Alexandra asserted. "I mean I like him. But I don't like, *like* him." She was nearly beet red with blushed embarrassment. She told an outright lie. Alexandra Reiniger did indeed like, *like* Brandon Meyer. Whatever her words indicated, her facial expression and stumbling speech told the truth. Perhaps even more than the other three, Alexandra knew that they were not viewing events from the past. She had never before skated with Brandon Meyer.

The music pounding against the walls of the skating rink slowed to a more soothing, less frenetic pace. The relentless beat of the dance music mutated into a saccharine, velvety groove intended to draw out all the couples. "All right, all you love birds," began the DJ, "it's time to find your sweetie and head out onto the floor for our last slow song for this evening." Ironically, the young diminutive DJ had no more experience with romance than the middle and junior high kids to which he was speaking. Alexandra and Brandon glided as gracefully as they could across the carpet until they reached the wooden surface of rink. From there, Brandon took the lead and pushed off with enough force to send them both rolling comfortably across the wood-covered rink.

The soft lilting music continued, peppered with the latest lyrical rendition of passionate, eternally committed love. And then, although none of three noticed—not Ming, he was consumed in defeat; nor Alexandra, she was lost in an undulating sea of sweet reflection watching herself skate with Brandon Meyer, the nicest best-looking boy she knew—that the lyrics originally written for the song ceased. Seamlessly, and in perfect unison with the undercurrent of the song's beat and instrumentation, Agnes began to sing her own rendition.

> I could hear from the bird's first calling,
> That you and I were meant to be.
> From the dawn of day until its falling,
> The sun shines but for you and me.

Lewis and Ming turned around and gave Agnes their full attention. She continued.

> The days of joy with bliss will flow,
> In greens and vibrant blues.
> But soon will come the dismal woes,
> In murky, purple hues.
> Not for me, not for you,
> Nor for friends both old and new,
> But for a pair of sibling twins,
> Blonde-haired with eyes of blue.

Finally, able to pull away from the romantic apparition, Alexandra too gave her full interest to her sister's beautiful yet harrowing song. She sang with deep, confident conviction and a lucid thoughtfulness well beyond her years. Agnes folded her hands neatly at her front and held her head high, crooning the melodious message in phrases of perfect length and copious emotion.

> The advent of the young oppressor,
> Who finds the passage deep and crude.
> Will lead his minions none the lesser,
> In sable capes and wrinkles rude.

And with that, the vision ended. Every scene of the roller rink disappeared in one silent movement from left to right. The kids playing video games, the girls gossiping over sipped sodas, the brilliant flashes, even Alexandra and Brandon, slipped away into oblivion. What remained was not much brighter than had been the vision of the shadowy roller rink. Lewis and his new friends stood in the classroom that they expected to enter before bearing witness to the roller skating party and Alexandra's fanciful adventure in romance. The classroom and all its normal contents appeared untouched. Snow covered the windows fully from corner to corner, blocking any daylight from entering in.

Lewis and the others left the classroom in thoughtful silence and returned to the hallway.

13

The Thief and The Hidden Treasure

"Wow!" Alexandra began. "Did that weird anybody else out?" She spoke up immediately upon reentering the hallway as if she were trying to distract the group from her romantic scene with Brandon.

"It sure was strange," returned Lewis calmly. "But to be honest, I am starting to get used to strange things happening. Anyway, I think that they are all intended to tell us something, almost like pages in a story."

Agnes stood serenely as ever. She gave no real indication that anything out of the ordinary had just taken place. Ming was quiet. He glanced around the lengths and edges of the hallway, almost in a daze. He was lost in a fog of emotion and thought. His young inexperienced mind and heart could not identify the nature of his feeling, let alone resolve their causes. It troubled him deeply to see Alexandra skate with Brandon. It wasn't Brandon himself. Ming liked Brandon. It was more what Brandon represented. The letter jacket took Ming back to his brother, his consistent success and haughty attitude. It reminded him of his father's incessant need to compare the two brothers and his need to point out Ming's every flaw.

Then he saw Brandon, in that letter jacket, walk up and confidently ask Alexandra to skate together. Brandon's manner was effortless, smooth, and cool (in reality it was not, but that's the way it seemed to Ming through the eye of his insecure heart). He wanted to skate with Alexandra. He wanted to wear the letter jacket and hold hands with the most wonderful, beautiful girl in the school.

At the same time, Ming understood that Alexandra was not interested in him. She likely would never be so. It wasn't as if he and Alexandra had made their lifetime vows of unremitting love and then she walked away. There was no relationship to betray, no promise to break. So with this in mind, Ming didn't feel exactly jealous. It was a mixture of jealously, sadness, and anger. All three of those emotions swirled around in his mind and heart. He was angry but didn't know at whom or what. Of the three, sadness was the clearest emotion to grasp and account for; Ming had feelings for Alexandra. It hurt his tender heart to see her skate with someone else but him.

"If that's true," continued Alexandra, "what was the purpose of us seeing ourselves at the roller skating party? I mean, like I said, I've never skated with Brandon before."

"Right," responded Lewis. "That's true, but you said yourself that you liked him."

"No, I didn't!" asserted Alexandra. "I never said that."

"Yes, you did," corrected Lewis. "Ming, didn't she say that she liked him?"

"Huh?" asked Ming, slow and foggy as if coming out of a daze. Lewis ignored him and continued.

"Okay, okay," said Lewis. "You said you liked him but that you didn't like *like* him."

"Yeah, that's right," said Alexandra in an increasingly annoyed tone. "So what? I like lots of people."

"Well, follow me through on this. You said that you've never skated with Brandon before. We just walked into the classroom and saw you skate with him."

"Yeah? So?" Alexandra shot out the words like cannon balls.

"My guess is that we were seeing something from the future, something that will happen but that hasn't happened yet."

At this point, Ming joined into the conversation. "Okay, but what was the point?" Ming asked this question with an air of frustrated resentment, not at Lewis, but rather at the vision itself. He could have done without seeing his love skate with Brandon.

"Remember the song that Agnes sung, that one line, 'not for me, not for you, nor for friends both old and new, but for a pair of sibling twins, blonde-haired with eyes of blue'?"

"Yeah," started Alexandra. "I remember. And?"

"Oh, c'mon," said Lewis in a mocking quality to his voice. "You and Brandon skating together all sweet. Then come the sibling twins from Agnes's song." He motioned his hands out and then back toward himself as if he were trying to dig a reaction or perhaps the correct answer from Alexandra.

"Now wait a minute, buster!" demanded Alexandra. She drew in a deep breath and raised her thin nimble arms up to her hips like a mother catching her children in the middle of mischief. Her face turned a deep burning shade of red. The heat of her angered, embarrassed fever dissipated from the edges of her rounded pink ears, hidden beneath her long locks of brown hair.

Lewis looked over at Ming for support. "Makes sense to me," said Ming, bolstering his friend's conclusion.

"What are you talking about, Ming?" questioned Alexandra. "What did you see? You weren't even around. You were off in the bathroom getting beaten up!"

Ming didn't react to Alexandra's remark. He pondered his own reaction to Lewis's idea. *Why did I agree with Lewis?* he thought. The vision of a taller older boy skating with Alexandra disturbed him. Ming couldn't bear the idea that someday Brandon and Alexandra would get married and have a set of twins. He hated that future! In his gut, Ming wanted to join with Alexandra to reject the idea against Lewis.

At the same time, however, it felt better, comforting somehow, to make light of it. It soothed the pain in his smarting heart to dig at Alexandra and to watch her squirm with mortification. Ming tried his best to swallow his cast down spirit and forced a jovial smile.

Lewis offered a satisfied grin to see that his friend was in his corner.

"And you!" accused Alexandra, turning her murderous look in Lewis direction. "You weren't there at all! What do you know?"

At this, Ming stopped smiling and turned inward. His mind came to a sharp halt as if he were riding his bike and had come upon a deep rain-filled pothole. "That's true, Lewis. You weren't there."

"Yeah!" affirmed Alexandra, happy that Ming had changed sides.

"No, no…I mean, you weren't there…at the skating party," added Ming.

"That doesn't mean I'm wrong," contended Lewis.

"I'm not talking about what you're saying about Alexandra," started Ming. "I mean, why weren't you there at the skating party?"

"Who knows?" pondered Lewis out loud.

"Well, it was probably a party for the whole school," began Alexandra, starting to understand Ming's point (and oh, so pleased that the focus was no longer on her and Brandon). "Why wouldn't you be there?"

"I don't know," declared Lewis, shrugging his small shoulders. "Maybe I was sick. Maybe I was out of town. Who knows? Who cares?"

Lost in the confusion of the verbal melee, neither Lewis, Alexandra nor Ming noticed Agnes's unobtrusive movement past them and toward the end of the hallway. Upon reaching the end, Agnes stopped and turned sharply around toward the other three, intending to garner their collective attention. Lewis and the others stopped their conversation and stared directly at Agnes. She stood dispassionately in place, her feet together, and her left arm hanging stiffly. Alexandra's silent little sister raised her right arm and pointed firmly up the staircase leading to the second floor, the very same staircase Wyatt had taken not long before.

Agnes reached the end of the staircase and the second floor first, followed closely by her protective sister. The boys brought up the rear. They were greeted at the top by a series of creaks and smashes. They gathered from the distance of the sound, and the fact that they saw no one in the hallway meant the sound must be emanating from one of the classrooms, and specifically the one on the left side. The companions assumed that it must be Wyatt. Ming pictured Wyatt pounding Dylan to a pulp somewhere in the middle of the desks. Alexandra imaged Wyatt raising a student desk over his head and threatening Dylan for the sheer pleasure of watching his terror.

Agnes walked calmly and confidently up to the door to the classroom from where the sound emanated. With the speed of a striking cobra, Alexandra vaulted forward after her sister, reaching her just before Agnes was able to grab the doorknob.

"What are you doing, Aggie?" she questioned at a whispered volume. "Wyatt's in there. We don't want to go in there!" Alexandra firmed up her tenuous hold on her sister and pulled her back from the door. Lewis and Ming advanced up toward the door, stopping close to the girls.

Not quite struggling, Agnes stretched against her sister's greater strength and reached out toward the door. Her fervent expression and fully extended arm gave the impression that she wanted at least to touch the door, if not open it. The crashes and creaks continued. In addition, the four could also now make out faint but impassioned murmurs.

"Give me the, the, thing," mumbled out the understated voice.

"Is that Wyatt?" asked Lewis. "It doesn't sound like him."

"Who cares?" asked Alexandra rhetorically. "We're not going in there. Do you remember what happened with Wyatt and Dylan downstairs in the hallway?"

Agnes continued to struggle and pull from Alexandra in the general direction of the classroom door.

"There have got to be some things in here," muttered the voice. "I just have to find them. Where are they? Where are they?"

"Ming, look through the glass in the door!" mandated Lewis. "Can you see what's going on in there?"

Ming moved up close to the classroom door and angled his body in such a way as to have the best chance of obtaining a clear and comprehensive view. He swayed back and forth and popped up and down, adjusting his position. "Well, it's dark like the other classrooms. You can still see light coming in from outside. So the snow is not up to the windows on the second floor yet."

"Do you see Wyatt?" solicited Lewis, ungrateful and slightly perturbed at his friend's impertinent information.

"No," he returned simply. "But some of the desks are turned over. There's stuff all over the floor."

"Where is the stuff, the things?" babbled the unidentified voice. "There are always things in the desks, things in the rooms."

"Can you crack the door a little and get a better look?" queried Lewis, his face bearing a hopeful expression.

"No way you are opening that door, Ming!" shot in Alexandra in her best stern-mother voice. "Don't you dare!"

Mindful of Lewis's idea, Agnes relaxed her muscles and ceased striving against her sister's irresistible restraint. She began to nod rapidly, expressing her decided agreement with and support of Lewis's initiative. First she nodded to Alexandra, then Lewis, then Ming. Lewis produced a gratified smile on his young face, expressing the joy that someone liked and supported his idea. Ming reached his hand up to the door and wrapped his hand around the silver metallic handle.

"We are not opening that door!" proclaimed Alexandra, trying to supply her words with the appropriate force, while at the same time keeping her voice to a safe whisper.

Agnes continued to nod.

"C'mon, Alexandra," whined Lewis. "I think we should trust Agnes. "We'll crack it just a little to see better. Maybe there is something inside that Agnes wants us to see, something that will help us get out of here."

Alexandra drew in a full complement of air, preparing to respond to Lewis's words. She stopped short of doing so and stared straight out into space, not looking at any of the other three. She was thinking. Agnes pulled from her slowly and gently, and before Alexandra realized it, Agnes was close enough to the wall to touch. Agnes gracefully extended her arm and touched the cool cement wall that divided the classroom and hallway. In simultaneous action, Agnes looked intently but tenderly into her sister's eyes. It was clear that Agnes wanted inside.

"Okay, Ming," conceded Alexandra with a resentful fume emanating from her face. "Open it just enough to see inside. Just a crack and no more!"

Having obtained the endorsement of the unofficial decision maker of the group, Ming grasped the door handle enthusiastically and gave it a slow, tender pull. Ming's effort produced a narrow aperture between the frame and door, and thankfully, no sound. Ming pulled a bit more. Still no cracks or whines from the door. He breathed a sigh of relief.

At this point, Ming was able to move his head between the door and the frame to get a more complete view of the state of the classroom and the activity inside.

It wasn't Wyatt. Jeremiah Strickland, whom they hadn't seen since the gym, was meandering about in the classroom, moving from desk to desk. At each desk, he opened the lid, rummaged and bit and, having determined it was devoid of anything he deemed valuable, released the lid to drop closed on its own. As Ming had seen earlier, desks all over the other classroom were turned over, their contents strewn carelessly on the classroom floor.

"There must be something for me. Something to have. Some to make me happy," murmured Jeremiah.

"Ming," started Lewis impatiently. "Let me take a look!"

"There's no room," returned Ming with his eyes still fixed on Jeremiah.

"Well, I want to see what's happening," said Lewis.

"Will you two stop talking!" demanded Alexandra. "I really don't want to meet whoever is in there."

"It's Jeremiah," said Ming, turning away from Jeremiah for a moment to inform Alexandra.

"Ming, get out of the way," started Lewis. "My turn!"

"No…no…okay…okay…shush," offered Ming, keeping his voice low. "Hang on just a second." Ming slid the fingers of his right hand to the inside of door and gradually pushed the door open, taking great care to prevent creaks of any kind. When he had produced an opening wide enough to allow his own body to pass, he took a quiet step into the classroom.

"What are you doing?" questioned Alexandra in a shocked and terrified tone. "Don't go in there! Come back! Come back!" She waved her hands toward herself, directing Ming to return.

Ming ignored her. He didn't know why, and at that moment he didn't stop to consider the reason. Perhaps it was the excitement of the moment, the thrill of standing in the presence of danger, only to take another step closer. Perhaps it was nothing more than youthful idiocy. Maybe he ignored Alexandra in order to show her and himself that he was just as big, as grown-up, as brave as Brandon Meyer, maybe even more so, more so than even his brother, Hui.

He bent his legs and arched forward slightly in the expectation that doing so would render him less visible. Brave or not, he had no desire to get up close and personal with Jeremiah. Ming waited until Jeremiah turned his back. Then he darted from the door and ducked behind the clothing and backpack area in the back of the classroom. The area included a wooden construction that opposed the back wall and stood from the floor to the ceiling. It provided full and excellent cover.

Having safely arrived there, Ming turned back to Lewis, who by this time had positioned himself in the open door, and waved him into the classroom. As did Ming, Lewis watched for a safe moment from Jeremiah and then moved next to Ming within the clothing and backpack area. Now kneeling side by side, the two friends could not help but offer one another an excited smile, embracing the thrill of their precarious situation, the danger they did not yet fully appreciate.

In the hallway, Alexandra was beside herself, incensed and disbelieving. She stood up straight and moved with controlled rapidity over to the door. Looking through the opening, she saw Lewis and Ming smiling at one another. She considered how poor and ineffective the security at the local zoo must be to have allowed these two monkeys to escape. She wondered if their families would really miss them, or if she could be satisfied with merely beating bumps on their ignorant risk-taking heads.

"Must have something…something…then I will feel better," mumbled Jeremiah as he plunged his hands into another desk.

Settled in their places, Lewis and Ming peered from the opposite sides of the clothing area. For the most part, Jeremiah appeared physically unchanged. His clothing and general appearance were slightly disheveled. But this was likely due to his voracious uncontrolled digging about in the classroom. Lewis and Ming did notice his hands. They were larger than normal. What's more, from what they could see, they had lost their normal form. Each of Jeremiah's hands still had a palm, thumb, and four other fingers, but there were no knuckles or fingernails. His hands were puffy and disturbingly smooth. They were enflamed into a bright pink. It appeared as if someone had stuck a hose into each hand and compressed air into it like a helium balloon.

Lewis and Ming looked at one another, as if the explanation for Jeremiah's odd alteration would magically appear on the other's forehead.

Outside in the hallway, Alexandra looked on, trying to gauge the circumstances of the entire classroom from the expressions on Lewis and Ming's faces. She didn't like what she saw. Having given her attention fully over to the disquieting events in the classroom, Alexandra had released her gentle but resolute grip on her sister. With no intention of being secretive, Agnes nonetheless walked away from Alexandra's immediate presence without drawing attention to her departure.

Back in the classroom, Jeremiah continued his impassioned searching. "Must have something...there is something here...then I will feel better...where is the *something*?" muttered Jeremiah as he threw his hands into the bowels of another student's desk. He rummaged a bit inside the desk, turning his head back and forth to obtain the best vantage point. He then pushed both hands like shovel spades into the middle of the desk's contents. His arms pushed outward from the center of the desk, hurling the contents to both sides.

A blue mathematics book flew across the room, its pages flapping in the air midflight like a crazed bird. An assortment of pencils, pens, erasers, and paper clips filled the air in the other direction. On both sides, a variety of loose-leaf papers arched in the air and then landed strewn across the classroom floor. A few were pristinely flat and white, others late homework assignments, others nothing more than mindless doodling to pass the school day.

Having realized that this desk, like the others, held nothing of interest, Jeremiah lost his patience. "Something must have something. I need it. I feel bad. I want to feel better!" he cried. Jeremiah's enlarged rosy-pink hands clasped the sides of the desk like an eagle's talons around a field mouse. As effortlessly as one might lift a dinner plate from the table, he hoisted the desk over his head. Like a toddler having a temper tantrum, Jeremiah hung the desk behind his head just slightly and then pitched it furiously across the room at the window side wall. "That's what you get for not having something for me! I need something. Then I will feel better!" Lewis's eyes widened, and he clenched his hands tightly around the coat rack's wooden body. His heart raced. Ming reacted in a similar fashion.

Granted incredible momentum by Jeremiah's newfound and unnatural strength, the desk remained in the air for only a brief moment. Twice it flipped at lightning speed and then gave a terrific smash against the wall. Two of its legs pierced the window's glass, allowing the cold silvery snow to flow quietly in. The desk's main body impacted the cement blocks, which composed the inside of the outer wall, pulverizing the one that received the most direct blow and cracking three others into pieces. To see the potency of his work provided Jeremiah with a satisfying blast of vengeful catharsis. He gave a wide unreserved smile. "You have nothing now. Where is your nothing now?"

The frightful vision of Jeremiah's monstrous might affected Ming such that he pushed off backward from the coat rack in an unconscious act of self-preservation. He lost his balance and fell backward. Ming landed first on his rear end and then rolled clumsily until his back hit the wall. The audible impact drew Jeremiah's attention immediately. Lewis turned quickly toward his fallen friend in order to verify his well-being and then spun his head back around to monitor Jeremiah.

"Is there something there for me?" Jeremiah questioned to himself in a low guttural tone. "Yes, there is. It will make me feel better!"

Certainly, Jeremiah's approach was enough to terrify the two friends. But then their young eyes beheld such a ghastly sight as to cast them both irretrievably into paralyzing horror. As Jeremiah walked intently toward the coat area, still unaware of the bump's origin, his face came into full view. Jeremiah's eyes and surrounding portions of his head had grown three times their original size! Additionally, they bulged out from their sockets like a nearly flat balloon, squeezed in a child's hand. It appeared horribly painful, and the skin that surrounded his eyes was hot red, much like his hands, with folds of skins wrapped around each tortured eye.

Lewis's belly heaved and tightened in reaction to the fear. Jeremiah was drawing closer, following the sound of Ming's fall. For his part, Ming was struggling to regain his feet and take in the current predicament. He did so and reached his full standing height just in time to hear Lewis's warning. "Look out, Ming!"

Ming had no need to turn to Lewis for an explanation. It was clear. To Ming's near-immediate left, Jeremiah Strickland loomed large, his arms and swollen titanic hands arched with malicious intent.

"Ming," began Jeremiah with a ravenous expression on his face. "Yes, you have the something I need to feel better. I will find something and feel better!"

Ming turned toward Lewis to make his escape, but it was too late. As he pulled away, Jeremiah's left arm shot out like a spear, and his bulging hand grasped Ming's shoulder with vicelike tension. Not only was Ming unable to break the hold, but the pressure sent a sharp invasive pain down his shoulder and into his side. Ming made his most herculean effort to bat down Jeremiah's arm with his own. Nevertheless, there was no escape. Jeremiah's power was too great.

Jeremiah brought his other gargantuan hand to bear on Ming and turned his body like a rag doll until the two were facing one another. "You have something. It will make me feel better!" Jeremiah positioned both hands around Ming's, and he was able to offer no resistance. At this point Lewis stepped up and dug his own hands between Ming's neck and Jeremiah's lethal grip. It took every ounce of Lewis's strength to achieve any sort of effective grip on Jeremiah's hands. Once he had it, Lewis stiffened his legs and leaned backward, attempting to add his own body weight against the strength of Jeremiah's.

"Let him go, Jeremiah!" demanded Lewis. "He can't breathe!"

"He-he, maybe you have what I need. It will make me feel better," said Jeremiah with a calm, unaffected manner. "Just wait, I will get to you."

Just then, a soft lilting voice invaded the collective consciousness of the three.

> Jeremiah?
> Jeremiah?
> Have you found what will make you feel better?
> Good and right, down to the letter,
> Warm and beautiful, filling your soul,
> Have you found the soft, fertile soil to fill the hole?

There at the head of the classroom, in front of the middle of the whiteboard, pure and gentle, in stark contrast to the stormy chaos of books, pens and pencils, papers and other items strewn about the classroom, stood Agnes Reiniger, upright and seemingly impervious to the danger and calamity around her. She continued.

Jeremiah?
Jeremiah?
How your hands have grown!
Do they close abide when you're alone?
Large and mighty they search and grab,
For all the things you'll never have.

At this, Jeremiah began to slowly loosen his maleficent clasp around Ming's neck. For the first time in nearly a minute, Ming was able to once again draw air into his lungs. Lewis could sense the relaxation in Jeremiah's grip as his fingers slid more deeply into the crevice between Ming's neck and Jeremiah's bulky hands. Still holding Ming, Jeremiah fixed his attention upon the soothing siren at the head of the class.

Jeremiah?
Jeremiah?
Now! Without delay, the arrival of your plight,
Your hideous eyes with all their bulging sight,
Cannot prevent or even long forestall,
The advent of your doom, the coming of your fall!

So dulcet her melody and supple her tone that Jeremiah was transfixed. Despite the admonishing nature of the lyrics, Agnes's singing produced a savory tear in Jeremiah's eye. However, now there was no longer any pretending. Jeremiah had no illusions as to the purpose of Agnes's song. There was no sympathy there, and he would offer none in return. He fully emancipated Ming from his terrific hands and turned his own body fully in Agnes's direction. Ming dropped to the floor like a sack of potatoes.

Jeremiah's face turned as angry red as his hands. His overstretched lids strained to pull down over his bloated eyes to remove the tear, like windshield wipers casting off an intermittent sprinkle. Still their normal size, Jeremiah's eyebrows pulled together and pinched down in between his eyes, and his nostrils flared. Were it not for Jeremiah's harrowing intent, his appearance would have been quite comical. Nevertheless, there was nothing comical in neither his manic mood nor his enraged commitment to undo Agnes.

Jeremiah began a rampaging run toward Agnes. As he had with Ming, Jeremiah raised his large hands into the air and arched his arms. Agnes had stopped singing and stared directly at her assailant. Even when he initiated his charge, Agnes remained motionless and placid. She calmly crossed her petite hands and stood undaunted. Intent on his quarry, Jeremiah continued his run into the area where he had overturned all the desks and strewn their contents. So overwrought was he with fury, Jeremiah completed only two full bounds before stepping onto a pile books and other sundry items. He lost his footing and immediately fell face first to the ground.

During the intervening moment since his release, Ming had regained his breath and stood upright once again with the aid of his friend. He rubbed his tender neck, still smarting as a result of Jeremiah's great grasp. Seeing Jeremiah fallen to the ground and vulnerable, Ming took the opportunity to move against him in order to protect Agnes. Ming tore off from Lewis, ran fleetly toward Jeremiah, and then cast himself into the air in order to land heavily and squarely upon his adversary. Ever the quintessential example of more guts than brains, Ming misjudged the distance and landed on Jeremiah's legs as opposed to his back, the intended target. However, it was enough. Although Jeremiah's hands and eyes had grown, the balance of his body remained at its original size and weight. As such, though he was older and larger than Ming, Ming was able to hold onto Jeremiah and prevent him from standing up again.

"Agnes, get out of here!" charged Ming, looking up toward her as he worked to wrap his arms around Jeremiah's kicking legs.

Ming's counsel was not needed. Alexandra had made her way from the back door of the classroom where she had been observing Lewis and Ming, up to the other door when Agnes had entered in under her notice. Alexandra dashed in, grabbed her sister's arm and pulled. "Let's go!" cried Alexandra. So still had Agnes been standing that the sudden movement caused by her sister's yank made her appear as a stone statue come to life. The two left the classroom in a swift dash.

"Now, now I know that the singer has what I need, what I need to feel better!" yelled Jeremiah from the floor. He kept his eyes on Agnes and Alexandra even as they exited the room. Simultaneously, Jeremiah kicked his legs back and forth. He pulled them up and pushed them out using all strength to dislodge his unwanted burden. "Do not go far. You will not go far. You have what I need to feel better!"

Despite his most heroic efforts, Ming's desperate grasp was no match for Jeremiah's stronger limbs and impassioned intent. Gradually, Jeremiah pulled from Ming until his arms held nothing more than the ankles and feet.

"Help me, Lewis!" demanded Ming. "I'm not strong enough to hold him!" Ming curled up his body, drew up his legs, and pinched them around Jeremiah's ankles. Ming hoped that, in addition to his arms, this might be enough to restrain Jeremiah, or at least delay his departure after the girls. *What is Lewis doing?* thought Ming.

Strangely enough, Lewis didn't move over toward Jeremiah to add his weight and strength to Ming's in this struggle to detain their monstrous opponent. Instead, Lewis quickly made his way over to Mr. Brewer's desk and yanked open the large drawer on the right side. Mr. Brewer used one of the oldest desks in the building. It was bulky and heavy, fashioned in real solid wood. The drawer was burdensome and stiff, requiring more than a little effort to open.

"I need help here!" reasserted Ming in a desperate and loud voice. "What are you doing, Lewis?" Ming had no idea, but he was sure that Lewis was not helping him. He needed him.

Jeremiah continued his unrelenting struggle and had managed to liberate his right leg from Ming's grasp. Discouraged, but committed, Ming held tightly to the one remaining limb and squeezed with all four of his own.

"Soon, soon, I will feel better!" exclaimed Jeremiah. He still had his gaze fixed out into the hallway, the last place he had seen Agnes and Alexandra. Despite his brutal kicking and pulling against Ming, Jeremiah never once turned to look at his opponent. He was obsessed.

The contents of Mr. Brewer's right-side desk drawer were no surprise to Lewis. A deep and varied array of small toys filled nearly two thirds of the drawer's rectangular hallow. Mr. Brewer had a strict, relentless zero tolerance policy when it came to students carrying toys, cards, radios, or any other such items to school. If he saw it, you lost it. He consistently indicated that the item would be returned to the offending student at the end of the school day, with the stern caveat that it never happen again. However, this often didn't occur. Sometimes Mr. Brewer forgot. Sometimes the student forgot. In truth, there were also times that Mr. Brewer had a particular frustration with a student such that he would consciously retain the item, knowing full well the identity of its owner.

He had a number of such keepers in that drawer as reminders of students that gave him behavioral trouble through the years of his teaching at James Madison Elementary. A dark and immature slice of his personality relished those items and the sadness that their loss inflicted upon the students. It was his way of getting the last dig. It wasn't so hard. Many of the students who had items confiscated were too fearful of punishment from their parents to even ask for the item at the end of the school day. They simply wrote the item off as the cost of getting caught with it, figuring it was a small price to pay.

Not so with Lewis. Last Christmas, Lewis received a toy racetrack from his grandmother, Imelda. He loved it. It featured interlocking plastic track strips, which could be connected in myriad configurations to produce differing races. The set also included a set of adhesive decals that Lewis applied himself and lent the track an added air of realism. He felt proud and satisfied at how perfectly he had applied them, not allowing any portion of the sticker to sit out of place.

Thirdly, the track included a spring-mounted launch device, which one used to propel the set's most enchanting and valuable parts: two brand new, never previously released die-cast metal race cars. One was fashioned as a red Corvette, complete with a hot and bossy flame job in brilliant color across the hood. The other was an equally impressive blue racer, featuring a single seat, bright white lightning running down its sides and tiny dual exhausts out the back.

As the reader might expect, Lewis brought his beloved cars to school, and Mr. Brewer confiscated them. Lewis was angered and heartbroken and was lost in a vise grip of indecision regarding the cars. He wanted them back desperately but feared Mr. Brewer's reaction, and more importantly, the gut-wrenching shame that Imelda's reaction would produce. He wanted neither of those. So the following morning before the school day commenced, Lewis sat calmly at his desk and waited for Mr. Brewer to step out into the hall as he often did to commiserate with the other teachers regarding troublesome students or low pay or to refill his coffee mug. One particular morning Mr. Brewer did just that. He grabbed his cup and exited the classroom in pursuit of his favorite black caffeinated beverage. Lewis shot up from his desk, dashed to the classroom door to verify that Mr. Brewer had indeed left the area, and well, you can guess the rest.

Back on the classroom floor, Ming remained undaunted. Jeremiah bent his one free leg so that its foot rested flatly on the tile. He used this foot to add strength to his struggle against the stubborn and increasingly annoying Ming, clamped to his other leg. Ming was curled up in a ball so that at the end of Jeremiah's leg, he appeared as a spherical lollypop, swung to and fro as in a child's carefree hand. He would not let go. His eyes remained in closed darkness as he focused all his attention and strength on halting, or at least slowing, Jeremiah's nefarious pursuit of Agnes and Alexandra.

Jeremiah's free leg allowed him to draw closer to the classroom door. However, this rate of progress was too slow for the transformed miscreant. Sick and tired of his unwanted, newly attached parasite, Jeremiah turned his swelling eyes away from the door and shot a hateful gaze toward Ming. Ming, having his own eyes closed, was unaware of the change in Jeremiah's focus but did notice that his opponent had ceased to pull. The young hero immediately looked up at Jeremiah, retaining his herculean body grip. Ming was terrified to meet Jeremiah's daunting stare, with its knuckled pulsating eyeballs, red hot with anger, and nearly bursting from their sockets.

Before Ming could think, Jeremiah leaned forward onto his seat and swung his arms out to the sides, extending to their full range of motion like a fierce bird of prey taking to flight. In a flash, Jeremiah's hands finished their circle and came together at the sides of Ming's head—his ears more specifically—in a vicious, thunderous blow. In addition to the dull pain inflicted against Ming's skull, the wallop also created a sudden but potent vacuum inside Ming's ears. It sounded like being inside a car when someone slams the door, but a hundred times worse. Ming's tender defenseless eardrums reacted with a slightly delayed grievous agony and a shrill, high-pitched ring inside his head.

Ming reacted to the cruel smite just as Jeremiah had hoped. He pulled his gargantuan hands away from Ming's head and watched as he winced, gnashed his teeth, and cupped his palms over his ears in one rapid self-protective movement. Naturally, Ming was no longer able to maintain his hold on Jeremiah's ankle. Jeremiah yanked it away from Ming fleetly and popped to his feet, all the while wearing a vengeful smile that spread widely under his knotted eyes. Satisfied that Ming was no longer an issue, Jeremiah turned and dashed out the doorway to renew his pursuit of the girls.

Lewis stopped what he was doing for a moment to attend to his fallen friend. He stood with one hand on the desk drawer handle, and the other bracing himself up off Mr. Brewer's broad desktop. He looked at Ming writhing on the ground. He wanted to move to him immediately and tend to him, at least to make sure he was all right. However, Lewis knew where Jeremiah had gone, who he was after, and would not allow his mind to imagine what Jeremiah might do if he reached his wicked goal. As much as he cared about Ming, Lewis understood his first priority. Imelda's grandson dug deep into the pockets of his personal character and found the fortitude to hear but ignore his friend's moans and cries. He knew what he had to do first.

Pulling out the front portion of his shirt, Lewis extended it forward as far as it would reach. He then proceeded to fill the shirt with as many confiscated toys as could fit. First, he grabbed Stewart Morris's stack of superhero trading cards, then Meredith Reed's booklet of reusable stickers and her sparkled Chap Stick with its violently obnoxious perfumed smell, Juan Gonzales's plastic lion, Pearl Henderson's set of five marble-colored rubber balls, and so on. Lewis topped off his overloaded shirt, pulled its lip back toward his chest to secure the pilfered items, and stuffed an additional two toys into his right-hand pocket.

Jeremiah's newly found vigor and enthusiasm, which accompanied his emancipation from Ming were dampened when he found the school hallway empty. He had hoped to at least *see* Alexandra and Agnes running down at the end of the hall, perhaps entering a classroom, or turning a corner, anything that would help him to continue giving chase. Nothing. He turned around in a tight swivel and moved to the staircase that adjoined the two lengths of the school wing. Hanging his head over as far as he was able, he scanned and searched, looking for some clue as to their whereabouts. As he hung, the gravity and energetic movement of his head caused a solitary moisturizing tear to dangle and then drop from Jeremiah's left eye. It fell silently and altogether unnoticed until impacting on the tile floor below with a final circular splash.

"I will find them. Then I will feel better, then I will feel better. I must feel better," muttered Jeremiah in a frustrated, lonely tone as he opened the doors to the classrooms nearby. He gave each classroom nothing more than a cursory search, ducking in his head and popping it out again. He surveyed the bathrooms in the same fashion. This was all his obsessive impatience would allow. Nothing. He then returned to the center of the hallway where he had begun.

"Where, where, where are they?" questioned Jeremiah out loud into the empty hallway. His greed-soaked mind was ablaze with disconcerting consternation over his inability to locate his prey. His search left only one remaining unopened door. The two bathrooms on this floor were positioned on both sides of a drinking fountain like bookends. To the fountain's immediate right was the janitor's closet. Its door was tall and broad, made of dark-brown wood and complete with a charcoal-black cast iron handle from the school's original construction.

When executing his search for the girls, Jeremiah had initially disregarded it, assuming it would be locked, as usual, and impossible for Alexandra and Agnes to choose as a temporary, if ultimately fruitless, refuge. Now Jeremiah reconsidered it, wanting to give it due attention before leaving the area to begin a broader search.

He knelt down slightly and offered his bulbous left eye to peer through the cold metallic keyhole. The augmented strength of his changed eye returned nothing but darkness. "Is it empty? Are they in there? Will I find them and feel better?" mused Jeremiah in a hushed volume. Unsure, Jeremiah returned to his full upright stance and extended his right hand toward the door's nearly spherical round knob. As with the classroom doors he had just searched, Jeremiah's monstrously mutated hands were unable to grasp the knob normally. Jeremiah gently, slowly wrapped his enlarged thumb and forefinger around the cool black metal, making considerable effort to avoid making noise. At an even cautious pace, he turned the knob to the right, trying to ignore the rusted clicks and drags that the old metal produced.

Having reached the end of the knob's rotation, Jeremiah pulled lightly in the voracious hope that the door would open. It didn't.

"Where are they?" he cried. "I will feel better. I will find them! *I will feel better!*"

As he raised his voice and strangled it to a high pitch, Jeremiah took a step back from the closet door and raised his monstrous hands into the air. Like catapult, they snapped forward; his tightly balled fists pounded against the wooden closet door with a terrific unified crash. The door shook from top to bottom and produced various creaks and rattles from its hinges and mounts.

"Aaaieeah!" wailed a high-pitched voice from inside the closet. Then silence.

"Are you in there?" questioned Jeremiah. "Yes, you are. I will get you. Then I will feel better. *I will feel better!*" He continued with his fists in the same manner. Pounding his enormous fists against the door's wood and iron. Wallop after wallop, he brought his full strength and fury against the door's well-built stability. He was obsessively committed to breaching the door and accessing his prey. To any other teenager, even a fully grown man, this was folly, a fool's errand. However, Jeremiah had undergone a transformation. He was now endowed, or perhaps cursed, with hulking hands and strength to match their size. And, for whatever reason, he was certain that Agnes held the key to his "feeling better."

Inside the closet, Agnes and Alexandra did their best to maintain their sanity against the whirlwind of aggression and chaos, which ensued just beyond the door. They sat on the tiled floor of the closet in near-total darkness, a sable cloak pierced only slightly by the scant hallway light coming in under the door. So furious and impactful were Jeremiah's blows against the door that the sliver of light shining through its bottom shook with each terrific crash. Alexandra held her sister tightly, trying to convey some form of peace and calm to a sister she assumed would be overwrought with fear.

"Leave us alone, Jeremiah!" demanded Alexandra in a fear-wearied cry. "Go away!"

Jeremiah ignored her miserable plea and continued to torture the door with whacks and smashes, rattling the door on its hinges, and showing no signs of fatigue. Despite Alexandra's shrieks, Agnes remained characteristically calm. She sat in Alexandra's amazingly strong warm embrace and stared immovably at the door. She appeared completely unaffected by the impending doom, which loomed no more than three feet away.

It took only a few torrential blows before what Jeremiah hoped and Alexandra feared happened. With a particularly mighty wallop, Jeremiah's fists produced a long divergent crack in the door's wood, which ran from just above his head to just above his waist. It looked like a river on a map, wild and unpredictable, and sounded like an old dead tree branch, cracking beneath a hiker's boot.

"Stop!" yelled Alexandra. "*Go away!*"

Jeremiah didn't give Alexandra's wishes a second thought. In fact, the fissure now present on the door's face only served to fuel his tempestuous rage against it. He gave a wild smile and continued, whapping the door with renewed strength and commitment. The blow that followed weakened the door and widened the crack, such that light seeped in, sending a fledgling beam of pale glow across the inside of the closet just above the girls' heads. The light ran from the door all the way to the back wall of the closet and revealed small particles of dust that floated through the beam, visiting its illumination for a brief instant, and then returning to the darkness.

Alexandra had no illusions. She understood that Jeremiah could, and would, certainly breach the door. It was only a matter of time. Alexandra was prepared to do whatever she could to protect her sister. At the same time, she realized she could offer no real resistance to any creature able to pound through a solid wood door. She tightened her protective grasp on Agnes and watched the light grow larger and larger.

"Hah, I have found them!" exclaimed Jeremiah like a prospector having just discovered gold. "They are here! *I will feel better!*" Then, just as he was about to deliver another smash to the distressed and splintered door—perhaps the blow that would breach it utterly and leave the girls defenseless—Jeremiah felt something from behind hit his right shoulder. It produced no real pain but was enough to take his attention from the door. He gave a sharp, rapid turn to the rear.

"Maybe this will make you feel better," suggested Lewis in a mocking tone. Imelda Warner's grandson stood at the doorway between Mr. Brewer's classroom and hallway. His attention was unalterably fixed on Jeremiah. His hands were occupied with the toys he had garnered from Mr. Brewer's desk, the left suspended his shirt that cradled the toys like a forager, gathering woodland berries, the right held one of the items high in the air, cocked and ready like a stone.

The reader may assume that Lewis intended to merely pepper Jeremiah with toys in the hope that such treatment would either subdue him altogether, or at least to drive him off. However, Lewis had something else in mind, something deeper, simpler. Although he couldn't identify it as such, Lewis had a special gift for understanding people, a natural insight into their reasons and motivations. Consider the way that one student may understand mathematics more easily than another, and that student finds science or English grammar quite simple. They seem to grasp it with little effort and have success more quickly than others. Lewis has such a natural ability with regards to people.

Instead of tossing another toy at Jeremiah directly, Lewis simply skipped one across the floor next to him. As Lewis expected, it drew Jeremiah's immediate attention, and the large-handed lummox drew himself away from the splintered door and bent over to retrieve it. Jeremiah drew the toy up to his planetoid eyes and studied it fastidiously, almost as if he had never seen one before. Satisfied that he had found something of great worth, Jeremiah swallowed the toy in the palm of his huge hand and looked up ominously at Lewis. Lewis knew what to do.

"You like those, don't you Jeremiah?" queried Lewis, staring directly at Jeremiah. "These will make you feel better. You need more."

Interested, but not entirely convinced, Jeremiah stepped slowly toward Lewis, twice turning his gaze back to the closet as he did so. Lewis shoved his right hand into his makeshift bag of toys and randomly drew one out. Not pausing at all to identify it, he pitched the toy in Jeremiah's general direction, but this time beyond his immediate reach, hoping to direct him away from Alexandra and Agnes. It worked. Fascinated by the prospect of another toy, Jeremiah made the necessary movement in order to retrieve it. Like the first, Jeremiah stored it in the recess of his giant palm.

"Yes," coaxed Lewis in a warm inviting tone. "These will make you feel better."

Convinced of the ingenuity of his plan, Lewis threw two more for Jeremiah in the same fashion and with the same result. He then decided to take a further step and hurled the next toy not merely outside of Jeremiah's reach, but down the hallway. It was Juan Gonzales's plastic lion. Lewis heaved it at a slight arc, and upon landing, its plastic form slid across the smooth cool tiled floor until reaching a full stop nearly at the middle of the far hallway.

As he had with regards to the other toys, Jeremiah took an immediate interest. His head snapped with ravenous interest down the hallway, and then his body following in one enthusiastic leap. However, after a few quick steps down the hallway, he slowed and then came to an immediate stop. When Jeremiah started down the hallway, Lewis's face produced a pleased and relieved expression. Now it registered disappointment and even fear.

There was good reason. Jeremiah arched over a bit as he turned back in Lewis's direction. His malicious piercing eyes seemed trained upon Lewis even before his head made the complete turn. "I want more toys! I will have them *all*! And then I will be happy!" hissed Jeremiah.

Lewis's own eyes widened to their maximum capacity, and he froze in place. Jeremiah looked like a descending eagle, swooping down as he lifted his arms and massive hands up to shoulder level. Naturally, the toys that he had collected and stored in the abscess of his palm dropped to the floor. Jeremiah paid them no mind. His attention was fixed upon Lewis and the generous garner of toys in his shirt. Jeremiah was like a beggar, dropping two nickels upon discovering a one-hundred-dollar bill.

Lewis was terrified. He stood motionless with both hands at his shirt, one suspending the garment by its lip, and the other cradling the weight of toys. Jeremiah approached him step by ominous step, moving much more slowly than he was capable, almost enjoying the tortured look upon his face.

"They are almost mine!" babbled Jeremiah. "I will have them soon. Then I will be happy. I will feel better!" Jeremiah's oversized fingers dangled down from his hands and arms, arched just slightly higher than his shoulders. The fingers twitched and flipped with anticipation like those of a gothic organ player just above the keys, waiting to play. Jeremiah's bloated eyes seemed to sweat with avarice, appearing almost as highway headlights, and mesmerizing the young Lewis in a terrific trance.

Purely on instinct, Lewis ducked to his left just before Jeremiah was able to wrap his enormous talon-like hands upon him. Jeremiah's arms swooped down where Lewis had stood with breathless speed in the passionate expectation of grasping their prey. Lewis stumbled to the end of the floor where it joined the staircase. The stairs led down to a small landing, turned one-hundred-and-eighty degrees, and then continued down to the first floor. The turn in the staircase created a diminutive aperture through which one could see the first floor below, the same opening through which Jeremiah's eye had dripped a tear only a bit earlier.

With his back against the wall, Lewis jabbed his right hand into the cradle of toys and proceeded to toss them over the side of the staircase, sending a spray of assorted items down to the first floor like a frantic farmer trying to seed the waiting soil late in the growing season.

"No!" shrieked Jeremiah as he watched the toys drop to the tile floor below. Hysterical agitation gripped his mind, like a pirate watching treasure poured over the side of a ship into the abysmal sea. No longer were Jeremiah's arms arched over. He stood up straight in one drastic heave, like a cobra about to strike. His bulbous white eyes seemed to pulsate and shake back and forth in a mindless rage. "Do not throw down what I need to feel better!" he begged in a miserably hurt tone. "I will have the toys! Then I will feel better!"

Lewis tossed another handful of toys over the side, keeping his fearful attention on Jeremiah rather than the descending plastic items. Action figures, metallic cars, stickers, and the like all flew with a slight arch, bounced off the walls and stairs and landed on the cool unmerciful tile below. Lewis had pitched three volleys, yet still had more in his makeshift bag than he had thrown over.

Jeremiah seemed to have a sense of this fact, and after snapping his head toward the flocks of flying toys, making their helpless way to the first floor, fixated himself wholly upon Imelda Warner's grandson. Jeremiah's expression was a vicious amalgam of hate, frustration, and fear. He stared at Lewis with the most condemning air, enraged that this enemy had "taken" what would make him happy, vexed that he would not willingly surrender the quarry, and terrified to see the toys fly down to the floor below like the last precious sands of his life flowing through an hourglass.

Lewis knew what was coming. He considered throwing another stream of toys downward but realized that Jeremiah was beyond that now. Horror gripped his paralyzed mind, but it was a new breed of fear, one that he had never previously experienced. He feared when bullies troubled him in the bathroom or the park. He knew dread and apprehension when Imelda or one of his teachers caught him in some mischievous act. Those were controlled, though. There were limits. A bully might leave him with disheveled clothes, a bruise, or even wet pants. Imelda or a teacher might leave him with fewer privileges or a nagging sense of shame. Jeremiah knew no such boundaries, and Lewis understood this fully. The truth of his predicament soaked into his young mind and soul like a long heavy rain saturates the earth. It was deep, cold, and undeniable.

Lewis looked down at the stairs to his immediate right and seriously considered running or even falling down them in order to fashion his escape. However, he was off balance, and his hands, occupied with the toys, were unable to assist. The delay of consideration was too long and provided Jeremiah time to gain purchase on Lewis's relatively small form.

"No more toys down the stairs, Lewis!" exhorted Jeremiah. "They are mine. They will make me feel better!" Jeremiah trapped Lewis in a nauseatingly intimate embrace. His bloated mighty hands pinched Lewis's shoulders like a vice on tender newly chopped wood. Jeremiah trained his globule eyes so close to Lewis's face that their sweaty warmth poured over his terrified cheeks, nose, and forehead. Jeremiah's intense, putrid body odor invaded Lewis's nostrils like a foreign army. Widened with fear, Lewis's own eyes witnessed the blood vessels that ran through the pristine white of Jeremiah's eyes like erratic crimson rivulets, cutting through a fresh blanch snow.

"T...t...take them!" blabbered Lewis, overcome with fright. He released his slight paltry hold on the shirt and allowed the remaining collection of plastic gems to fall feebly to the floor. Lewis's most sincere desperate wish was that this action would offer Jeremiah satisfaction, and thereby, his own eventual release and renewed safety. It did not have the desired effect. Jeremiah dropped his eyes down to the floor almost in unison with the falling toys and watched them scatter. He then returned his gaze to Lewis. The impatient anxiety had left Jeremiah's face, but now it was replaced with increased resentment.

In its warped obsessive state, Jeremiah's mind assumed that Lewis had dropped the toys with the intention of mocking him with a final inconvenience, as if to say, "Okay, have your stupid toys, but you're going to have to pick them off the floor." As the reader might expect, this was not Lewis's purpose at all. He merely wished to surrender the toys as quickly as he could. Jeremiah's victorious smile twisted into a vengeful sneer. He increased the already considerable pressure on Lewis's arms and shoulders. Lewis closed his eyes and winced.

"Stop, stop!" Lewis begged. "Let me go!"

Jeremiah's face seemed to light up at Lewis's expression of agony. The pressure on Lewis's limbs was such that they began to turn numb. He lost control of and then even the sensation in his lower arms and hands.

"Yes, yes," wheezed Jeremiah gleefully as if his mind had just answered the world's most profound question. "Yes, Lewis, I will let you go. Then I will feel better. I will feel better."

In an instant, in a flash, like a beam of heroic light, Lewis saw salvation turn the corner from Mr. Brewer's classroom. Ming dashed toward Jeremiah at an incredible rate, like the fleetest of leopards driven to its prey with voracious hunger. Ming charged at Jeremiah, curling his arms and shoulders, his entire body into a rocketing battering ram, unleashed and unyielding.

By this point, Jeremiah had carried Lewis like a rag doll away from the wall and over the hole in the curved staircase that dropped to the first floor below. Jeremiah saw Ming coming and, seized by the new threat, released Lewis carelessly to the ground. Unaffected by this partial victory, Ming completed his charge and plowed into Jeremiah like a freight train, like a rookie football player hungry for the tackle. He struck Jeremiah hard and solid, delivering an effectual blow, which carried all his weight, strength, frustration at himself for failing to protect the girls, and anger at seeing his friend in danger.

Totally unprepared and off balance, Jeremiah impacted against the partial wall of the staircase under the force of Ming's charge. With his arms still in the air, Jeremiah hit the partial wall at his waist and flipped over it, falling headlong. His adolescent body slid gracelessly between the narrow aperture running down between the flights of stairs. In terror, he groped fruitlessly at the smooth painted walls that led to the floor. His arms flailed in a gloomy rhythm with his pulsing eyes as he closed the last few feet to the floor. In an instant, it was done.

So enthusiastic and irresistible was Ming's charge, it took the partial wall and some effort of his own to avoid falling right behind Jeremiah. He caught himself at the wall and leaned over it slightly until all the momentum was gone. In the process, Ming got a full view of Jeremiah's end. Lewis had fallen in relative safety down only the first flight of stairs and stopped unharmed on the landing. Overwhelmed with curiosity, Lewis shot up to his feet and moved fleetly to the staircase to share Ming's view.

Jeremiah Strickland lay flat and motionless on the first floor tile. His condition was unclear. Ming and Lewis looked up at one another more than once in stunned silence. Both of them swung back and forth between two ideas in their respective minds. On one hand, their tender innocence hoped and begged that he was simply unconscious. On the other, their collective fear and anger shared an unspoken wonder if it was more.

14

Do I Get A Letter For This?

"Are you okay, Lewis?" asked Ming, pulling back from the partial wall and trying to release the intense emotion using deep throaty breaths.

"Yeah," returned Lewis in a soft tone. "Thanks, Ming." Lewis looked at Ming with a tender, grateful expression. His eyes bore the start of some serious tears, tears in reaction to Jeremiah's mindless aggression and the expectation of real harm.

"Don't worry about it, buddy!" said Ming, trying immediately to lighten the mood.

"No, I mean it," asserted Lewis. "I don't know…I, I just didn't know what he might, what Jeremiah might…" Lewis knew. He knew exactly what he wanted to say, but it was too much. Saying it would have made it too real.

Lewis and Ming continued to look at one another for what seemed to both of them like an eternity. They didn't want to speak anymore but felt gratefully obliged to at least linger in the moment, the uncomfortable moment, to share their appreciation for the other. Then they gave a final appreciative smile and moved to the next order of business.

Thanks to Jeremiah, the door to the janitor's closet was a splintered shamble, beaten and divided down the center. So wide was the divide, Agnes and Alexandra could be seen, albeit unclearly, shadowed in the mixture of darkness and the light seeping in from the hallway. Ming gave the door a playful knock.

"Good afternoon, ladies," greeted Ming in a cool, detached tone, seemingly unaffected by the recent events. "May I ask what you're doing in the janitor's closet?" Ming knew exactly what they were doing in the closet. Nevertheless, he wanted to play and had heard adults ask similar questions many times before. May I ask what you are doing outside? May I ask what you are doing in your brother's bedroom? May I ask what you are doing with that ketchup bottle?

The door produced a deliberate low-pitched click as the lock mechanism released. The doorknob turned slowly and offered the expected, unoiled creek. Agnes, and then Alexandra emerged from the shadows. Agnes darted unswervingly for Lewis and gave him an unabashed embrace, burying her smooth tear-moistened cheek into his chest. It was more than gratitude, but not exactly love. Agnes was indeed grateful but more *relieved* that Lewis was all right, as if they shared a profound long-standing connection that had no past, a relationship outside of reality.

"Hey, what about me?" questioned Ming in a dejected voice. "I saved Lewis! What about that!"

Ming attended mainly to Agnes and Lewis. Yet in the corner of his right eye, he saw Alexandra approaching in slow grace like a long-awaited sunrise. Ming understood that Alexandra was walking out of the closet, but it wasn't until she stood immediately close that he realized she was walking up to him. Ming turned to face her but didn't dare look up at her. His crush forbade it. He was the loyal subject abating his gaze before the regal queen. Alexandra closed the remaining distance and stopped.

"Ming," said Alexandra in a calm harmless voice.

Ming then did look at her face-to-face as if he had returned from some perilous quest and her voice had given him leave to look upon Her Majesty.

"Thank you for saving us," offered Alexandra. Her expression was warm, calm, and shined with peace. Then she leaned forward slightly to close the distance, the difference in their height that age had created, a difference that one day he would surpass. Alexandra moved slowly until she looked at Ming just inches from his face. She placed the left side of her face gently upon the left side of his and whispered, "You are very brave, Ming Lee."

Her soft brown hair draped smoothly over his nose and blocked his vision. He didn't mind; his eyes were closed anyway. Ming breathed in the sweet smell of her shampoo and whatever perfume her parents would allow. Then

Alexandra Reiniger gave Ming Lee an unromantic, but nonetheless, affectionate kiss on the cheek. She pulled away unhurriedly and returned to a normal upright posture, her hands folded demurely in front.

Ming closed his eyes and remained in the event, even as Alexandra stepped away to greet Lewis and attend to Agnes. Ming stood in place and reflected on the stupendous treasure he had just received from Alexandra. The kiss served to push away all the troubling negativity of the day—the cold endless snow that fell outside, their inability to leave the building and get home, the vestiges of anxiety that lingered in his heart after the struggle with Jeremiah. He felt as if he stood one hundred feet tall, as if a strong, courageous wind had opened his heart and filled it with the highest, mightiest mountain on the earth.

Ming opened his eyes and turned toward Agnes and Alexandra. He realized that they were safe now, due in large part to his heroic selfless choices. He turned his mind naturally to his older brother, Hui. *Finally, I have done something that Hui hasn't done,* mused Ming. Maybe Hui was one of the top students in his school; but had he ever tackled Jeremiah Strickland with those bulging, changed eyes? Perhaps Hui was a star athlete; but had he ever saved two girls from danger? Had he ever saved his friend? These were satisfying questions, and he smiled. Maybe Hui wasn't so much better.

Ming thought of Hui's letter jacket and the metal decals that decorated it. *Could I get a letter for restraining Jeremiah?* he thought. *Could I get one for pushing Jeremiah over the side of the stairs?* A small golden football decorated the letter on Hui's jacket, indicating his success in that sport. *What sort of metal pin would represent what I did today?* he pondered.

Ming imagined himself on the stage in the gymnasium, receiving his letter jacket. The whole family would be there, except for Hui, of course. Who had the honor of laying the letter jacket across his strong proud shoulders? Alexandra, naturally. And there, pinned in the middle of the large embroidered J for James Madison Elementary School, would be a shiny gilded replica of Jeremiah Strickland's head, complete with bulbous large eyes. Ming was glowing with joy.

Earlier, Ming had wished that all of this—this adventure with Lewis and the girls—was just a dream. He wished that the snow, the gloomy creatures outside, the changes that took place with Dylan, Wyatt, and Jeremiah, all of it, was a mirage in his imaginative mind, was something from which he could just awaken. However, he knew that it wasn't, and now he was glad for it. He hoped that they could get out of the school and see their families again. That would be the highest good for the others. For Ming, however, he wanted to get home in order that his father would have to admit, finally acknowledge, what his son had done, what he had accomplished. Then his father would be ashamed, disgraced for always favoring Hui. Then the shame would pass, and his father would give Ming the fullest, closest embrace any son had ever received.

15

The Hole Starts to Fill in the Space

Ming was the only one of the four who still stood near the opening to the janitor's closet. Consequently, he saw it first. It most definitely took his attention and pulled him from his ecstatic dream over Alexandra's kiss. On the far wall, deep in the shadowed black of the closet, a rectangular purple glow appeared. It took shape in the same fashion as had those around the classroom doors; it began as a small dot at the bottom center, extended in both directions simultaneously, and finally wrapped around at the top until the two lines met at the top center. Unlike the classroom doors, this rectangle was considerably smaller.

"Hey, check this out!" spouted Ming, keeping his eyes on the glow but gesturing to the others.

Lewis and Alexandra walked over. Agnes stayed in place. The three looked intently at the hypnotic glow as if they were waiting for something to happen. "What do you think it is?" asked Alexandra. Lewis and Ming turned toward one another and shrugged their shoulders in ignorance. Drawing on his newly acquired potent infusion of courage,

Ming walked with a slow but purposeful pace into the closet and toward the glow. As he did, Lewis and Alexandra close behind, the radiant shape intensified in brightness. They took a step closer. The gleam, a step brighter. This happened three times until they quickly reached the back wall of the closet.

The closet itself was unremarkable. It contained two mops, one bucket that read caution in three different languages, and a large assortment of paper towels, toilet paper, liquid soap, and a copious array of other cleaning/ toiletry products. Additionally, there was a utility sink with a steel basin attached to the wall. Its bottom was well-used and filthy. A morbid rainbow of grays, dark blues, and gloomy greens covered its inner sides and bottom. It was a visual history of countless pours: emptied mop buckets, sopped-up vomit, and drained paint cans, just to name a few.

When the three were close enough to touch the back wall, they realized that the rectangular glow wrapped around one of the bricks located about waist high to Lewis and Ming. Almost as a matter of course, and as if no ill could possibly come of it, Lewis reached out to touch the brick.

"No, wait!" started Alexandra. "What are you doing?"

Lewis stopped and turned sharply to Alexandra. He pulled his hand back a bit. When he did, the shimmer that surrounded the brick pulsated once and then returned to its stable intensity. Lewis considered the glow, again looked up at Alexandra, but this time decided to move forward with his plan. Lewis Warner placed his fingers on the brick. It was cold and stony, covered with cracks and minor pock marks. As he expected, the glow blazed with increased power in reaction to his touch.

The slight pressure, which Lewis's fingers conveyed, was enough to move the brick slightly. This Lewis did not expect, and he jumped slightly. Ming and Alexandra drew in inaudible gasps of shock. Lewis yanked his hand back, wondering if he hand done something wrong or triggered some perilous consequence. There was none. Overcome with curiosity, Ming poked his right hand forward to touch the brick, and upon connecting with its dead rough surface, he began to move it side to side, gauging to what degree it was loose.

Ming discovered that the brick was quite loose indeed, and guessed that, given the correct maneuvering, it could be removed. He pushed it side to side, narrowing the light on one side and increasing it on the other. Despite his efforts, Ming was unable to press his rounded fingers between the brick and those neighboring it. Realizing what Ming intended to achieve, Alexandra produced her relatively slender fingers and attempted to slide them into place. To her delight, they fit. She wiggled her index, middle, and ring fingers from both hands into the separations on either side of the brick. When she believed that she had sufficient purchase, she pulled the brick, and her face gave a luminescent expression that rivaled the purple glow coming from the wall.

To their extreme disappointment, the blazing purple light ceased at the moment Alexandra cleared the brick from the wall. "What happened?" asked Ming with a sad, almost whiney, tone. "I thought there would a jewel or a glowing stone or something…something cool!"

Ming looked away in dejection, and Alexandra turned to place the brick in the sink. Lewis continued to look into the small rectangular hole where the brick had been and noticed a slight reflection of the light coming into the closet from the hallway. The reflection was understated and seemed natural, as opposed to the captivating purple glow, which had suddenly ceased.

Lewis squinted and moved closer to the hole. "There's something in there," he offered. Lewis examined the contents of the hole, weaving his head back and forth to gather as much information as he could. He noticed that the reflection moved when he did and surmised that its source must be metal or perhaps glass.

Wasting no further time or effort, Lewis jabbed his right arm into the space with stunning speed and agility. He took hold of the object, reflecting the light and pulled it into view. It was largely what Lewis expected, a small glass bottle. It was dusty, covered with a flurry of brick powder, and sealed at the top with a twist-off cap.

"Look at this!" charged Lewis, shoving it in front of Ming and Alexandra.

As Lewis moved the bottle, it became apparent that it was not entirely empty. A spare amount of auburn, brown liquid sloshed back, forth, and around as Ming tried to seize it from Lewis for a closer look. "Give it back!" mandated Lewis, not giving an ounce of quarter to Ming's actions.

"Hey, turn it over," mandated Alexandra, using a tone that suggested she would not be at all surprised at what the other side would reveal.

Lewis yanked the bottle free from Ming's rude grasp and did as Alexandra suggested. The bottle's opposite side bore a rectangular label, which featured the product name, Pale Moon Whiskey, in broad colorful letters. The remainder of the label included a serene woodland camping scene and a small pale moon in each corner. What else would the corners have?

"Whoa," put in Ming. "Somebody around here is drinkin' whiskey!"

Behind them, in the quiet shadowed space of the hallway, Agnes began to croon with a mournful tenor.

> Brick and wood cannot restrain,
> The ceaseless drip of auburn rain,
> Which longs to cover nagging voices,
> The bottled haunts of shameless choices.

"I wonder if there is anything else in there," exclaimed Ming.

Without request or even a glance in Ming's direction, Lewis handed him the bottle and reached—this time with a bit more caution—into the dark recess. Lewis retrieved one, and then two, bottles. These two bore the same label as the first but were bone-dry. "That's it," started Lewis, dusting off his right arm and arranging the two newly retrieved bottles on the ground at his knees. "That's all there is in there."

Agnes continued almost inaudibly.

> Can a heart or mind long carry,
> What you tried here once to bury?
> The lies you spun, the world to scam,
> Left you a broken, lonely man.

"Well," Lewis began. "I think we were certainly intended to find those bottles."

"What makes you say that?" asked Ming.

"Notice how the brick was surrounded by the purplish glow that shot around the sides and then stopped when we pulled it out," answered Lewis.

"Yeah, what about it?" countered Ming.

"It was the same color and glow that surrounded the classroom doors," returned Lewis. "And with each one of those, there was something we saw, or learned, or had to do."

"So what's the deal with the bottles," inquired Ming. "Who's the one that was drinking?"

"Isn't it obvious?" asked Alexandra rhetorically, cutting off Lewis who was just about to respond to Ming's question. She was increasingly intimidated with Lewis's growing acumen and desired deeply to reassert her greater intelligence and wisdom. In her mind, this was the natural order of things; she was the oldest.

"Yeah, I think so," added Lewis. "Are you thinking what I'm thinking, Alexandra?"

"Yes, who else could it be?" responded Alexandra.

Lewis and Alexandra looked at one another. Lewis first, and then Alexandra, gave a timid, shameful grin. They both knew the answer and, indulging their playful sense of cruelty, held back the answer, allowing Ming to sit in painful suspense. Ming's face snapped back and forth from Lewis to Alexandra and then back again in frantically quick motion, as if his pants were on fire, and he needed to know which of them had the water. Finally, Ming gave up on the two and glared at Agnes, hoping that she might have something to say. As they all expected, Agnes was stone silent, offering Ming nothing but a warm smile.

After another excruciating instant, Ming sounded off, "Oh, I know. Mr. Jenski was drinking. Those bottles are his."

"Yeah," started Alexandra. "Remember Mr. Cohen's office, the paper storm and the letter that fell conveniently at Lewis's feet?"

"Sure," replied Ming. "I can see the connection, but why do we need to know about Mr. Jenski's drinking, his getting fired, and the bottles he kept in his closet?"

In almost perfect unison, the three looked directly at Agnes, anticipating that she must have some idea. Agnes responded predictably with an unaffected, nearly blank expression.

"I don't know," responded Lewis, "But I can guess we'll find out."

Alexandra glared at Agnes, certain that her sister had some innate insight into all that was taking place. Equally certain that Agnes had no plans to speak, Alexandra instead studied the minute, sublime nuances of Agnes's expression. *Aggie, what's happening here?* she thought. Alexandra retreated mentally into a memory at home with Agnes, playing that game in which one person hides an object for which the other searches. The one who hides the object says over and over "you're getting colder" when you're far away from the hidden item, and "you're getting warmer" when you get closer.

16

I Can See Tomorrow in Yesterday

It didn't take long before the group's attention was snagged by the increasingly familiar purple glimmer. It emanated again from under a classroom door, one the group had yet to pass. The staircase and bathrooms were included in an area that connected the two lengths of hallway. Behind Lewis and the others was located a long hallway adjoining two classrooms, in one of which the group had encountered Jeremiah. Before them extended another long hallway, and like the one behind, adjoined two more classrooms. The room on the left included the door from which the recognizable hue came forth. All four of them knew what it meant.

"Ach!" belched Ming. "I am sick of these purple doors."

"Don't you want to see what's behind it?" asked Lewis with a slightly disappointed mood to his voice.

"No!" shot back Ming immediately. "I don't want to see what's behind it. What have they brought us? Every time we open a door, something bad happens. Why don't we just leave the doors closed and try some more to get out of the building?"

"I don't think that's really an option, Ming," put in Alexandra.

Ming wanted to snap back at Alexandra with all his fear and frustration, but he didn't. He held back. In his mind, the moisture of Alexandra's hero's kiss was still extant on his cheek. Whether it was in reality or not, the scent of her perfume remained as a sweet lingering remnant in his love-struck nostrils. He produced a more congenial response.

"What do you mean, Alexandra?" questioned Ming.

"Did you see the snow and the way that it was packed up against the windows in the last classroom?" responded Alexandra. "That was on the second floor, remember, not the first."

"Yeah," continued Lewis. "I don't think there is any getting out of the building, at least not right now. Besides, I have a feeling that snow or no snow, there is something or someone that wants us to see the things we are seeing and do the things we are doing."

"I guess," replied Ming, dropping his face a bit. "I don't disagree. I just want to go home. Don't you guys?"

"Sure," responded Alexandra with a sweet consoling air. "I think we all do. But I have to agree with Lewis, and we all have to agree with the snow." She walked up to Ming and put her hand on his shoulder and gave a smile, hoping that it would be contagious.

It was. Ming brightened slightly and took a full deep look at Alexandra. *I have to remember to fight off mutated bullies and complain more. It has great results,* he mused.

Seeing his friend in a lighter mood, Lewis brightened to a much larger degree and spoke up enthusiastically. "Awesome! Now let's go check out that classroom. Maybe there's something really great in there!"

As the four moved toward the door, no one took notice of the unreserved change that took place on Agnes's face. Upon hearing Lewis's expectant remark regarding the contents of the classroom, she turned to him in mournful silence, losing her smile and generating an expression of sad empathy.

Lewis took the lead this time and flung the door open with vigorous anticipation. The sounds coming from inside the classroom were so stark and of such a volume that the four wondered if they might have begun even before Lewis opened the door. Lilting melodies came in scintillating harmonies from birds, flying or alighted on high electrical wires. Incoherent speech could also be heard at various volumes and, at least by appearance, from differing distances.

Without doubt, the predominant noise was produced by the fleetly moving traffic. It included the unchanging hum of tires, hugging the hot, solid road, the complaining of old mufflers and other engine parts, aching from old age or lack of maintenance, and impatient whiny horns snipping between cars and their careless or enraged driving.

Inside the classroom, it was sunny and warm. The golden rays of light poured forth from the confines of the room and pierced the shadowed, unilluminated winter gloom of the hallway. The sky was a fresh dome of cool baby blue, dappled with a perfect portion of fluffy clouds that looked like pillows begging for a tired head.

The source of the traffic racket became immediately clear. A chaotic array of sedans, trucks, and motorcycles buzzed up and down the street. The four made their way cautiously into the classroom and took a position safely on the sidewalk immediately adjacent to the four lanes of traffic. Everything normally present in the classroom was gone, or at least hidden. On the other side of the traffic, the four observed another sidewalk, very much like that on which they currently stood. Both sidewalks bore an array of casual pedestrians, walking at assorted rates of speed, but all taking their time. Behind the sidewalk on the other side of the street lay a simple, green park, replete with lush towering trees, yapping dogs, cyclists, and other relaxed folk.

By all appearances, the four had entered into a beautiful summer day, busy with people passing and recreating in what could be any town or larger city of which one could conceive. Lewis and the others took in the general feeling of their surroundings in silence and relative calm until a most shocking noise disturbed every soul in sight.

The four heard a sudden earsplitting crash that sounded from their right side. Every face in the area on both sides of the street snapped in the direction of the violent clatter. A considerable number of gasps could also be heard, including one from Alexandra. Although the cars most directly involved in what sounded like an auto accident were still too far away to see clearly, Lewis and the others made every effort to discern the details of the collision as best they were able, craning their collective necks and waving their heads back and forth. The crash was followed by a high-pitched skidding of tires against the pavement and simultaneous fanatical revving of the car's engine.

"Can you see the car that did it, Lewis?" asked Ming, tiptoeing to the point of hopping in order to see over the grown-ups in front of him.

"No," returned Lewis. "It sounds like the car is coming this way though."

Every eye in the area was trained in the same direction, looking down the street in anticipation of the coming car. With each passing second, the engine's roar increased like the winds of a thunderstorm slamming against the walls of a tiny house. Amidst the rolling growl of the engine, a high-pitched screech sang out like a whining banshee, trapped forever in some celestial tornado.

Although his attention was fixed primarily upon the oncoming car, Lewis did notice the most colorful group of helium balloons take aimless flight into the air. The balloons seemed to begin their skyward ascent the instant the metallic din sounded forth from down the street. Up they went bopping into one another floating carelessly, unaffected by the drama ensuing on the street. The white stream of cords that dangled from the balloons flopped and waved as the vibrant bouquet ascended in a broken, erratic diagonal line. The tangled rope looked like a monkey's tail gliding limply as the animal leaps from branch to lofty branch.

Sooner than expected, the car came into view, almost surprising the crowd despite their vigilant stares. It was a long dirty sedan and, as one might guess from the cracking skid noises, carried a half-detached front bumper, barely hanging on from the passenger's side. The car moved at a recklessly quick pace, such that the dangling metallic bumper produced a hail of bright orange sparks. The sight reminded Alexandra of sparklers that she and Agnes enjoyed every Independence Day at Uncle Aaron's house. Sprays of starlet fire leapt from the bumper as it scraped against the unforgiving pavement. Intermittently, the bumper encountered the occasional chink or hole in the street, popping the bumper into the air for an instant, and creating a brief hiatus in the sparks.

Each of the onlookers was transfixed on the harrowing circumstances before them, but Lewis more than anyone else. It was the sound of the speeding car most of all. It pulled at his memory like a horse's reign. Images of the balloons danced in his recollections as well like rainbows in a dream or yellow spots that flash behind your eyes during the worst of headaches.

"Sweetie, no!" came a woman's voice from across the street. Most of the people in Lewis's immediate vicinity stole their attention from the oncoming car in favor of the shrill pained cry.

"Oh no!" cried Ming, stiffening his limbs as he took in the new situation.

A small boy—presumably the one who had released the balloons—had stepped away from the relative safety of the sidewalk, heedless of the impending danger in order to fetch the flying bulbs. The youngster appeared no more than two or three years old.

"Son!" shouted the boy's father. He threw off his wife's hand and plunged unreservedly into the street after his child. The man charged with such sudden and enthusiastic energy that he slipped as he left the curb. The smooth sole of his casual walking shoe met with cement sidewalk under the full weight of the man's body and failed to gain purchase. Uncontrolled forward momentum caused the man to fall to his knees with predictable and painful results. Solid grainy cement ripped into the material of his thin dress pants, and left a rosy smarting collage of abrasions.

Lewis did fear for the boy but was disturbed equally so by the toddler's familiarity. His features, gait, and skin tone, the shape of his ears seemed like they belonged to a best friend that somehow he had never met. The memory was strong and relentless, yet it continued to slip from the exactitude of his perfect recollection like a greased pig, evading a butcher's grasp.

Despite the increasingly loud, and now nearly deafening, sound of the oncoming car's engine, the toddler attended dutifully to the balloons, at this point almost halfway across the street and certainly beyond his reach. He bopped step by diminutive step further into the street, his arms flailing desperately in the air in a vain effort to reach the florid grouping of helium jewels.

His father ignored the sharp sting in his knee and rose to his solid feet and strong long legs. He burst forward again with, much like his son, his arms fully extended outward. The boy was unaware of his loving father's salvific efforts and was instead consumed in the pitiful realization that his balloons were beyond hope, beyond all his love and affection. He dropped his short precious arms to his sides, spun in a clumsy circle and produced the most woeful wail of his short life. "Naaaaahhhhh!" he howled.

To see the man and woman, the father and mother, started in Lewis an indiscernible emotional memory. It was like looking for your slippers in a dark room in which you have lived your whole life. You recognize everything you touch, and it all seems to be in the right place; yet you can't seem to get a clear, full image.

"The car, the car!" the mother shrieked in desperate horror. "Sweetie, come back!"

Completing two long deep steps, the father was nearly to his son. Unfortunately, so was the car. It closed with diabolical speed and, by all appearances, had no intention of stopping. Its engine roared in deep angry howls like a starving lion in midleap for its prey. Shimmering lines of citrus-orange sparks flashed across the sun-heated street. The little boy could almost feel the engine's hotness, pouring forth from the car's grill like a runner's steamy breath.

"Get him! Get him!" his mother yelled.

I know him. I know that boy, thought Lewis.

The little boy's heaving lungs dragged in a sampling of his salted tears, and the bitter taste ran in tiny rivulets around the surfaces of his tongue. Finally, he understood the real trouble, the true reason to cry. His father's lidless eyes and his mother's insane shrieks evidenced the reason for fear. It was also obvious from the motionless attention offered sympathetically by the onlookers from the safety of the sidewalk. His head snapped to the right as the car was merely yards away. With the dangling spark-covered bumper, the car's façade looked like the cavernous mouth of some ravenous monster, clamping open and shut, open and shut.

Finally, the memory came clearly to Lewis like the frigid sobering air of a kitchen freezer opened on a summer's day. "That's me!" he shouted.

Then there was no time to speak. There was no air to breathe. All became tense and empty. The car was nearly upon the father and his boy; and the few remaining yards were closed like the final falling sands in an hourglass. What other choice was there? The boy felt his father's vicelike hands grip his small body under the arms. His tiny feet left the ground, and he felt cool air waft across his face as his father swung him around.

In one mighty, deft motion, the father tossed his son into the air toward his mother on the sidewalk, out of the street, away from certain death. Perhaps the father would have had ample opportunity to take the boy, turn, and reach the sidewalk in time to avoid the car, but he hadn't been sure he could accomplish all that. So he chose the only option that would ensure his son's certain safety.

While the boy was still flying in midair, the car gave its first indication of awareness, but it was long after too late. The driver of the car slammed the butt of his palm down on the middle of the steering wheel, and the car's horn produced an ear-splitting wail. The brakes clamped down on the spinning wheels like the toothless jaws of a hungry bear. It helped to reduce the car's velocity, but not nearly enough.

Every eye was bare and every lung breathless as the car struck the boy's father. The father didn't look at the car as it reached the point of impact. Not because he was afraid, but rather because he had his full attention focused on his son. The screeching of the wheels began before the impact and continued even afterward. The horn ceased and left a deadly hollow. So powerful was the collision that it sent the father flying a good twenty feet in the air before landing, rolling, and then reaching a complete stop. He lay motionless and face up.

Despite having all of the father's passionate, protective strength, the heave was not enough to carry the boy all the way to the safety of his mother's arms. He landed a few feet in front of her, about where the street meets the lip of the sidewalk. The stiff rough cement was unforgiving, and the boy landed on it with all his weight. Fortunately, most of the impact was borne by his knees, hands, and left shoulder. But the shock and pain was more than enough to send him into deep howls and flowing tears. His mother closed the distance in an imperceptible flash, scooping her beloved son into the warmth of her arms, and raising him from the rough ground.

After the car made contact with the father, it continued to slow, curving slightly to the left. The car weaved back and forth, suggesting that the driver was working to gain control of the vehicle and straighten its direction. When the car's direction was more or less even, its engine revved sharply and loudly, seeking to regain the speed lost before the accident. It achieved one gear, then another, and pulled down the street.

"No!" yelled the man's wife, holding her injured son close to her. She pulled his head to her shoulder and ran as quickly as she was able off the curb and down the street toward her fallen husband.

"Daddy?" voiced Lewis, staring directly at the unmoving man. He set out from his own side of the street, stepping off the curb and walking toward the man directly, but still with some hesitation. As Lewis drew closer to the man, the mystery faded away in layers; the injured man's identity became increasingly clear and sure. With each successive step, he was more certain that this was his own father, struck down, and apparently unconscious.

He took another step, and a warm electric sensation coursed from the bottom of his back to the top of his head. It felt like certainty, like some archeologist discovering an ancient artifact and gently brushing off the final specks of dirt. It was like the dawn, revealing the truth of all things with its revealing illumination. But to see his father this way made it more like the dusky dawn of night. There was no soft warm sunshine climbing over the dew-covered hill with morning promise. This was the apocalypse of gloom, the news of the end.

The woman reached her husband, bearing her son in a nearly immovable embrace. She fell carelessly with her knees on the hard street next the man and began checking immediately for signs of life.

"Talk to me, baby!" she started, holding her son in her right arm, and reaching out to her husband with the other. "Are you okay?"

Lewis moved to within five feet of the family. He took in the reality that this was his father lying on the ground. He owned it. His mother was tending to her husband, overwhelmed with shock and grief. Her tears fell from her soft face, hit the man's clothes beneath, and soaked away into nonexistence. After shaking her husband a bit more with one hand, the mother released her son and stood him up on his own tiny two feet on the street immediately next to her.

The boy's position was such that Lewis was finally able to secure an unobstructed view of him. He knew immediately that he was gazing at himself, the features, skin tone, and posture made the reality unmistakably clear, undeniable. For Lewis, it was like rummaging through a box of memorabilia lost in your attic or closet. You unearth an old drawing you did in school, finger paintings from kindergarten, Christmas cards you wrote to your parents when you were a child. To see himself at this younger age was like discovering a little brother he had never had.

"I got Lewis, sweetie," started the woman, speaking between sobs. "You saved him. Look, sugar. He's right here. Lewis is here." She leaned back and pulled the little boy up close.

"Yes, Daddy," began Lewis. "I'm here."

This wasn't the little Lewis who lost the balloons speaking. This was the Lewis of our story. His throat tightened as he spoke the words. This was the first time within his recollection that he had said this to his father. Doing so felt familiar and real, like discovering your favorite color or pulling on shoes that fit perfectly. It suited him and felt comfortable, and yet it shattered his heart.

Lewis's utterance triggered a change in the surroundings. One by one, portions of the mirage that filled the classroom began to disappear. First it was a group of bystanders on Lewis's side of the street. Then the park behind the street from which the family of three had come was gone. The street lamps faded away, one by one. Ming and Alexandra stared in amazement as the disappearances revealed the interior of the classroom in its original form. For her part, Agnes gazed undistractedly at Lewis, bearing a sympathetic expression on her sweet silent face.

Individually, and then in groups, all the people disappeared. The clear blue sunny sky overhead evaporated and left behind the classroom's white rectangular ceiling tiles. All the traffic on the street also went away, including the reckless car that struck Lewis's father. It raced away at an ever-increasing speed, still dragging (but now just barely) the metallic sparking front bumper.

"Momma?" said the eleven-year-old Lewis, now nearly close enough to touch her.

"No, sweetie," his mother sobbed, leaning over her husband and giving no indication that she was aware of Lewis. "No, sweetie, please don't go away. Don't leave me and Lewis behind."

Lewis took a final long-reaching, purposeful step toward his mother and reached out to touch her shoulder. As his fingers were about to make contact with her clothing, his mother disappeared, just like the trees, the people, and the sky. Lewis's younger self followed suit almost immediately, leaving Lewis there with his father.

"What! No!" Lewis shouted. "Come back!" Lewis stepped forward into the space just held by his mother and waved his arms around wildly as if somehow by doing so, he could pull them back from wherever they had gone.

He eventually stopped the fruitless flailing and was then gradually overcome by a broad, potent clarity, a lucidity that seemed to pierce the visceral storm of desperate grief in his head and heart. He looked down at his father on the ground and realized that it was never about his mother, never about his younger self. It was about his father and him.

Lewis had no memory of ever embracing his father, ever holding him.

When he knelt down and wrapped his arms around his father, however, it seemed like the most normal, customary experience he had ever had. Lewis's arms slid effortlessly around his father's broad strong chest until his hands reached the stony cold street beneath. He pulled in close until his body rested on the bottom end of his father's motionless rib cage. Lewis rested his young face on the center of his father's chest and listened. The material in his father's shirt muffled his hearing just slightly.

"I'm here, Daddy," Lewis whispered. "I'm here, Daddy."

For a brief sweet moment, Lewis embraced his father fully. He shut out all the trouble and mayhem that surrounded him: the cold miserable snow, the relentless shadows in the school hallways, the menace created by the three bullies, and he nuzzled his face deeply into the softness of his father's shirt. He shut out what he knew to be reality—that his father was not really here, that he was merely enjoying the indulgence of this illusion.

Lewis didn't care about reality now. Without reservation, Lewis stayed in the moment. He was with his father. How many hugs had he missed in the intervening years between his death at the hands of that driver and today? How many mistakes could he have avoided with the aid and advice his father would have given him? How many walks in the park? The void in his heart endeavored to fill itself with the goodness of this rare opportunity. Lewis held his father's body tight and dreamed.

The moment was too short. Lewis could feel the solidity of his father's form soften. He knew what was coming.

"No, Daddy," cried Lewis. "Don't go. You can't go."

Lewis pulled his head up from his father's chest and noticed immediately the small tear-soaked spot where his head had been resting. His arms were still partially wrapped around his father's body, and they remained so even as the image faded away into emptiness. Then Lewis was left there alone, down on his knees with his arms curved in an imperfect circle. As he watched his father's body fade away, Lewis felt as though the world was ending. A part of him wished he had never had this second chance. Another part longed deeply for just another moment. He scanned the outline of his father's body, its colors and size, trying desperately to etch the image indelibly into his memory.

He pulled his arms back and then reached out into the space where his father had laid, speaking almost imperceptibly, "Daddy, don't go. Come back."

17

A Blast from the Past

"Are you all right?" asked Alexandra in a soft consoling tone. She was the first to step up and address her broken-hearted friend. Her steps were slow and regular. Then she stopped, reached out toward Lewis, and placed her warm long fingers on his shoulder.

"I don't think so," answered Lewis. His answer found its source half in sadness and half in ironic bitterness. He felt cheated. Part of him wished he had never entered this room. He wondered how they might be faring now if they had found some means of leaving the school and venturing out into the cold waste of the afternoon winter. *Anything would be better than going through this*, he thought.

"I'm sorry," dropped in Ming, speaking as he made his way up to the two. "I'm sure it must have been awful to see that happen again."

"But that's just the thing," shot back Lewis, raising his face up to look Ming right in the eyes. "I haven't seen this before."

"But wasn't that you with the balloons?" asked Alexandra. "I heard you say as much while you were on the sidewalk."

"Yeah, but I don't remember seeing this," Lewis returned.

At that point, Agnes stepped to bear on the other three. As usual, his face bore a calm stoic expression, and she said nothing. However, her posture and palpable purposefulness of her gait suggested that she had something important to communicate. Agnes made her way around Ming and Alexandra until she stood squarely before Lewis, who was still on his knees. She looked deeply at Lewis and leaned in slightly with her neck and shoulders.

"What, Agnes! What is it? What do you want me to know?" asked Lewis, nearly shouting and with an unmistakably mocking air.

"Hey, cool it! She isn't saying anything to you," commanded Ming. He understood fully Lewis's frustration. Ming didn't like Agnes's silence and the way she crooned her cryptic songs, meandering about with her bland, unaffected expression. At the same time, Ming could tell that Lewis was being nasty, and he didn't care for it. What's more, it seemed so out of character for his friend. One thing he liked so much about Lewis was his even, tranquil demeanor. From it, Ming derived a degree of peace for himself, and Lewis's change took that away.

"You cool it!" snapped Lewis in return, giving Ming his full furious attention. "You didn't just see your dad run down on the street, did you? Besides, Agnes may not be saying anything to me, but she's staring at me, staring through my eyes like she lost her lunch money in my head or something."

When Lewis finished his remark, he smiled a bit. He didn't want to. His heart hurt, and the pain morphed easily into anger. It felt good to release a portion of the ire out, even if it was on someone innocent like Agnes. The smile made some of the pain go away, and fortunately, the grin was contagious. It spread from Lewis to Ming and then to Alexandra.

Agnes was unchanged. She continued glowering at Lewis in the same fashion.

"Lewis, I think that Agnes is staring because there is something she wants you to know, some conclusion that she would like you to draw from what you just saw," stated Alexandra.

At this, Agnes's face lit up. She even smiled slightly. The most noticeable change, however, was a rapid widening of her eyes as if she had just witnessed fireworks for the first time in her life.

"Is that it, Agnes?" asked Lewis.

"Lewis," started Alexandra. "I know you said that you don't remember experiencing any of what we just saw, but can you recall even the slightest little bit?"

"Well, some of it seems familiar," Lewis began, wiping the tears from his face and rising to his feet. "The balloons are familiar, and I remember the loud sounds of the cars that were going by."

"Uh-huh," said Alexandra, sounding a bit like a psychiatrist with her questions and compassionate tone of voice." The similarity was not lost on Ming.

"But that's it, really, and even the sounds are mostly feelings, like not really memories at all," returned Lewis.

"And that was your dad who got hit by the car?" asked Ming. "Man, that's really messed up."

Lewis looked at Ming with appreciation for his kindheartedness, but at the same time he thought, *Yes, I've seen it twice now, Ming. Thank you!*

"What about the driver of the car that hit your dad?" solicited Alexandra.

"What about him?" replied Lewis.

"Well, did they ever catch the driver?" asked Alexandra. "How do you know it was a man? Maybe it was a wo—" As Alexandra spoke the last word of her comment, an audible bump came from behind the teacher's desk.

"What was that?" asked Ming, using a slightly higher-tense tone.

Instantly Lewis, Ming, and Alexandra turned their full collective attention to Mrs. Connie Lathrop's desk. The large shiny rectangular placard on the desk's top bore that out. Like every other teacher's desk, Mrs. Lathrop's was immense and thick, fashioned from unprocessed wood and complete with a matching chair. Such a piece of classroom furniture could easily hide something or someone.

Alexandra turned to Lewis and Ming and brought her left index finger up to her mouth to indicate the necessity to remain quiet. Ming responded sarcastically by contorting his face into a ridiculous expression and turning his palms outward as if to say, "Uh, yeah." Positive change was occurring in Ming's friendship with Alexandra. At its start, his crush on her was so thick that he remained at a cold distance, fearful of saying or doing the wrong thing, something that might sour her regard for him. Now, although they had put the four in peril, their current circumstances had afforded Ming a chance to actually become friends with Alexandra. While previously, Alexandra was merely an image, a beautiful dream, now she was a real person.

All three took a step closer to the desk. Nothing happened. They took another step, one leg at a time, toe to heel, sparing no effort to remain silent. Each step brought the area between the desk and the wall behind it into fuller view. They knew that whatever lurked there was either behind or under the desk, and they would see it soon enough.

The matching chair behind the desk jiggled slightly and created a sound only audible in the pure silence, which the three maintained. All three stopped in perfect unison. Ming clenched his hands to absolute immovability. Lewis did the same, except he felt the tension in his back and shoulders. So stiff were his muscles, he felt he was carrying fifty pounds of wet cement. Alexandra pulled her fingers into fists and tensed up her elbows.

Being on the far right of the three as they approached the desk—and whatever unidentified creature lurked there—Alexandra panned slowly to the left to gain any ideas from Ming and Lewis that could be conveyed in silence, and to gauge their willingness to proceed. Lewis and Ming returned her gaze, stared at her face for an instant, and then each offered an affirmative, supportive nod to continue. Alexandra took the next step forward.

Mrs. Lathrop's chair made a rapid, violent move forward, slamming against the desk and producing a cacophonous rattle from its old oil-starved wheels. In fleet succession, a pale, nearly white hand, leapt up over from behind the desk and took hold on its top. All six eyes belonging to the three friends tuned in sharply to this newest appearance. There were four fingers, but they were soft and nearly chalk-white. Not one of them bore the slightest knuckle or fingernail, and appeared almost entirely smooth.

Nonetheless, the fingers tensed and pulled back somewhat, and with the hand, formed something like a grip around the back edge of the desk's flat hard top. Without a second's further delay, Dylan Pierce popped up from behind the desk with frightening rapidity. Without the aid of his familiar clothes, he would have been nearly unrecognizable to the three. The changes that had begun earlier had now come to full fruition. Dylan's head was now an almost perfect oval as if someone had replaced his natural head with an inverted egg. The pale hue, which his skin had taken, and which the four had seen during Dylan's deadly encounter with Wyatt, was now a powdery white, soft and pristine, covering his entire cranium without the slightest blemish. Not a single strand of hair remained in his scalp.

"Now just stay back!" hissed Dylan.

"Take it easy, Dylan," started Ming, "We don't want any trouble."

Dylan's face was nearly without feature. Not the smallest patch of eyebrow sprouted from above his eyes. In fact, even the pores that had previously held the strands of his eyebrows were gone. It appeared as if he had never had eyebrows; the skin above his eyes being as smooth and unblemished as the remainder of his blanched face. What's more, his nose was reduced to merely two small holes (presumably through which he breathed). Yet there was no protruding bone from his skull nor any cartilage to form a nose. It wasn't simply flattened. It looked more as if it had been ground down to nothing.

"Stay away!" howled Dylan with a noticeable terrified edge running through his voice.

"Just relax, Dylan," began Lewis in the best calming tone he could muster. "No one wants to hurt you."

This was a genuine inversion of previous bully-victim relationship. Never in a million years would Lewis have dreamed of trying to relieve Dylan Pierce of fear, certainly not fear of him or Ming. Yet things had changed. It was clear that Dylan was terrified. He appeared rattled, fidgeting with his hands all over Mrs. Lathrop's desk chair, snapping his attention to the left and then to the right as if he were expecting some terrific encounter or unwanted visitor. Whether he realized it or not, Dylan's head bore a thin rivulet of sweat, which took its start on his blanched bald scalp and trickled cautiously down his left temple.

"No, no! Don't lie to me," spat Dylan. "You're with him. You're going to take me to *him*!"

"Dylan, we don't know what you're talking about," said Alexandra. "Who's him?"

"Him, you're going to take me to him. Wyatt, *Wyatt*!" shouted Dylan. As he did, Dylan squinted and pulled his head and neck back into his shoulders as if he were trying to protect himself. He pursed his red slender lips slightly and appeared to be at the verge of crying in an effort to release the nervous fear.

"Really, Dylan, it's true. We don't know where Wyatt is," said Alexandra. "And we're not at all interested in running into him."

"Yeah, and what happened to your—?" started Lewis.

Before Lewis was able to complete his question, Dylan's already kinetic state boiled over into a full frenzy. He clamped both white hands down on to the back of Mrs. Lathrop's desk chair and slammed it into her desk. As the wooden seat smashed into the desk, Dylan raised both hands into the air in front of him and covered his face.

"No. *No!*" wailed Dylan. "You will not take me to him, not to *him!*"

The three were stiff with confusion and expectation. Dylan delayed no further. He ran out from behind the desk and headed toward Alexandra. It made sense, given that she was closest to Dylan and was the only thing blocking his escape (although in reality, Alexandra had no plans to prevent any such attempt). Dylan must have reverted unconsciously to his football training. With both arms tucked tightly into his sides, he plowed full force into a completing unsuspecting Alexandra. Upon reaching her, Dylan exploded with his arms, knocking her backward. She was helpless and wholly off balance. Impacting her squarely in the chest and shoulders, Dylan caused her to fall headlong backward.

Instinctively, Alexandra reached out forward with her arms. Before she was able to move her arms backward to support her fall, Alexandra's head crashed against the hard cold uncarpeted classroom floor. So fierce was Dylan's blow that after hitting her head, Alexandra slid across the smooth tile over ten feet, until the wall adjoining the hallway stopped her with unforgiving abruptness.

"Alexandra!" cried Ming.

He rushed over to tend to his fallen friend. Agnes darted over just as quickly, but in complete silence. Dylan's cowardly collision into Alexandra barely slowed him down. He pivoted slightly toward the left and shot out through the classroom door and into the hallway.

"Alexandra?" asked Ming, kneeling down next to her and checking for signs of life. Agnes did the same, drawing Alexandra's bangs from her head and laying them gentle alongside the rest of her auburn locks. Ming and Lewis worked together to straighten out Alexandra's body, which, having slammed against the solid cinder block wall, rested in an odd contortion that looked extremely uncomfortable. Agnes assisted by supporting her sister's head as Lewis and Ming extended Alexandra's limbs and straightened her back. As Agnes moved her diminutive hands around to the back of her sister's head, she felt something warm and wet. Agnes rested Alexandra's head on the floor and retracted her hands to examine them.

"Oh no!" offered Lewis, after drawing in a startled breath.

Nothing bleeds like the head. Agnes's hands were covered with blood from her beloved sister's scalp. As she examined the surrounding area, Agnes noticed spots of blood on the wall and the floor. She surmised that Alexandra must have sustained the injury when her head hit the floor as opposed to the impact of the wall. Alexandra wasn't speaking. Agnes knew why. A part of Agnes's mind was disturbed by the blood's warmth and the odd, morbid comfort it offered.

Another part traveled back to kindergarten, to finger painting. She recalled having hands covered in a similar color, drawing Valentine's Day hearts on white paper for their mother.

Overwhelmingly, however, fear and anger percolated in Agnes's young heart, and it grew.

"Alexandra, wake up!" cried Ming. "We need you!"

That wasn't exactly what he meant or what he was thinking. However, he didn't have anything better to offer. He just wanted her to wake up.

For Lewis's part, he sat on his lower legs in silence. He didn't know what to do, and it left him intolerably ill at ease. Until now, Lewis was able to produce some degree of courage in the face of all that had happened. He recognized now that much of that recently manufactured courage was based on the foundation of Alexandra's age and maturity. Now that those elements were out of the picture, Lewis's strength seemed to fade away like the flames of a dying fire on a cold autumn evening, like the setting sun. He scrambled for something to do, some manner in which he could contribute and add to the solution. All he could think of was this television program he had seen once, which taught that raising an injured person's legs above their heart can help get blood back to the organs. He didn't know if it would actually make any difference, but he tried it anyway.

As Lewis took hold of Alexandra's ankles and prepared to lift, he noticed a sudden stark increase in the temperature around Alexandra. In the course of a few passing seconds, it became clear that the thermic rise was not generalized. The air to his left had not heated up, but on the right, it had. Agnes was on the right. Lewis looked over to his right to see what was happening with Alexandra's sweet younger sister.

Agnes's eyes and face were filled with wet streams of salty tears. Her tiny supple cheeks were flushed with emotional red. Agnes's expression did register sadness, but not weak despondent sadness. Instead, her facial features all seemed to harmonize into one solid air of resolution and strength. Her face was hard, almost mean. Lewis lowered Alexandra's feet to the floor and leaned back slightly, partially in reaction to the rapidly intensifying heat flowing off Agnes in undulating waves, but also the unnatural and quite disturbing visceral atmosphere, which emanated from this otherwise gentle, innocent child. The atmosphere could only be described as a controlled bestial resolve.

Lewis's eyes widened as they watched Agnes. She placed her hands calmly on the cool tile floor to facilitate her ascent up to her feet. Then she pivoted on her feet, almost robotically, and walked around Lewis toward the door through which Dylan had run. As she passed, Lewis continued to sense the heat that radiated from her, and he noticed a series of intermittent, tiny flashes of light from her hair and face. He wondered, hoped really, that it was merely the light reflecting off Agnes's tears. He longed for it to be nothing more than light, reflecting off her sweat-soaked hair. But he knew better.

By this time, the heat was so pervasive and distracting that Ming noticed it as well. "Why is it so hot in here?" he asked, partially curious and partially annoyed that something would draw his attention away from tending to Alexandra.

"Ming," said Lewis, pointing slowly toward Agnes.

Ming turned and looked. Agnes curved around Ming and reached the door. Any hope of light, sweat, and tears evaporated with the first flame that danced across Agnes's head like a victorious golden imp. Soon, other flames followed until her head was a blazing pyre of heated wrath. So strong was the heat emanating from Agnes that Ming had to move for the sake of his cooking back. He slid over to the safety of Lewis's side. They both stared mesmerized as if they were having a sleepover, sitting in front of the television, and watching some terrifying horror film, which their parents had forbidden.

"Agnes?" asked Lewis.

Agnes stopped at the door with frightening suddenness. She snapped her head to the left in response to Lewis. When Lewis saw Agnes's full countenance, he knew exactly what was coming. He realized there was no stopping her. Her hair flopped and danced in flaming waves, and her eyes were surrounded and filled with glowing fire. Even the eyes themselves were consumed in an orange fervor. Lewis knew the look. He had seen it before. His mind raced back to the gymnasium and Mrs. Lagrange's musical. He remembered the stupefying experience of Agnes bellowing his name with awful impatience.

"What is going on?" demanded Ming in bewilderment.

Agnes expanded her eyes into jewels of volcanic beauty. This caused her hair to fly into a tempest of fiery licks and slaps. Every lock seemed to conflux into a harmony of fiery glory. She turned again toward the door and stepped through.

Dylan was still close. He had moved to the other end of the hallway, near the closet where the girls had hidden themselves from Jeremiah. Dylan seemed confused, stumbling forward and backward, from one side of the hallway to the other. His movements didn't suggest disorientation, more like lack of clear direction. The rapidity of his efforts made clear that he wanted to go; he just didn't know where. He looked pathetic and desperate, like a roach discovered in the midnight kitchen light.

Agnes positioned herself in the middle of the hallway, facing Dylan with slightly forward arched shoulders and a head full of flaming hair. "Dylan!" she bellowed.

Dylan Pierce gave a noticeable start and swiveled in place. His bald powdery white head stuck out like a sore thumb against the lightless hallway and the tan-painted cinder blocks. Upon seeing Agnes, Dylan squinted to ascertain at whom he was looking and then produced an immediate expression of relief, as if someone heard a suspected intruder and then discovered it was only a mischievous cat. "What do you want Agnes?" he started in a condescending tone. "Are you angry 'cause I pushed your sister down?"

"Dylan!" Agnes shouted out. "Do you see the fire? Do you sense your cleansing?" Flames licked out from Agnes's head and hair in an effervescent rage. Her facial complexion took on an eerie glow, such that her cheeks, forehead, and nose appeared no different than her dazzling coif.

"I don't know what you're talking about, little girl," began Dylan. "But you better shut your tiny trap right now, or we are going to have a problem!" As he spoke, Dylan turned to face Agnes directly and took a step forward, intent on intimidating this diminutive child less than half his size.

"Your time has come, Dylan Pierce. How long have you annoyed and vexed others to feed your pride? Where is your pride now?" spoke Agnes. She stood undaunted, unaffected by Dylan's cruel tone and aggressive posture.

"Where is my—?" asked Dylan. "Are you making fun of my face, little girl? Are you lookin' to get hurt? You got it!" Dylan sneered in humiliated anger as he leapt into a run toward Agnes. His thin red lips twisted in a hateful expression, and his eyes glared with avaricious malignity.

What happened next put the impressive flames emanating from Agnes's locks to undeniable shame. Agnes stopped dead in her tracks, but not from fear. She opened her mouth to its maximum capacity and dropped her chin down deeply, such that it all but touched her chest. At the same instant, her eyes widened once again, this time even larger than before. From her mouth and eyes came forth sparks and flame so bright and pure that it illuminated the hallway fully, from top to bottom and end to end. Not one inch of the space was left in the slightest shadow. The blast traveled down the corridor at a fearfully rapid pace and grew wider as it passed.

"Do you see now the purity, Dylan Pierce?" scolded Agnes. "*You will be cleansed!*" Remarkably, Agnes was able to speak in concert with the unrelenting discharge of heated ferocity coming from her mouth and eyes. It shot forth from her mouth, casting sparks and licks of flame, which bounced chaotically off the inner sides of her cheeks. The flames coursed in between her teeth with breathtaking heat and force, yet did not injure her supple flesh in the least little bit. Her eyes produced and guided similar fire, and like her mouth, remained unsinged in the face of this scalding parade of thermic terror.

Through the formidable blast of fire, Agnes could see Dylan's face, and his dramatic reaction to Agnes Reiniger's destructive capacity. He shuddered in horror, fear expressed with a deep gasp, a gaping maw, and eyes just as wide as Agnes's (although for another reason). Agnes's flaring discharge impacted hard and solid against Dylan, hitting him squarely in the torso. Initially, Dylan stood his ground, and the flames curled around his strong body like glowing yellow vines growing up a flagpole. He tried valiantly to step forward in vengeful aggression toward Agnes.

"Is this what you wanted, Dylan? *Let the flames answer you!*" cried Agnes.

With those words, the power of Agnes's flaming belch doubled, and Dylan was thrown back with decisive force. His body arched slightly in the air and then landed with a low thud. He slid a bit across the floor, rolling slightly, clothes smoldering with a few remaining flames.

When Dylan was sufficiently lucid to try gaining his feet, he leaned back on his smoky hands and kicked his feet out forward a few times, slipping across the smooth tile floor and making an energized, but clumsy effort to stand. Reaching the stability of his feet and full height, Dylan looked down the hallway toward his antagonist. Agnes stared back in vigilant defiance. Wrathful yellow and oranges danced across her face and hair like victorious soldiers waving their hands in celebration. She took a bellicose step toward Dylan. When she did, all doubt ran screaming from Dylan's pensive, terrified mind. He tensed, turned rapidly toward the descending stairs, and darted out of sight.

"Aiee!" screamed Dylan "No! No! Not you!"

When Dylan had hurried away from Agnes and out of sight, it was only for an instant. Dylan came back around the corner into Agnes's full view, but this time, he was not alone, and he was not walking.

"Uh-uh, uh-uh, huh," giggled Wyatt in a brilliantly satisfied voice. He walked around the corner, grappling Dylan with his monstrously strong hands. Wyatt looked like a child who had just found his long lost toy. He lifted, twisted, and shook Dylan as if he were weightless. Wyatt's arms and hands bulged with unnatural power. "I have found you, Dylan! Now I will have your face! I will be you!"

"Let me go! Let me go! Let me go!" cried Dylan. He moved the free parts of his body as best he could. There weren't many of them. Wyatt clasped Dylan's right shoulder, and thereby immobilized the arm on the same side. With his other herculean hand, Wyatt clamped Dylan's legs together. Consequently, all of Dylan's energy caused his head, hand, and feet to wiggle wildly.

Having heard the commotion in the hallway, Lewis and Ming hesitantly left Alexandra in the classroom and shot after Agnes to investigate. It took some courage to walk away from her since they were as yet unsure of her condition. "Whoa!" bellowed Ming in shock. The two friends bore witness to the aftermath of Agnes's thermic brawn. Even as her hair continued to burn in lambent flaming beauty, any loose items lying on the floor smoldered and popped. The hallway floor between Agnes and Dylan (and now Wyatt too) sported a raven black scorch mark, which reflected the length and width of her destructive volley. The air contained a lingering heat and the smell of burnt paint. Agnes Reiniger stood indomitably, her hair in a fevered pitch, her eyes trained on Dylan and Wyatt.

"Little Agnes," said Wyatt in teasingly saccharine tone. "Did you put these pretty little burn marks on Dylan? That's not nice, not nice for little girls."

"Is that what you want, Wyatt?" asked Agnes. "Is that what you want to become?"

"Yes, little Aggie Reiniger," returned Wyatt. "I am him. I will become him."

"Look at his face," mandated Agnes. "Examine your chosen quarry!"

Wyatt looked down at Dylan, producing a tender expression but in no way loosening his vicelike grip. He took inventory of the reddened portions of his ears and nose, the charred bits of clothing, and the blackened tips of his fingers. "You have burned him!" cried Wyatt with increasing tension and volume. "You have burned me!"

Unconsciously, Wyatt flexed the enormous muscles in his arms and hands in angered defiance toward Agnes. This had the effect of producing an even more painful experience for Dylan, locked in the irresistible grasp of his captor. Dylan let forth an agonized, miserable wail as he felt Wyatt's gargantuan palms and fingers crush his shoulders and legs. At the same time, Wyatt also gave a maniacal sneer-bearing teeth and pulling the already overtaxed lids from his bulging eyes. The colored center areas seemed almost to shrink in focused rage, trained as they were on their diminutive target. Holding onto Dylan, Wyatt launched himself forward into a stampede-like run toward Agnes. Each step seemed to reflect an increase in Wyatt's formidable commitment to Agnes's demise.

Agnes was relentless. The playful rolls of flame that danced around her scalp and the simmering orange glow of her eyes grew immediately into a zealous display of flaming fervor. So bright and pervasive were the flames that waved across her head, neck, and hair that her facial features became partially indistinct. The cascading flickers, pops, and sparks flew out with even greater excitement than they had just previously with Dylan.

"Will you hold to your prize, Wyatt McKinney?" bellowed Agnes as the blast shot forth from her mouth and eyes. "Will you share the purification?"

The spinning cone of volcanic fire poured forth from Agnes with dreadful speed and force. First, from her widened gaping maw and then her eyes, the startling blast careened down the hallway in a heated stream both awesome and beautiful. This time, nothing between Agnes and her objective survived. The relatively unimpressive scorch mark on the hallway floor was replaced by an even larger darker scoring. This grew, widening out to the hallway walls, blackening every inch of the floor, and melting the wax and tile between Agnes and Wyatt. As Agnes continued to pour forth the heat, the floor underneath the tile also surrendered until nothing remained but a soot-covered trench dug out in the shape of her conical cry of combustion.

The walls fared little better. First to burn were the seventh graders' poster reports on foreign countries. Gloria Turner's well-fashioned poster on Uruguay caught fire instantly and was reduced to ash in seconds. Ellis Marshall's shabbily fashioned poster on Poland enjoyed a slightly longer life, suffering the effects of a few smoldering stray ashes before flaming up into a roll of embers and falling from the wall.

The last to go, naturally, were those hanging closest to Wyatt and Dylan. It made no difference in the end. When Agnes's fire reached Barry Ferguson's award-winning poster on Uzbekistan, a ray of heated sparks streaked across his pie chart, highlighting the country's agricultural production. Finally, the continued and increasing heat served to produce an effect on the walls similar to that of the hallway floor described above. The rest was smoke and ash.

For Wyatt and Dylan, the instantaneous, but no less spectacular, display of fire was primarily a harbinger of what was coming for them too. Fortunately for Dylan, the fire was sufficiently irresistible and intense as to consume him utterly within a few seconds. So bright were the flames and potent the heat, that Wyatt's hands were left empty. Wyatt had no time to protest. As the bursts of flames and heat slammed against him and Dylan, the latter began to disintegrate almost immediately.

Dylan looked up at his captor in stupefied awe, unable to grasp the grand hopelessness of his situation, let alone take any action toward self-preservation. While the mass of Dylan's very being thinned into nothing, Wyatt threw his arms out into the air with hands cupped. He looked like a clumsy child trying to catch his mother's favorite vase. But in this case, he desperately wished to hold onto Dylan. There was nothing left. In the end, Dylan was reduced to small tendrils of ash, running through Wyatt's massive fingers and falling from his hands.

"Oh man! Oh man! Oh man!" cried Ming, moving back quickly from Agnes.

Lewis did the same. They backed away for two reasons. They did so instinctually because the heat coming from Agnes's eyes, hair, and mouth was overwhelming even from behind. Second, they weren't sure what to make of Agnes's behavior. Like most people, Lewis and Ming felt comfortable quickly around people they assumed could do them no harm. Now that had changed with Agnes. This little girl had never hurt either of them, but she was more than just a little girl. They weren't sure about her any longer. They backed away.

Wyatt was incensed. He looked down at his hands with suspenseful silence, watching the last vestiges of white and gray ash trickle and drop from his fingers. "Naugh!" belched Wyatt, so consumed with ire as to be unable to formulate a simple no. "He is not gone! I am not gone!" Wyatt dropped carelessly to his knees and began to draw the chaotically strewn ashes into piles. The ashes puffed and blew as he smacked them together into a single mound. "He is still here! I am still here!"

There was brief silence while the reality of the situation chased Wyatt in his mind and left him nowhere to hide.

With all his gargantuan strength, Wyatt raised his right palm into the air as far as he could and then brought it crashing down on the recently formed pile of ashes. It produced a frighteningly thunderous rumble, which vibrated the floors and even caused loose chunks of the charred wall to fall. Lewis and Ming threw their arms out like wings to resist the sudden tremors, which destabilized them. Agnes was unmoved.

"You took him from me!" wailed Wyatt, offering Agnes a chilling stare. "You took him. You took me! He is gone! *I am gone!*"

With that, Wyatt raised his right leg up and put his palms to the ground. At first he appeared to be in the process of merely raising himself up to his feet. Instead, he remained in the semielevated stance, arching his back just slightly. With his face and eyes still trained unwaveringly on Agnes, Wyatt spread his large bulbous fingers out wide on the ground to solidify his balance. His humongous bulging white eyes throbbed in his head as vigilant planetary sentinels. Leaning his weight firmly on his strong arms, Wyatt lifted his legs into position so that he appeared like something between a sprinter at the starting block or the center of an offensive line, waiting for the starter's gun to fire or the quarterback's call to snap the ball.

Wyatt had come to idolize Dylan. It was more than simple hero worship. Wyatt McKinney envied Dylan Pierce for who he was, what he was. Now Agnes had taken the object of that hellacious envy away, leaving Wyatt with nothing but himself. Wyatt launched forward with the full energy of his venomous hate, set upon stamping out this thief of his most urgent and pathetic hope. His legs propelled him with such force that he all but left the ground. As he shot forth toward the diminutive Agnes, Wyatt lifted his arms up from the ground and curled them through the air, like a pair of hawk wings swooping in to snatch their prey.

"No, Wyatt McKinney," stated Agnes in a firm punitive tone. "You will stop here! There is nothing further here for you, nothing rude, nothing dark!"

Agnes produced the most harrowing and potent blast of wrathful fire yet. It came first and foremost from her tender mouth, a veritable fountain of terrific flame, a stream of yellow and orange purification as wide as her jaws could allow. Tendrils of chaotic flame and spark spit from the sides of her mouth, seeming to have a mind of their own, clawing with bestial impatience to escape. Auxiliary beams exited her eyes with the same awful combustion, shooting forth independently at first and then flowing into the larger stream teeming from her mouth. This time, the wisps of her hair were less passive. Like a driver's whip, each lock of Agnes's soft flowing hair curled forward with a vicious crack, adding its own share of yellow and orange to the flaming gust.

Wyatt closed his huge eyes against the intense light, but continued undeterred. His rage and offended sense of justice spurred him on. He would have his quarry in Agnes Reiniger. His anger-addled mind could produce no discernable speech. Wyatt merely croaked out grunts and growls in his own confused language of bitterness. Agnes met his rage and progression with further heat. With each step that he achieved in his march to reach her, Agnes expanded the aperture of her gaping maw, widened her innocent oval eyes, and increased the frequency of her flame-hurling locks.

Even from behind, the heat became overpowering for Lewis and Ming. Lewis fainted outright from the intense thermic blasts, and a stray tendril of spark and flame ignited Ming's pant leg. With frantic rapidity, Ming pulled his leg away from Agnes and began to slap at it, often enough to beat it out, but seldom enough to avoid burning his hand. Once the flame was safely extinguished, Ming jumped over behind the door that adjoined the classroom and hallway. In the next instant, he reached out for Lewis, grabbed his arm, and pulled him to relative safety.

"Throw your heat, little girl!" growled Wyatt. "I will still reach you!"

Wyatt took another three staggered steps toward Agnes. They were slow but sure. He wasn't finished yet. He threw up his massive right hand and forearm in an effort to block Agnes's thermic blasts. It helped some. His forearm and the soft side of his palm looked like the bow of a boat, cutting courageously into the torrential waves of an ocean squall. He pulled the forearm closer to himself to more effectively protect his face, especially the large protruding eyes.

Then something happened, which was able to draw away Ming's attention from the frenetic drama that ensued in the hallway. From the corner of his left eye, Ming noticed slight but undeniable movement from Alexandra. She was conscious. Satisfied that Lewis was protected behind the classroom door, Ming crawled quickly but cautiously over to Alexandra. He edged up to Alexandra and cradled her head just as she took her first steps into lucidity.

"Are you all right?" asked Ming in a slow genuinely tender voice. "You took a good hit and fell pretty hard."

"Yeah, I think so," moaned Alexandra. She curled up into a seated position and began to rub the back of her head with her right hand. "Where is everybody? And why is it so hot in here?"

"Well, that's a bit of a long story," answered Ming, fishing for the right words. "It would probably be easier to show you than tell you."

Back in the hallway, Agnes continued to pour forth the flame like a vengeful island volcano, belching hot lava on a disobedient people below. Wyatt's expression of hateful confidence began to morph slowly into pained distress. It was clear that the heat and flame was taking its toll, especially upon the arm and hand, which he employed as a shield against Agnes's thermic onslaught.

"There is no contest, Wyatt McKinney!" scolded Agnes with a deep solid voice. "There is no chance to overcome this!"

Further provoked by this little girl's defiant words, Wyatt dug deep to the base of his voluminous rage for one last bellicose salvo. He produced a bestial growl from his cavernous lungs and heaved his body forward with two final steps. He threw his arms up into the air like tiger's claws and reached out in unrestrained aggression to lay hold of Agnes. Taking his protective arm away from his face allowed the full complement of Agnes's fire to splash forcefully against his face. It left Wyatt unaffected. He was all in totally committed to reaching Agnes with enough passion-fueled strength to push his head and face within two feet of her. His bulbous pulsing eyes gleamed at her with a rounded blanched fire all their own.

It was at this very moment, when Wyatt stood toe-to-toe with Agnes, his hands and fingers tensed against her fiery bursts, that Alexandra reached the hallway, followed closely by Ming. Here she bore witness to the spectacular grandeur of their collective circumstance and her little sister's awe-inspiring contest. As soon as she saw Agnes, her heart reached out with instinctive protectiveness. She embraced the reality of Wyatt's awesome strength and his massive hands and saw nothing of Agnes's but her diminutive tender form. "Agnes...sweetie. What are you doing?"

"Play your fiery games, little girl," bleated Wyatt in a malignant tone. "I will reach you! *My hands will get you!*" Wyatt gritted his teeth and pressed in toward Agnes, employing the final vestiges of his feral energy and nearly touched Agnes.

"No, Wyatt McKinney. *You will not!*"

Agnes responded in kind to Wyatt's heroic last effort by raising her own hands to meet his. Her gentle hands appeared almost laughably small compared to Wyatt's monstrous mitts. Yet after everyone present had seen what those hands would produce, there would be no further underestimation. In addition to the fire that poured and careened from her eyes, mouth, and flapping coif, dreadful flames and sparks began to shoot from her palms. Like her eyes had done just a brief time before, the fire from her palms initiated their own path through the space, but finally joined in with the others. Her mouth, eyes, hair, and palms all labored together to produce an irresistible detonation of heat and flame.

There was no contest. The initial explosion sent Wyatt flying backward like a rag doll. A rolling, thundering orb of orange fire carried his helpless body halfway down the hallway until it finally dissipated and dropped him carelessly on the scorched tile floor in front of the drinking fountain. A further blast of volcanic fury sparked and crackled from Agnes's head and hands. This one was cone-shaped and filled the hallway, bigger and louder than any before it. The blast's explosive force enveloped Wyatt in its irresistible might and continued down the hallway unopposed.

When it had finished with Wyatt and passed into the second half of the corridor, the conical blast assumed the shape of the hallway. Then it exploded victoriously, blasting the doors off their hinges and into their respective classrooms. Agnes's fire was still yet unappeased. It filled both classrooms and consumed anything that wasn't metal. It was only when the fire had burst through the classroom windows that it surrendered. Window glass shattered and splintered under the fire's heat and pressure. Heated shards flew outward with a muffled crash into the howling winter's snowstorm.

Down in the frosty snow-covered parking lot, the Rayaims snapped their heads upward at the site and sounds. Wiry impish grins curled the rough sags of skin on their faces. The fire that shot from the shattered windows danced across the sky and produced an orange glow over each of the creatures. Each of them raised their feet in monstrous delight and filled the air with their malevolent wails and cackles.

Up in the hallway, Wyatt came to his senses. He looked down the corridor and saw Agnes standing vigilantly. She was no longer hurling blasts of fire, but the dreadful flame still licked off her fingers. Her harrowing fire-orange eyes still lit up the hallway like a distant constellation in dark space, and the locks of her hair lapped back and forth in sentinel waves. Wyatt did not hesitate. He rose to his feet, draped in the hanging remnants of his scorched, tattered clothing, and dashed painfully out of sight and down the stairs.

Confident that the danger had passed, Agnes's fire diminished. She lowered her arms to her sides, and as she did, the flames that adorned her tiny hands abated as well. One by one, each lock of her youthful soft strands of hair ceased to wave and lap. Each gave up its flame and came to rest gently on Agnes's sweet head. At their completion, the flames and vestigial sparks left her with beautiful waves of brown hair as if nothing at all had happened.

"Aggie?" said Alexandra.

Agnes turned to face the three. As she did, her mouth closed and produced a kind smile. Her eyes returned to their normal state, the lids, lashes, and brows all intact and completely unaffected. Agnes augmented her grin into a toothy effervescent smile and opened her arms warmly to her sister.

Without hesitation, Alexandra dashed from behind the door and embraced Agnes with profound relief and unbridled love. "Aggie, sweetie," spoke Alexandra. "I'm so glad that you're okay!"

"Yeah, Lexie," started Agnes calmly. "I'm okay."

Then it dawned on Alexandra. Her sister spoke. She had spoken to Wyatt during their struggle, but Alexandra was so consumed in verifying Agnes's safety that she didn't notice the change. For the first time in a long time, Agnes spoke. It was Agnes's speech in particular that Alexandra missed. All this time, Agnes continued to sing. Her sweet melodic voice never stopped blessing the ears and minds of every one so fortunate to hear. However, Agnes has ceased speaking. Now for the first time in a long time, she spoke.

"Agnes, you talk again!" exclaimed Alexandra with a glowing, gleeful expression.

With these words, all four of them smiled from ear to ear, and a lighthearted atmosphere filled the hallway despite the residual heat, smoke, and soot. "I am so happy to hear your sweet voice again!" Given the difference in their respective height, Agnes's head came comfortably into Alexandra's stomach when they hugged, and that was just fine for the both of them. Agnes's warm head and soft rounded cheek fit quite nicely.

"Lexie?" asked Agnes in a calm voice.

"Yeah, sweetie," returned Alexandra.

"It's okay," stated Agnes with a piercing gaze.

"What do you mean?" asked Alexandra.

"It's okay," stated Agnes once again, using the exact same tone, and employing the same deep inexorable stare.

This time, Alexandra didn't speak. Instead, she allowed her head and heart to spin until the answer was reached. As she stood there, transfixed by her sister's potent gaze, Alexandra's mind swam through all her memories concerning Agnes. *What did she mean?* she thought.

Agnes seemed to know intuitively that Alexandra didn't quite yet understand. She continued to stare and repeated, "It's okay."

It was then that Alexandra reached it, the place in each of us where the head and heart come together. Alexandra then knew exactly what Agnes meant. It was the question that Alexandra never knew she had; she had never conceived of it, never even voiced it privately in her head. Yet, somehow, it was the biggest, most important question ever. Now her sister, speaking for the first time in over a year, had answered perfectly without even having been asked.

"I'm so sorry, Agnes," said Alexandra, pursing her face slightly, and the overwhelming emotion filled her. "I am so sorry that we left you alone in those woods. We never should have done that."

"It's okay, Lexie," assured Agnes. "I love you."

When those final three words, Agnes had given her sister full permission to let go; and she did. For Alexandra, a wave of peace, joy, and relief flooded through her soul, washing out every bit of hurt, self-loathing, and doubt. At once, it felt better than a headache fading away on a Sunday afternoon breeze, better than a burp to release the pressure of overeating, better than pounding a pillow when you're angry. It was all gone. Alexandra would no longer punish herself for leaving Agnes behind, no longer bounce back and forth between defending her choice to do so and judging herself to the point of dark, heavy, unrelenting shame.

The two sisters had laid down their arms. Agnes had come to speak again, and with her first words, she had broken down a wall of silent tension and discomfort that, until now, Alexandra didn't even fully understand. Agnes's courage and simple words had removed everything cold and chaotic from their sisterhood. Without those troubling, draining elements, there was nothing but a tremendous surge of tranquility.

"I love you too, Agnes," said Alexandra softly.

18

Now That I've Got You Talking

The same moment that Alexandra and Agnes were finally able to break away from their conciliatory embrace, Ming and Lewis were also pulled back to their present circumstances. All four of them took a look around at the remains of the school hallway following Agnes's victorious display of thermal might against Wyatt. The entire hallway, from where they stood to the opposite end, was a black charred, smoking mess. Residual chunks of wall dropped to the floor, finally surrendering to the irresistible destructive force of Agnes's onslaught. The few unconsumed pieces of wood offered tongues of flame intermittently. Many of them had already snuffed out to nothing more than narrow billows of gray smoke.

"Agnes, I'm really glad that you're talking again and all," began Ming. "But the coolest thing is the way you blasted fire down the hallway! That was awesome! How did you do that? How are you able to do that?"

"Yeah," dropped in Lewis. "And what can you tell us about Wyatt and the others? Why did they get so weird-looking?"

"I just thought it was cool the way you talked to them confident and bold! 'No, Wyatt, You will not!' and all. I've never seen anything like it. Where do you get those powers?"

"Give her half a second to breathe!" interjected Alexandra in a motherly voice as she pulled Agnes in close. "She's been through a great deal. We all have."

"Well, I know," conceded Ming. "But give us something. We're dying here!"

Agnes drew in a deep pacifying breath. "All the fire, glowing and sparking and everything, started back when Lexie and I visited our Uncle Aaron. I had some trouble there, and I haven't been able to talk since then. Sometimes, the coolest things happen when things are bad." Upon saying this, Agnes looked up warmly at her sister and simultaneously reached over and took her hand, intertwining her fingers with Alexandra's in order to remind her that all was well.

"I couldn't speak, but I still had a lot to say," continued Agnes. "Y'know what I mean?"

"All those spooky songs, right?" dropped in Lewis.

"Yeah, all those spooky songs," agreed Agnes with a sweet affirming smile.

"What do they all mean?" Alexandra asked.

"Look who's asking questions now, Alexandra," said Ming mockingly. "C'mon give her half a minute. She's been through a lot. We all have."

"Oh hush, Ming," rejoined Alexandra. She gave Ming the most haunting scowl and then returned her attention to Agnes.

"Each of them were things that needed to be said, or sometimes, things that someone needed to hear," answered Agnes with a searching expression that seemed to suggest that she was speaking candidly, but grasping for each answer only seconds before offering it.

"Did you make up those songs," asked Lewis.

"Yes, but kinda' no too," responded Agnes.

"Well, which is it?" questioned Ming.

"It's like I was singing and saying the words, and I knew what I was saying," began Agnes. "I understood it, but each word was a gift to me. Something gentle, but not me, kept the words going in the right way. Does that make sense?"

"Not really," returned Ming with a curt disappointed tone.

"It seemed like the songs fit what was going on at the time, like they seemed to explain it or something," added Lewis.

"Yeah, that's right," affirmed Agnes. "The words were something that needed to be said at that time and place, something that needed to be heard. When we were fighting with Wyatt and the others, the songs were things that they needed to hear for own good, and sometimes, for theirs too."

"Speaking of Wyatt and the others," dropped in Lewis, changing the subject slightly, "what happened to them? Why did they get all weird?"

"You mean weirder than they already were?" asked Ming with a playful smirk.

"Ming?" asked Alexandra, looking over at him with a disapproving groan.

"What do we know about those three?" asked Agnes, suddenly taking on a very authoritative air.

"They are all three jerks, bullies, who found pleasure in making our lives miserable," answered Ming, disregarding Alexandra's rebuke.

"That's true, Ming," responded Agnes. "But think about what each of them is."

At this, the other three seemed stumped. It was Lewis, finally, who came forth with an answer.

"Do you mean, like, what was different about each of them?" asked Lewis, digging for a clue.

"I mean, what did each of them really want?" responded Agnes.

Lewis dwelt on Agnes's words for a moment and then chimed in. "With Jeremiah, I know he was always stealing other people's things."

"That's exactly right, Lewis," said Agnes with an affirming smile on her face.

Lewis smiled too. "And why does he steal?"

"Let's see," said Ming, looking up to the ceiling to suggest that he was thinking. He raised his hands and pretended to be keeping a list. "He steals because he's mean, because he's selfish, because no one likes him enough to buy him anything. Shall I go on?"

"Because he's greedy?" dropped in Alexandra.

"Exactly!" exclaimed Agnes, looking over at her sister with affection. "What happened to his hands?"

"Did they change because of his stealing?" asked Lewis with an air of hopeful confidence.

"Yeah," answered Agnes. "They became so big because he steals."

"But that doesn't make any sense," stated Ming. "If he's stealing, wouldn't bigger hands mean he could steal more?"

"But they weren't just bigger," said Lewis. "They were also fatter and rounded. He didn't have any knuckles. His changed hands made it harder for him to steal, not easier. I think that was why he got so angry and started throwing desks all over the room. He dug around in the desks looking for what he wanted, but he couldn't get those big fingers around anything."

"Perfect!" congratulated Agnes. "Now, with the other two, think in the other direction."

"What do you mean, Agnes?" asked her sister. Alexandra was stunned with her young sister's acumen and wisdom.

"With Dylan and Wyatt, think about what changed about them first instead of why it happened."

"I see what you mean, Agnes," said Alexandra. "Dylan's face became really white and smooth. It lost all of its features, his nose, lips, everything!"

"But it was more than that," added Ming. "He became kind of a wimp. I mean, before, Dylan would never let Wyatt talk to him the way he did in the hallway. Dylan turned into a coward."

Lewis was briefly silent and then he began to shake his head up and down as if he were agreeing with himself. "Dylan was always the leader. He bossed everybody around, including Wyatt and Jeremiah."

"Yeah," started Alexandra. "And he always thought he was so good-looking. He used to come up to me, point to his own face and say, 'You're not dreamin' baby, but I'll still pinch you if you want'."

"Doesn't it make sense, then?" asked Agnes. "I mean, what happened to him, how he changed?"

"Yeah," responded Lewis. "He thought he was more handsome than anyone else and then all his good looks went away. He didn't really have any looks at all."

"And his strength, his courage, went away too!" dropped in Ming.

"Well," started Alexandra. "He acted like he was better than everyone else, but I wonder if he really believed that."

Agnes reached over again and took her sister's hand. She looked up to Alexandra with an approving, esteeming smile. This was the first time Alexandra received such a smile from her little sister. Usually, it was the other way around. It took Alexandra back a bit, but she liked it nonetheless.

"Agnes," started Ming, bearing a quizzical expression. "If this is all true, then what about Wyatt's eyes? Doesn't it make more sense that Jeremiah would develop those huge bulging eyes?"

"Wow, those are creepy!" interjected Alexandra.

Ming continued, "Wasn't Jeremiah the one who stole things? It seems to me that if Jeremiah wanted to steal the things that he saw, wouldn't *his* eyes change and get so big and bulging?"

"That's true, Ming," said Lewis. "But I think what Wyatt wanted was more than stuff. He's a bully for sure, but I don't think Wyatt was a thief, not like Jeremiah, anyway. I keep thinking about the time that we first saw Wyatt and Dylan in the hallway. Do you remember what Wyatt kept saying to Dylan?"

"It was awful!" exclaimed Alexandra. "Over and over again he said, 'Give me your eyes! Give me your face! I am you! Give me your ears!' and all that. It gave me the creeps!"

Lewis's face, his whole being lit up with excitement. "I got it!" he shot out. "But I don't got it." Upon this last remark Lewis's face dropped with disappointment.

"Agh, what!" asked Ming, making no effort to mask his frustration.

"What is that word, you know, when you want something that you don't have. Y'know, it's like an eating feeling. It almost hurts because you can't have what you want."

"Want, wish, desire?" asked Alexandra.

"No," responded Lewis. "It's meaner than that."

"Jealous, greed, spite?" offered Alexandra again.

"Envy!" said Lewis, nearly shouting. "Envy! Envy! Wyatt had envy for things."

"That makes sense," started Alexandra. "He didn't steal exactly, but I think he wanted to have what Dylan had. He wanted to be tough, good-looking, and in charge all the time."

"But he never was. He wanted what Dylan had, but he could never get it. Dylan always had just a little more."

Then there was silence. All four of them became lost in their own respective inner dialogue, trying to digest the answers they had just discovered. It was a pleasant feeling for each of them. After such turmoil with the three antagonists, it felt good to have a few answers; and the clarity of those answers afforded them a calming degree of control in the midst of a scary chaotic situation in which they had no control. They didn't get themselves into these circumstances, and they certainly had no idea how to get out of them. Now, at least, however, they understood it all a bit more.

After the four basked in the brief satisfying silence a bit longer, Ming chimed in, "Okay, but what now?"

"You mean, what are we going to do now?" asked Lewis, trying to clarify.

"Yeah," Ming responded. "It's great that we figured out about Dylan and the other two. But what do we do now? We're still stuck here in the school. The snow is still up over the windows."

There was another period of silence. However, this one brought no calm whatsoever.

"Well," started Alexandra with a pleasant, contented tone. "I'm just happy to have my sister back." She smiled widely, leaned over Agnes, and gave her a close hug.

Ming let his frustration get the better of him. "That's nice and all, but—"

Ming wasn't able to finish his rather inconsiderate remark. He was sharply startled by what he saw. Alexandra remained with her long, slender arms wrapped intimately around her beloved little sister's neck. Then, in a terrifically rapid flash, Alexandra yanked her arms away, leaned back, and stepped away from Agnes. Immediately, the reason became clear.

"Agnes, what's going on?" cried Alexandra in confusion.

Even before Alexandra was able to withdraw her hands from the vicinity of her sister's head and neck, the familiar thermic tendrils appeared once more all over Agnes's hair. They lapped and crackled as they had before in all their glory, at once beautiful and frightful. From the other side, Lewis and Ming saw Agnes's eyes adopt the now familiar hot yellow hue. Alexandra moved over next to Lewis immediately before Agnes broke into song.

Flames and crackles heat and burn,
O, how they bring the smoke!
They fetch the fear and stomachs churn,
The soot and ashes choke!
Though it may seem the day is done, our enemies in fire!
I do regret, one danger yet, before we can retire.

You've found two clues, the story told,
In paper and the bottle!
You found your courage, steady, bold,
When danger came to throttle!
More trouble still, it hides and looms, in this most loathsome mire,
I do regret, one danger yet, before we can retire.

Lewis Warner, hear these words,
The nightmare and the vision!
They linger long like flightless birds,
And cut with cold precision,
No mercy, peace or clemency, though bone and muscle tire,
I do regret, one danger yet, before we can retire.

"Okay, Agnes," began Ming. "You can come back now. Very funny! Ha-ha!"

"Yeah, Agnes. We were just starting to relax a little bit," followed Lewis.

But she didn't come back. Agnes remained completely still, eyes flushed in scintillating fire and flaming locks of hair whapping to and fro. Then in a chillingly mechanical manner, Agnes turned and walked down the hallway at a cool unaffected pace. She didn't hurry, nor did she tarry. She simply moved her diminutive, but no less disturbing, person down to the other hallway junction, which also connected to a descending staircase. At this point, it was the only usable passage. The other direction offered only scorched, smoky black impassable waste. Aside from the residual heat, it was not entirely certain that the floor in that direction would still support their weight were they to attempt traversing it.

When Agnes Reiniger reached the junction, she stopped, coolly spun in place, and looked back at the other three. In her movements, she looked like a soldier practicing marching drill, skillful and precise. All three remained as they were, just where Agnes had left them, lost in a fugue of confusion and aching frustration.

In a movement familiar at least to Lewis, Agnes swiftly snapped her left arm out to the side toward the descending staircase. Her arm moved not an inch further than she wished. Then a sudden impatient glare came forth from each eye, and the flapping locks picked up the pace. The message was clear. Lewis, Ming, and Alexandra shot down the hallway toward Agnes. By the time they reached her, she was already making her way down the stairs.

19

In Case of Fire, Please Use the Stairs

It didn't take the other three long to catch up with Agnes. She had started descending the stairs ahead of them, but she was keeping the same imperturbable even pace, which she employed in reaching the stairs. As her three companions followed, they eventually had to slow their sprint to a slow, almost annoyingly dawdling crawl. Step-by-step, the four descended the stairs, watching Agnes and following her directions. Following in her fiery wake, the other three gradually fanned out to the sides, overcome by the intense heat wafting from Agnes's hair.

"Agnes, where are we going?" asked Alexandra with a flash of annoyance.

Agnes was silent, offering nothing in return but a smooth, serene descent down to the first floor. The junction of the stairs and the first floor was a familiar sight. Not only the main entrance to the building, it was also the location at which Lewis and the others had come to fully realize the extent of the storm—seeing snow drifted up to the door's apex, and encountering the Rayaim who bashed and kicked against the glass, endeavoring to gain malicious access to the four.

"Agnes Reiniger," clamored her sister. "I am talking to you!"

To no one's surprise, the snow remained just as high as it had been the last time they were there. The cold, frosty piles leaned heavily against the glass and produced a lifeless gray shadow through the windows. The glass muffled the winds slightly, but it was unmistakably clear that the storm continued unabated. This sad but expected realization left each of them (well, at least Lewis, Ming, and Alexandra) cold and hollow. Each of them privately surrendered any hope of rescue or relief. The four curved unenthusiastically around the corner and continued downward to the basement in concert with Agnes's slow steady pace.

Upon taking the first step in the final set of stairs, Lewis heard a quiet thought sound off in his head, "Agnes. Purifier."

"Ming, what are you mumbling about?" asked Lewis, turning sharply toward his friend.

"I didn't say anything, Lewis," he replied.

"Agnes. Purifier," sounded the voice again.

Hearing it for a second time and having passed the initial shock, Lewis was able to determine that it was not the voice of anyone immediately present. Before they reached the basement floor, the voice resonated one final time. "Agnes. Purifier."

"Agnes, c'mon!" cried Alexandra, nearly shouting. "What's going on? I want some answers!"

"Alexandra," started Ming in a confident and gentle voice, "I know she's your sister, but I don't think she is going to answer you."

"Yeah, I don't think we have any choice but to follow her," added Lewis.

The final flight of stairs ended in a small junction that allowed two options. To the left, a hallway opened, offering another set of classrooms and offices similar to the first and second floors. To the right, a set of double doors opened to the school cafeteria. Agnes and her magnificent flaring locks made no hesitation. The set of solid windowless doors flew open, and Agnes marched into the cafeteria, bold and easy, without missing a beat.

The cafeteria at James Madison Elementary was practical and unremarkable. Its narrow long space was filled primarily with an innumerous fleet of wooden collapsible lunch tables, each surrounded by a group of multicolored plastic chairs, easily cleaned and nearly unbreakable. At the end of the cafeteria near which the four walked was the kitchen, a collection of ovens, stoves, closets, and refrigerators. It included two entrances, one for ingress and the other egress. A small podium, table, and microphone resided at the same end. From time to time, Mr. Cohen would use these items to address the student body or deliver awards. Agnes passed all of these with cold indifference and led the group toward the other end of the cafeteria.

As the group passed through the rectangular space, unaware of the destination to which little Agnes was leading, (let alone why) Lewis, Ming, and Alexandra ceased attempting to pry the information from her and simply followed. Like the majority of the rest of the school building, the cafeteria was nearly dark, filled with the same drab grayish hue. A small modicum of light succeeded at piercing through the thick snow and shined through the rectangular windows at the top of the walls. This provided enough light for the group to navigate. However, something told Lewis—based on the indivertible manner in which Agnes walked—that she could have traversed the cafeteria even if it were left in total darkness.

Ming was struck by the haunting emptiness of the cafeteria. He understood that it remained vacant most of the day, but generally speaking, he was always in class when the cafeteria was empty. This sad hollow state of the space afforded Ming an inexorable sinking feeling deep in his heart. He looked around at all the empty chairs and pictured himself sitting and eating lunch with his classmates and friends. He also reflected on how many times he had stared across the cafeteria at Alexandra Reiniger, dreaming of what it would be like to stand next to her, perhaps even to talk to her.

Now, in the midst of this scary ordeal, he had achieved both. What's more, she had even kissed him. He imagined what it would be like to tell his friends about that kiss over lunch. And then, he decided he wouldn't. Something inside Ming told him that he should never share that. The charge came from a place in his own heart and mind, a place with which he wasn't too familiar. Nevertheless, he liked his own advice. It made him feel strong, solid. The kiss was for him to keep. It was between the two of them, and that is where it would stay.

Agnes led the group to a most unremarkable and unanticipated destination. At the back end of the cafeteria were located two storage areas, one on each side of an ascending staircase that led to the gymnasium and the street outside. Both of the storage areas were large, and each was accessed by a simple door. Alexandra's diminutive sibling halted about five feet in front of the door leading to the storage area on the left.

"What are we doing here?" asked Lewis, showing a rare expression of impatience and frustration. It was clear that all of this was finally getting to him.

"Sweetie," began Alexandra, trying to add a diplomatic touch to the situation. "What's this about? Why don't we try taking the stairs up and seeing if we can get outside onto the street?"

Agnes heard them both but offered no response. She stepped up intentionally to the door and gripped the knob.

What happened next became for Lewis an example of the difference between amazement and surprise. Agnes gave the knob a stiff right turn but was stopped immediately by the lock. She gave the knob an equitable turn to the left and then went into action. In a relatively understated fashion, the locks and subtle curls of Agnes's hair flapped and whirled as they had before.

Lewis noticed that her eyes also took on the evocative bright glow, which the three had previously witnessed. Because she was facing the door, he wasn't able to see Agnes directly, but Lewis discerned that her eyes had taken on a radiant glimmer because the door reflected their ocular light. The glow was warm and comforting, like summer sunshine beaming gloriously through a morning window.

When the light produced by Agnes's eyes reached the apex of its luminosity, the doorknob took on the same color, but with an added intensity. It gleamed brilliantly in Agnes's small hand and illuminated the entire end of the cafeteria. Ming wondered if the light also produced heat, and if that heat affected Agnes in any way. He decided it didn't.

Just as sharply and calmly as she approached the door and knob, Agnes now stepped back slightly. The light from Agnes's eyes and the secondary glow that it produced on the doorknob abated. With smooth unintimidating fluidity, the knob turned in its correct functional fashion, and the door released. It opened slowly, giving just a begrudging few inches, and produced a clear, evocative creek, which pierced Lewis, Ming, and Alexandra to their very souls.

Hopeful that Agnes had perhaps reached a point of taking questions, Ming chimed in, "Agnes, what's the point of coming to this room? Nobody comes down here. This room hasn't been used in decades and probably hasn't even been opened in years."

Lewis and Alexandra had the same question and waited impatiently with Ming.

"My time has passed," began Agnes. "My work is finished. All that remains is for Lewis. The rest is up to him."

With that, Agnes stepped out of the way. The unnatural manifestations which took place in her hair and eyes subsided. She offered Lewis a friendly smile, but the expression bore an unmistakable detachment. Before ceasing movement altogether, Agnes extended her left arm and pointed toward the door, inviting Lewis, and only Lewis, to take the next step.

Lewis was lost in bewilderment. *What could she possibly mean?* he thought. *Haven't I done enough? Isn't it enough that I got locked in the middle of this nightmare out in the middle of this storm? I just saw my dad get run down by some nut. What more does she want from me?* As Lewis dashed through the corridors of his mind and heart, he experienced an aggressive procession of emotion pressure and anxiety over what would now be expected of him, fear over what could lie beyond the door, then finally, anger over falling into circumstances that he didn't choose. Lewis stood unmoved.

"Go ahead, Lewis," Ming mandated. "We'll be right behind you."

Lewis took comfort from his friend's words. He believed him. Lewis took a short cursory look at the door. He then stared downward, not wanting to enter. Naturally, his thoughts flowed back to his grandmother, Imelda. He pictured her sitting on the couch in their small home on the corner, looking out the picture window. He imagined her locked in bottomless heavy fear, waiting for an afternoon school bus that would never come, or at least not with him on it. He imagined her staring sadly into the relentless waves of snow, buffeting the houses and trees, and offering no hope of her grandson's return.

Then, strangely enough, the image in his mind changed. Imelda wasn't fearful or helpless, pondering hopelessly some tragic scenario. Instead, Lewis pictured her standing brave and tall, no, not brave—proud. She stood tall and proud, fully aware of her grandson's predicament, but also fully confident of his ability to face and overcome it. She still looked out the picture window in the front room, but now her face wore an imperturbable smile. Her heart pierced through the impenetrable undulations of wintry blight and reached her beloved grandson, offering him all her love, pride, and confidence.

"Let's go," said Lewis.

20

The Dust Covers But Never Destroys

Lewis stepped boldly forward. In one uninterrupted motion, he grabbed the knob and pushed the door inward, swinging it out to an aperture sufficiently wide to allow the four to enter. As the door gave way, it also offered another long eerie creek, which rose to an uninviting zenith in both pitch and volume, more of same, as Agnes had encountered earlier. Lewis steeled himself against any vexation from the creepy sound and proceeded far enough into the chamber to allow the others to follow in turn.

The contents and condition of the room made it clear that Ming was spot on with his assessment. Clearly, nothing had been disturbed within for decades. There was a thick visible layer of dust over everything in the room; and it was even, suggesting that nothing, from the front where they stood to the room's deepest recesses, had been touched in quite a long time. Alexandra reflected on something she had learned recently in science, that dust is composed primarily of human skin. She wondered how many people had come and gone from this chamber, how many different samplings of skin were represented in the pale white particles that heaped up high enough to create dust. How many of those people were still living and shedding dust somewhere else? How many of them weren't?

Another clue to the room's old and neglected state was its contents. From wall to wall, the chamber housed desks, chairs, easels, sports equipment, and odd planks of wood and metal. In one corner there was a hanging chart, which teachers used to present word components: vowels, diphthongs, consonant blends, and the like. There were even a couple of bed frames and mattresses, likely used in the school office for the occasional vomiting kid. It wasn't so much the items themselves, but rather their make and production company, which suggested their protracted tenure in this locale.

The four could tell from the design of the students desks, which were stacked as high as safety allowed, that they were no longer in use within the school and had been replaced. The same was true of the chair and teaching tools. Only Alexandra could recall seeing one of these items ever used by one of her teachers. The memory created a brief moment of emotional bliss in the midst of their current vexing predicament.

A small rectangular window, exactly like those in the cafeteria, sat at the top of the far wall. It offered only meager, insufficient light—no more than what the snow would allow. The spare thin beams of gray illumination were enough to allow safe navigation by foot, but insufficient to expose every nook and cranny, which darkness, junk, and time had created.

Most of what resided in the room did not offer the four any great surprise, with the exception of another door. This door did not lead outside, but rather to a smaller closet inside the room. Lewis gave the door a committed stare then turned around and looked directly at Agnes, expecting, or perhaps hoping, for some confirmation or refutation regarding the door. There was none. Agnes stepped innocently toward Alexandra, wrapped her arms around her taller grown-up sister, and offered nothing but a warm tender smile. *Absolutely useless,* Lewis thought.

Imelda's grandson stepped toward the closet door and turned the knob. Opening the door revealed nothing else than more of what they saw in the main room: a couple of desks and a stack of chairs. Lewis was almost disappointed. Then, just as his elevated heart rate began to slow, Lewis bore witness to imagery, which blocked out the desks and chairs and consumed the entire inner space of the closet. Now the closet appeared empty and much cleaner. Based on the condition of the walls and floor inside the closet, Lewis guessed that whatever he was seeing now took place some time ago. Suddenly, a man appeared inside the closet almost immediately in front of Lewis.

"Hey, check this out!" charged Lewis, gesturing over his shoulder.

Ming squeezed in between Lewis and the door frame. Alexandra looked in over his shoulder. Agnes stood back in the main chamber, completely unaffected. The man was of average height and build and looked to be in his late forties or early fifties. His hair was black and graying, cut short, and balding slightly on the crown of his head. He wore dark navy blue coveralls with a white dingy T-shirt underneath.

"Who is that?" asked Ming.

The man turned around and stood up so immediately they wondered if he had heard Ming's questioned. The three drew in a rapid shallow breath. The man stood up tall to his full height and seemed to look over them, in the direction of the door, leading to the cafeteria. Realizing that he wasn't looking at them, and that this was merely an image, the three calmed.

Aside the near heart-stopping start, the man's movement also afforded the three an answer to Ming's query. When he turned to face the door to the cafeteria, the three were able see clearly an oval patch located on the upper right side of his chest. The name was inscribed using a cursive, ornate style *Frank* in thick black letters, all inclined to the right. Below the oval patch were six words embroidered in bright orange thread, Head Custodian: James Madison Elementary School.

"Hey," shot out Ming. "Isn't that—?"

"Shush!" charged Alexandra. "Do you want him to hear us?"

Ming grew suddenly annoyed and wondered if Alexandra understood how ridiculous her question was. He decided not to address it.

Satisfied that he was alone, the man pivoted back in the other direction. Once there, he reached over to his right and took hold of a long (nearly as tall as Alexandra) object wrapped in a light brown, well-used canvass tarp. The man cradled the item in his strong left arm and used his right hand to unwrap it, starting at the top, and working downward until it was nearly half-bare. His effort revealed a shiny metallic car bumper.

The three gathered that it was not too old or overused (aside from a flurry of pulverized bugs), with the exception of two unmistakable points of damage, which sent chills of terror up their spines. On the far right end of the bumper, along its bottom edge, there was a rough blackened area about two feet wide. Its coarse, chaotic character suggested that the bumper had been burned or scraped along something harder than itself for a considerable period of time. What they saw at the center of the bumper removed the last clinging vestiges of calm from their already-troubled minds.

The man denuded the bumper far enough to reveal a grand dent at the halfway point. So profound was the effect on the bumper it was not merely dented but in fact bent in two. Wrapped in the undulating canvass tarp, the three didn't notice the bend at first, but it was now unmistakable.

Not located in the exact center, or bearing a premeditated form, the dent and bend left the three with no doubt that whatever car this bumper belonged to must have run into something.

Lewis felt nauseous, but curiosity stayed his weakening legs.

The man ran his free hand down the side of the bumper, taking time to give the blackened edge and the dent special attention. Then he looked again over his shoulder and proceeded to rewrap the bumper. He cradled the long item and moved it over to a spot in one of the left side corners of the closet. After he had adjusted the bumper into such a position that made him confident of its stability, the man moved calmly over to the other side of the closet and took hold of three or four spare planks of wood. He leaned the planks over the bumper and then did the same with a desk, three chairs and various other items.

If someone had asked Lewis at this point if there was anything to which he might bear witness that would more thoroughly and profoundly have astounded him, he would have most certainly answered in the negative. He would have been wrong. Just as the man in the navy blue overalls had nearly completed his work of burying the bumper within the sundry planks of wood and old furniture, a soft pale light poured over his back and filled the room with a chilling glow. The apexes of the light's intensity and the shadows which it created left no doubt that the glimmer originated from somewhere on the right side of the closet, behind the man in the overalls.

At first he didn't notice, being wholly consumed in the task of concealing the bumper. However, once he stepped backward to survey the results of his efforts, the man saw the warm pallid lights crawl over his shoulders and form hazy shadows on the items he had arranged. He gave a committed revolution with his entire body and leaned in toward the light to investigate. As he did, it became increasingly clear to him that accessing the source of the glow would require moving a few items that sat before it.

Lewis and the others watched as the man removed a box, then another, then a small stool, another box, then a chair, and so on. With each obstruction that he removed, the light behind was less inhibited, casting an increasingly intense glow across the man's face, shoulders, and chest. Alexandra couldn't help but remember the recent experience upstairs in the janitor's closet after Jeremiah's attack. She recalled the warm purple light gleaming from the back wall, beckoning for, almost demanding, attention. The man in the overalls seemed to be having a similar experience.

"Hey, that's just like when—" started Ming.

"Shush!" shouted Lewis and Alexandra in unison. They both whipped their heads back in Ming's direction like lashes flagellated against a stubborn beast (and having the same effect).

When the three had turned their collective gaze back toward the man and his discovery, they saw an unabashed childlike grin split across his face as he reached out toward the source of the waxen glow. Because of the man's location in the closet in relation to the light, Lewis and the others were unable to see the object of his reach. Instinctively, the three edged slightly to the left to gain a more complete view.

The man took hold of an object no larger than his hand. Given the transfixing brightness of its light, the three assumed it must be a jewel of some sort—rare indeed! As the man brought his new treasure toward his chest, the air of his body became almost motherly, like an innocent child having discovered an injured bird in the park. He drew it close, cradling the item with tender care. With the item tucked so deeply in the man's protective arms, it failed to produce the same degree of light toward Lewis and the others. What's more, given their position, they were again unable to see precisely what the man was holding.

When they moved slightly forward, almost inside the closet, a deep sobering sense of disappointment invaded each of them. This was no rare jewel, no unearthed diamond; it was, rather, the most mundane of articles, a small canvas sack, fastened shut at the top by a short thick length of twine. Nevertheless, this simple item gave off the most incredible, spectacular white illumination and did so with increasing intensity as the man pulled it up even closer to his face. It seemed to offer the added glow in reaction to the man's interest and affection. His face reflected the radiant glow, nearly bereft of features in the consuming luminosity.

As the three expected (and in reality, hoped) the man proceeded to pinch the body of the canvas sack in the tension of his right hand fingers and employed the combined might and dexterity of his left hand fingers to loosen and detach the twine. At the end of a few pulls, twists, and agitations, the twine surrendered and became sufficiently loose as to be removed. Without an instant's hesitation, the man upended the sack with manic enthusiasm and dumped the contents into the cupped palm of his left hand.

"Seeds?" blurted out Lewis.

This time, it was Ming and Alexandra. "Shush!"

One might assume that the seeds, being removed from the confines of the canvas sack, would offer an even brighter light, painting the room with its warm glow, and piercing every hidden nook and cranny. Strangely, just the opposite happened. When the last seed descended from the sack's rough and rippled mouth, they ceased giving light altogether and seemed to become nothing more than any other diminutive pile of kernels, resting peacefully in the man's hand. The four friends were left in relative dark.

Then, dimly, almost unnoticeably, one seed gave a bashful glow. Another followed suit. Soon, every seed in the pile was glowing and then diminishing intermittently like a department store Christmas tree. The effect left the man mesmerized with interest, but not for long. When the alternating flashes emanating from the seeds reached a rapid but steady rhythm, tendrils of energy poured forth from the pile and began to crawl from the palm of his hand and then up his arm. The effect on the man was sudden and excruciatingly painful.

Still down in his knees as he had been to access the sack, the man tensed with every muscle in his body. His torso straightened, and he threw his shoulders back in reaction to the agony that coursed through his spine. The three clinched their teeth in near unison and drew in shallow hisses, almost suffering along with the man. The shock relented, and the pale white tendrils drew back into the pile of seeds.

Certain (or at least hoping) that the danger had abated, the man drew in a deep relaxing breath and took to his feet. As soon as he stood straight, a second shock emanated from the seeds, this time more powerful. The tendrils of energy shot out from his palm and popped up and down over his arm shoulder and nearly the entirety of his chest. This time it was more than he could handle.

The man gritted his teeth and pulled his arms into himself, making every effort to avoid unconsciousness. It was no use. His eyes closed, and in one fluid motion, his knees failed, his legs buckled, and the entirety of his body flopped helplessly to the floor. Falling in their general direction, he landed immediately in front of Lewis and the others. Left unconscious by the overwhelming shock, the man released his zealous grip on the seeds. The pile dumped from his palm and scattered in every direction before the children.

When the seeds scattered, Lewis and Ming standing in front instinctively stepped backward to avoid the seeds as they rolled and slid. So compelling was the imagery that the three had to remind themselves that what they were viewing was not real, at least not presently. When the entire collection of seeds came to a complete stop, a few of them took on a most disturbing change. A few in center of the scattered constellation began to glow in intermittent flashes as they had just a bit earlier.

Unlike the previous instance, however, these seeds glimmered with a purple light, now seeming to have taken on a hue, mixed with gray and red. The purple that had previously gleamed around the school classroom doors with a comforting purity now appeared corrupted, defiled. It was itself, yet impure. The spoiled purple hue reminded Lewis of used paint water. Ming looked at the seeds and recalled filthy snow just before the spring warmth, dirty and cold, struggling with all its might to remain while the whole world is waiting for its frozen corruption to melt.

One of the seeds that flashed its putrid version of purple then began to grow slowly but noticeably. It was Alexandra who discerned first that the change was much more than mere growth. When the seed was about the size of a baked potato, it started rolling back and forth under its own power, like someone on fire trying to extinguish the flames. As it rolled back and forth, small extensions grew from the sides of the seeds, two larger in the front and two in the back.

At the same time this was taking place, the other glowing seeds now began to grow as well, in the same manner as the first. The first seed progressed. The two larger extensions in the front curled outward, and upon reaching a certain length, produced five smaller extensions of their own. The two smaller extensions in back followed the same process.

"It looks like a bug or somethin'," offered Ming.

"Gross!" interjected Alexandra.

The changes continued. By now, all of the glowing seeds had ceased to glow; all were increasing in size, each at a different rate of speed, producing extensions similar to the initial seed. The first seed rolled over on its side one last time and seemed to wait for its extensions to fully mature. When they did, the end result became disturbingly clear to the group. The seed had taken on an almost human form, like a newborn infant. However, there was nothing tender or endearing about this creature. Its skin was not warm, pink, and smooth. Rather, it was wrinkled and coarse, almost like leather, with enflamed stripes of irritated tissue.

"Kick it!" demanded Alexandra, reacting with the fright that was starting to get the better of her.

"It's not really there," stated Lewis, keeping his eyes on the grotesque creature with an obsessive fixation.

All three of them watched with indivertible awe as the first creature's transformation continued. Its four extensions at top and bottom were now fully defined. The lower two extensions developed feet and toes; the upper two, hands and fingers. Then, even after the legs and feet had ceased growing, the hands and fingers continued, becoming monstrously large in relation to the feet. It appeared as if a fully grown man's hands had been affixed to a baby's wrists.

Within the duration of the creature's limb development, its body had matured as well. The original narrow shape of the seed widened to form a back, expanding in each dimension and filling with muscle. Its torso developed through a horrific harmony of muscle and bone, intertwining toward a menacingly large result. Not as surprising as the hands, but much more disturbing, was the creature's head. Rather than extending upward, the neck grew from the creature's torso in a horizontal direction moving outward from the body. Ultimately, the creature's head and face arched forward such that its head added nothing to its total height. The other seedlings followed in the exact same pattern.

When it appeared that the first creature's maturing had reached its end point, it rolled over onto its front. Lewis, Ming, and Alexandra were waiting for the monstrosity to roll backward onto its feet and stand. It didn't. Instead, the creature ignored its relatively useless feet all together, planted its mighty hands on the ground at its sides, and pushed up. The three took in a long awful breath.

So massive were the creature's arms and hands that, when fully erect, its legs and feet dangled freely in the air beneath its muscular torso. Alexandra looked closely at the creature's toes and suddenly reflected on Agnes as an infant. The creature's legs were, at least in size, somewhat reminiscent of an infant's. However, this creature's legs were grossly muscular, covered with rough wrinkled skin, and terminated with stubby toes, ornamented with sharp rot yellow nails.

Finally, all of the seeds finished their transformation and produced terrific, diminutive humanoids. Each one of them stood firmly on their hands, their smaller legs and feet dangling uselessly in unorganized, imperfect circles. Their stubby toes wiggled and squirmed like night crawlers at the bottom of a fisherman's cup. Then the lead creature offered a muffled grumble to the others and gestured with one foot toward the man in blue overalls. The lead creature shuffled on both hands over to the man in overalls. The stubby humanoid proceeded to take an action that, when completed, made his identity hauntingly clear.

Needing the dexterity only present in its hands, the lead creature lowered itself down gently to its smaller less stable feet and reached out toward the man. With brutal disregard for the man's well-being, the creature yanked at the man's left-arm shirt sleeve and wrapped it around his own diminutive body. It continued in this manner until it had managed to create a suit of makeshift clothing.

The creature then gestured once again toward the others, leading them over to do the same for themselves. As the others ambled near, the lead creature tore one final piece from the man's clothing and wrapped it around his head. The piece was sufficiently large as to not merely cover its head, but rather to enshroud its entire head and face.

All of the creatures, fully suited and shrouded, leaned proudly back on their hands and kicked their feet into the air with bold playful enthusiasm. As they did, the entire group bellowed out one cacophonous "raugh!" in malevolent harmony. Their vile revolting tone sent shivers running up and down the three friends' collective backs. The tone was an obnoxious combination of a dog's bark, a child singing off-key, and the sound of a thick pile of dinner scraps being chewed up in the kitchen garbage disposal.

Alexandra covered her ears.

Quietly, passively, the man in the now-shredded navy blue overalls vanished. The remaining seeds, scattered all over the floor did the same. Then, in midscream, one by one, the creatures all disappeared. To vanish cut their shrieking short, leaving a haunting echo hanging in the air, like a hungry carrion bird searching for a place to land.

21

Haven't I Seen You Somewhere Before?

A thick palpable silence hung in the air. The lack of sound seemed almost like the air pressure in a balloon not merely filling it but also pressing outward. So it did with the four friends. For a period that seemed quite a bit longer than reality, the four remained entirely speechless, allowing all that they had just witnessed to sink in, to take its toll. The door to the closet hung open; everything inside it was just as they had found it before the images began. Presently, there was no longer any evidence of the imagery, save the clear indelible memories etched in their brains.

"Those things that grew from the seeds were the grossest, nastiest things I have ever seen!" asserted Alexandra, supporting her words with enthusiastic and expressive body language.

"Yeah, they were pretty nasty!" agreed Ming.

"But they kinda' filled in the gaps, don't you think?" asked Lewis.

"What do you mean?" asked Alexandra.

"Did you notice what they did with that man's clothes, the way they took strips of it, and formed them into hoods? Doesn't that remind you of anything?"

"Sure," affirmed Ming. "I think they are like baby versions of those weirdos we saw in the gymnasium, like those we saw out in the parking lot with Mrs. LaGrange."

"Right!" acknowledged Lewis.

"But what do they have to do with that guy in the blue work clothes?" asked Alexandra.

"Well, remember where they came from," Lewis directed. "They grew from the seeds that were in the man's hand."

"Do you think the man put the seeds down here?" asked Ming.

"No, I don't think so," answered Alexandra. "He looked genuinely surprised when he discovered them."

"How did the seeds even get there?" asked Ming.

"I don't have the foggiest," admitted Lewis. "I think the more important question is why did they give the man a shock?"

"I think the more important question is who is the man?" asserted Alexandra.

"That one's easy," said Lewis, soberly.

"How so? I don't get it," said Alexandra with a small but noticeable tone of annoyance that Lewis, being younger, would discern something before her.

"That was the man that ran down my dad," said Lewis stolidly. After annunciating this simple sentence, there was a repressive silence, almost as if it would have been wrong to speak too soon after such a dramatic and startling revelation.

Lewis looked at their faces and saw the mixture of disbelief and confusion. "Yeah, think about it," he mandated. "Think about what we found. First, there was the letter in Mr. Cohen's office punishing Mr. Jenski for coming into work drunk."

"Sure, but what—?" started Ming.

"What was his first name?" interrupted Lewis, using a tone that suggested he already had the answer.

"Franklin!" dropped in Alexandra.

"So the guy we just saw in the closet," began Lewis. "He was wearing janitor clothes. Do you remember the name on his little round patch?"

"Frank!" dropped in Ming, smiling with a bit of pride.

"Then, later, we found an empty liquor bottle in the janitor's closet when Aggie and I locked ourselves in there," added Alexandra.

"And it tucked into the wall like someone was trying to hide it!" stated Ming with growing excitement.

Presently, Alexandra's expression grew soft and sympathetic. Her eyes seemed to become rounder, more vulnerable. She stepped slowly but decidedly toward Lewis. "Then, in the other classroom, we saw your father get hit by a car, and the car was out of control, speeding and swerving back and forth." She reached out and tenderly placed her supple palm on Lewis's cheek. It was warm, and Alexandra wondered if tears were to follow.

"The bumper!" interjected Ming, marveling at his own ingenuity. "The car that hit your dad was dragging a bumper! There were sparks coming off it because it was scraping on the ground." Ming said nothing further. He simply glanced over into the closet, remembering how Mr. Jenski had tried to bury the bumper, to hide the evidence of what he had done.

"I am so sorry," consoled Alexandra, embracing Lewis. Agnes walked over and did the same.

"Whatever happened to Mr. Jenski?" asked Ming. "Did anyone ever find out what he did? Did he ever get arrested?"

"Not that I know of," answered Lewis, pulling away from Alexandra and Agnes. "My grandma just told me that my dad was killed in an auto accident. I don't think they ever found out that Mr. Jenski was the one that did it."

"As far as where he is today," started Alexandra. "I don't know, but I would guess that he either got fired or quit. He hasn't been around for a long time, and good riddance!"

Then there was brief pause in the conversation. It seemed as though all four of them needed a minute to process. Ming was the first to start again.

"I wonder," said Ming, sporting an inquisitive expression, and looking directly into the closet.

"What?" asked Lewis.

"Don't you want to know?" asked Ming.

"Know what?" asked Alexandra.

"Well, if the bumper is still here, of course," responded Ming.

Neither Lewis nor Alexandra had thought of it yet, but as soon as Ming invoked the question, it began to peak their curiosity. Ming charged into the closet without hesitation and started displacing the boxes, chairs, and boards that filled the room, the same items in fact, which Mr. Jenski had placed there years before. Alexandra and Lewis reflected on how odd it was to see Ming unstacking the sundry items. It was spookily reminiscent of what they had witnessed in the imagery just moments before.

Before long, Ming reached the back corner of the closet. Sure enough, beneath the boards, chairs, and boxes was a long, narrow piece that appeared to be the bumper. Ming grabbed it and began to remove the tarp in the same fashion as had Mr. Jenski. The canvas tarp almost fell from the bumper, flimsy and affected as it was by the passing years. Ming's rabid curiosity and subsequent efforts revealed what they had all suspected. He turned around and gave the other three a solemn look.

"Well, at least we know it really happened," he said.

"And if the bumper is real, then that means that those stumpy beasts are real too!" asserted Alexandra, giving a tremulous shrug from her shoulders. "Those things are the creepiest things I've ever seen!"

"Well, maybe not the creepiest," croaked a hauntingly familiar voice. The voice was deep, mockingly calm, and almost certainly within the room.

The four of them jumped with fright. Then, barely able to swivel their necks on account of a sudden stiffness of muscle and tension of bone, they all turned around. There, standing in the doorway, blocking the only exit from the larger room, was Wyatt, wearing a cruel grotesque smile, and glaring at the four friends with his humid bulging eyes. Both ocular globes pulsated and throbbed as he pulled his vile grin out to the corners of his face.

"No, not the creepiest." said Wyatt.

22

I've Got More Than My Fists

Lewis and his friends were struck numb and motionless with fear. Wyatt stood as a relentless sentinel statue, blocking the only exit from the room. They knew he had no intention of allowing them to leave. An impenetrable black terror gripped each of the four as they took in the reality of Wyatt's presence, his round pulsating eyes—seeming to have a consciousness of their own—almost breathing with impish delight. His darkly glad smile peeled away from his teeth, putting forth an expression that was at once satisfaction, delight, and avarice.

"We don't want any trouble with you," offered Ming confidently, and at the same time trying not to provoke Wyatt.

"Oh, but I want trouble with you," responded Wyatt, allowing a throaty rattle to trail from his voice. It was clear that he sensed their fear, and he savored every ounce of it.

Wyatt took a step forward sharply, intending to intimidate the group. It worked. The four took another jump, even Agnes this time. So close was Wyatt to his prey that the four could see the thin shiny coat of liquid gleam off the surface of Wyatt's eyes, working desperately to keep the enlarged organs moist and lubricated. Additionally, his smile had so fully retracted his lips that his teeth were evident. One could even obtain a clear sense of the shape, size, and texture of each tooth in the front of his mouth, smooth white in some places and decaying yellow in others, decorated with the remnants of Wyatt's last meal.

"Y' see," Wyatt started, "I got no idea how I got this way, with my eyes pokin' out, and my head all big. But I had somethin', somethin' in my hands that woulduh' made it all better. That was all I wanted, and you took it from me. She took it from me!" Wyatt pointed directly at Agnes, and his cruelly wry smile morphed into a scary expression of disgust and hate. "I had it. I had it in my hands!"

Instinctively, Alexandra stepped in front of Agnes, throwing her arms backward to protect her. Alexandra was consumed in her duty to shelter Agnes, and therefore had nothing but cold contempt for one who would dare to injure her beloved sister. Ming had stepped forward into a role of conciliation, hoping that somehow his cool self-assured voice could prevent a confrontation, or at least delay it.

Lewis, for his part, was free to experience the emotions of the moment. Without a doubt there was fear; he had seen Wyatt's obsessive rage and its violent results against Dylan. He knew that he—even he and Ming—could not offer any real resistance to Wyatt, at least, no real chance of overcoming him.

At the same time, in the safer places of his heart, the places that Imelda had nurtured—nurtured against the loss of his father and mother, nurtured with hugs, soft words, and warm support, nurtured with comforting bowls of lemon pudding—Lewis felt compassion. Neither Lewis nor his friends had invited or caused the snowstorm, the rapscallion creatures, or any of the other aspects of their current mysterious situation, but neither had Wyatt. And to the extent that Wyatt was passive in these affairs, Lewis was sympathetic. He hurt *with* Wyatt.

Belying his tender age, Lewis guessed that deep in the recesses of Wyatt's heart and mind, buried under the rage, frustration, and vengeful motives, Wyatt was afraid and despondent, thoroughly confused with regards to how his head and eyes came to change size, and if any of this would ever end. While Lewis feared Wyatt, even more so now that before, he hurt for him and wished away his turmoil.

Ming dug deep for courage. "Look, Wyatt, why don't just leave us alone," he began. "We don't know what's going on around here anymore than you do. This is a big school, and there is plenty of space for all of us. We can just leave each other alone and wait until help comes."

"I don't think so, Ming," replied Wyatt, not giving his idea an instant's reflection. "I've never been too patient.

There's something here that I want. I'm going to have it. That's all that matters."

"Lexie," whispered Agnes with a shaky voice as she pulled herself close to her sister. "Don't let him get me."

"He's not going to get you, Agnes." Alexandra said assertively. "I won't let him."

"Oh, I am going to get her," stated Wyatt, "and anyone who gets between me and her."

Wyatt took another impatient step forward. The four moved back from him quickly. It appeared as if Wyatt had pushed them back himself. "Not so proud now are you, little girl? Huh? Where are your lights and sparks now?" Wyatt asked with a vengeful sneer.

It occurred to Ming. "Yeah, where is that now, Agnes?" he said. "Why can't you just blast him like you did before?" Ming turned his head slightly as he addressed Agnes, trying to keep Wyatt's approach in peripheral view.

Agnes didn't respond.

"Ming, leave her alone!" Alexandra blasted.

"No," replied Ming. "Not too long ago, she blasted Wyatt out of the universe! It would be really nice if she could do that again! What do you think, Lewis?"

"Yes, that would be my vote," answered Lewis with a tremulous vote.

Wyatt took another step forward, broadening his grin as he sensed their group's increased anxiety.

"I can't do it anymore," stated Agnes in a simple unassuming voice.

"What do you mean you can't do it anymore?" asked Ming sharply. "This is not a good time to take a break. We need heat! Let the heat fly!"

"I could do that before, but I can't now," said Agnes, trying to appease Ming the best she could, although honestly, Ming's disappointment was not her greatest concern.

Wyatt took another step forward. His grin wanted to grow, but it had reached its malevolent limit. "Hi, Agnes," said Wyatt with a repugnantly false sweetness. He offered her a small wave, like a kind old woman waving to her friend through a patio window.

The four took another step backward to offset Wyatt's advancement, but that was the last step they could take, and they knew it. Lewis and Ming had nearly reached the back wall of the small room, and Alexandra and Agnes were already there. In fact, Agnes gave a minor start as her tiny back came into contact with the cold, coarse cinder block wall.

"Last chance, sweeties," offered Wyatt. "Give up the little sister."

"You will not touch my sister, Wyatt," stated Alexandra.

With that, Wyatt arched his arms up and leaned his head back like a cat poised to pounce. They all knew what was coming. They could see it clearly in Wyatt's eyes even before he wound up. Agnes closed her eyes and ducked behind Alexandra. Ming was lost and out of options. Alexandra steeled herself in anticipation of Wyatt's charge and in defense of her cherished junior sibling. However, it was Lewis, and only Lewis, who stepped forward to prevent Wyatt's assault, and in a most unexpected way.

"Wyatt?" put in Lewis, in a voice calm but slightly elevated to gain Wyatt's attention and to break his momentum.

"What is it, jerk?" asked Wyatt, still carrying his arms high in the air.

"What if you do get Agnes," asked Lewis evenly. "What then?"

"I will get her!" asserted Wyatt.

"Okay," Lewis conceded. "What then?"

"What do you mean what then?" inquired Wyatt, beginning to lose interest in this delay.

"Well," started Lewis, "Agnes isn't what you wanted. You wanted to *be* Dylan, remember? And when Agnes is gone, you still won't be Dylan."

At this, Wyatt lowered his arms and gave Lewis his entire attention more than Imelda Warner's grandson ever wanted. It became clear that Lewis had hit a nerve, a live wire, something in Wyatt's mind and heart that turned him away from his quarry. This was Lewis's plan.

"Just what are trying to say, squirt?" asked Wyatt in his now familiar bully tone, a tone that reminded both Lewis and Ming of their confrontation in the boy's bathroom.

"Don't you remember?" asked Lewis. "In the hallway, 'I want your eyes, your face,' you kept saying to Dylan." In restating Wyatt's speech, Lewis did not dare attempt to mimic his tone.

"Yeah. So?" dug Wyatt.

"You wanted to be Dylan," stated Lewis. "In fact, I think you actually said that. But Dylan's gone now. Whatever might happen to Agnes, you can now never be Dylan. He's gone."

Hearing these words—the description of a reality of which he was already fully aware—Wyatt dropped his arms completely in submission and emotional destitution. He literally shrunk in stature, now hunched over under the onerous weight of Lewis's cutting revelation. Wyatt stared deeply at Lewis, like a child pining for the approval of a dismissive parent. Consumed in Lewis's speech, Wyatt almost entirely disengaged from the others.

"It makes perfect sense to me," continued Lewis. His voice took an almost contemptuous tone. "I can understand why you would want to *be* Dylan. I mean, he was always the leader. Why wouldn't he have been the one in charge? He was the strongest, the most confident, and the most intelligent."

"But I am smart too!" exclaimed Wyatt.

"Sure, sure, Wyatt," patronized Lewis. "I am sure you are, but not like Dylan. He always had the meanest cracks. No one could be cruel like Dylan. I mean, when you three would bully the rest of us in the bathroom. You and Jeremiah annoyed us, but Dylan was the one we were really afraid of."

"No!" spat out Wyatt. "You were afraid of me too!"

"Not really," replied Lewis. "You can think that if you want, but Dylan terrified us. I used to have nightmares! Whoa, that Dylan, he sure had it all. Brains, strength, confidence, good looks. He was the perfect bully!"

Initially, Ming and girls were confused by Lewis's actions. The more they listened, however, the more they understood his tactic. Lewis was working to distract Wyatt from Agnes. And, at least for the time being, it was working. Wyatt had not given the other three a glance since Lewis started speaking to him. The immediate danger had abated. However, there was still no clear means of escape. Lewis and Wyatt were nearest the door, the only door. There was no way the others could evacuate the room without drawing Wyatt's attention.

"Wait!" demanded Wyatt. "You take that back! I am just as good a bully as Dylan was!" The statement marked a slight but undeniable change in Wyatt's emotional state. He was no longer merely forlorn and broken. Driven by jealously, he had not taken his first step out of dejection and toward destructive rage.

"No," asserted Lewis. "You might be better than Jeremiah. Perhaps with more time, you could have been close to Dylan, but now we'll never know. I guess you'll always be second best."

"Shut your mouth, Lewis," mandated Wyatt, heating up with anger and curling his fingers into fists.

During the conversation, Ming had kept his eyes on Lewis, waiting for some sign, some glance or wink to indicate the next step in the strategy. It came. Squelching his ever-increasing fear of Wyatt's wrath, Lewis calmly offered a furtive glance to Ming. Ming got the message. Ever so slowly, Ming turned in place and reached out to Alexandra. He took her hand and moved just a single step toward the door, watching Wyatt like a hawk for any sign that he had noticed their attempt to escape. All three took a second brave step.

Lewis kept the rattling jibes coming in order to retain Wyatt's attention. "Yeah, even though Dylan is gone, you'll never be more than just his shadow. He had the strength and the confidence. But don't worry, Wyatt, you've definitely got the eyes."

"That's it!" howled Wyatt. "You are done!"

"Go, Ming!" cried Lewis.

"Huh!" growled Wyatt.

Ming and the girls tore off for the door, doing their utmost in the process to avoid coming close to Wyatt. In utter stupefaction, Wyatt turned at his torso to follow the three as they ran behind him. His arms were already in the air against Lewis. Ming and the girls were moving quickly, but Lewis could tell that there was still a chance for Wyatt to reach them. He also sensed that there were no more jibes that would prevent Wyatt from pursuing the others. Lewis tensed his muscles and squatted down slightly. He pictured the football players he had seen on television, especially the one in the center that hikes the ball to the quarterback. He allowed this image to take charge of his body in order to prepare for action.

Like a cat, Lewis sprang up and slightly forward to catch Wyatt precisely at his midsection. It worked. With his attention on Ming and the girls, and his body askew at the waist, Wyatt was caught off-guard and wholly unprepared for Lewis's tackle. Lewis plowed into Wyatt with all the force his body would offer, and he wrapped his arms tightly around Wyatt's waist, locking them immovably with his hands. The force of Lewis's tackle knocked Wyatt squarely off his feet, and the two of them went crashing into a row of portable storage boxes towered up against the wall.

Ming and the girls stopped immediately to see to Lewis. When Wyatt realized that he had been fooled, he growled with volcanic rage and didn't waste an instant in working to free himself from Lewis's grapple. Lewis closed his eyes and tightened his grip on Wyatt's waist.

"Ming, get the girls out of here!" Lewis mandated.

"No way, Lewis!" replied Ming. "We're not leaving without you!"

Wyatt pulled against from Lewis, keeping his feverish eyes on the other three, Agnes in particular. Lewis redoubled his efforts to keep a tight hold at Wyatt's waist.

Wyatt moved his hands down to Lewis's hands and began working at the fingers in an attempt to split the vicelike grip and get free. Lewis wouldn't be overcome. Wyatt bellowed in feral anger, whipping his arms out to the sides chaotically and bashing the floor with his fists.

"Ming, get going!" shouted Lewis.

"I can't leave, Lewis," Ming replied. "We can't leave you here alone."

"I've got him!" exclaimed Lewis. "Now go!"

"You've got nothing!" growled Wyatt.

Wyatt made another attempt at Lewis's interlocked hands. It was no use. Something in Lewis's mind and heart, more than his middle-school arms gave him all the strength he needed to retain his hold on Wyatt. Wyatt produced a frustrated gargle and returned to bashing the floor with his fists. Something unusually powerful came over Wyatt as well. Incredibly, despite his inability to release Lewis's arms, Wyatt's fists began to produce cracks in the tile floor. The blows continued to flow and those cracks quickly developed into fist-sized craters.

"Lewis," begged Ming. "Please, let me help you!"

"No way, Ming," asserted Lewis. "I've got him. I'll be right behind you. We gotta take care of the girls!"

Lewis squeezed harder. Wyatt increased his flailing such that he looked like a toddler in the middle of a tantrum. His fists continued to impact the floor, creating more cracks and craters in the tile around the two of them so that they looked like a snow angel with shattered floor tiles for wings. Lewis could feel the wrathful heat coming from Wyatt's body as he grew more and more angry. The blows kept coming. With the added rage came increased results. Wyatt's next few blows sent harrowing vibrations through the floor underneath Ming and the girls' feet, and caused everything loose in the room to rattle: the window, the light fixtures, the shards of broken tile.

"Let's go!" demanded Alexandra for the first time. She didn't know what else to do. She was torn between a basic desire to save her sister above all else and the realization that Lewis could not possibly resolve the situation with Wyatt to a positive conclusion. Seeing that Lewis was immovable in his conviction to remain and resist Wyatt, Alexandra made the only choice she could.

Wyatt continued to pound. The next two blows not only sent waves of destabilizing vibrations through the entire room, such that Ming and the girls had to brace themselves to avoid falling, they also produced two splintering cracks in the very floor, one extending from each of Wyatt's fists as they landed. Still, Lewis held on.

Impressed with his own incredible and increasing might, Wyatt tried one final time to release Lewis's stalwart grip around his waist. It was no use. If rage and frustration were affording Wyatt unnatural strength, something was doing the same for Lewis. Lewis cared for his friends, and so he wondered if that alone was providing his brawny powers against Wyatt. Perhaps it was pure protective passion, or perhaps something else.

Despite Lewis's unbreakable hold, Wyatt's new might was such that he was able to get to his feet. Lewis, locked irresistibly around Wyatt's waist, hung like a needy child on its mother. Wyatt scanned the cracks his fierce blows had produced and gave a smile of wicked delight. He wanted more. Maybe he couldn't release Lewis, but his anger would have its ventilation. Wyatt raised both fists in the air and stepped broadly over to the wall. He brought both fists down against the wall with brawny force. The blow created a deep crater, which nearly breached the wall. What's more, the impact generated a thin fissure in the wall that reached floor to ceiling.

Still, Lewis held on.

Lewis was in no position to stop Wyatt; he was merely holding on to him. At the same time, his strategy was producing its intended result: Wyatt had lost interest in Agnes and was wholly consumed in his furious tantrum. Lewis had no idea what he would do when Wyatt finally fell down exhausted, but at least he wasn't threatening Agnes.

The next minute brought Ming to the toughest decision of his young life, one on which he would dwell for the rest of his life. Wyatt examined the impressive cracks his wallops had left on the wall and was left transfixed. He set about to demolish the rest of the room. Wyatt flailed against the other wall, this time leaving similar craters and fissures and causing a set of mounted shelves to fall, helplessly crashing to the floor. Ming saw that neither Wyatt nor Lewis would relent. He didn't know what would happen next, but he was sure that he and the girls would be safer outside the room. With a fearful and heavy heart, Ming led the girls to the door and ushered them out. Ming remained at the doorway, watching.

Wyatt's chaotic flailing continued, and each blow seemed more powerful than the last. His infuriated might had left cracks and craters on every surface of the walls and floor, and now, for the first time, the ceiling. Wyatt then left the walls, bruised and beaten as they were, in search for some pristine surface to assault. He walked to the center of the room, Lewis still relentlessly in tow, and settled upon a section of tile he had yet to damage. The first impact of his fists left a predictable crater in the floor. A second blast caused three ceiling tiles to drop, and another two were left dangling.

"This is awesome!" cried Wyatt.

The next set of blows dropped the dangling tiles and brought down the heating duct, suspended above the room. Wyatt smiled with fevered delight and caught a glimpsed of Ming, still standing vigilantly. "Hang on just a minute, Ming," the bestial villain exclaimed. "I'll be right there."

Lewis opened his eyes long enough to see the new danger. He saw the fallen ceiling tiles, the collapsed ductwork, the fissures in the walls, and realized that Wyatt might, intentionally or otherwise, bring the room down on top of them. However, he couldn't have the alternative. He wouldn't release Wyatt to pursue Agnes.

"Not bad, Wyatt!" started Lewis with a patronizing tone.

"Quiet you!" replied Wyatt.

"No, I mean it," added Lewis. "I'm impressed! Dylan would be so proud. What you've done to this room is almost as good as he would have done. Keep trying, Wyatt. I know you can do it! I believe in you!"

The mocking praise sent Wyatt over the edge, and that was exactly Lewis's intent. Wyatt didn't even respond verbally. Maintaining his position, Wyatt began to beat the floor mercilessly one fist at a time. Right, left, right, left, he pounded. The last remaining ceiling tiles fell to the floor. Then the entirety of the ductwork fell as well with a thunderous crash. Wyatt's fury was filling the room with fallen objects, a few of which had come close to hitting both Wyatt and Lewis. Outside the room, in the cafeteria, even Agnes and Alexandra witnessed the effect of Wyatt's destructive ire. Cracks came from under the walls and separated the tiles beneath their feet. A few of the ceiling tiles above them threatened to fall as well.

Lewis knew what was coming. There were no illusions. He renewed the strength of his hold on Wyatt's waist and ducked his head into his back in an effort to protect himself from falling objects. Another series of Wyatt's monstrous wallops to the floor dropped part of the wooden framing above down onto Wyatt's head and back. He ignored it, knocking the boards away with disdain. Lewis saw the boards fly and looked up. Certainly, the wood framing would soon fall, perhaps even the floor above. He wondered if Wyatt's rampage would ever stop. *Will he ever get tired?* Lewis thought.

Then Lewis looked over at his friend. Ming saw Lewis's eyes. No words were needed. Ming gave a difficult swallow, giving in to the feeling that accompanied the reality he now understood. It was heavy and dark, all-consuming and relentless. The emotion led Ming to recall the sadness of losing the family's cat, coming to that realization that it was over, there would be no recovery. It was a bit like holding a half-opened birthday present and realizing that you hadn't received what you wanted. It was like watching the sun go down on the last day of summer vacation.

What Ming felt as he looked at Lewis for the last time was like all of these rolled together. He hated the feeling, the reality. He hated it mostly because he could do nothing to change it. He just had to accept it. There were no tears, but plenty of heated eyes, furrowed brows, and the intense tingling that accompany an anxious mind.

Ming gave Lewis one last look, turned, and ran out toward the girls.

"No!" growled Wyatt as he watched Ming run out after the girls. "I am going to get her!" He stopped pounding on the floor and pulled away from Lewis toward the door.

"Where are you going?" asked Lewis refocusing his attention on Wyatt. "You're not done with the walls, the ceiling! Oh, I understand. Not only are you weaker and slower than Dylan. You're also a quitter. I guess that makes sense. Dylan wasn't a quitter."

"That's it!" howled Wyatt. "Enough!"

Just as Lewis planned, Wyatt's rage skyrocketed again. More importantly, his focus shifted from harming Agnes and returned to convincing Lewis (and the rest of the world) that he wouldn't stand in Dylan's shadow. He returned to bashing the floor.

"Where's Lewis?" asked Alexandra out in the hallway.

"He's still in there," answered Ming, offering the first thing that came into his overtaxed brain.

"I know he's still in there, Ming," rejoined Alexandra with a sarcastic tone. "What's he doing in there? What's happening with Wyatt?"

"Alexandra, he's holding Wyatt back. There's nothing we can do!" said Ming, stepping just slightly in front of Alexandra.

"Maybe there's nothing you can do, Ming," returned Alexandra. "We can't leave him alone in there!"

With that, Alexandra swatted Ming away and stepped toward the door, leading back into the room. She was stopped short suddenly as the door slammed shut. Alexandra reacted with a start. From the cafeteria's side, it was difficult for the three to discern the cause of the closure, but they could guess. Just prior to the door's slam, there was a loud crash from above, and something heavy impacted against the door from the inside. When Alexandra recovered her wits, she braced herself and tried forcing the door open. It wouldn't budge. Ming stepped in next to her to offer his strength. Nothing.

Inside, Lewis was acutely aware of why the door closed. More of the ceiling fell, and a couple of heavier beams crashed onerously against the light hollow door and wedged it closed. There would be no opening the door from the cafeteria's side or from Lewis's side without first moving the beams.

Seeing the beams fall against the door afforded Lewis new assurance that it was just a matter of time, just a matter of blows, really. And so it was. Wyatt's mighty fists came down once, then a second time, then finally a third. The first two started a series of loud creeks, which served as the sentinel of things to come. Wyatt paid the creeks no attention. He was consumed fully in the thrill of giving vent to his rage and laying waste to the room.

Lewis, however, was fully aware of the ceiling's moans and complaints. He was mindful of what they foretold. He gave Wyatt one last unbreakable squeeze. He thought about his new friends and hoped that his efforts would save them. He hoped that they might find a way to safety. He thought about his beloved grandma, Imelda. He thought about bowls of lemon pudding, cold snowy days together, and her hugs. Finally, before it all came down, Lewis thought about his dad. Mentally and emotionally, he was at the park with the balloons, the crowds. It was the speeding car, his mother screaming, and again, his dad.

Lewis made his decision.

Then it all came down. A few lighter pieces struck Lewis in the legs and one in the arm. Finally, one of the heavier beams fell squarely on the top of his head. He immediately released his hold on Wyatt and fell to the ground. There was a brief pause before the pain set it. His head throbbed. Boards, beams, and plaster continued to fall. Wyatt was able to protect himself for a short time, but finally, he fell too. Lewis was tuned into Wyatt as his vision gradually surrendered to darkness.

The darkness came to Lewis in two waves. First, the boards and beams were so numerous that they eventually covered Lewis, buried him really. He lay motionless under the rubble, pinned down under metal, wood, and plaster. Then the darkness came in its second wave. The blow Lewis had sustained offered him only a brief period of remaining consciousness. The time now was up. After his eyes went completely dark, his ears took in another two or three seconds. Lewis lay helplessly under the weight of the rubble, hearing the last few boards fall. Wyatt bid a spiteful final groan. Lewis heard the walls and the ceiling release their final dropping and offer their final cracks, whines, and creeks.

And then...

Silence.

23

Hellos and Good-byes

The symphony of thunderous crashes, which buried Wyatt and Lewis, sent Ming and the girls into a terrifically agitated state. They each gave their own rendition of a startled yelp, yanking their shoulders inward with fright. The concern they shared, which was previously focused mainly on Wyatt's malicious intentions and the falling ceiling structures, shifted decidedly in favor of the latter. Whatever fell from the ceiling and produced such a harrowing racket must surely have spelled the end for Wyatt just as much as Lewis. The immediate threat was over.

Coming to his senses, Ming pulled his arm in like a running back cradling a football and threw his entire body weight incautiously. "He's in there! He's in there and probably hurt. We have to get him out!" he shouted.

Alexandra didn't hesitate and added her efforts to Ming's working to synchronize her impacts with his for maximum effectiveness. It required few blows to get into a perfect, united rhythm. At about the third effort, Agnes joined in as well. However, given her size and the dearth of door area, Agnes succeeded merely in plowing into Alexandra's legs.

"C'mon!" cried Ming. "He could really be hurt badly!"

The three thumped against the door, but it was no use. Where previously their heroic efforts against the door had at least caused it to shake and rattle, their combined strength could not even budge the door, and it produced only a thick dull thud in reaction to their shoulder-driven assaults.

"Stop, Ming," mandated Alexandra. She pulled away from the door and began to rub her shoulder tenderly. "It's no use. That door is not going to move."

Given that Alexandra stepped out of the way without telling her sister, Agnes plowed with full force into Ming's body, bouncing off and tumbling to the side. She gave a startled grunt, stumbled, and finally regained her feet.

"We have to get in there!" shouted Ming with a dejected breathy voice. His face offered an expression that comingled sad frustration and frantic anger. He didn't know whether to cry or scream. He chose neither. After giving the door one more spiteful blast, he conceded its superior strength and relented.

"Whatever is behind that door, it's not movin'," exclaimed Agnes.

Alexandra stepped up assertively and started rapping aggressively against the door. "Lewis! Lewis! Can you hear me, Lewis?" she asked.

Alexandra stopped, waiting for an answer. There was nothing but vacuous silence. She tried again.

"Lewis! Say something. Yell out so that we know you are okay!" she demanded. She cracked her knuckles against the wood soundly. Still there was nothing. Alexandra stopped, leaned her head back, and exhaled emphatically. She dropped her knocking hand to her side like the other.

Before either Ming or Alexandra could continue, Agnes stepped up. She shuffled to the door fleetly and gave it a series of slightly softer, but no less passionate, raps. "Lewis," she said. "C'mon, you have to say something!" Hearing nothing in response, Agnes pulled her tiny fist backward to knock again. Before her knuckle hit the door again, three solid thumbs sounded softly but clearly.

Ming placed his ear to the door. "Lewis?" he started with a renewed vigor. "Is that you? Keep knocking! We can hear you!"

Similar thumps came again. This time there were four.

Alexandra pulled away from the door with a puzzled expression. "I don't think those knocks are coming from in there," she said.

"Of course they are, Alexandra," stated Ming with a hint of annoyance. "That's Lewis!"

"No, I don't think so," affirmed Alexandra. "Listen."

The three waited in total silence just briefly before another volley of thumps reverberated through the air. When they did, Alexandra turned her face rapidly toward Ming. She said nothing, but her expression seemed to further assert her idea and also ask Ming's opinion at the same time. Alexandra's inquisitive stare had the desired effect. Ming paused for an instant, then nodded.

"Wul, if it's not Lewis, where is it coming from?" asked Ming.

"I think from in there," answered Agnes, pointing toward the double doors just to their right.

The three were listening intently now, listening to locate the source.

Three more thuds sounded.

Without hesitation, the three darted to the double doors and bashed them open like the three strongest players on a football team's defensive line, plowing through the opposition and toward the quarterback. The doors swung open rapidly, knocking noisily against the walls on the other side. They shot up the short flight of stairs and reached another set of doors. These were larger, thicker doors, main doors, doors to the outside!

Just as Agnes's relatively shorter legs had carried her successful to the top, another series of thuds sounded, this time louder and more defined, confirming that they had reached the right place. Instinctively, Ming returned the thuds, which clearly were coming from the other side of the left center door, with three knocks of his own.

"Hey!" Ming shouted. "Is anybody out there?"

Alexandra grimaced at the silliness of such a question, but under the circumstances, she chose not to address it.

"Yes," answered an unfamiliar male voice. "This is Officer Lawrence of the county sheriff's department. Is anyone hurt in there?"

Ming didn't know how to answer. He looked at the girls for help. They were fine, but what about Lewis? "I don't know," answered Ming. It was the best he could think of, and it was honest, at least.

"Well, I'm gonna' need you to push on the door from that side," stated the officer. "We dug out the snow, but we don't have a key of the building, and Mr. Cohen isn't here yet."

Agnes lit up with relief and joyful expectation. Alexandra was suddenly lost in thought. *Dug out the snow*, she mused. She remembered that the snow outside had packed all the way up to the windows on the second floor, at least on the other side of the school. There was no way they could reach the door without digging first. She wondered if perhaps the snow had drifted higher on the other side.

Ming's arms snapped out forward, and he gripped the ice-cold crash bar that hung across the door. He ignored the skin-numbing sensation and pushed against the door with all his anticipating, youthful might. The crash bar gave a metallic whine and surrendered, allowing the lock to release. Opening the door required just a bit more effort from Ming than normal, given that ice had formed on the outside of the door, indicated by intermittent cracks and breaks that sounded as the door finally gave way.

It was an overwhelming experience, and each one of Ming's senses participated. The timid winter sun had set, replaced by the detached mechanical illumination of the street lamps. Nonetheless, it was light, beautiful light. The lamps pressed hopeful beams though the gloom of the chilly night. Along with it, a bitter cold wind weaved its way through the opening and wrapped its frosty tendrils around all three of them, sending arctic chills to the marrow of their bones, and leaving each of them with a mighty case of goose bumps. However, the wintry wind was a welcome intruder. The cold air meant the door was open, and the open door meant help.

Alexandra closed her eyes and let her mind relax in the atmosphere of salvation and safety. Agnes stepped over to Alexandra and embraced her sister at the waist. Alexandra returned the squeeze, holding her close. Ming saw Officer Lawrence and smiled. Two other officers stood behind Officer Lawrence, one to the right and the left. One smiled back at Ming, the other gave a reserved wave. Behind them stood a cadre of unidentified men, about six of them from what Ming could see. Each of them was bundled tightly in winter wear and brandished a shovel.

Ming had so many things to tell the officers. The officers had a million questions. But all that would have to wait. Ming moved toward Officer Lawrence. Daryl Lawrence knew what to do. He opened his arms just before Ming reached him. Ming landed against his cold, snowy standard-issue, sheriff's winter coat. Daryl Lawrence pushed all his questions to the waiting room in his mind and wrapped his strong arms around Ming. Ming's cheek chaffed against the rough icy material of Daryl Lawrence's coat. He didn't mind.

Ming released a few tears, but just a few.

24

New Friends at the Lunch Table

Friday lunch at James Madison Elementary School cafeteria was intended to be the "fun" meal. That is, the meal in which the full priority of nutrition was thrown to the wind (or at least tossed gently to the side) for one day of the week. The kitchen staff's latest rendition of this policy was soy hamburgers along with diced pears, pickles on the side in a little paper cup, milk, and chocolate pudding. Whatever "fun" was gained at the cost of nutrition by the choice of soy burgers was lost on certain three friends, sitting together for the first time.

"I wasn't aware that it was possible to take soy beans and change them into a burger," stated Ming with an unreservedly sarcastic tone. "I think I might just eat the bun and save the burger for later in gym class. We're playing hockey."

"They're not too bad," shared Agnes. Her soy burger was still technically such but now appeared more like a fast-food volcano buried underneath at a least a pint of ketchup, mustard, and mayonnaise. She lifted the burger to her mouth and bit down with famished enthusiasm. Condiments squished outwardly from the sides of her mouth in rivulets of red, yellow, and cream white. She looked like a rainforest frog devouring a juicy fly.

"So what did Mr. Cohen ask you?" interrogated Alexandra, changing the subject suddenly and staring directly at Ming.

Ming paused for a silent instant.

"He asked if I was okay, and if my family was happy that I was okay," Ming answered. "He asked if I knew anything about the broken window in the gymnasium or anything about what happened to Mrs. LaGrange and her car."

"What did you tell him?" prodded Alexandra rapidly, not giving Ming a chance to breathe.

"I told him that some kids from the neighborhood broke the window into the gymnasium and that it was probably the same kids that tried to hurt Mrs. LaGrange and broke into her car."

"Did he believe you?" inquired Alexandra.

"I don't know," answered Ming, shrugging his shoulders. "He seemed to, but I wasn't about to tell him the truth that a bunch of black-hooded weirdos smashed through the glass, attacked Mrs. LaGrange and did the same to us. What did you say?"

"Pretty much the same thing," responded Alexandra calmly.

"Has anyone talked to Mrs. LaGrange since all this happened?" inquired Ming.

"I haven't. How about you, Aggie?"

Agnes Reininger just shook her head and continued devouring her condiment volcano. For a moment, Alexandra forgot that Agnes wasn't silenced anymore. She could speak, and had been speaking (quite voluminously, in fact) since their encounter into the hallway with Wyatt. However, since then, every time that Agnes communicated nonverbally, it disturbed Alexandra. She never wanted to lose her sister's voice again.

"I haven't talked to her either," offered Ming. "I guess she's okay, but every once in a while, I see her staring off into space in total silence. She never did that before, at least not so often."

"Yeah, and sometimes I catch her staring at me, and then she will quickly look away," said Alexandra. "It's like she wants to ask me something, but then she just turns away."

"Dylan, Wyatt, and Jeremiah are like that too," added Agnes between succulent bites. "They look at me down the hallway from a distance, or across the parking lot, but they never come over. It's weird."

"What's weird is how they found them," asserted Ming.

"Yeah, they found Jeremiah on the floor right where he had fallen," offered Alexandra. "He was totally fine. They had to dig Wyatt out from the room over there, but he was fine too. He didn't have a scratch!"

Ming gestured to the room in the back of the cafeteria.

"I can't believe they found Dylan too!" exclaimed Agnes. "He was just a pile of ashes when we, I mean I, left him. But they found him asleep on the floor right where he had fallen from Wyatt's fingers." Agnes gave a gleeful smile when she expressed herself and jiggled proudly in her seat when she thought about her victory over Dylan.

There was another brief silence and a few bites of food and gulps of milk.

"What do you make of all that we saw about Mr. Jenski, especially the seeds that fell from his hand and so on?" asked Ming, looking directly at Alexandra.

"Well, if he was the man driving the car who hit Lewis's dad, and I think he certainly was, it seems like Mr. Jenski, Lewis, and all that happened to us must be related somehow."

"What do you mean?" asked Ming.

"Do you remember all those songs and poems that Agnes sang when we were walking all over the school?" asked Alexandra. "They seemed to be about things that we needed to know as we were moving and dealing with everything. Do you remember how Agnes helped us to find the clues that led to seeing Mr. Jenski in the closet with the bumper and the seeds? I don't think that was accidental. I think we needed to see all of that, or at least Lewis needed to see it."

"Speaking of Lewis," injected Ming.

"Any ideas?" asked Alexandra.

"None," responded Ming. "When they dug Wyatt out, I was sad that they didn't find Lewis, but I can't say that I was totally surprised."

"Why not?" asked Agnes quizzically.

"They found Wyatt unconscious, but he was unhurt, and his eyes had returned to normal. Something weird was going on with all that. So it's not too shocking that something strange happened with Lewis as well."

"Yeah, I guess," returned Agnes mournfully.

"And the police's explanation was totally ridiculous," asserted Alexandra. "I mean, why would Lewis just leave the school in the middle of the snowstorm and just run away?"

"Well, whatever happened, I sure do miss him," offered Ming tenderly.

"I do too," added Agnes.

When she did, Alexandra leaned over as far as her red plastic chair would allow and gave her sister a warm hug, nuzzling her head close to Agnes's.

"Do you think we'll ever see him again?" asked Agnes desperately.

"I honestly don't know," answered Alexandra.

25

Silence.

Whatever lay across his body did so with unbelievable weight. It's unyielding girth had pinned his legs in place fully with the exception of his left below the knee. He wiggled it to the left and right to ascertain that he still could. Little good that leg would do him though. The other leg was immovable under the stone, and there wasn't enough room for the free leg to pull up.

"Puh, puh, puh," he breathed, blowing a dusty mixture of dirt and stony powder.

Each successive inhalation and exhalation was smaller and smaller as the weight on his back bore down. He could feel his ribs expanding under the weight and his chest pushing out to the sides. Yet his arms were free. He tried pulling them inward with the hope that, in doing so, he might be able to push off the ground and release the huge weight from his back. He tried and found that whatever space he was afforded in this makeshift tomb wasn't enough to get his arms up to his sides.

"Puh, puh," he breathed, but this time more shallowly and with more times between breaths.

Then, to the slight ringing in his ears and the sound of his own breathing, was added the speech of at least two people. He couldn't identify the voices or be sure of how far away they stood, but they were close enough to be understood.

"I tell yuh, mandatory overtime," started one male voice. "Don't that beat all?"

"I know it!" added a second male voice. "And I had plans for this weekend!"

"Well, I guess they gotta get this place up and running," said the first man with a resigned tone.

Underneath the gargantuan weight, he took hold of a renewed, hopeful excitement. Calling together every bit of energy and resolve, he endeavored to make himself known to the voices he heard. At once, he drew in the fullest breath his lungs would allow, feeling his chest and muscles labor under the weight in this effort to fill his lungs to the last inch. Simultaneously, he began flailing his arms out to the sides in the hope that he might move enough of whatever held him down and draw the men's attention. He looked like a young frog, whipping its new legs outward for a first swim.

"Hulf, helf, help!" he cried, exhausting the last vestiges of air in his crushed lungs.

"Hey," exclaimed one of the men. "Did you hear that?"

"Yeah," affirmed the other. "I think it came from over there by that pile of bricks."

His effort worked. The two men shot over to the pile of bricks and saw his hands poking from beneath.

"There's somebody under here!" cried the first man.

"Don't you think I know?" asked the second man. "Start diggin'!"

As the two men worked feverishly to disinter him from the pile, he could feel the weight of the bricks lift from this burdened chest one by one. It was a glorious relief, and nearly too late. They moved from his head and chest out to his extremities, finally displacing a sufficient number of bricks in order to allow the man full movement. Their considerable exertion revealed a fully grown young man with dark-brown skin. He was covered in a reddish powder, no doubt from the bricks under which he previously lay. Other than a few minor abrasions, he appeared quite healthy and unharmed. In fact, from the looks of his clothing, he had not been trapped beneath the bricks for very long.

"C'mon, fella," said the first man, offering as much tenderness as his middle-aged masculinity would allow. "Let me help you up."

The man gladly accepted the help from the other two. He leaned heavily on their considerable combined strength and worked to pull his legs out from the bricks and then under himself. Having achieved this, he stepped cautiously away from the pile of bricks to the flat uncluttered ground.

"How did you git yerself under there?" asked the second man.

"I...I don't know," he answered, waving his head back and forth in a vain effort to clear it.

He brushed his arms gently to rid them of the dry reddish brick dust. He leaned back to a normal full stature and took in his surroundings. They were new to him but oddly familiar, like a cousin you see but once a year. His eyes panned across the horizon and absorbed everything. He stood in the middle of a vast clearing, man-made and devoid of grass.

To the right and left stood rows of apartment buildings, built and finished in a uniform design. In his immediate vicinity, there were piles of building materials: wood, bricks, aluminum siding, and the like. This explained the two men. Off in the distance, at the end of one row of apartments, standing high next to the road was a sign that read "Bridgeview Apartments: Under Construction and Currently Accepting Applications for Summer Move ins."

In another direction the man saw three other workmen laying asphalt for a playground, and in its foreground, two others were placing the finishing touches on a large sandbox, located in the middle of a rare plot of land that still retained its grass.

"Wul, uh, what's yer name, fella?" asked the first man politely.

The man pushed through the fog in his head and set aside the disconcerting familiarity of everything before his eyes in order to produce the answer.

"It's Lewis…Lewis Warner."